NEVER SAY NO

"Are you saying I should ignore you? I can't." Colter's voice was husky. His hand was cupped under her chin, preventing her from moving away.

"Kiss me," he commanded against her mouth.

He was being deliberately provocative, tantalizing her lips with the nearness of his without kissing her. She felt an incredible hunger to know the elemental mastery she had experienced before.

"No," Natalie said, fighting with every stubborn bit of resistance she possessed.

The arm around her back tightened with seductive force. "Kiss me," Colter coaxed.

from "Fiesta San Antonio"

BOOK YOUR PLACE ON OUR WEBSITE AND MAKE THE READING CONNECTION!

We've created a customized website just for our very special readers, where you can get the inside scoop on everything that's going on with Zebra, Pinnacle and Kensington books.

When you come online, you'll have the exciting opportunity to:

- View covers of upcoming books
- Read sample chapters
- Learn about our future publishing schedule (listed by publication month *and author*)
- Find out when your favorite authors will be visiting a city near you
- Search for and order backlist books from our online catalog
- Check out author bios and background information
- Send e-mail to your favorite authors
- Meet the Kensington staff online
- Join us in weekly chats with authors, readers and other guests
- Get writing guidelines
- AND MUCH MORE!

**Visit our website at
http://www.kensingtonbooks.com**

LOVER MAN

JANET DAILEY

ZEBRA BOOKS
Kensington Publishing Corp.
http://www.kensingtonbooks.com

ZEBRA BOOKS are published by

Kensington Publishing Corp.
119 West 40th Street
New York, NY 10018

All Kensington titles, imprints, and distributed lines are
available at special quantity discounts for bulk purchases for
sales promotion, premiums, fund-raising, educational, or insti-
tutional use.

Special book excerpts or customized printings can also be created to fit specific needs. For details, write or phone the office
of the Kensington Special Sales Manager: Attn.: Special Sales
Department. Kensington Publishing Corp., 119 West 40th
Street, New York, NY 10018. Phone: 1-800-221-2647.

Zebra and the Z logo Reg. U.S. Pat. & TM Off.

ISBN-13: 978-1-4201-0666-4
ISBN-10: 1-4201-0666-X

First Printing: July 2009
10 9 8 7 6 5 4 3 2 1

Printed in the United States of America

Contents

FIESTA
SAN ANTONIO

Chapter 1

The black velvet sky was studded with diamond stars, twinkling in a cloudless Texas night, warm and languid. But there was a crackle of excitement in the air along the banks of San Antonio's famous Riverwalk as watchers focused on the parade.

A man stood in the crowd, but he seemed somehow apart from the festive throng. Tall, whipcord-lean, he was aloof, expressing an aura of detachment. The chiseled lines of his handsome face belonged to a man who rarely smiled, or who had found no reason to smile for a long time.

Thick light-brown hair fell carelessly over his forehead in waves streaked with burnished gold from long hours in the sun. Tanned, with attractive lines, his face had the look of being carved from wood, dispassionate and indifferent, without a soul. His eyes were a changeable color between green and blue, but there was a hint of frost in them.

A lavishly decorated barge floated under the stone footbridge, its bright lights blazing for the benefit of the crowd gathered along the river's bend at Arenson River Theater. A murmur of appreciation rippled through the spectators. The young girl standing in front of the man glanced quickly at him, her eyes shining.

"Look at that one, Daddy," she breathed in awe. "Isn't it beautiful?"

"Yes." There was a suggestion of an impatient sigh in his agreement, but the girl didn't seem to notice. Her attention had returned to the parade.

His gaze flicked uninterestedly over the float and back to the child in front of him and the single, plain braid nearly touching the waistband of her dress. Colter wondered how long it had been since her hair had been cut, then chided himself silently for not remembering.

He glanced at another little girl standing nearby, whose braid had narrow, colorful ribbons threaded through it in an intricate design. Her doting grandma gave a gentle tug on the neatly curled tail and the little girl looked up with a smile.

Colter felt a little guilty. He considered himself ahead if he got Missy to comb her hair without complaining. Beribboned braids—no one would expect a single dad to go that far.

Or so he hoped. His thoughts drifted and he began to wonder what he was doing here, anyway. The family atmosphere was getting on his nerves. People stood elbow to elbow, craning their necks for a glimpse of the floats when they could have stayed home and had an unobstructed view of the parade on TV.

Not the same as participating. Unbidden, Flo Donaldsen's statement came to mind.

Yes, it was his aunt who was to blame for his presence in the crowd. But his own conscience pricked him. He'd done the best he knew how over the years, but had he paid enough attention to Missy? His daughter had never wanted for anything. She had beautiful clothes, plenty of food, a fine home on thousands of acres. He had never sent her off to boarding school. She'd lived under the same roof with him since the day she had entered the world.

What else was he supposed to do? He didn't understand his own uneasiness.

This shy, quiet child with the sensitive face was his daughter. Yet Colter Langston felt no surge of emotion when he looked at her now. He cared for her, as much as he could, but there was no bursting warmth of pride to take away the emptiness within him.

He let himself think, just for a moment, that maybe parenthood wasn't as incredibly important as everyone made it out to be. Kids grew up too fast anyway, almost like weeds. Blink, and they turned into teenagers who knew it all and had everything. Missy was only a few years away from that. He wasn't looking forward to the inevitable back talk and bad behavior, and he didn't see any reason to imagine he would somehow be spared. Even if she'd never been anything but good.

Colter glared resentfully at the slow-moving minute hand of his watch, knowing the parade had barely started and wishing it was over. His lean jaw tightened as he reminded himself that he'd committed to accompanying Missy to all the activities of Fiesta Week, the celebration marking Texas's independence from Mexico. The river parade was the first major event and he was already bored. Standing around gawking at events he'd seen before wasn't his idea of a thrill.

He would have to admit that he tended to be easily bored. Growing up an only child, son and heir to the vast Langston holdings in the Texas hill country north of San Antonio, he himself had been denied nothing as a kid, a wild teenager, or a young man. Now at thirty-four, he realized that hadn't been to his advantage. Life held no surprises. Sex, love, marriage—been there, done that, what now? The lasting happiness and satisfaction a man was supposed to find in all that had eluded him, when it came right down to it.

For the last five years, since his father's death, he had been the sole owner of the Langston Ranch and its numerous investments. The power of the family name was his to command and he had influence. Colter Langston had grown accustomed to being obeyed. He didn't mind it. Someone had to be in charge.

Matt Langston had taught him that every man had a price, monetary or otherwise. Colter had admired and respected his father, but they had never been close. His mother had died when he was six and he had only photographs to recall what she looked like.

As for his wife Caroline, she had married him for the wrong reasons. It hadn't taken Colter long to realize that. Within the first year of their marriage, she had died in childbirth, their newborn daughter her last link to the Langston power and wealth. Her diary had callously stated that she'd never loved Colter at all, only his money and name. Looking back, Colter had to admit that he hadn't loved her either. He'd lusted after her, sure. Her beautiful face and body had dazzled him. He'd wanted to have her all to himself and she'd made it clear that he'd have to marry her to do that.

Love had nothing to do with it. Hell, he wasn't certain he knew what it was, except that it made people act like damn fools when they thought they were in it.

He couldn't say that he'd truly loved anyone, not even himself. No one loved him. Missy tried, just as Colter had tried to love his father. Maybe the one who'd come the closest to caring for him had been his aunt Flo. When his mother had died, Matt Langston brought his widowed sister to Langston Ranch to look after his son. She'd stayed on to care for Missy.

But no longer. His mouth moved into a grim, forbidding line. At the end of this month, Flo Donaldsen was leaving, figuratively if not literally. She was a strong, proud woman who spoke her mind and Colter had been told what she thought of him—not much—before he and Missy left for San Antonio.

"I don't like what you've become, Colter," she had told him. "Do you know how cold and inconsiderate you can be? You show more kindness and attention to your horses than you ever do to anyone, including your own daughter, and it isn't right."

He'd listened, stone-faced. What else had she said? Nothing very nice.

"You may be my nephew but I'm ashamed to see that your heart has turned to stone, if you ever had one. Missy needs her father, not just a weary old great-aunty who's not going to live forever. You ought to provide her with a mother. And I don't mean one of your useless girlfriends. I'm talking about a *mother.*"

As if he could just go pick a perfect mom off the shelf, Colter had thought bitterly. Too bad life didn't work like that. But was it worth pointing that hard fact out to Flo?

His aunt had rattled on, finishing up with a statement that wasn't exactly a declaration of independence. "According to your father's will, the cottage by the creek is mine whenever I want it, along with a pension. I'll be moving into it at the end of the month."

Colter hadn't argued. Eventually he knew he could work his way around her. He had no qualms about using the affection she held for him and his daughter to gain what he wanted. Yet he had to admit that she was right— Missy ought to have a mother.

Deirdre, the definition of what his aunt meant by "useless girlfriend," would love to give it a try, but that was never going to happen. Granted, he found her company stimulating, at least for the time being, but Colter knew that Deirdre only tolerated his daughter. The sensually attractive redhead was a man's woman, definitely not the domesticated type. When her physical interest in him ebbed—as it undoubtedly would, because, yes, she was that shallow—she would probably take her vengeance out on Missy. No, he wasn't going to marry Deirdre.

Candy tossed from a float landed at his feet, missing the outstretched hands that tried to intercept it. As Missy bent down to pick it up, someone else's small fingers reached it first. A pair of dark brown eyes peered through the mop of brown hair falling over his forehead, their expression reluctant and hopeful.

"Was this yours?" The little boy's clenched fist opened to reveal the paper-wrapped candy, offering it to Missy.

Colter watched the movement of his daughter's mouth into a timid smile, noticing how easily she related to the other kid, who was probably half her age.

"No, you can have it," Missy assured the little boy.

The small palm remained outstretched as the boy fixed his gaze on the candy. "Nonnie said I wasn't supposed to take things that belong to someone else, and I'm not supposed to take things away from girls, ever."

Missy gave Colter a shy, adult smile before turning a solemn face back to the boy. "You found it, so you can keep it."

Bright brown eyes studied her for an instant longer, then his fingers closed protectively over the candy. For precious seconds he held it in his fist before he began reverently unwrapping the paper.

"My name is Ricky," he said a little thickly after he'd put the candy in his mouth. "What's yours?"

"My name is Missy and this is my father," she replied.

The boy named Ricky had to tilt his head way back to look up at Colter's face. One corner of Colter's mouth turned up in wry amusement at the open inspection he was getting. He rather liked the boldness of the boy's look, forthright and not easily impressed. Nor intimidated, it seemed.

"I don't have a father," Ricky announced, "but some day I'm going to have cowboy boots too."

The two thoughts didn't connect for Colter, but obviously they did for the boy. Colter wondered where his mother was, and then thought briefly of what it would be like to have a son like this. Would he and Missy have been closer if she had been a boy instead of a girl? It seemed mean-spirited to speculate, but it was only a thought. He doubted it, though. Colter probably would have been irritated by the demands and natural competitiveness of a son.

He looked over the heads of the crowd to see if anyone was making their way through or calling for a lost kid. Nope. Everyone stayed more or less in place, craning their necks to see better. He'd keep Ricky with them until someone showed up or he could turn him over to a police officer.

"Did your mother bring you to the parade?" Colter heard Missy ask.

He was a little surprised at her interest in the kid. She'd never seemed to pay much attention to the other children she went to school with, although she seemed to like little Josh Harris. Still, Colter had presumed she was a loner like himself. The one trait they shared.

"Nonnie brought me," Ricky said, adding with a shrug, "but I think she got lost."

"Are you sure you're not the one who's lost?" Missy smiled.

"I don't think so." He screwed up his face in a puzzled frown. "I know where I am, but I don't know where Nonnie is. So she's the one who's lost."

Colter assumed that Nonnie was his grandmother. He looked over the crowd again for a woman of the right age in search mode, with no luck.

Then it was Colter's turn to frown as he saw his daughter touch the little boy's arm and bend slightly toward him in a solicitous movement.

"Yes, but you see, Ricky, your Nonnie knows where she is, but she doesn't know where you are. I'll bet she thinks you're the one who's lost," Missy explained.

He screwed up his face again. "I'll bet she'll be mad," Ricky sighed.

"Where did you last see her?"

Colter guessed where his daughter's questions were leading. The last thing he wanted to do was get involved in a search for whoever had brought the boy to the parade. Old Nonnie should have kept a closer eye on him.

"Over there somewhere." Ricky waved a hand in the general direction of the footbridge. "I was thirsty and she was going to get me a drink."

"And you were supposed to wait for her," Missy concluded astutely.

The boy shamefacedly tucked his chin in and answered in a very small voice. "Yes."

"Give me your hand," Missy instructed him, "and we'll go see if we can find her."

"Missy!" Colter's voice rang out more sharply than he intended as his hand closed over her shoulder. He lowered his voice quickly to a firmer, less abrasive tone. "We are not going to search this crowd."

The hurt look in her accusing eyes hit home, as did her words. "We can't just leave him. He's only a little boy, Daddy."

"Did I say we were going to leave him?"

"I'm not so little," Ricky inserted proudly. "I'll be six pretty soon."

Colter nodded and turned back to his daughter. She had withdrawn again into her shell, a remote resentment clouding her calm blue eyes.

"Look," Colter sighed. He hated being backed into a corner, but he knew he was right. "We'll take Ricky to that policeman over there. The woman who brought him probably already knows that he's lost and will have notified them. That's the right way to do it. And the safest for him."

"Couldn't we take a few minutes to look first?" Missy suggested, glancing hesitantly at him through upcurving lashes.

"No."

His jaw tightened when Missy flinched at his tone. Fleetingly, he had to acknowledge that Flo had been right when she'd said he hurt people without meaning to do it. Well, whatever. Tact had never been one of his virtues. He did have a few, if anyone needed to know.

He told himself to snap out of it and turned to the boy. "Come on," he said crisply. "We'll take you to the policeman. He'll help you find your—"

"No." Ricky shrank back. "They don't know where Nonnie is." His lower lip jutted out in a trembling pout.

Colter stared at him for an instant, then reached down and swung the boy into his arms. Tear-wet brown eyes studded his face, now at eye level. Tears or no tears, Ricky wasn't intimidated by the forbidding set of Colter's jaw. He just wanted his Nonnie and that was that.

Colter's expression revealed nothing, or so he hoped— but he had to admire the kid's impertinence. Just why he did wasn't clear to him, but it didn't change anything. He turned toward the distant police officer, aware that Missy was dragging her feet as she followed him. Enough of this. He wasn't required to be her hero, not under these circumstances, and legally speaking, he had to give the kid to an officer or risk seeing his face on an Amber

Alert billboard. As far as he was concerned, it was enough that he'd brought her to the Fiesta. There were a thousand reasons they couldn't get involved with a lost child.

A small, grubby hand used Colter's shoulder to balance while Ricky took in his improved view of the crowd and the river parade. Then the boy's fingers tightened perceptibly.

"Wait!" he cried. "There's Nonnie!"

Colter turned in the direction Ricky indicated, his alert gaze immediately picking out the woman frantically searching the crowd. As she drew nearer, his eyebrow rose thoughtfully. Nonnie was no grandmother. She didn't even look old enough to be a mother. If Colter was any judge, she was barely over twenty and Ricky himself had said that he was almost six years old.

He could be wrong about all that. She wasn't that close to him to see for sure.

But she was really pretty, Colter decided, far above average, despite signs of exhaustion and strain etched in her features. He guessed it wasn't just losing Ricky temporarily that had told on her—something had been stressing her out for months.

Then her hazel eyes, almond-shaped and tilted up at the corners, spied Ricky in Colter's arms. A wide smile of relief spread across her sensuously full lips as she hurried toward them. There was an untouched look about her that kindled a fleeting fire of desire in him until he remembered the kid in his arms. He had his pick of available women everywhere he went, women who didn't have children to complicate their lives. Single motherhood was a deal-breaker. He had enough problems being a single father as it was.

The crowds were so thick that Natalie was terrified when she discovered Ricky was not where she'd left him.

The grandmotherly type who'd offered to watch him was borderline frantic when she realized it too.

He usually did exactly what he was told. What had happened? The excitement of the parade must have been too much for his adventurous nature to ignore.

A flying chunk of candy hit her shoulder and bounced off. Aha. Ricky would do anything, absolutely anything for candy. He must have been chasing down a piece.

Somehow she knew he wouldn't stray out of sight of the footbridge. Her fear had been that she'd walk by him in the throng of people and not see him. Only by the merest chance had she spotted Ricky in the stranger's arms and then only out of the corner of her eye.

"Oh, Ricky!" she exclaimed with a laughing cry as the stranger handed him to her. "I told you to stay by the bridge with that nice lady—you didn't listen to me!"

Her relief at finding him unharmed was too great for Natalie to be as angry as she should have been with him. Tears filled her eyes, tears of relief and exhaustion. She brushed them away and proudly raised her head to thank the stranger.

Her breath caught in her throat, her body automatically stiffening at his appraisal of her and the suggestion of . . . there was no other word for it . . . contempt. His self-assurance bordered on arrogance. Natalie's initial impression had been that the man was handsome, but close up, not so much. His intense gaze seemed to strip away her pride, for one thing.

And then there were his fancy clothes. Big deal, she thought. The hand-tailored, ultra lightweight leather jacket he wore had cost serious money. He was undoubtedly aware that her clothes came from a discount fashion outlet.

"Thank you so much for finding Ricky." Her expression of gratitude lacked sincerity, the result of his derisive look.

"You're holding me too tight," Ricky whispered loudly in her ear.

It was his way of saying that he was too big to be cuddled like a baby in her arms. Reluctantly Natalie let him slide to the ground, keeping a firm hold of one small hand.

"He was no trouble." The low-pitched masculine voice drawled lazily, a contradiction to the watchfulness of the man's gaze. "We were taking him to the police officer over there."

She knew it was the correct thing to have done, but she would have stayed with a stray, to reassure the kid and herself. Not this guy. He didn't look like the type to get involved with a lost child, certainly not to the extent of participating in a search for her.

Natalie knew she was being a little unreasonable—he couldn't have done both—but his attitude put her off.

Ricky tugged at her hand. "They threw candy from the floats. I found a piece and Missy let me keep it. Was that all right? I already ate it," he added as an afterthought.

"Missy?" Natalie repeated blankly.

She followed his pointing finger, seeing for the first time the quiet young girl standing beside the stranger.

"That's Missy," Ricky explained, "and that's her father."

Compassion touched Natalie's heart. If the girl's father was as arrogant as he looked, it was no wonder Missy seemed so sensitive and withdrawn. The girl was just reaching that awkward age when she needed the reassurance that somebody cared. Natalie remembered those heartbreaking years. If it hadn't been for her brother—but her brother was gone. Natalie could only hope that the girl's mother was a vast improvement over her father.

"Can I have my drink?" Ricky asked.

"I dropped them looking for you. And that's about it for our fun money, kiddo."

A passing vendor overheard and proffered a small

bottle of icy-cold water from the cooler he lugged. "For free, lady. For you and him."

Natalie murmured a heartfelt thank-you as he pushed on. Ricky did too, then watched her struggle with the cap.

"Let me."

She didn't look at the stranger when he spoke. "That's okay, I got it. Here, Ricky."

The little boy put the opened bottle to his lips and glugged it blissfully. He left her some water, but not much, wiping his mouth with the back of his hand. At that instant, Natalie noticed the marked silence of the stranger and realized he probably only wanted her to take Ricky and leave. Squaring her shoulders, she turned to him.

"Thank you again," she offered. He nodded curtly in acknowledgement and Natalie tightened her hold on Ricky's hand. "Come on. Let's go watch the parade."

Her forced smile immediately changed into one of genuine loving at the sight of the bright brown eyes gazing back at her.

"Would you—" a hesitant voice began, stopping Natalie and Ricky as they began to turn away. "Would you like to watch the parade with us?" Missy faltered.

Natalie saw the look of reproach that the man gave his daughter and knew he wanted to be rid of them. She had guessed correctly, as it turned out. Gold fires flared for an instant in her eyes before she quickly banked them to meet the girl's wavering gaze.

"Thank you, but I don't think so," Natalie said.

At the sideways look the girl gave her father, Natalie was aware that Missy had guessed the reason she had refused. There was a rebellious urge to stay just to spite the man, but Natalie knew she would be uncomfortable in his presence.

With more haste than was necessary she led Ricky

through the crowds to the footbridge. Their previous vantage point right next to the river was taken, much to Ricky's dismay. Natalie succeeded in finding a spot along the low, guarded rock wall where she could sit with Ricky on her lap. The minute she relaxed, an aching tiredness swept over her, throbbing through every muscle and nerve.

Going to the parade had been her idea, a wonderful thing to do with Ricky that was free, thank God, and a distraction from her problems. It had barely begun when Ricky had gotten himself lost and left her frantic with worry. What little energy she possessed had been expended in the search for him. She knew the stranger must have silently condemned her for leaving the boy even for an instant. But the kind grandma standing next to them had promised to watch Ricky for her—the old lady hadn't realized how quickly a small boy could wriggle away, evidently. Natalie was struck with fear when she came back with drinks and saw he was gone, and the grandma was horrified. Natalie had dropped the drinks and dashed into the surging crowd to find him. She'd always been able to count on Ricky doing what he was told, so she hadn't dreamed he would stray from the spot. But what had gone right for her lately?

His small brown head leaned against her shoulder and Natalie rested her cheek against his fine, silky hair. Her lashes fluttered tiredly. If only she had someone to lean on. She gave a heavy sigh. Her exhaustion was mental as well as physical. Sinking her teeth into her bottom lip, she tried to hold back the waves of despair.

That terrible weekend four years ago when her brother Ned and his wife had been killed outright in a car crash . . . then it had seemed so logical and natural for Natalie to take her little nephew Ricky to raise. It was either that or make him a ward of the courts to be placed in a foster home. At the time she'd had a secure job and was sure she'd be able to pay for child care. She couldn't have guessed that the company would go out of business within a few months when the national economy suddenly tanked, and she hadn't realized the constant expenses of being a single parent.

As the clothes, medical, and babysitter costs mounted, Natalie was forced to take nearly any kind of work to try to make ends meet. The last one she'd had was through an agency that provided daily help to homes in the area.

Just last Friday they had fired her when she was falsely accused of stealing from one of the homes. The client, an alcoholic, judging by all the empty bottles of booze Natalie had found, had undoubtedly lost whatever was missing, but it was her word against his, and the agency hadn't wanted to lose his payments. On top of that, her weekly paycheck, no matter how frugal she was, had never succeeded in lasting till the next one. The few groceries in their tiny apartment would get them through the end of the week and no longer. She had to find another job and soon.

The weight of the small boy on her lap seemed to increase, numbing her legs into leaden sticks. When the last float emerged from under the footbridge, Natalie realized that Ricky had fallen sound asleep. As she smoothed the straight brown hair from his forehead, she knew all her efforts had been worth it, and all the future ones would be too. Ricky was strong and healthy, intelligent and happy, trusting and loving, and totally confident that she loved him. There was no hint of the shyness, unhappiness, or uncertainty in Ricky that she had seen in Missy.

Gently Natalie enfolded Ricky in her arms, his hands automatically circling her neck in sleep and hugging her tightly. There was a warm sensation of love in the way the small body clung to her. Rising to her feet and carrying the heavy burden of the sleeping child that felt strangely lighter, Natalie followed the milling crowds that had begun to leave the Riverwalk area.

The street leading to their apartment was full of people and well-lit, one of the main thoroughfares to downtown San Antonio. As Natalie walked past a parking lot congested with cars attempting to leave, she wished she could spare the money to take the bus. But it would cost as much as a dollar meal, plus tax, at a fast food place, a big treat for Ricky. She sighed. It was going to be a long walk home.

A white luxury car pulled out of the parking lot, accelerating by Natalie. She had a fleeting glimpse of a thin, sensitive face pressed against the window and staring at her before the streetlights reduced the two occupants of the car to silhouettes, one large and one small. Red lights at the rear flashed a danger signal as the car braked and eased against the sidewalk curb ahead of her. Natalie shifted Ricky in her arms, her heart pounding with fear— or pride.

The driver's door was opened and immediately slammed shut. As Natalie drew nearer to where the car was idling, she saw the arrogant stranger's long, impatient strides eating up the distance that separated them. She could only guess his daughter had insisted they stop when she recognized Natalie and the sleeping Ricky.

For all the annoyance she had sensed in his hurried movements, the chiseled face in front of her was remarkably calm. He stopped directly in her path, forcing her to stop too—and acknowledge him.

"Hey, can we give you a ride home?"

The offer was made in a bland voice. Natalie decided that it had been a long time since this man had let his true thoughts show on his face.

"No thank you." She spoke concisely and with no hesitation.

She didn't want him to believe for an instant that she might be impressed by his obvious wealth or even his attention.

"With your son and my daughter as chaperones, you don't have to worry," he said briskly.

Natalie started to correct him by saying that Ricky was her nephew, then changed her mind. Let him think what he liked. He probably wouldn't believe her if she told him the truth.

"My daughter is really anxious about you getting home safe," he added.

"It was her idea and not yours to stop, am I right?" Natalie's eyes flashed.

"Of course," he said, letting her know for sure that the thought never would have occurred to him, just as she'd guessed. "And I don't look forward to the prospect of sitting up half the night trying to convince her that you and the boy made it home okay on your own."

Natalie glanced at the car. The streetlight illuminated the fearful expression of the young face that watched them. He had a point. The girl was obviously concerned.

"We'll accept your offer," Natalie said a little ungraciously.

The slight twist of his mouth informed her that he'd expected no other decision. He didn't wait for her as he walked to the car and opened the passenger door. Missy gave him a darting smile of gratitude as she scrambled into the back seat, leaving the front seat vacant for Natalie.

The cheap cotton of Natalie's dress slid nearly up to mid-thigh as she tried to negotiate getting in without waking Ricky. Tugging her skirt down, she felt her cheeks stinging with embarrassment, conscious of those eyes of his that watched everything. Then her door was closed and he went around to the driver's side, sliding behind the wheel.

"Is he asleep?" Missy leaned forward on the leather armrest in the middle of the front two seats.

Natalie answered quietly, "Yes, it's past his bedtime."

The car was in motion, the man at the wheel concentrating on the traffic and ignoring Natalie completely.

"The parade was nice, wasn't it?" the girl said timidly as if she wasn't sure of her own opinion.

"Yes," Natalie agreed. "Ricky enjoyed it. It's the first time he's ever seen one."

"Me too. Except on television," Missy qualified.

"Where do you live?"

Natalie was brought up sharply by the masculine voice, hating herself for forgetting to tell him her address, a situation that she quickly corrected. "Do you know where that is?" she inquired as an afterthought.

"I've lived near San Antonio all my life. There are few places in it I don't know," he replied evenly.

And yet it was the first time his daughter had been to a Fiesta parade, Natalie thought. Her arm brushed the expensive leather upholstery. Couldn't have been due to a lack of money, she was sure of that.

"Have you lived here long?" the girl whispered. Natalie had the impression that she spoke very softly because of her father, not because of Ricky being asleep.

"For the last few years," Natalie admitted in an equally quiet voice.

"It's nice. I like San Antonio."

Then Natalie recalled the slight qualification the man had had that he lived "near" San Antonio. "Ricky said your name was Missy, right?"

"Missy Langston, short for Melissa," she explained. Her

hand made a slight movement in her father's direction. "Th-this is my father, Colter Langston."

The name registered vaguely in Natalie's memory as belonging to an important family. She glanced in his direction and found steady, blue-green eyes returning her look. The knowing glitter in them forced her to look away. He had seen the faint glimmer of recognition cross her face.

"My name is Natalie Crane." She identified herself for no other reason than to fill the oppressive silence.

"Ricky calls you Nonnie, doesn't he?" Missy replied.

A tender smile curved Natalie's mouth as her fingers touched the head of the boy sleeping against her shoulder.

"When he was really little, he couldn't say Natalie. That was the closest he could come to it."

"Which of these places is your home?" Colter Langston had made the turn off the main thoroughfare onto the side street where she and Ricky lived.

"The third house on the right," Natalie answered.

The windows of the large structure were dark except for one small light in the rear. Natalie was glad. Lights would only make the old monstrosity of a house, broken up into apartments years ago, look as shabby and neglected as the darkness hinted. She wished now that she'd asked to be let out on the corner. She'd caught the faint note of derision in his question.

The car stopped next to the curb. Natalie was groping for the door handle as the headlights and the motor were switched off. Her startled gaze watched Colter Langston get out of the car and walk round to her side. As she realized that this show of courtesy was for his daughter's benefit, her mouth tightened grimly. When her door was opened, she swung her legs around to step out.

"Give me the boy," Colter ordered, his strong hands reaching for Ricky's small waist.

"I can carry him," she said, drawing back from the outstretched hands.

"And get your key out of your purse and fumble with the lock?" He ended up taking Ricky. "I sincerely doubt that you want me rummaging through your purse for the key."

Without being encumbered by Ricky's weight, Natalie was quickly out of the car, looking resentfully at the man holding her sleeping nephew. She walked over the broken concrete sidewalk, too familiar with it to trip or stumble, hearing Colter's long, catlike strides keeping pace behind her. For once the key didn't stick in the lock but turned instantly, opening the front door. A step inside, Natalie turned to take Ricky but was refused.

"He's fine," Colter said. "Just point out your apartment."

"It's upstairs," she sighed, wondering if it gave him a feeling of superiority to see how humble her home was. She was simply too tired to care.

As she started toward the stairs, a door into the hallway opened and the rheumy eyes of her landlady peered out. An overplucked brow arched upward as she spotted the man with Natalie.

"I have told you repeatedly, Miss Crane, that I will not allow you to entertain men in your apartment. This is a respectable house!" Her landlady's voice rang out harshly.

Through sheer force of will, Natalie didn't lose her temper. The first of the month wasn't far away. If she hoped to gain a couple of days' grace to scratch together enough money to pay the rent, she couldn't afford to get angry.

"He's only carrying Ricky to my room. He'll be leaving immediately, Mrs. Thomas," Natalie answered, not daring to glance at Colter.

"Well, see that he does!" the woman snapped, and closed the door.

Natalie didn't want to guess how Colter might've interpreted the exchange he'd been forced to observe. If she knew, she would almost certainly tell him just what she thought of his lordly ways.

At the top of the stairs, she unlocked the door to her one-room apartment and reached for Ricky. Colter handed him to her without protest.

"Thanks for the ride," she said wearily.

"I'll pass that on to Missy. It was her idea."

A subtle reminder that Natalie truly hadn't needed. But it wasn't worth getting her licks in. Colter was already going back down the steps. In another few seconds, he was gone.

Chapter 2

"You sit here quietly, Ricky, and eat your sandwich," Natalie instructed. "And don't bother anybody."

"I won't," he said cheerfully as he crawled onto the long bench, his chin barely above the wooden counter. "Aren't you going to eat with me, Nonnie?"

"No, honey, I have to work." Her hair was curling around her face and neck from the heat of the grill, trying to escape the hairnet she had to wear. She pushed a wayward lock back under it.

Under the influence of her encouraging smile, Ricky picked up the sandwich, cut into sections for his small fingers to handle, and began eating with his usual gusto. Her smile faded as Natalie turned away. Her temples throbbed from the heat and noise. She longed for a cool breeze to sweep it all away, but the air was still and stifling, and the setting sun promised no relief.

A country-western band was playing a rousing tune in the main square of La Villita. The music was loud enough to be heard over the steady din of voices and laughter from the milling crowd. "A Night in Old San Antonio," part of the Fiesta Week activities, transformed La Villita, a recreation of the small settlement that once existed there, into four nights of perpetual chaos. Every available inch of space was used for booths to sell ethnic food and drink, and handicrafts made by Native Americans and descendants of long-ago immigrants.

It was in a stand located in the Frontier section that Natalie had at last found work. Temporary, unfortunately, but it was money she desperately needed. The stand's owner had raised no objections when Natalie asked to bring Ricky with her as long as he stayed out of the way. Doing that saved the considerable expense of a babysitter even if it did mean keeping Ricky up much later than she liked. It was only going to be for four nights and he could always curl up on the bales of hay in her sight if he became too tired.

Flipping another steak on the grill, wishing Jeannie, her replacement on the next shift, would show up soon, Natalie wearily wiped the sweat from her forehead. She had an awful feeling that she was never going to get out of the financial sinkhole she was in. All her efforts seemed to get them nowhere and in the last year, everything had gone from bad to worse.

She had grown to love Ricky tremendously and she refused to grumble at the responsibility of taking care of him. If only she could have an hour's rest from the pressure and stress, she thought wistfully. If only she didn't feel so unbearably tired and worn out all the time, maybe a solution to her problems would come to her. Besides, it would be fun to join in the excitement of the hundreds of merrymakers roaming through La Villita, seemingly without a care in the world.

Dully Natalie glanced over her shoulder to be sure that Ricky was still sitting at the counter. At the reassuring sight of his silky brown head, she started to turn back, only to freeze into stillness as her gaze became locked by a pair of blue-green eyes. A wildfire of dislike raced through her—Colter Langston wasn't someone she'd expected to see or wanted to see.

His calm study of her was annoying and Natalie didn't want to get into a staring contest. She looked away from Colter to his daughter Missy, who had sat herself down on the bench next to Ricky, smiling shyly and talking to him in a low voice.

Averting her head with a jerky movement, Natalie concentrated her attention on the small steaks on the grill. It was so *not* a thrill to see him again. The feeling was mutual, Natalie was sure—that is, if Colter possessed any feelings. His handsome face was chiseled into strong lines made stronger by years out in the Texas sun, and the incongruous glacial color of his eyes didn't soften them. Tall, lean, and powerfully muscled, he gave the impression of some big animal surveying its domain from a high rock—a cougar or something.

Yes, Natalie decided, not without a trace of an inward smile, there was a lot about him that reminded her of a predatory big cat. The proud and withdrawn look in his expression, the air of supreme independence, the strength that was held in check until it was needed and unleashed with lightning swiftness, the dangerous claws that remained hidden, the indifference to others' wishes unless he felt like granting them, and, most of all, there was that hint of a primitive animal, untamed and hating civilization.

The smoke and fumes from the grill must be getting to me, was Natalie's troubled thought. Yet she had to acknowledge that Colter Langston possessed serious animal magnetism, with a dash of danger.

Natalie shook her head firmly to clear her mind of her fanciful imaginings. It was sheer chance that she'd seen him again, chance and his daughter's acquaintance with Ricky, and the Fiesta. Her mouth twisted wryly as she realized that for a few moments her money worries had been set aside.

"Nonnie?" Ricky's voice rang clear and loud, only a tad apologetic for interrupting her.

After dishing up two more plates, Natalie self-consciously wiped her hands on the gingham checked apron and went to the counter where Ricky was seated, deliberately ignoring the man standing behind him.

"Hello, Missy," she greeted the girl, and received a timid but friendly little nod in return.

"I ate all my dinner." Ricky pushed the clean plate forward for her inspection. Before Natalie could comment, he rushed on, "Missy said she would take me around and show me everything."

"I'll keep hold of his hand all the time so he won't get lost," Missy inserted anxiously.

"I'm sure you would be very careful, but—" Natalie glanced unwillingly at Colter Langston's face. He seemed relaxed, actually. She wasn't. "Missy, I think Ricky should stay here with me. It's very crowded tonight."

"Daddy!" Missy turned her anxious gaze to her father. "Please explain to Mrs. Crane that we would take really good care of him."

He was about to answer when one of San Antonio's finest, a female police officer who'd stopped in for a steak a little while ago, stepped up. "It's okay," she said to a startled Natalie, "I can vouch for both of them." She turned to Colter and his daughter. "Hey there, Missy. How's the Safety First champ? She won the county prize for knowing all the rules a couple of months ago," the officer said to Natalie.

"That's great, Missy," Natalie said. But she wasn't exactly surprised that the sheltered little girl took safety so seriously.

"And how are you, Mr. Langston?" The female officer's

tone was jokey, and Natalie wondered if she knew him from somewhere else besides the countywide kid-safety contest.

"Just fine."

The officer winked at Natalie. "He was also known as Colt 45, back in the day. For all the wrong reasons."

Colter grinned. "You had to remind me, Officer Olivera. Also known as Teresa. And yourself?"

"Can't complain," she laughed. "Hey, the chief said he saw you walk by him, talking to your daughter."

"Why didn't he say hello?"

"He had a *churro* in his mouth," the officer laughed. "Got himself all covered with powdered sugar. Now, I don't crave sweets like the chief does. Give me a steak every time. You going to have one, Colter? They're good."

He shook his head. "Not right now. I made too many promises. Missy wants to wander around and this little guy here is her new best friend."

"Oh, okay." The officer gave Ricky a big smile. "He sure is cute. Is he yours?" she asked Natalie.

"Well—yes," she said, not wanting to get into a long explanation. Colter was looking at her a little smugly, as if he had just received the official recommendation of the San Antonio Police Department and a shiny fake badge.

Missy beamed at all three adults, looking happy, but Natalie squirmed inwardly, feeling like she was in a difficult position because, well, she was.

She didn't have to hear him say yes to Missy to know that he was just doing it to please his daughter. The last thing Colter Langston wanted to do was babysit her nephew. He smiled at the cop, and then his aloof gaze swung to Natalie, who steeled herself to say no.

"He'll be safe with us. We'll return him as soon as

we've made the tour, Mrs. Crane," he said, with a trace of mockery on the word "Mrs."

"It's Ms. Crane. Ricky is my nephew." The look Colter gave her made Natalie regret that she'd corrected him. "Now if you'll excuse me, I have to get back to work."

"Right. We'll bring Ricky back in an hour," Colter responded smoothly.

"I didn't say he could go!" Natalie turned back in astonishment.

"He doesn't have much to do while you're working," Colter said. "What's the harm?"

Resentment flared in her eyes, but it made no great impression on him.

The police officer tried to be tactful. "Really, it's okay. Colter actually never broke a law in his life. Me and him went to the same high school outside of San Antone. He was too damn good to be true even then," she laughed.

Natalie didn't feel like she could stand there and argue the point, especially in front of the two children watching the exchange so closely. Indecision hovered in her mind until she met the little boy's pleading brown eyes, so loving and full of mischief. It would serve Colter Langston right to take Ricky.

"Okay," she sighed. "I expect him back in an hour."

Afterward she wondered if she had done the right thing to agree. The officer's reassurances aside, Natalie really didn't know Colter Langston, even if his daughter was a sweetie, regardless of how respectable he seemed on the surface. Respectable—somehow it was hardly an adjective that could be applied to him, not with any degree of certainty.

She didn't want to believe her impression that Colter had been indulging his daughter's whim, using Ricky to entertain her so he wouldn't have to. But the more

Natalie thought about it, the more it seemed like it could be true.

As the hour neared its end, Natalie kept searching the crowd, now so big that they were elbow to elbow as they jostled their way to the various cultural booths. The sky had darkened to purple-black and La Villita was illuminated by strings of brightly colored lights strung across squares and alleys and atop the booths. The time for her fifteen-minute break was approaching, precious minutes that she wanted to devote to Ricky.

Then, through the mob of people young and old, Natalie saw him perched again on Colter's arm as the three wound their way to the stand. Colter kept Missy in front of him with a hand on her shoulder, listening to Ricky, whose brown eyes were wide and wondering at all the things he had seen. She knew he would talk nonstop for an hour to share everything with her. Even Missy's face was unusually animated and happy.

Ricky almost leaped into her outstretched arms. "Did you have a good time?" Natalie smiled.

"Terrific!" he exclaimed, and would have launched into a full account then and there, but Missy broke in.

"We brought him back safely," she said earnestly.

"Yes, you did." Her gaze flickered automatically from the girl to her father, her smile turning a little more reserved under his lazy but piercing look. "Thank you."

Natalie stood Ricky up on an empty corner of the counter bench, tucking his shirttail back into his pants. "You should've seen the pretty eggs," he told her excitedly.

"*Cascarones,*" Missy added. "Like eggs but filled with confetti."

"Oh, I know what those are," Natalie said.

Ricky interrupted eagerly, "You break them over people's heads!"

His dark, bright eyes rounded still more as Ricky

passed on that startling discovery to Natalie. She couldn't help laughing at his amazed expression, the laughter erasing the lines of concern.

Missy reached into the small straw purse she was carrying and took out two *cascarones*, one red and one blue. "You can take these home with you if you like, Ricky," she offered.

Natalie's hand was resting lightly on Ricky's back. She felt him stiffen slightly and stand up straighter. She glanced at his solemn expression as he stared at the brightly colored things in Missy's hand.

"Nonnie and me, we don't accept charity."

A warm flush of embarrassment crept up her cheeks at the gaze—Colter's—that was directed at her. It was so obvious that Ricky was repeating something he'd heard her say many times. She felt even worse when she saw the hurt look steal over Missy's face, the sparkle leaving her blue eyes.

"It's not charity." Colter's low voice got Ricky's attention. "It's a Fiesta gift, like when people play Secret Santa at Christmastime. Just a little something for fun."

Barely moving his head, the boy turned to Natalie for a confirmation of Colter's words. When it had been a simple, well-meant gift from Missy, Natalie hadn't minded Ricky accepting the *cascarones*. Now that her father had involved himself, she wanted to refuse. Her denial wouldn't matter to Colter Langston, who was only backing up his daughter just as Natalie would've done had she been in the same position. But it would be one more treat she couldn't give Ricky herself. Which was selfish of her, she thought. Too bad innocent children couldn't have their small pleasures without grownup second thoughts getting in the way.

"That's right, Ricky," Natalie agreed a little reluctantly. "And you can go get your truck and show it to Missy.

Some girls love trucks." She gave the girl a wink that was meant for her alone and not the little boy.

Carefully cradling the *cascarones* in his hand, Ricky took off like a shot for the toy truck placed for safekeeping behind the counter. Apart from that one comment, Colter left himself pretty much out of the three-way conversation between Natalie, Missy, and Ricky. But Natalie never lost her awareness of him and her nerve ends tingled whenever she felt his dispassionate gaze directed at her.

Her break was over and she was back working at the grill when Missy said good-bye to Ricky. Natalie doubted that Colter Langston had joined in the farewell. She was certain any courtesy had been extended by Missy.

As she'd hoped, Ricky curled up very willingly on the bales of straw—to watch the people, he said. At ten o'clock, she saw his head drooping in sleep. A few minutes later, he shifted into a horizontal position, snoozing away, completely unmindful of the din that hadn't let up since the gates of La Villita had opened late that afternoon.

Officially, the Old San Antonio celebration ended at 10:30 each night, but it was close to that before Jeannie showed, talking a mile a minute as she pitched in to clean the grill. Natalie wasn't able to leave until 11:30.

She was dead beat. The last three days she had conducted an exhaustive search for a new job. That combined with almost six straight hours on her feet over the sapping heat of the grill made her feel too weary to take another step. Time enough to collapse when she reached home, Natalie told herself. She picked up Ricky and his toy truck and her purse to trudge to the gates of the Alamo Street entrance.

Just as she walked through them, a tall figure pushed itself away from the stone walls of La Villita. Her tired brain identified Colter Langston a second before he lifted the sleeping child from her weary arms.

"My car is across the street."

"You don't have to—" Natalie began weakly.

His head was drawn back a little, heightening the effect that he was looking down at her. "Would you like a ride home? A plain yes or no will do." The pitch of his low voice didn't change, yet there was an uncompromising quality to it.

The prospect of the long walk to her apartment seemed more daunting than a short ride with Colter Langston. Besides, in her overtired state, she found his strength and vitality intimidated her. Natalie held his expressionless gaze for an instant.

"Missy's idea, I suppose," she sighed, unable to acquiesce completely. He didn't deny her observation. Wearily she pushed the hair away from her face. "Okay. What the hell. I accept."

"My car's across the street."

Natalie had no trouble finding the white luxury car in the half-empty parking lot. Once she was in the passenger seat, he handed the sleeping Ricky to her and walked around to the driver's side. As Natalie tried to shift Ricky into a more comfortable position on her lap, his eyes blinked open.

Craning his neck, he looked into the back seat, then at Colter. "Where's Missy?"

"She's in bed, asleep." Colter answered the question as if it had been asked by an adult.

"I'm tired too," Ricky said, and settled his head against Natalie's shoulder, dropping off almost instantly to sleep.

Natalie leaned her own head against the rich leather cushions, half-closing her eyes as the powerful car accelerated into the street. The darkness and quietness closed around her like a warm cocoon.

"I never realized silence could be so beautiful," she murmured aloud, "or so peaceful."

The unceasing din of the crowds took on the aspects of a nightmare that was only barely remembered. Out of the corner of her eye, she studied his profile. The cushy seat relaxed her tired muscles, lessening their ache, and Natalie felt a twinge of conscience that she hadn't expressed her gratitude for the ride.

"I really appreciate your taking Ricky and me home, Mr. Langston. I hope your wife doesn't object."

The last remark, spoken without much thought, twisted the hard line of his mouth into a mirthless smile. "I doubt it. She passed away several years ago."

The blunt statement astounded Natalie. "I—I'm sorry," she said, for want of any other response.

"Are you? Why?" His gaze never left the street. "Because she's dead or because I can't pretend to feel grief over something that happened more than ten years ago?" Colter asked with asperity.

There was no answer Natalie could give to any of those questions, so she subsided into an uneasy silence the taciturn man at the wheel seemed to endorse. She got the picture. Colter Langston didn't indulge in idle conversation. He was totally frank and straight to the point. Her blunder into his personal life was thoughtless, true enough, but his tightlipped comments about his late wife begged a lot of questions.

As soon as she got home, she was going to look him up and get the whole story on her barely functioning laptop, if she could get it to work. If it didn't, she'd go to the library first chance she had, drop off Ricky at story hour, and research Colter online.

When they arrived at the house where she lived, Colter took Ricky from her again while she retrieved her key from the scant contents of her purse. The landlady's hallway door opened a crack for her stern face to peer out, but mercifully she said nothing, letting her disapproving presence serve as a reminder of her admonition the night before.

As Natalie hurried up the stairs to her apartment, her tiredness tripped her up and she stumbled over a step near the top. Instantly a firm hand came under her elbow, righting her. The hard strength and warm support that it represented was so overwhelming Natalie wished she could lean against it if only for a moment. She pushed away the impulse and the hand withdrew almost immediately.

The door of her apartment opened wider than she intended, allowing an unobstructed view of the sparsely furnished but clean room. In the short time it took to transfer the sleeping child from his arms to hers, Natalie had the feeling that every detail of her existence had been memorized by Colter. Her thanks were self-consciously offered and quickly shrugged aside as he turned back down the stairs before she had closed the door.

Each succeeding night of the Old San Antonio festivities was a repeat of the first. Colter and Missy arrived at about the same time and Missy spent most of the evening entertaining Ricky while Colter looked on. At closing, he was waiting outside the gates alone to give Natalie a lift home.

Her one offer to pay had been rejected with no more than a shake of his head. After the third night, Natalie stopped conjecturing that his actions might be more than a way to ease his sensitive daughter's concern for her and Ricky's safety.

At least she had managed to look him up online, jiggling the ancient laptop, a refurb, until the hard drive came to life and she could pick up a free wi-fi signal. He was who he seemed to be: a rich, well-connected, dyed-in-the-wool Texan, whose social-butterfly wife had died in childbirth. He'd never remarried, didn't have a specific girlfriend, though he'd been photographed with lots of gorgeous women at various events, got a lot of favorable press, and hadn't ever been arrested for anything.

So what and why do you care, she asked herself. Working nights, searching with no success for a permanent job during the day, and caring for Ricky didn't leave any free time to analyze his possible motives for being with her.

She'd brought up his name to Jeannie and gotten an earful, solid information and pure gossip culled from the glossy magazines her fellow cook read avidly. It all matched up with her online research and gave her about a thousand more reasons to wonder what on earth he saw in her.

It was close to midnight when Colter brought her home on Friday, the last night of the festivities at La Villita and the last night of her job. She had a fleeting thought as she took Ricky from his arms that there was little likelihood she and Ricky would see Colter or Missy again.

Before Natalie could say a final good-bye, though, he was reaching around her for the doorknob and she realized that he probably couldn't care less if he saw her again.

That was fine. Neither did she. She'd only been thinking that Ricky might miss his daughter. She murmured an edgy "Good night," and stepped into the apartment, adding the pressure of her free hand to the back of the door he was already pulling shut.

Weak and exhausted, wanting nothing more than to crawl between the covers of the daybed she shared with Ricky, Natalie instead walked to the tiny kitchen above and put a kettle of water on the stove to boil. As it heated, she spooned instant coffee into a cup, gathered pencil and paper and the pay envelope from her purse, and set them all on the small table. She knew she wouldn't be able to sleep until she worked out the true state of their finances.

Sipping the deliberately strong coffee later, Natalie studied the figures. It didn't seem to matter how many things she eliminated as non-essential. There simply wasn't enough money to carry them through the next week. In the three years Ricky had been with her, the future had never looked as bleak and hopeless as it did at that moment. Burying her face in her hands, she began to cry softly, tired sobs and stinging tears that didn't ease the pain of despair.

The click of the doorknob turning brought her head up in frightened disbelief. A blurry but very masculine outline filled the doorway. When she blinked away her tears, the blur resolved itself into the one and only Colter Langston.

Damn. Why now and why him? And how had he gotten in?

His keen eyes missed nothing, not the tear marks on her face, or the small stack of money meticulously counted out, the scribbled sums on the paper, and last but not least, her sagging shoulders and air of defeat.

"What are you doing here?" she breathed.

"You forgot to take the key out of the lock."

Metal clinked as he tossed her key onto the table. When her stunned gaze turned to it, he took the few steps necessary to reach the table and placed a paper package in the middle.

"W-what's that?"

"A sandwich."

"For me?" Natalie stared at the impassive man towering above her.

"I had dinner this evening. Did you?" A thick brow arched inquiringly. "Or did Ricky get the meal you were entitled to for working at the stand?" Her indrawn breath was the only answer he needed. "Thought so."

His tone sparked her pride to answer. "I'm not hungry," Natalie asserted, trying to ignore the tantalizing aroma of whatever was wrapped in the paper package.

"I don't believe you." With one swift move, his long fingers tore it open to reveal two sliced halves of French bread mounded in the middle with barbecued beef. He slid it in front of her, disregarding the neat stack of money he toppled. "Eat that," he commanded. "It'll do you good."

Something in his expression told her that he meant well, even if he wasn't Mr. Gracious. But even so . . . torn between the desire to throw it in his face before he had a chance to dodge it and to appease the hunger sapping her strength, Natalie gave him a cold stare.

"What do I owe you for your generosity?" she demanded.

An uncomfortable heat warmed her face when she realized that statement could be interpreted in more than one way. The corners of his mouth quirked, but he didn't take the opportunity to say something stupid, only looked sympathetically at her for a few seconds. Her cheeks still showed traces of the tears she had shed—was that what triggered his pity?

She didn't want it.

"At least you've learned nothing is for free," he said finally. "But all I want right now is a few minutes to discuss something with you once you've eaten."

"That's all?" Natalie was wary of his vague qualification.

"For now," Colter said, smiling in a way that she guessed was supposed to be friendly. But she wasn't in a warm-and-fuzzy mood, and she didn't smile back.

"The eventual outcome of our discussion will be strictly your decision," he went on. "Does that satisfy you?"

Natalie flinched at the question. "Not really." Her eyes were unwillingly drawn to the tempting sandwich.

"Eat. And relax a little, okay? I don't bite."

His blunt remark took the edge off her appetite, but not enough to lessen the tightness in her hungry stomach. Natalie wasn't going to argue with him, despite her vague feeling that she would be wiser not to get into the discussion he proposed. At her first bite of the sandwich, Colter moved away from the table.

Natalie swallowed quickly. "What are you doing?" She turned in her chair as he walked behind her to the kitchen alcove.

"Getting myself a cup of coffee."

"Let me do that." She set her sandwich down to push away from the table.

But his effortless strides had already taken him into the small cooking area. "Why, Mother Hubbard? Because your cupboards are bare?"

She cringed inwardly.

"I'd already guessed it," he said. As proof he opened the top door beside the sink to reveal the nearly empty shelves. Her pale cheeks flamed as she watched him take a cup and spoon some instant coffee into it. The kettle heated up again and he poured the steaming water into the cup. As he turned to her with it, Natalie subsided quickly into her chair.

When he wandered back to the table, there was only a faint hint of pink in her cheeks. She studiously avoided looking directly at him as he reclined his lean body in the straight chair opposite her, relaxing with negligent ease. Eating under his watchful eyes wasn't doing wonders for her digestion.

Natalie started visibly when he leaned forward suddenly, his hand reaching to one side of her. Then she saw what had captured his attention: a framed photo of her brother, his wife, and Ricky that sat on the shelf beside the table.

"My brother Ned and his wife Susan. That was taken on Ricky's second birthday," Natalie explained defensively when his glance turned on her.

"Then he *is* your nephew."

"Yes, he is." Her chin lifted in proud defiance. "Ned and Susan were killed in a car crash a few weeks after that was taken."

"And Ricky had no other family?"

"Our parents are dead and Susan's mother was an invalid," she responded, wondering why she was answering his nosy questions at all.

"You must have been quite young yourself." Colter continued to study the photograph.

"Eighteen, if you really want to know." She was rewarded for her sharpness with an immediate narrowing of his gaze.

But otherwise his expression remained completely unruffled. "That makes you twenty-one or twenty-two?"

"Twenty-two."

The tone of the last exchange didn't fall under the heading of idle conversation, but Natalie couldn't begin to perceive what he was getting at. She could only guess that it concerned something he wanted to discuss with her.

"No boyfriends?"

As if it was any of his business. "No," she answered.

She was unable or unwilling to explain that raising Ricky on her own had put an end to her social life. A kind of loneliness, however reluctantly acknowledged, had become her constant companion.

"Young guys lose interest when a kid is part of the package," Colter observed dryly. "Too much of a reminder of some other man, I guess. Plus a single mom can't pick up and go just like that."

He had put his finger exactly on the problem, but his accurate perception didn't ease her wariness. Natalie refused to acknowledge the truth of his statement and remained silent.

"You're sacrificing a lot for the sake of the boy." He'd replaced the photograph and was leaning back in the chair, tilting it onto its back legs.

"'The boy' has a name. It's Ricky," Natalie said, hating the way Colter kept referring to her nephew as if Ricky was an inanimate object. "And I don't regard it as a sacrifice. It isn't Ricky's fault that his parents were killed."

"Nor yours, although you seem determined to make up for it."

"What do you suggest I do?" Natalie demanded angrily. "Turn him over to court custody to be shuffled from one foster home to another? He'd never know the security of a real family. And I'm all he's got."

"I don't imagine there was anything else you could do under the circumstances." Colter set the chair back on all four legs.

Despite his statement, Natalie sensed that he didn't agree with her. She thrust what was left of the sandwich aside, losing her taste for it.

Chapter 3

"Would you mind telling me exactly what it is that you wanted to discuss?" Natalie's voice held a note of challenge. She was tired of playing the game of being mouse to his cat.

He nodded, while she studied his face. The only life in his expression was in his eyes. And even those gave nothing away. She told herself to be careful. Figuring out a strong, silent type was too much trouble.

His hand moved the coffee cup away from the edge of the table. "This evening," he began, "Missy told me that she wished her mother hadn't died giving birth to her. Understandable, of course, but what she really meant was that she would've liked a little brother or sister. She's become very fond of your nephew in a great big hurry."

Natalie nodded. He had a disconcerting way of saying things—important things—as if the person he was talking to would understand instantly. "Kids will do that sometimes—take a fancy to someone. She'll probably get over it. I'm sorry if it's inconvenienced you," she added crisply. She felt nothing but sympathy for Missy, who'd undoubtedly learned not to expect too much affection from anyone, especially parents.

His gaze narrowed. "We live on a ranch. My aunt Flo, who lives with us, looks after Missy," Colter continued. "But she's getting too old, or so she says, to shepherd my daughter through the next phase."

"Which is?" Natalie wasn't quite sure what he was getting at.

"The teenaged years. To me and maybe to you, she's still a little girl, right?"

Natalie nodded. "A sweet and gentle little girl."

Colter sighed. "Doesn't matter. Dear old Flo says all hell is going to break loose before I know it and I'd better be prepared. I think supervising a household the size of mine is what's getting to Flo, but there's no arguing with my aunt. Anyway, if she wants to retire, she's entitled to do so."

"I see," Natalie murmured. The picture had begun to form in her mind. He was looking for a live-in replacement for his elderly aunt. Someone a whole lot younger with the energy to take care of his house and his daughter. "And that's what you want to talk to me about."

"Exactly." There was a faintly friendly look on his face. "If you'll pardon the understatement, it's clear to me that life hasn't been easy for you and the boy lately. And from the frantic scribbles on that paper, your future doesn't look very bright either."

"If the question is do I need a job, the answer is yes."

"I'm not offering you a job."

It was difficult for Natalie to hold his level, ever watchful gaze. She took a deep breath, feeling weary of trying to match wits with someone who was one step ahead of her.

"Then what is this discussion all about?"

"I want you to marry me."

She blinked and frowned. "Is that some kind of a joke?"

"I'm completely serious." Now that the announcement

had been made, he seemed a little more relaxed. But she wasn't.

"*Marry* you? That' s just crazy. I don't love you and you don't love me," she said in blank confusion. "And we barely know each other."

He shook his head and tapped his fingers on the table. "Doesn't apply in this case—but, oh hell, let me explain." But he didn't, not right away.

Natalie eyed him warily. He looked sane enough. The explanation was probably going to be interesting. She took a deep breath and composed herself.

He leaned forward when he'd gathered his thoughts. "Here's the story. My aunt Flo holds very conservative views about a lot of things—kind of like your landlady—and if I hire a young woman, I don't want her thinking that I'm trying to take advantage of the situation."

"Uh-huh. But that doesn't mean you have to marry that young woman—I mean, marry me—just to make Flo happy. That doesn't make any sense at all."

"It would if you knew Flo. She's been a widow a very long time. Sometimes I think she gets her ideas about men and women from romance novels, if you really want to know."

"Oh." A few titles she'd seen in drugstore racks floated into Natalie's mind. "You mean like *The Rancher Hearts The Nanny.* And *Kiss Me, I'm Pregnant.*"

He grinned. "I found my personal favorite on the porch glider where she left it. Got my award for dumbest title ever. *The Billionaire City Boy and The Flat Broke Cowgirl.*"

"How did I miss that one?" Natalie asked wryly.

"Consider yourself lucky."

She shook her head. "I wish I had time to read. But scientific studies show that paperback romances definitely warp your mind."

"Must be why Flo reads them in secret. Hey, I don't

really care and it's none of my business. But I still think she takes them too seriously. Whatever. She's from the generation where men were supposed to do the right thing just after they did the wrong thing."

And what does that say about your generation? Natalie was dying to pop that question but she didn't.

"Anyway, she doesn't think highly of my abilities as a father."

"And why is that?" Natalie had to ask.

"She'll probably tell you as soon as you meet her—but she'll also tell you that I'm not crazy or a menace to society. Just that I need help."

"I see." Natalie took a deep breath and folded her arms across her chest. That statement could be interpreted in several different ways.

Looking at her defensive posture made him smile, but he didn't say anything.

"I'm sorry, but I really don't understand what you're getting at," she said. "You started by saying that you needed a housekeeper and someone to look after Missy," she reminded him with a trace of anger. "That's reasonable."

"Glad you think so." He gazed at her calmly. "That's why I want to marry you. Temporarily."

"Oh. Temporarily." She blew out a breath. "Huh. I have to say, it still sounds crazy."

"Makes sense from my point of view. Missy would have someone around who wouldn't up and quit in five seconds."

"Has that already happened?" Natalie asked cautiously.

"No. There's always been Flo, and only Flo. She's a tough old bird and I respect her. If we get married, she won't blow a gasket, that's all."

"Why would she? I mean, I'm not sliding on a pole at the Bim Bam Boom Room. I'm a line cook in a hairnet with a little kid to raise."

Colter flattened out his inadvertent smile into a frown. "She's the protective type."

"You don't look like you need any protecting to me."

"It's you she'd be protective of. You're young, single, and pretty."

"I beg your pardon?"

"Don't you like compliments?"

Natalie pressed her lips together and took her time about answering, finally deciding to let him talk.

"You can bet she'd give me hell for bringing someone like you home as her replacement," Colter went on. "She'd accuse me of wanting something from you, and so forth. I don't want to get into it with her."

"Oh. Go on."

"But if I can wave a marriage license under her suspicious nose, she'll be assured that everything is perfectly respectable."

"Let me get this straight." Natalie unfolded her arms. "Your aunt would rather see you come home with some strange woman that you just up and married than a—"

"Yes," was his curt reply. "Can we move on? I'm sure you want to know what's in it for you."

"I wouldn't put it quite that way, but—"

"A very good salary. Room and board, of course. And breathing room for you and the kid while you figure out what you want to do and where you're going in life."

"All well and good, but how is the last thing you mentioned going to provide stability for Missy? If that is what you really want."

He exhaled a long, slow sigh. "Interesting you should put it that way."

"Kids don't do well when caregivers come and go. You're her father. You should know that. Am I wrong?"

He stiffened a little, as if he were totally unaccustomed to someone talking to him like that. Natalie looked at him coolly, giving him a chance to make the right reply to her pointed question. Or get egg on his face by saying the wrong thing.

"No, you're not wrong," he said after a while. "But until Flo decided to retire, I didn't have to think about it too much."

"So you picked me. A woman you've known for, what, five days?"

That hit home. He looked like he was about to growl. But he shook his head instead. "I trust my instincts. You're great with kids, you have a lot of energy and you've got guts. Missy likes you a lot. Shy as she is, she said so."

"I like Missy."

He held her eyes for almost a minute. She didn't flinch—and neither did he. "Okay, you have the job, if you want it. Under my conditions."

She threw up her hands. "One of which is that I marry you? I still don't believe I'm hearing this."

"I am serious."

Her mouth felt dry and cottony. With a flash of irritation, she rose from the table, taking her cup and walking into the small alcove for more much-needed coffee.

"I'm afraid I don't see your reasoning," she said as she fussed with the coffeepot, milk, and sugar. "You don't have to acquire a wife to get a housekeeper."

"They're not mutually exclusive," he pointed out.

"Don't make me throw this coffee at you, okay?" Natalie returned to the table with her cup, stirring it vigorously. "It's awfully hot."

"Sorry. That remark was out of line." He watched her take a few sips.

"It sure was." She finished it quickly and stared into the cup, then at him. "What about if I say yes to the house-keeper part and no to the wife part?"

"No deal."

"Aha. Then what if I say yes to the wife part and no to the housekeeper part?"

A goofy grin started up on his face, but he quickly suppressed it. "Good one. You know how to bargain, Natalie. But I know what I want."

"The whole idea is ridiculous. Look, it's late and both of us are tired. Can we talk about this some other time?"

When Colter had mentioned that he wanted a housekeeper, she had wanted the job, her heart leaping at the thought of Ricky living in the country and herself being there whenever he needed her. But an impulsive marriage to a man she didn't know, just to pacify his straightlaced Aunt Flo—she reminded herself that she didn't know his elderly aunt either, both of them could be crazy as bedbugs—she wasn't going to do that.

But still. There was something about Colter Langston that made her want to trust him and his proposal. *Be careful,* she told herself. *Very, very careful.*

"Look," he was saying. "Check me out online before you answer. Unfortunately, the Langstons get a lot of media coverage, so we don't have any secrets. And go to that site where you can look up legal records and all that." He held up his hands palms out and gave her a rueful look. "I am who I say I am."

"Right. Jeannie told me you were one of the Langstons." She added mentally, as in *filthy rich and used to getting your own way.* She didn't mention that she had already looked him up online.

"Who's Jeannie?"

"My fellow steak-flipper. An authority on Texas society, believe it or not."

"Well, then, she can tell you that you'll come out ahead. And so will the boy. Starting with the basics—food, shelter, clothes, all included, plus a salary, instead of a hand-to-mouth existence."

"Whoa." She held up a hand. "What's in it for you?"

He almost smiled at her. "That's a blunt question."

"Well, it has to be asked," Natalie said.

He nodded. "Of course. Look, you hardly know me and you're pretty young, even though I'd bet you know more about life than a lot of people older than you." He looked around the sparsely furnished apartment. "Got a laptop?"

"Yeah. It's a clunker, but it works, sometimes."

"Then investigate me."

"I did." She thought for a second, ignoring his grin. Then she paused, studying him. "Is it just me or is this the weirdest conversation you ever had?" She imitated his deep voice. "Hey, want to get married? You can look me up online."

"Point taken." Colter made a wry face. "And no, it's not just you."

"So, do you do this a lot?" she asked conversationally. "Ask women to marry you just like that, I mean."

"No."

She cleared her throat, stalling for time. His direct questions and blunt answers nonplussed her. "Okay, well—that's a good thing, I guess."

"I like you, Natalie. And I'm hoping—" He didn't finish that sentence. "Anyway, do what you have to do. Keep on researching me. If your laptop won't cooperate, I have two. I'll drop off the new one. I haven't figured out how to use it yet myself. Too many bells and whistles for me. I'm old-fashioned, I guess."

Natalie looked at him with curiosity. "Really?"

Colter frowned. "Could we get back to business?"

"Okay."

"I can sweeten the deal, if you like."

Natalie shot him a suspicious look.

"It's clear to me that Ricky's happiness means everything to you."

She was taken aback. Had he been paying that much attention?

Colter continued. "I can set aside money in a gift-to-minors trust, make you the sole trustee with complete control over it, and he'll be able to afford a college education when the time comes."

Lately, Natalie's perilous finances had kept her from thinking ahead any more than, oh, a day or so. If that. She couldn't imagine what it would be like to make enough money to save. Or to give away.

Ricky going to college seemed far in the future. But her nephew would, her sister would have wanted it and she would make it happen somehow. Colter's offer was incredibly tempting. But it still seemed unreal.

"You don't have to say yes or no right this minute, Natalie."

She smiled politely. "I wasn't planning to."

"I'll explain just a little more, then. You won't have a worry in the world. You'll have nothing to concern yourself about except taking care of Missy. Other than the times the boy is in school, he'll be with you constantly."

"It's insane," Natalie said, staring at her cooling cup of coffee.

"It's logical."

She shook her head, trying to clear it. "I really do need time to think." Although she wasn't sure what there was to think about, except that she was reluctant to say no.

"Let me know. Missy and I are leaving for the ranch on Sunday morning. I have to explain the situation in advance to a few people, and I can't postpone that indefinitely."

"Right," she said with more than a trace of irritation. "No pressure. Thanks so much."

"I don't see the point of indecision, if you really want to know."

"Well, I'm not you," Natalie replied, nervously running her fingers through her brown hair.

"What are your alternatives?" he asked, a thread of impatience in his voice. "You and I both know what the future holds." His sweeping glance around her shabby little place said more than words. He shrugged and got up to leave, his long strides carrying him to the door without a backward glance.

At the click of the doorknob, something made her say the word. "Yes."

He turned but stayed where he was. "For real?"

She swallowed hard. "If you're for real. And I do intend to look you up some more and not just on Google. There's LadiesYouHaveBeenWarned.com and some others."

"Have fun." He favored her with a big grin. "You won't find me on any. You can double-check with Officer Olivera. She has access to some really interesting databases." He waggled his fingers at her. "And she can pull up my prints, believe it or not. I got inked when Missy did, for her school child safety program. I'm clean, Detective Natalie. Nothing to hide. My hell-raising days are long over."

"Maybe that's because you're a parent." Somehow *dad*, that friendly-sounding word, didn't quite fit him.

"Maybe so." Had she insulted him by not saying he was a dad? His face was impassive and she couldn't read his eyes. "I'll pick you and the boy up at eight tomorrow morning." Again his gaze made an all-encompassing sweep of the room. "You want to take any of this?"

She pressed her lips together. "No."

"Okay. Then you have time to vet me online to your heart's content." He seemed annoyingly confident. Without giving Natalie a chance to reply, saying a swift goodnight, he was out of the door and heading down the stairs.

She sat there, stunned. What had she just done? Said

yes to the most outrageous proposal she'd ever heard. Unbelievable.

On the other hand, yes was only a word. And she didn't have to go anywhere or do anything she didn't want to if she changed her mind.

If there was just one little thing she found online this time that she didn't like—one tiny discrepancy—she could take Ricky and go to a women's shelter and . . .

Natalie went looking for her laptop.

Two hours later, she'd followed up on every mention of Colter and looked at every photo of him ever published with this or that female on his arm, generally glamorous. She explored a link to a Texas magazine that gave the particulars of the Langston family going back several generations. His aunt Flo even rated a mention, confirming his description of her as a rock-ribbed conservative.

So he had a life, a full one, and he wasn't lonely or weird. As far as she could tell, Colter Langston was indeed who he said he was. She even found a photo of him with the beaming woman cop and the San Antonio chief of police, handing over a healthy donation in the form of a gigantic check to their youth group fund.

So far, so good.

But getting married to him . . . that was a sticking point. It just seemed like such an outlandish thing to do in this day and age.

She thought again of his offer concerning Ricky, and rose to look at the sleeping child.

"Am I doing the right thing?" she murmured aloud, then turned her eyes toward the ceiling. "God, let me know." The only response to her question was Ricky's peaceful sigh.

If she married Colter tomorrow morning, she rationalized, it could be easily annulled if things didn't work out. After all, it wasn't like he'd mentioned sex. Clearly, he'd had a string of girlfriends who completely outclassed her. So that probably wasn't going to be an issue.

Unless . . . She told herself firmly that she wasn't going to do anything dumb like fall in love with him. They were going to have an—an arrangement. That was all. She got ready for bed, her eyes bleary from staring into the flickering screen of her poor old laptop. But it had told her at least part of what she needed to know. As for the rest, well, starting tomorrow, she was going to take the only chance she had to get out of this dump and make a fresh start.

She expected to spend a restless night, but for the first time in recent memory, she awoke feeling refreshed and rested without that heavy weight of her endless problems pushing her down. A marriage of convenience didn't sound quite as strange as it had last night.

In a way, what they were going to attempt was probably much more honest than lots of real marriages. This for that. No romantic, gooey nonsense. Just clearly outlined expectations and responsibilities.

There really wasn't much to pack. But the process wasn't speeded up by Ricky's unbounded excitement, generated not by Natalie's announcement that she was going to marry Missy's father, but by all the changes that would bring.

"Can I really have a pair of cowboy boots?" he asked, for the hundredth time, Natalie was sure.

"Yes." She smiled patiently, unable and unwilling to dampen his enthusiasm. "As long as you behave. Are you sure you have all your toys in the duffel bag?" Not that he had many.

"Yes." Ricky sighed contentedly.

Apprehension tightened her stomach when Colter knocked on the door promptly at eight o'clock. Before the doubts could take hold, he had them and their few belongings stowed in the car, and the landlady cuttingly dealt with.

The entire day was a whirl of efficient organization, never allowing Natalie more than a passing opportunity to think about what she was doing. An entire wardrobe had been chosen by Colter, from the most intimate lingerie to accessories for an evening dress. While Natalie had her hair shampooed, styled, and set, the same impersonal attention was given to Ricky's clothing needs, fortunately including a pair of cowboy boots.

She had barely caught her breath at lunch before Colter was whisking the four of them on to a chartered jet bound for Laredo and ultimately, by rented car, to Nuevo Laredo across the border in Mexico, where she and Colter were married. In the car and on the flight to and from Laredo, Missy and Ricky had kept up a steady stream of chatter in which Ricky always included Natalie but Colter was left out.

By that evening, the events of the day had taken on an unreal quality, as if none of it had happened except in a dream. Breathing deeply of the warm night air, Natalie glanced at her pants suit, the elegant lines complementing her slender figure.

It *had* all happened. There was a heavy gold band on her finger to prove that she was Mrs. Colter Langston. And there was Ricky standing in front of her beside Missy, staring down again at the pointed toes of his shiny new cowboy boots.

They were back in San Antonio now watching another parade as her gold-flecked eyes looked curiously at Colter a foot or more to her right. As he had all day, he seemed aloof, detached from the group while in command of them. As if sensing her inspection, his eyes swung to Natalie from the precision drill teams entertaining the crowd.

"It's too late for second thoughts," he told her quietly.

Under his compelling gaze, Natalie couldn't look away. "It's too soon to say whether I regret it," she answered truthfully. She tilted her head to one side, her face softly illuminated by an overhead street light, her hair highlighted with a golden glow, the total effect feminine and alluring. "Do you?"

The mask of his expression didn't vary as his gaze raked her from head to toe. "I never regret anything," Colter replied.

"How wonderful it must be to be that confident," she mused.

"The only time you regret something is when your emotions are involved."

"And you don't have any emotions?" Natalie mocked the implacable mask.

"No, that curse wasn't put on me when I was born."

Automatically her gaze shifted to Missy, protectively holding Ricky's hand. "You don't feel anything?"

He guessed she was referring to his daughter. "Responsibility for her." Amusement flickered faintly around the corners of his mouth. "That shocks you too, huh?"

"It's just hard to comprehend." A frown of concentration drew her finely arched brows together. "Haven't you ever cared deeply for anyone—your parents, your wife?"

His muscular shoulders moved in a careless shrug as he turned away, letting a sideways glance slide back to her face. "I don't particularly care for myself. It's just as well you should discover that about me now, Natalie."

It still sounded strange to her to hear him say her name. It sounded as if he wasn't actually talking to her, just happening to mention a name that belonged to someone else.

"That way you won't expect very much from our marriage," he added.

If her imagination had entertained any thought that something might grow between them, it died with his statement. She felt a slight easing of her conscience at the same time. It wouldn't necessarily be a loveless marriage. No, it would be a true marriage of convenience where each of them got what they wanted for as long as it lasted and expected no more.

"Look, Nonnie!" Ricky said excitedly. "The parade is going to start."

Obediently Natalie directed her gaze to the street and the university marching band that had assembled. Beyond them and the crowd lining the opposite side of the street was the spotlighted façade of the Alamo, the cradle and shrine of Texas liberty, and the focal point of all the Fiesta activities commemorating Texas's independence from Mexico. The strategic Long Barrack stood watch to the side.

A drum roll from the band silenced the crowd as it anticipated the first notes of the song. In the hush of the Alamo, the strains of "The Eyes of Texas Are Upon You" filled the air, inspiring and proud. As Natalie stood a little bit straighter, she was conscious of a pair of Texas eyes on her. She glanced at Colter, applause and cheers rippling through the crowd when the song ended. His vague air of boredom dampened her enthusiasm for the Fiesta Flambeau, the night parade marking the official end of the annual celebration.

This time Ricky stayed awake through the entire parade, although by the time they arrived at the hotel, his eyelids were beginning to droop. Hotel rooms during the famous Fiesta had been booked months in advance, but Colter had used his money and his influence to obtain a room with twin beds on the floor below his.

This was not how Natalie had ever envisioned her wedding night, with her husband one floor above her, but then she had never expected to be left with Ricky to care for when she'd indulged in romantic fantasies of wearing white. Her dreams had been all about the dress and the veil and the beribboned bouquet—the man waiting at the altar had had his back to her in every fantasy. She'd had no one in particular to play that role, but she also hadn't expected to marry a man she didn't love. Reminding herself that it was temporary and for the sake of appearances, she slipped the expensive, flimsy nightgown over her head and climbed into one of the beds. Ricky was happy and safe, and that was all she had a right to ask for.

It was midmorning before she awoke. Natalie doubted she would have then if it hadn't been for him. Ricky hopped on her bed, hungry and eager to be off to the ranch that Missy had told him about. Colter and Missy were both in the lobby when she and Ricky hurried down.

"I'm sorry. I overslept," Natalie apologized.

"You needed the rest." Colter dismissed her apology in that offhand, indifferent way she was beginning to expect. "If your bags are packed, the front desk will send the bellhop up for them. We'll leave as soon as you and Ricky get some breakfast."

Natalie assured him that they were good to go. Her nerves fluttered wildly as she watched him walk away, realizing that within a couple of hours she would be on his ranch, in charge of his home. And his daughter, she added.

Missy was already taking Ricky by the hand to lead him into the hotel restaurant. The fact of her father's sudden marriage hadn't seemed to register with her yet. The only one Missy seemed interested in was Ricky. Natalie guessed it was because the young girl could give him the affectionate attention that came naturally to her, something her father didn't seem to want or care about.

Colter joined them at the breakfast table for coffee. Natalie discovered to her surprise that she wasn't at all nervous with him. She had expected to be. They were married, but they were strangers. For the next few years, if it all worked out to their mutual satisfaction, they were going to share the same house and food, even if not the same bed. It was a marvel that she was taking the situation so calmly. Maybe the shock of taking a leap like that hadn't worn off yet.

With all four of them sitting around a circular table draped with a snowy cloth, they looked like a complete family. Not boisterously happy, just quietly happy, because Missy had that shy, withdrawn look she always wore in public places, and Colter, taciturn and sipping coffee, held himself aloof. Yet the naturalness of their togetherness wouldn't leave Natalie.

As soon as the meal was finished, they left for the ranch. Some of Ricky's excitement over their soon-to-be-seen new home rubbed off on Natalie. She longed to ask Colter about it, but she decided not to. He might consider her questions more mercenary than curious.

Once the city of San Antonio was left behind, the scenery claimed her attention. It had been so long since she'd been in the country that the spacious expanse of blue sky stretching above rolling, piney hills took her breath away. They'd gone far, considering the suburban sprawl that now surrounded the old Texas city. More spectacular were the limitless fields of spring wildflowers, sometimes dotting, sometimes filling entire valley meadows. Brightening the green of the grass, they were vividly colored in whites, oranges, yellows, pinks, and the perennial favorite sky-shade of the bluebonnets.

"How much farther?" came the inevitable question from Ricky in the back seat. He was squeezed in between the extra bags that wouldn't fit inside the already full trunk.

"A few more miles," Colter replied.

"How far is the ranch from San Antonio?" They seemed to be a world away from the city's bustling streets and quaint lanes, and Natalie couldn't stop herself from asking the question.

"Somewhere around sixty miles." He was slowing the car and turning on to one of the ranch roads that intersected the main highway.

"Well, that's a ways. But you could have driven back and forth to the Fiesta," she responded without thinking.

"Missy thought she wouldn't get the whole experience if we did that." Colter glanced in the rear view mirror at his daughter who was listening patiently to Ricky. "The only thing she might have missed was meeting your little boy."

Something in his tone forced Natalie to ask, "Are you sorry?"

"No." A brow arched briefly in her direction. "Are you?"

"No," she answered quietly, feeling strangely tranquil.

Within a few minutes, the car slowed again and turned onto a gravel road, gliding dusty white between tall crossbars that marked the entrance to Langston Ranch. The road sloped gradually upward leading to a stand of tall trees. Through their branches, Natalie glimpsed a dark red roof, and, as they drew closer, cream-white walls. Guessing at Colter's wealth had not prepared her for the sight of the ranch house beneath the towering trees.

Though modern, its style was traditionally Spanish with curving roof tiles in terracotta and smooth stucco walls, set off with scrolling wrought iron at the windows. Flowering bushes and shrubs grew in profusion, their vibrant flowers accented by the enormous white blossoms of a magnolia tree. The gravel road meandered on in the direction of the house, built through the stand of trees that partially concealed it. The car descended the slight slope it had climbed, and they came out in front.

"We're here," Missy announced.

As Colter braked to a stop by the stone walkway leading to the house, a man came walking through the trees toward them—tall, broad-chested, wings of silver mingled with otherwise dark hair beneath a battered but serviceable Stetson, older than Colter, maybe in his late thirties.

"When did you get back, Colter?" the man said as Colter stepped from the car and walked to greet him. "I was just coming up to the house to check."

"Just now—"

Missy and Ricky were faster getting out of the car than Natalie, who dawdled to get a longer look at the sprawling but luxurious ranch house that was her new home. She missed hearing the rest of Colter's reply as she closed the car door.

"Did you enjoy the Fiesta, Missy?" The man tugged at the young girl's long braid as she walked by him to her father.

"Yes," she answered politely, giving him a shy smile.

Ricky had been impressed by the size of the house too and for once lagged behind Missy. His silky brown head was trying to turn simultaneously in all directions and still see where he was going, without success.

"Hello there," the man said when Ricky almost ran into him. "And who are you?"

"My name is Ricky," he announced unabashedly, taking his measure of the stranger. "I think I'm going to live here."

The man glanced inquisitively at Colter, then caught Natalie's approach out of the corner of his eye. The boy was forgotten as he studied her, and Natalie felt herself blossoming warmly under his admiring gaze. His brown eyes were telling her, respectfully, that he found her very pretty, but they didn't leave her with the feeling that she'd been secretly undressed. Going on feminine instinct, Natalie knew she was going to like this man, whoever he was.

"Travis, I'd like you to meet my wife Natalie. Her

nephew has already introduced himself, I believe," Colter said. "Natalie, this is my foreman, Travis McCrea."

If a thunderbolt had struck him, the good-looking stranger couldn't have been more shocked. As self-conscious pink began to appear in Natalie's cheeks, he tried to hide his amazement.

"Forgive me," he said to Natalie. "I didn't realize Colter had any plans to marry again."

"That's quite all right," Natalie replied after Colter failed to comment on his foreman's observation.

"Travis usually eats with us if he's around the house at mealtimes," Colter informed her. "You can file that away for future reference."

"If you have any objections to setting an extra place," Travis said hastily, "I can make other plans."

"None at all," Natalie assured him with a genuine smile. "I hope you'll continue coming around, Mr. McCrea."

"Travis," he corrected her, smiling back. "We aren't formal at the ranch."

"Then call me Natalie."

"Thank you, I will." There was a curious glint in his dark eyes when he glanced briefly at Colter, but it was gone when he directed his warm brown gaze at Natalie. "You'll be anxious to see your new home. I won't keep you, Colter." He touched his hat with his finger and went back the way he had come.

"You liked him, didn't you?" Colter commented as they turned to follow the children to the house.

"Is there any reason why I shouldn't?" Natalie wondered why she had to feel defensive simply because she had immediately liked Travis McCrea.

"No."

"Then why did you ask?"

"A lot of women find him attractive," was the only reply she received.

"I would imagine so," Natalie said, striving for a non-committal tone.

His inscrutable gaze took her in. "Feel guilty?"

"What? No, I don't." She wished she knew exactly what was on his mind, though she could guess.

"There's no need to be ashamed of feelings like that," Colter said dryly.

"How would you know? You don't have any feelings," she shot back, unaccountably angered.

"Don't confuse feelings with emotions." He answered in the same level voice as before, not reacting to Natalie's anger. "I see, touch, hear, smell, and taste as keenly as the next man. Sexual attraction between men and women is physical. There is no emotion in desire."

Chapter 4

A cold finger ran down her spine. She hadn't liked Colter's detached implication that she might be attracted to Travis McCrea. The carved walnut entrance door stood open and Colter moved aside for Natalie to go first.

As she stepped across the threshold, she forced herself to remember that their marriage wasn't real, merely a convenient arrangement. It was clear that Colter had no intention of abiding by the traditions of a bride and groom; to do that would be a mockery. There had been no kiss after the wedding ceremony and now he was letting her walk into her new home instead of carrying her. Thank heaven there was no need to pretend, she told herself.

Cool white walls confronted her, accented by dark walnut wood. The floor was tiled in large squares of black and white. Natalie's glimpse of the living room extending out from the foyer gave her the idea that the interior of the house was as elegantly casual as the outside. But most of her attention was focused on a plump older woman seated on a straight chair, her hand holding Missy's fingers. Her head turned at the sound of their footsteps on the tiles, her blue eyes curious and alert.

"So this is your bride." The woman addressed Colter in a no-nonsense tone as she rose to her feet.

There were few age lines on the woman's face, confined mainly around her eyes and mouth. Her features were stern but unlike Colter's, her mouth gave the impression that it smiled frequently. It was a strong face and its beauty was in its strength rather than simple prettiness. This was a woman whose friendship was not lightly given, Natalie thought.

"Yes, this is my wife Natalie," Colter said, then introduced the woman. "My aunt, Flo Donaldsen."

"Hello." Natalie smiled as her hand was enclosed in the woman's firm grip.

"I hope you'll like it here." The tone of Flo Donaldsen's voice said that she doubted it, as her eyes flashed a speaking glance at Colter. "Would you like a bite to eat?" she asked Colter with routine politeness. "I've already put away the lunch food. You said you would be back this morning."

"That was my fault, Mrs. Donaldsen." Natalie spoke up. "I overslept this morning."

"Rolls and cold cuts will be fine until dinner," Colter stated, subtly letting Natalie know there was no need to apologize. "While you're fixing that, I'll show Natalie the bedrooms where she and Ricky will be sleeping. Everything ready?"

There was a silent challenge in his voice, almost daring his aunt to make a personal comment. The woman's mouth tightened just a little before she answered yes.

Walking down the hallway on the east side of the house, Missy shyly pointed out her own bedroom to Natalie and Ricky, a feminine room with pastel flower prints everywhere. Ricky's room was next to hers, its single bed draped with a red, white, and blue spread with matching curtains and throw rug. But it was the toy train set in the corner that caught his attention, and he waited impatiently while Missy showed him how to operate it.

"Was it yours?" Natalie asked after Colter had suggested they leave the children while he showed her where she would be sleeping.

"Yup. Years ago."

It was difficult for Natalie to picture him as a little boy. She guessed that he'd always seemed older than his years and not at all the happy-go-lucky, open-hearted kid that Ricky was.

As Colter opened the door across the hall from Ricky's, her idle musings were replaced by admiration. Beautifully crafted oak furniture dominated the room, its rich patina reflecting the sunny shade of the area rug. The warm shades were repeated in the drapes and sheers framing the French doors leading out to the patio.

"W-was this your aunt's room?" Natalie was unable to take her gaze away from the attractive décor.

"No. She's always used the room off the kitchen, which was meant to be for a maid or cook. I was never able to persuade her to take one of the bedrooms in the main section of the house once Missy was grown. She insisted that she wanted her privacy," Colter said.

"Maybe I should stay there," Natalie said hesitantly, really wanting to enjoy the luxury of this room while wondering at the same time whether she was asking too much. Essentially she was only the housekeeper.

"No. You're my wife. Your place is here in this room," he said calmly. "Besides, you'll want to be near Ricky until he gets used to his new surroundings. The paperwork for his Universal Gift to Minors Act trust is in that folder." He pointed to a small desk.

"Right. Of course," Natalie agreed, silently glad that his logic had vanquished her doubts. "I'll look it over tonight."

"Any questions, ask me."

Yes, sir. Was she supposed to salute?

"Missy will show you where the dining room is. Flo should have a snack set out by now." He turned toward the door, expecting Natalie to follow, which she did.

"Aren't you going to join us?" she asked.

"I want to check on a few things with Travis."

Natalie lingered in the hallway, watching Colter as he disappeared in the direction of the foyer. He had been away from the ranch almost an entire week, she reminded herself. Stood to reason that he would be anxious to be brought up to date. She glanced at the other closed doors leading off the hall, wondering which one was his room. No doubt it would be as austere and masculine as he was.

Then the wonderfully old-fashioned sound of a toy train, little chugging wheels and tiny whistle and all, drew her into Ricky's room. Going in, she gave Ricky a few minutes to show her how he could operate the train without derailing the small cars before she suggested that Missy take them to the dining room. The next item on her agenda after some food and a cold drink was to have Mrs. Donaldsen explain the household routine.

At the dining table, Natalie said no to the pecan pie Flo offered in favor of a tall lime cooler. Missy was much less reserved around her great-aunt, eagerly responding to her questions about the San Antonio Fiesta, while Ricky began devouring his pie after the first polite bite. When his plate was clean, he pushed it toward Flo.

"May I have another slice?" he asked brightly.

"No, Ricky," answered Natalie before Flo had an opportunity to reply. "One is enough."

"Okay," he agreed, not put out by her refusal as he took a big swallow of the lime drink. "Are you ready, Missy?"

"I have to help Aunt Flo clear the table first," the young girl replied.

"If you don't mind, Missy," Natalie said gently, "I'll help Flo and she can show me where things are in the kitchen. Maybe you could show Ricky around the house and yard."

Missy hesitated for an instant, glancing at Flo Donaldsen for approval, which was given with a slight nod. Excusing herself from the table, she took Ricky's hand and began leading him from the room.

The older woman didn't say a word as they stacked the few dishes and carried them through to the kitchen, a state-of-the-art one with every appliance. On the counter sat a colander full of squeezed lime halves next to a juicer.

"The limes were fresh?" Natalie murmured in surprise.

"Colter likes everything fresh." The explanation was given tersely. "He sends a truck to the Rio Grande Valley every two weeks for fruit and vegetables."

"Couldn't he buy them locally?"

"He could," Flo admitted, "but he wants to be sure they're the best."

"That must be expensive." Natalie set the dishes on the counter by the sink, the full extent of Colter's wealth slowly sinking in. The place was so well-run she figured there were invisible servants—only the best invisible servants, of course.

"He can afford it," the older woman sniffed.

"Yes, I suppose so."

Flo's blue eyes studied her intently for a long moment before the subject was set aside and they put the plates and cutlery into the dishwasher. Flo added detergent and switched it on, and then briskly explained the household routine.

Wiping the already immaculate table that stood in the middle of the kitchen, Flo concluded, "I've already had most of my things moved to the cottage after Colter called me yesterday. I'll stay at the house tonight to help you with supper and fix breakfast in the morning. After that you're on your own."

Disapproval of their hasty marriage was clear in the rigid lines of Flo's shoulders as she went to the stove to wipe the top off. Her capable hands halted their circular movement as she turned to Natalie.

"I know why Colter married," Flo said grimly. "When it suits him, he can be very persuasive. I didn't see any love or even pretend love in your eyes when you looked at him. What did you marry him for? Was it his money?"

The blunt question caught Natalie by surprise. She hadn't expected the older woman to say exactly what was on her mind. She stared at her fingers for a moment, studying the plain gold band while the other woman's gaze stayed on her. The silence was awkward.

Tossing her head back proudly, Natalie met the look. "It was a matter of convenience. He needed someone to look after his house and daughter, and Ricky and I needed a home. So, no—it wasn't his money, exactly. More like a promise of security."

Flo stared at her for a little while longer before she breathed in deeply and turned away. "I raised Colter from a boy, you know. I blame his father for always reminding him that he was a Langston and different from other people, but I think Colter was naturally different from day one. He's cold and heartless. You're likely to regret the day you married him."

A shiver raced over Natalie's skin as she took in the absolute quality of the woman's statement. No wiggle room whatsoever. It was a flatly spoken prophecy with the ring of truth. Which made it doubly depressing.

A small hand tugged impatiently at hers, demanding her attention. Mentally dismissing Flo's pronouncement, Natalie glanced at the boy standing at her side. A smile appeared immediately at the sight of a little face brimming with happiness.

Colter's approval or affection didn't matter to her. She would be his housekeeper and look after his daughter. Her reward would be in the shining contentment of knowing Ricky would have all the things she wanted to give him: a home, security, and a future.

"What is it, Ricky?" Natalie asked.

"Come and look at the swimming pool!" he exclaimed. "There's one in the backyard!"

"I'll be there in a minute. I have to help Mrs. Donaldsen first."

"Run along," the woman spoke up. "I'll start making dinner around five. You can come and help me then."

"Please, you have to see it," Ricky insisted.

"All right." Natalie gave in with a laugh, unable to resist the sparkle in the little boy's eyes.

The front of the house had only hinted at the beauty to be found around the back. Honeysuckle vines covered the rock walls, their sweet fragrance mingling with other heady scents. The oleanders were covered in scarlet-pink blossoms, showier than the more delicate dusty pink of the mimosa tree. At the end of a walled patio was a swimming pool, its smooth waters reflecting the vivid blue of the sky.

A slatted bench swing was suspended from the thick branch of a live oak. Natalie couldn't resist and Ricky scrambled up to sit beside her, soon joined by Missy. Listening with half an ear to Missy's chatter, Natalie drank in the tropical serenity of the garden, inwardly smiling at the thought of ever regretting the events that had brought her here.

The relative inactivity of just swinging soon bored Ricky, and Missy obligingly produced a large beach ball for a game of catch while Natalie looked on. Relaxed, her worries gone, she didn't notice the shadows getting longer until she happened to glance at her watch and saw the hands pointing to half past four.

With a start of surprise at the quick flight of time, Natalie slipped out of the swing, calling to Missy and Ricky that she was going into the house to help Mrs. Donaldsen prepare dinner. As she stepped through the French doors into the living room, she heard the sound of a car speeding into the driveway, followed by the strident blare of its horn. Curiosity brought Natalie across the room to the windows looking out to the front entrance.

Pushing the sheer ivory curtains aside, she saw Colter and Travis McCrea approaching the house through the trees. A dust cloud was just settling around the wheels of the dark green sports car that had ground to a halt in the drive. A woman with long, shimmering curls of red-gold emerged from the car, wearing an emerald-green crop top and lowslung white jeans.

The house's thick walls muffled her words of greeting, but Natalie knew exactly who they were meant for when the gorgeous redhead glided over the ground to Colter.

Natalie breathed in sharply when the woman didn't stop at an over-the-top hello. Her manicured fingers touched Colter's chest as her head tilted back to smile at him. Then her hands twined around his neck while she suggestively pressed her body against Colter's. His mouth quirked at the corners before Miss Gorgeous stood on tiptoe to claim an obviously passion-filled kiss.

Natalie's blood ran cold at the sight of Colter's hands resting lightly on the woman's bare waist. His complete lack of resistance kindled a fiery rage that didn't ease when his head rose slowly from the woman's kiss. Not until she saw his gaze turn toward the house did Natalie let the curtain fall into place, suddenly aware that if Colter hadn't seen her at the window, Travis McCrea sure as hell had.

She fought to get a grip on her frustration and—she had to call it what it was—her fury. If Colter had married her to stop the gossip that would have been inevitable if she'd merely lived in his home as a housekeeper, then she ought to be entitled to some show of respect from him as his wife.

Then she told herself that it was neither here nor there. He hadn't married her for that reason, but to be sure she wouldn't be free to leave whenever she chose. There had been no mention of any pretending to be married.

Her stomach lurched as Natalie realized that whatever women Colter knew, he would go on knowing. He hadn't even attempted to dodge the woman's embrace or kiss, even with Travis looking on. Which proved that he didn't care if Natalie got her feelings hurt or would be a bit of a joke to his guests.

It was a jolting discovery, a serpent in this Garden of Eden. Her pathetic assumption that as his wife she was entitled to an outward show of respect was a little ridiculous as well.

Her thoughts preoccupied her to the extent that she didn't hear the sports car churning out of the gravel drive. The opening and closing of the front door alerted her to the fact that she was still standing with her back to the window. Too late to move, she lifted her head in proud defiance, preparing to reject the pity that Travis's brown eyes would offer. But Colter walked into the living room alone, aloof, strikingly handsome, and arrogant, adjectives that consistently described him well. His gaze flicked from Natalie to the window, then back to her face.

"Deirdre decided against staying." His mouth moved into a humorless smile as he strolled into the room.

The smoothness with which he spoke the name of the

woman he'd just been kissing sent an electric surge of anger through Natalie's veins. Her eyes blazed with it.

"And Deirdre is?" Her brow arched in a haughty question. She was determined to show him she wasn't a total doormat.

"Deirdre Collins, the daughter of one of the neighboring ranchers," Colter explained, looking calmly at her. "And friend of mine."

Natalie's gaze was drawn to the hard line of his mouth, seeking traces of lipstick. "Is that all?" she asked mockingly.

Her indignation only seemed to amuse him. "Yes."

Again she was uncomfortably reminded of his coldness, his lack of compassion for another person's feelings. She averted her gaze from his.

"Where's Travis? I thought he was with you."

"I believe he was under the impression that you might be embarrassed." Laughter edged his voice. Not very nice laughter.

"Because I saw you kissing that woman?" Her shoulders moved in an uncaring shrug, as if the scene hadn't concerned her in the least.

"Actually, I was being kissed rather than the other way around." Colter corrected her with infuriating evenness.

"You weren't exactly protesting!" Natalie snapped, and immediately turned away so he couldn't see that he'd gotten to her.

"Does that bother you?"

"Of course not!" She tried to ignore the eyes she could feel burning into her back.

"Then why are you angry?"

Natalie was tempted to tell him that she wasn't, but she had already made the contrary clear. Curling her fingers into her palms, she turned back to him, subduing her temper to reply in an unruffled voice.

"I hadn't realized that you intended to broadcast the

fact that I was nothing more than a glorified housekeeper and babysitter, unworthy of any respect as your wife."

"Do you mean you want us to pretend that we care for each other?" His tone made his contempt for the idea more than clear. "Do we have to fake it?"

"No, I don't mean that at all," Natalie said vigorously. "I just don't want to be ridiculed in the community where Ricky has to grow up."

"Legally having my name will get you plenty of respect," Colter said.

Her mouth tightened into a mutinous line. "And make me the subject of a lot of gossip."

"Do you care what people say?"

"Only if it hurts Ricky."

"Aww. You must feel insulted because I haven't kissed you yet. I did say that you were very attractive at least once." There was a flirtatious gleam in his eyes.

"Nice of you. But I'm not longing to be kissed, believe it or not. I've already told you what I expect and that's respect. Nothing more." Her nerves suddenly vibrated at how very close he was standing to her, and how strong he seemed.

"Do you mean you didn't expect to be the first woman I kissed after we were married?" His amusement was unbelievably annoying.

Natalie flushed and his finger touched the heightened color in her cheek. She remembered expecting a duty kiss after the wedding ceremony, meaningless and dry, meant to keep up appearances. She'd been disappointed. She pressed her lips tightly shut rather than admit that. Glaring at him, she stayed still under the caressing strokes of his finger along her cheek and jaw, determined to show her complete indifference to him, even be as rude as he was being.

"Maybe I should make amends."

The words were hardly spoken when his hand closed firmly over her chin. Her eyes widened in surprise as her hands came up to his chest to push him away. But the attempt was wasted as his arm swept around her to check her movement.

The swiftness of his action was misleading—Natalie was well aware of the slow deliberation that controlled Colter. When his hard mouth began to descend to hers, she didn't dodge. No reaction was the best deterrent for an unwanted kiss.

The pressure of his lips caused an involuntary and tiny gasp of surprise. His coldness, remoteness, and lack of emotion had not prepared her for the warm, sensual experience of his kiss. Natalie had expected his lovemaking to be skillful, even powerful, but certainly not this seductive mastery that evoked such a strong response in her. An enveloping warmth swept through her body as his hand slipped from her chin to the vulnerable curve of her throat.

His expertise intrigued her and she was reeling a little when his head rose from hers. Had she kissed him in return? Of course you did, she scolded herself, feeling dazed when she looked at his face. He radiated masculine satisfaction as his eyes examined the parted fullness of her lips, still trembling from the firm imprint of his mouth. Then he looked into her wondering eyes.

"Been a long time since you've been kissed, hasn't it?" he asked, relaxing his hold on her throat so she could move away.

"Yes." From somewhere she dredged up the strength to reply, seizing on his comment as the reason that his kiss had inexplicably moved her. She had never been a prude. A man's kiss had always been pleasurable if not exciting.

"That's a pity," Colter drawled lazily. Indifference

subtly altered his expression, but his face was starkly handsome all the same. "You might be quite good at it with a little more practice," he added.

Natalie sputtered indignantly before telling herself that her temper was wasted on Colter. He had already released her and stepped away.

She let out her breath and turned to go into the kitchen. "I'm going to help Mrs. Donaldsen fix dinner."

"Where's Missy and the boy?"

"Ricky." Her teeth gritted as Natalie emphasized her nephew's name. "Missy and Ricky are playing ball in the back."

Flo was the soul of brisk efficiency when Natalie met her in the kitchen, launching first into the arrangement of items in the well-stocked cupboards. While Natalie prepared a fresh pineapple, the older woman started cutting thick slices of ham to be broiled with the pineapple rings.

If she noticed the glow in Natalie's cheeks, she didn't mention it. Her comments on their marriage had been made. And Natalie was too determined to show Colter's aunt that she wasn't a novice in the kitchen to allow her mind to wander back to the disturbing kiss.

As Natalie began collecting the plates and glasses to set the dining room table, Flo said, "I had Juan—he's the handyman and gardener—take your suitcases up to your rooms. I would have unpacked them for you, but I thought you'd rather do that yourself later tonight."

"Thank you," Natalie responded, silently wondering if Flo was implying that she and Ricky would be better off to leave them packed. Shaking away that thought, she chose to say something nice. "The gardens and the house are beautifully kept up."

"Humph," Flo sniffed, lifting the lid of one of the pots on the stove to check the vegetables being steamed.

"What's the old saying? Stone walls do not a prison make. Yes, that's it."

Glancing apprehensively at the older woman, Natalie decided to ignore the comment. She could hardly regard herself as a prisoner in this house. She'd come here of her own free will, the decision made with a full understanding of the relative permanency of her position here, at least until Ricky was grown. Or she wanted out. Either way, her nephew would have money for college.

The first meal in her new home was a success, at least from the standpoint of the food being delicious and the company pleasant. Travis McCrea dominated the conversation with his easy, confident charm, with Ricky occasionally competing for control of the subject matter.

For the most part, Travis talked about Fiesta Week in San Antonio, getting shy Missy to share her observations of the goings-on and chuckling at Ricky's boldness. Travis steered the conversation away from personal inquiries into Natalie's life or how she'd happened to meet Colter.

For his part, Colter restricted his comments to Ricky's questions about the ranch. He seemed to be prepared for Ricky's interest, and Natalie wondered silently how long his patience would last under Ricky's insatiable curiosity.

When the dinner dishes were cleared and the strawberry dessert placed on the table, Ricky leaned forward to look past Natalie at Colter seated at the head of the table.

"Will you take me to see the cows and horses tomorrow?" he asked, but the question was closer to a demand. "Missy wouldn't take me to see them today. She said we weren't allowed down there."

"Ricky!" Natalie said in a shushing tone, sure that he'd gone too far by asking Colter for a personal tour of the ranch. "Mr. Lang—" Her sideways glance caught Colter's reaction to her almost formal reference to the man who was her husband. "I mean Colter," she corrected quickly, feeling an embarrassed warmth climb up her neck. "Colter will be too busy tomorrow to show you around. So you'll just have to wait, that's all."

"Really?" Ricky asked, wanting to hear Colter say no, ignoring Natalie's frown.

"I probably will be busy tomorrow," Colter said, "but there's the day after. We'll see."

"Can I ride a horse?" Satisfied with his half-promise, Ricky went off on another tangent.

There was a trace of exasperation in Natalie's sigh that brought an amused glance from Travis McCrea, who was seated across the table from her.

"Have you ever ridden a horse before?" Colter asked him, not missing the smiling exchange between his wife and his foreman yet totally unconcerned by it.

"No." Ricky seemed to think it didn't matter.

"Have you?" Colter's compelling blue-green gaze turned to Natalie.

"Years ago, but I'm hardly experienced."

Colter nodded. "Pick out some suitable mounts for them," he said to Travis.

"I think I know just the pair," the dark-haired man replied, winking at Ricky, who was beside himself with glee.

"Do you ride, Missy?" Natalie asked, trying to include the young girl so she wouldn't feel left out of the activities.

Missy darted a nervous glance at her father, who answered for her. "She used to. She was thrown from a horse two years ago and dislocated her hip. She hasn't been on a horse since then."

His shy daughter turned crimson at the detached-sounding criticism in Colter's reply. Natalie felt nothing but sympathy for her. That kind of fear was difficult to overcome. Missy wasn't naturally adventurous, which only made it worse.

Chapter 5

Coffee followed dessert for the adults while Ricky and Missy excused themselves from the table to enjoy the last of the sunlight outdoors.

A scarlet-orange sun was hovering over the treetops when Natalie finished helping Mrs. Donaldsen with the last of the dinner dishes and went in search of Ricky. She listened to his halfhearted assertion that he wasn't tired, but a yawn accompanied his statement and Ricky followed Natalie to his bedroom.

There was a bathroom situated in the hallway between his room and Missy's. While Ricky bathed, Natalie unpacked his suitcase, barely filling the empty drawers of the bureau and the roomy closet. She was just turning down the covers of his bed when he padded into the room.

"Will you read me a story? I brushed my teeth and washed." He held out his small hands for her inspection.

Long, curling lashes fluttered down over his brown eyes long before the Three Bears discovered Goldilocks in their woodland cottage. Natalie tucked the bedcovers tightly about him, brushed a kiss to the forehead covered with silky brown hair and tiptoed out of his room, leaving the door slightly ajar in case he called for her in the night.

Before Natalie returned to her own room, she looked in on Missy, who was sitting in bed with a book propped on her knees. Her hair was free of its braid, flowing down her shoulders to her waist in crisp waves. Its length made the young girl's face look thinner and even more narrow. Natalie silently resolved to persuade Missy to have her hair cut into a shorter style—in the future, when they knew each other better.

Natalie smiled. "Good book?"

"Uh-huh. Pretty good. Is Ricky in bed?" Missy asked.

"In bed and already sound asleep, and he wasn't tired," she laughed softly, receiving an answering smile of understanding at Ricky's initial reluctance to go to bed.

Then the smile faded from Missy's face as she darted a shy look at Natalie. "I'm . . . I'm glad you and Ricky came to live with us."

"So am I." Natalie nodded calmly, knowing this was not the time to grasp too firmly at Missy's tentative friendship. "Good night, Missy. Sleep well."

"Good night—Natalie."

As Natalie opened the door to her room, there was a satisfied gleam in her eyes. Ricky was adapting easily, as only a child could, to his new life, and Missy was on the verge of accepting them both completely and without reservation. The future seemed rosy. So far.

Her suitcases stood at the foot of the bed. As she approached them to begin her own unpacking, she saw the door to what she had thought was a closet, standing ajar. The glimpse of lush carpet and shining porcelain revealed that it wasn't.

Curious, Natalie stepped through the open doorway, gazing with pleasure at the spacious private bath. In contrast with the three white walls, the fourth was covered with a photomural of a green landscape. But the most striking feature of the bathroom was the sunken tub, luxuriously deep and large.

Thick bath towels hung on a gold rack. A glass shelf near the tub held a dish of yellow-gold soap in the shape of rosebuds. Beside it was an unopened container of lavender-scented bath salts, no doubt a peace offering from Mrs. Donaldsen.

The prospect of lazing in the sunken tub filled with fragrant bubbles was infinitely more inviting than unpacking the suitcases in the adjoining room. And, Natalie told herself, she could always unpack after a relaxing bath.

Thus convinced, she turned on the gold taps and adjusted the water temperature, liberally adding the lavender-scented salts. In her bedroom, she shook out the lounging robe from the smaller of the two suitcases and carried it and the cosmetic case into the bathroom.

Nearly three-quarters of an hour later, Natalie stood in front of the vanity mirror above the gleaming porcelain sink, feeling clean and refreshed and blissfully feminine. Fluffing the ends of her shining honey-brown hair with a comb, she tried to recall the last time she'd felt free to spend so much time on herself. It seemed very long ago.

The lapels of her robe revealed the delicate hollows of her collarbones and the graceful curve of her throat. The rich color of the robe intensified the sparkling amber lights in her hazel eyes. Her features were no longer etched with worry and tension, but soft and alluringly beautiful. A little security did wonders for her. Without the pinched look of strain, Natalie didn't look nearly so thin.

With a satisfied smile at her reflection, she switched off the bathroom light and walked back into her bedroom.

She froze at the sight of Colter standing near the bed in the act of tossing his shirt on the chair.

"What are you doing here?" Natalie demanded in a

less than commanding tone as she stared in disbelief at the leanly muscular and naked chest.

He spared her a sliding glance of unconcern as he unbuckled his belt and slipped it out of the loops of his jeans. "Getting ready for bed."

"But . . . but this is my room." She faltered, her heart beating wildly.

"Yes, it's your room too," Colter agreed, emptying his pockets on the dressing table.

"Too?" she echoed weakly, still in the grip of surprise. "But I thought—"

Colter turned slowly, dispassionately examining her startled expression. "What exactly did you think?"

Natalie turned away from his compelling gaze, her hand clutching the zippered front of her robe. Striving to achieve a calmness she was far from feeling, she breathed in deeply.

Colter only laughed.

"You honestly didn't believe this was going to stay one of those in-name-only marriages, did you?"

"Yes, I did," she said indignantly. But she was thinking along rather different lines. *You wished that your relationship with Colter would stay the same—distant—until you were good and ready to get closer, didn't you?* "Last night," she began.

But he interrupted with cutting swiftness. "Last night accommodations with suitable privacy couldn't be arranged."

"You might as well know right now that I have no intention of going to bed with you." Natalie tilted her head to a defiant angle. "We may have gone through the formality of a marriage ceremony, but we aren't really husband and wife."

"Not yet," qualified Colter, his hands resting complacently on his hips.

"Not ever!" she flashed, moving away from his half-naked, unmistakably masculine presence.

With the swiftness of the cougar she'd mentally likened him to, Colter pounced. His grip on her arm was impossible to shake off. Yet he was gentle in a way also as he turned her around to face him. His intense gaze was just as impossible to avoid.

"You're a beautiful woman, Natalie. Why would you expect me to—" he hesitated. "Hey, I'm not going to force you."

"Then let go of me."

He did . . . but she didn't bolt from the room, just stood there, waiting to hear what he would say next.

"Any man would do his damnedest to get next to you."

"Somehow I don't find that flattering, Colter," she said tightly. "Any man at all?"

"Okay. I'll narrow it down. Me. I would do anything—"

"Can we stick to our agreement?" she interrupted him.

He thought it over. "Only if we rewrite those vows."

"Those vows didn't mean a thing and you know it," she snapped.

He ignored her jab. "For starters, we'll have to take out the to-have-and-to-hold part."

"Fine with me."

He fell silent, observing her. Natalie took a step back. "You can't just have me because you happen to want me," she said sharply. "You may have provided me and Ricky with a place to live and security, and I'm doing everything I can to make a home for you and Missy in return, but that doesn't mean you own me. Is that clear?"

He folded his arms across his bare chest and nodded. "Yeah. It is, actually. But did you expect to live in this house the dozen or so years before Ricky is grown without me ever trying to, you know, touch you?"

She fumed.

"Is the word 'touch' on your not-allowed list?" he asked sarcastically. "I need to know. Maybe you could write down everything I'm not supposed to do. See if you can keep it to one page. That way I can keep it in my shirt pocket for easy reference—"

Natalie glared at him. "Unfortunately, you don't have a shirt on right now."

He grinned at her. "Put that on the not-allowed list too."

She wanted to shriek at him, throw things, but Missy and Ricky weren't far away. And truth be told, he hadn't done anything.

The awful part was that she didn't really want him to keep his distance indefinitely. Just right now. Until she got used to this odd arrangement and thought about just what it was she wanted out of life, now that she wasn't desperate and totally broke.

Keeping house for Colter Langston was more complicated than she'd let herself think.

He was rubbing his bare upper arms lazily, as if to keep warm. But the slight motion drew her attention to the swell of his biceps. Colter seemed to be waiting for her to make the next move.

So make it. Go to him. How wonderful it would be to have him hold you, that voice in her mind whispered. *Why not say yes?*

Because . . . because her every instinct said to keep him at a distance. For now, she would have to stall.

"You know something, Colter?" She looked him right in the eye. "I don't think you actually want me. It's just that I'm here, in your house, so you think you have to try. It's a guy thing. Am I right?"

He shrugged. "I'm not ruled by passion, if that's what you mean. But there's one question I'd like to ask."

"Go ahead," she said, forcing a note of bravado into her voice.

"Have you ever been with a man?"

She gasped as an unexpected panic coursed through her. Her deep, dark secret was out—or at least he'd figured it out. Well, hell. It wasn't anything she had to be ashamed of, was it?

"If you let me, I'll be gentle."

Right. Sure. His voice was almost a growl. Or was she just hearing it that way?

He reached out for her and her heart pounded so loudly she swore he had to be able to hear it. But she didn't push him.

His arms enfolded her. Underneath the gentleness was a whole lot of strength—tamed. For the moment. Natalie felt the nakedness of his skin warming her through her robe, melting her will to resist. Her breath came in tiny gasps for air through parted lips.

"How can you do this when you know you don't really want to?"

He gave an almost inaudible chuckle. "That was your theory. Not mine. The question is"—he nibbled the outside of her ear as he whispered into it—"what you want, Natalie. Got an answer for me?"

"N-no."

His free hand moved caressingly to her throat. "Meaning, no, you don't have an answer? Or no, stop it?"

His touch against her sensitive skin sent shudders of intense pleasure through her. Foolishly Natalie didn't guess his intention until she felt the zipper on her robe start to slide slowly down.

"Colter!" She reached up a hand to impede the

zipper's progress and he bent down to brush kisses against the back of it.

What on earth is the matter with me? Why can't I just say no? she thought wildly.

He didn't let her go and the front of her robe fell open. His hand slid inside and cupped her breast. Natalie's eyes closed at the wave of erotic sensation and she leaned into him, almost helpless.

He seemed to take that as a yes. Colter swung her off her feet and into his arms. She murmured something that was far from a protest and he answered with tenderness, but exactly what he'd said, she didn't know. He carried her to the bed and set her down, stretching out beside her.

Two or three seconds later, her robe was on the floor. His jeans were flung over it and they lay together, not quite touching.

A moment to catch her breath, that was all she needed, she told herself, and stiffened as she felt the warmth of his lips tracing the cord of her neck. His strong hands brought her body closer, keeping her on the bed beside him—not that she wanted to be anywhere else in the universe.

She relaxed, not knowing how to fight such pleasurable sensations—or why she should.

Immediately his mouth took possession of hers, branding her with sensual thoroughness, claiming her for himself. At some point in the provocative mastery of his kisses, a whirling, erotic void opened up . . . and Natalie went into it, abandoning herself, giving up something she no longer had need of: her innocence.

It was much later before Colter rolled away from her, though not until he had savored her involuntary cries of pleasure one by one. For interminable seconds, Natalie lay weak and spent, struggling to surface from the fiery sensations that swamped her consciousness.

In one part of her mind, she felt nothing but regret for getting so carried away. He hadn't had to do much persuading. Natalie had practically fallen into his arms.

But, she told herself, she hadn't fallen in love with him. This was—what they did was—just something that happened all the time, and now it had happened to her. Maybe it was better to get it out of her system at the beginning, so he couldn't exert that kind of power over her again.

The rest of her mind was still reeling, though, from the sensual shock of his lovemaking. The aftermath, physically at least, echoed with the pure pleasure he had given her. As sexual initiation went, she'd have to guess that he was good at it.

Very, very good.

Rolling on her side, she felt the sense of regret grow all-consuming. Because sex was all that had been and nothing more. Not love. If tears could have erased the memory of how good it felt, she would have cried. Instead she curled into a tight ball of misery.

The moon had risen above the treetops. Its light was streaming through the sheer curtains at the window, making a silvery path across the bed. The droning song of the cicadas sounded in the distance, punctuated by the call of the bullfrogs, and a night bird trilled to the stars. The world should have stopped, but it hadn't.

"You're likely to regret the day you married him." Flo Donaldsen's words came back to her.

She thought of the Fiesta. Natalie had married Colter on the last day of Fiesta San Antonio, a celebration of independence. How ironic. The gold band on her finger was a symbol of the exact opposite. Natalie realized that she had made a mistake. He had correctly gauged how incredibly needy she was—and not just about money, if she was going to be honest with herself, she thought miserably. Everything.

She'd been on her own too long, struggling to raise her sister's child when she'd never had a chance to grow all the way up herself, and just plain lonely. Natalie couldn't say whether he'd been trying to do the right thing or not, but lying here in this bed, she knew it didn't feel like she'd done the right thing.

No matter what, she resolved silently, even if she and Ricky had to walk all the way back to San Antonio, she would not stay in this house another night.

"Natalie."

Colter's fingers closed over her arms as he spoke. His tone was detached and impersonal, as if they had not shared the ultimate intimacy only moments ago.

A shiver of sensual awareness danced over her skin, igniting an answering spark within her. The involuntary response of her body angered Natalie and she wrenched her arm free of his touch.

"Leave me alone," she demanded tautly.

His reply was physical: he took hold of her shoulders and pushed her gently back onto the bed. Natalie lay rigid, unresisting, keeping her head turned away from him.

"Look at me," he said. When she didn't comply, Colter took hold of her chin and moved her face to his. "What's the matter?"

Resentment flamed brightly when Natalie focused her gaze on his face, the moonlight shimmering on the sun-bleached hair falling across his forehead. His eyes were cool steel and she trembled under his gaze.

"You don't want to know," Natalie told him.

Colter studied her for a long moment. Then his other hand slid over her silken skin to the swell of her breast, effectively reminding her that he had made her his in more ways than one.

"You like that, don't you?" he said softly when she arched to his touch.

"No."

"Hmm. Could've fooled me."

She pushed his hand away without replying.

Colter sat up. "Okay. I can guess what's on your mind."

"Really?"

"You're thinking about running away," he answered. Her lashes fluttered slightly in surprise, but there was no other admission from her that his guess was anywhere near accurate. "Where would you go? Not back to that apartment—that bitchy landlady wouldn't take you back. And you don't have enough to cover first and last month's rent plus a security deposit somewhere else. Without a job, how do you intend to support yourself and Ricky? Or were you planning to leave Ricky here?"

"Of course not," Natalie retorted. Her teeth sank into her lower lip, too late to bite back her giveaway words.

"What would you accomplish by running?" Natalie refused to respond to the quiet mockery in his question. "Would it change what happened tonight? Would you be able to forget that it ever happened?"

He knew the answers to his questions before he asked them and she closed her eyes tightly to avoid seeing the truth he was trying to force her to admit.

"Nothing's really changed, you know," Colter said. "You still have the security you wanted for you and the boy, no financial fears, a decent home. New clothes, even."

"But look at the price I had to pay." This time her voice was choked with emotion, her eyes still closed to shut out the image of his handsome face—only to have her mind's eye visualize it.

"My apologies," he said, an edge in his voice. "I didn't know there were any virgins left. It isn't my fault that you were one. And that was something I had no way of knowing until tonight."

"It's your fault that I'm not now!"

Colter sighed heavily. "Guilty as charged. But you weren't exactly fighting me. I would call that sweet surrender."

She offered a few choice curse words in reply.

Colter grinned. "Okay, maybe you're not all that sweet. But even so, you were more than willing. Deal with it."

Natalie rolled over and buried her face in the pillow.

"Did you intend to remain, I believe the word is pure, for the rest of your life?"

She could imagine his derisive smile.

"Or were you going to go for something on the side and ignore me, your lawfully wedded whatever?"

Whatever is right, she thought furiously. Certainly not a husband. Did hasty marriage vows count if one or both of the parties had second thoughts at a time like this?

"Answer me, Natalie."

She lifted her face out of the pillow and hugged it without looking at him. "Unfortunately, I didn't think about it much at all. For sure, not in those terms." Her reply was truthful.

Her relief at having Ricky's future secured and her personal responsibility lessened had overwhelmed her better judgment. It was true, though, that Colter had rescued her when her back was to the wall. She owed him for that—but she drew the line at giving away herself, body and soul.

Until tonight, he'd been distant to the point of indifference often enough. And that had lulled her into believing he wouldn't do what any man, as he'd said, would do under the circumstances.

"We're married. That's a fact you can't ignore," Colter said.

"I guess you don't intend to let me forget it," Natalie responded bitterly.

"Not yet. I think I stand a chance with you," Colter replied. "Of course, I could be wrong. It's happened before."

"Really?"

He laid a hand on her back and rubbed it absent-mindedly. Even affectionately. Like a husband, she thought for a fleeting second, before she pushed the notion from her mind.

"Natalie, this was your first time," he said after a while. "I guess I get why you'd be upset—"

"And I guess I'm your first virgin." She rolled over to glare at him. "And by the look in your eyes, I'm right," she said with fury. "So spare me the understanding talk. I don't need or want a lecture from you."

Colter had enough sense not to smile. His expression was sober. "Okay. But you don't have to have hysterics either. I know I gave you pleasure—"

"You arrogant bastard!" She scrunched up the pillow she'd been hugging and tried to hurl it into his face, but he took it from her with ease.

"Quit it. There's no reason to pretend you didn't like it." His tone was dry. "And leaving here would accomplish nothing and change nothing. Go to sleep, Natalie, and let someone who's a more convincing actress play the role of the outraged female."

With a cry of anger that she quickly stifled, Natalie withdrew under the covers, silently daring him to lay down beside her. If he did, she would . . . she stiffened herself. It was her reaction to him that was the problem. He hadn't done anything she didn't want him to do, from the sweep-her-off-her-feet part to the ecstatic climax. Yes, he took her there, with so much tenderness she'd forgotten all about it being her first time.

He got into the bed. She waited. It was a wonder, but he didn't even try to touch her. Natalie was so tired and over-emotional that sleep swiftly claimed her—and granted her some wild dreams into the bargain. She didn't have another conscious thought until daybreak, when she became aware of the sunlight trying to shine through her closed eyes and the sensation that someone was in the room with her.

The events of the night before came racing back and her eyelids sprang open, her gaze focusing on the empty pillow beside her.

"So you're finally awake." But it was a woman's voice and not Colter's that spoke.

At the sight of Flo Donaldsen across the room, Natalie pushed herself to a nearly upright position in the bed, dragging the covers with her. A telltale warmth invaded her face and she raised a hand to brush the hair away from her forehead to conceal her self-consciousness for a moment from the woman's sharp gaze.

"What time is it?" asked Natalie.

"Almost ten. Colter said to let you sleep this morning," Flo added in explanation. "But I thought you'd want a chance to shower and dress before lunchtime. I'll be staying on to fix it, so you needn't worry about that."

"Thank you," Natalie murmured as her gaze slid away from the older woman's discerning face only to rush back a second later. "Where's Ricky?"

"Colter took him along this morning. Do you want anything for breakfast?"

"No, just coffee."

Flo nodded and left the room. Her muscles protested as Natalie slipped from the bed and hurried into the bathroom, craving a hot bath that would relax her and help her face the day ahead of her.

Her mouth tightened at Flo's pronouncement that Ricky was with Colter. She had a feeling he was covering all the bases: she'd let him know she wouldn't leave without Ricky.

He always seemed to be one step ahead of her. Even letting her sleep late had been a means of hinting to Flo that they had slept together. Some hint. He was about as subtle as a brick.

After bathing and dressing, Natalie stripped the sheets from the bed and put on fresh ones from the linen closet in the hallway that Missy had pointed out the previous day. Then she made her way to the kitchen where Flo was preparing lunch. Natalie was setting the dining room table when Ricky came bursting through the front door.

"Nonnie! Nonnie!" he cried excitedly as he rushed toward her.

Automatically she kneeled down to get his exuberant hug and stayed in the same position to be on his level. Her smile was heartfelt as she looked into his bright brown eyes, loving the happiness she saw there.

"Nonnie, you shoulda been with us!" he exclaimed. "I got to see the horses and barns and pet a dog and everything! And C-Colter"—he glanced over his shoulder as he struggled for a second with the name—"is gonna take me out to see the cows and their babies this afternoon," Ricky concluded gleefully.

Natalie's gaze swept past Ricky to the man standing in the archway of the dining room. Colter's blue-green eyes held her. All she could think was that Colter wasn't above using Ricky to ensure the little boy would never want to leave the ranch.

"Ricky's more than welcome to come along," Colter said

amiably as he stepped farther into the room, "providing you don't have any objections, of course."

"I can go, can't I?" Ricky pleaded.

Natalie shot an angry look at Colter. "I don't really have a choice, do I?"

His gaze narrowed, the warmth in his eyes turning frosty. "If you've made other plans, then say so."

Deliberately Natalie ignored his challenge as she flashed a tense smile at the small boy standing in front of her. "Go and wash your hands, Ricky. We'll talk about it after lunch."

He hesitated, as if wanting to argue about it right now and not wait, then scampered away when he caught a warning look from Colter. Natalie straightened, her head lifted at a defiant angle.

"You don't play fair," she said in an accusing undertone.

"I don't 'play' at anything," Colter replied.

Without her meaning it to, her voice rose. "You know exactly what I mean. Every little boy from Texas dreams of being a cowboy, and you're making sure that Ricky thinks his dream will come true if we stay here."

"Is that in doubt?" He lifted one eyebrow in lazy regard. "Nobody tells me anything around here. Didn't see any suitcases waiting by the door, though."

A stab of pain laced through her as Natalie realized she had tacitly accepted her situation. It was disturbing to discover that all her protests were only bold talk that she had no intention of backing up with action. She was ashamed of her helplessness, her not-so-hidden neediness, and the lack of strength that'd prompted her to accept his offer of marriage without giving any thought to the consequences.

Despite Colter's insensitivity, he was strong. In the short time she'd known him, Natalie had learned what it was like to have a man to rely on, someone decisive, so she didn't have to feel so much like everything, absolutely everything was up to her.

All the same, she intended to let him think that someday she might leave, she told herself, and some day she would find the strength to do it.

He was still waiting for her answer, that quality of alertness more pronounced than ever at her silence. She felt an odd satisfaction in knowing that he wasn't entirely sure of her reaction as he met her searching look. Without replying, Natalie turned away, a mysterious smile flitting over her lips.

When Natalie didn't—and started to walk away—his hand closed over her arm and turned her around.

The hard pressure was like a catalyst, suddenly causing a rush of vivid memories, recalling the way he'd caressed her so intimately and sensually the night before, and her own instinctive reaction to his touch . . . recalling everything.

Immediately she tried to pull free of his hold, hissing angrily, "Don't touch me!"

When she couldn't do it, she raised her hand to strike his lean cheek and the taunting curve of his mouth. But the movement was stopped before she connected—he had her wrist in his fingers and he hauled her against him.

"Don't! You're out of control, Colter!"

"Yeah? That makes two of us."

"What?"

"You were a little wildcat last night. I enjoyed taming you. Sorry I didn't get around to telling you that until now. You were too busy having a hissy fit."

The instant of pleasurable immobility at the hardness of his body against hers was over, chased away by his obnoxious comments. She knew it was no use, but Natalie struggled against his hold anyway.

"Let me go!" she demanded hoarsely. "I can't stand you! I don't want you to touch me!"

The last cry vibrated in the air. There was a movement behind Colter and for a frightened second Natalie thought it was Ricky witnessing their argument. Then her face flamed in embarrassment when she saw it was Travis McCrea, his brows drawn together in a concerned frown. She sensed his indecision, uncertain whether to step forward and interfere, or leave before his presence was noticed.

Colter turned his head to see the reason for her disconcerted expression. Natalie gazed tensely at his almost impassive face, noting the challenging gleam in his eyes as Colter silently dared Travis to come between them.

Then her look slid back to Travis. His frown was gone, and a humorless smile curved the mouth that had been grim.

"Your first fight, huh?" Travis said casually as he walked into the dining room. "That was fast. I've heard that's always the first sign the honeymoon is over."

Not commenting on Travis's observation, Colter studied Natalie's averted face, its color only just beginning to return to normal.

"Still want to run away? Go ahead," he jeered, lowering his voice because of Travis. "I won't come after you. I don't want all this drama, if you really want to know."

There was no sign that the dark, rugged foreman had heard him. As Colter finally loosened his grip on her, Natalie pulled away, saying self-consciously. "Enough. I have to help Flo in the kitchen."

It was a feeble excuse, but the only one she could think of with the two men looking at her.

Chapter 6

Life fell into a comfortable pattern for Natalie. Although her pride demanded that she pretend otherwise, the undemanding routine of cleaning house, taking care of Missy and Ricky, and preparing meals was truly enjoyable. She had never had the time to give much thought to what she wanted to do in life, from figuring out a career to finding a soul mate, and at the age of twenty-two, neither seemed like critical concerns. Her being at the ranch turned out to be exactly what Colter had promised: a breather from a life that had been lived on the edge, financially and emotionally speaking.

She felt a true sense of fulfillment in taking care of others, and there was no reason on earth she had to be ashamed of that facet of herself.

Not that everything had gone smoothly. Initially there had been confusion when Flo Donaldsen departed for her cottage, but Natalie had soon found her way around. And then there had been a real milestone event for her and her nephew: enrolling Ricky in the afternoon kindergarten class at the local school for the rest of the term.

Colter gave her almost free rein, handing her sets of keys to his luxury car and a more utilitarian vehicle as well, providing a list of the stores where the Langston name was on account, and generally letting her do as she pleased as long as she maintained their bargain.

During the day, Natalie was never alone with him, since he only appeared at mealtimes and then in the company of Travis McCrea. In the evenings he was in the house most of the time, but those were the hours she spent with Ricky and Missy. Colter never requested her company nor indicated the least desire to establish a more companionable relationship between them.

When they were alone, Natalie didn't hide her mixed feelings for him—she couldn't be that dishonest. But he kept right on trying and for some reason she let him. The sensuous warmth of his kisses always produced a reaction that was purely physical and hard to control.

Natalie had just returned the vacuum cleaner to the utility closet when she heard the front door open and close. She glanced at her wristwatch, wondering if she'd lost track and Missy and Ricky were home from school.

But it was nowhere near time for them, so she moved curiously to the living room. Her steps halted abruptly at the sight of the redhead in the room, walking around the furniture as if she'd always known exactly where it was.

Natalie remembered her. Oh, yes. *That* redhead. The woman whom Colter had identified as Deirdre Collins. The woman who'd thrown herself into his arms the first day Natalie had arrived at the ranch.

"Hello," was all Natalie said, knowing her voice and demeanor were stiff and cold. She didn't care.

The redhead turned, a superior look in her green eyes as she openly surveyed Natalie. Poise, sophistication, and wealth were stamped in the clothes and hairstyle of this strikingly beautiful woman.

Natalie set her chin at a slightly defiant angle. The

action elicited an immediate smile of satisfaction on the other woman's glossed lips.

"You're the new Mrs. Langston, of course," the redhead murmured with feigned friendliness. "I'm Deirdre Collins. I wanted to meet you and offer my congratulations. I hope you don't mind me barging in this way." A manicured hand waved the air in apology. "I'm just so used to coming and going as I please. It never occurred to me until now that Colter might not have mentioned me."

"Well, he has. Your parents are our neighbors, aren't they?" said Natalie. Her temper was slowly reaching the boiling point, thanks to Deirdre Collins's patronizing attitude. "As a matter of fact," she added boldly, "I believe you were here the first day Colter and I returned after we got married. I'm so sorry I didn't get to meet you then."

The woman's gaze narrowed slightly as she met Natalie's eyes. Her glare meant the exact opposite of her courteous words to the redhead.

"I hope," Deirdre hesitated over what she wanted to say, "that my appearance that day didn't upset you or anything."

"Not at all. I mean, you weren't aware that Colter was married. To me."

Deirdre stared at Natalie for a long moment before letting her emerald gaze drift idly over the room. "Colter has such a beautiful home. It is kind of high-maintenance, though. Are you the domesticated type?" The sarcasm gleamed out as if from a see-through veil.

"Yes, I am," Natalie admitted without any apology.

"I can't stand housework myself. I would make an awful wife—you know, the traditional kind of wife. Dishpan hands and dusty hair, whapping at everything with a stringy old wet mop. No man should have to see a woman like that."

Natalie made a noncommittal sound, wondering how much longer Deirdre was going to go on.

"I'd much rather be pampered. I like a man to wait on me and treat me right, seven days a week. Know what I mean?"

Natalie knew exactly what Deirdre was hinting at and she realized that she had unconsciously known all along that Deirdre had probably been Colter's girlfriend. Main girlfriend, she corrected herself silently, feeling even more miserable.

But what if Deirdre was insinuating something more? Like . . . Was she still his girlfriend?

Colter could've had a dozen Deirdres for all Natalie cared, but if he expected her to welcome them into her home—and she had begun to think of it as hers and Ricky's for now, and it certainly was Missy's home—then he was in for a rude awakening.

"I'm sorry Colter isn't here. I know he'll be sorry he missed your visit." As tactfully as possible, Natalie tried to suggest that Deirdre leave. Under no circumstances was she going to play the perfect Texas hostess and offer the redhead refreshments.

Deirdre laughed throatily. "You're right about that. With his sense of humor, he would have found our meeting really funny."

"Oh?" Natalie kept her cool, fighting for the respect that Colter seemed intent on denying her, directly or indirectly.

The one-word question was ignored as Deirdre smiled sweetly, silent laughter in her green eyes at Natalie's equally silent bristling.

"Okay. Gotta go. With all that sla-a-aving around the house the way you do, there must be a thousand things that need to be done, so I won't keep you, Mrs. Langston. How strange that sounds."

Never mind the last snotty remark—saying she, Natalie, was slaving was just plain mean. Natalie cringed inwardly when she heard Deirdre drag out the word. She had the fleeting impression of a cat cleaning its whiskers in satisfaction as Deirdre started toward the front door.

"Give Colter—" The redhead hesitated as if she was on stage playing a part. She glanced over her shoulder at Natalie with a knowing smile. "Give him my love, will you? I'll stop in to see him another time."

Natalie was rooted to the floor, frozen by her anger, an anger directed in equal parts at Colter, Deirdre, and herself. When the door clicked shut, it took her a full second to realize that Travis McCrea had walked in as Deirdre walked out. His kind brown eyes searched her rigid but false expression of unconcern.

"Are you all right?" Travis asked in a low voice.

"Of course." But there was a brittle edge to her airy reply.

The immediate tightening of his mouth made Natalie realize that she had betrayed herself. She quickly turned away and walked over to needlessly plump a pillow on the couch. Natalie had never been one to give way to hysteria, but she was possessed by a frightening urge to throw herself on the couch and sob out her humiliation.

"Was there something you needed, Travis?" She tried to sound cheerful and together, but her response was forced and it showed.

He stayed in the hallway, watching her from there. "No," Travis responded. "I noticed Deirdre's car in the driveway."

Natalie met his velvet gaze, her own swinging over the strong, broad face, the thick brows, and the silver wings in his jet black hair. Not for the first time in the last two weeks, she silently wished that instead of making a loveless match for Ricky's benefit, she could have married this strong, quiet man instead of Colter. Her timing sucked and her luck was worse. But hindsight never changed anything.

Shrugging self-consciously, she said, "Deirdre stopped over to offer her congratulations."

"I bet she did," Travis said. "What she really wanted was to meet the woman who snared Colter when she'd failed."

"Snared? That's a joke," Natalie laughed bitterly. "I'm the one who's trapped." Immediately after the words were out, she regretted them. She sank dejectedly in the nearest chair, wearily pressing her fingertips to her suddenly throbbing temples. "I'm sorry. I shouldn't have said that. It's not true."

"You can't pretend in front of everyone, Natalie." Although he was still standing in the hallway, his voice seemed to reach out to touch her in reassurance. "Being at the house as often as I am and eating with you and Colter, I did notice that you two don't act like newlyweds."

"Please." Her head moved in a negative shake. "The way I feel right now, if you say another kind word, I'll burst into tears." As quickly as she slumped into the chair, she pushed herself out of it, squaring her shoulders with determination. "I have what I wanted and I'm not going to start complaining because my loaf of soft bread has a hard crust."

Travis nodded in understanding, a glint of admiration in his eyes. His head turned slightly at the noise of the door just as it opened.

Colter walked in. His gaze swung from Travis to Natalie and back to his foreman.

"Is something wrong?" Colter asked, pulling off his leather gloves and tossing them on the small table.

"No, I was just leaving," Travis replied, and set his battered Stetson on his dark head. "I'll see you tonight, Natalie," he offered in good-bye as he opened the door.

When it closed seconds later, Colter stared at it in a

thoughtful silence that grated on Natalie's nerves. She stiffened instinctively as his gaze flicked to her.

"Travis doesn't usually come to the house during the day," she stated defensively. His attitude was annoying—but she reminded herself that she'd been jealous of Deirdre.

"Neither do I," he reminded her. "But today I want to shower and change before I drive to San Antone."

He turned from her and started down the hallway to their bedroom, his fingers making short work of the buttons on the front of his shirt. Anger raged within Natalie—why was he casually ignoring her? She was in no mood to be brushed aside, and she followed him down the hall.

"Are you going with Deirdre?" Natalie asked with deliberate softness as she stopped just inside the door of their bedroom.

Colter gave a low laugh. "I wondered how long you would take before you got around to her."

"Well, she was here earlier."

"I know." He unbuttoned his cuffs and sat on the bed to remove his boots. "I was just leaving Flo's cottage when Deirdre stopped by to see her. Was that why Travis was here? To rescue you from her clutches?" He rose to his feet and stripped the shirt from his back. The never-before-seen scratches from her fingernails were now visible on his naked shoulders. "Maybe he doesn't know you can defend yourself."

"He's more of a gentleman than you are," Natalie retorted.

Colter's alert gaze studied her indifferently. He tossed his shirt to her. "Throw that in the dirty clothes basket," he ordered.

Had she been able to pick him up bodily, he would've gone right in there with it. Fuming, Natalie wadded the shirt in her hands, toying with the idea of throwing it back at him or on the floor, only to dismiss it. There had to be a better revenge, but she couldn't think of it.

He was watching her face, seeing her silent arguments with herself in her eyes, and his mouth quirked in satisfaction.

That did it, Natalie hurled the shirt back and it landed at his feet. "Throw your own dirty clothes away! I'm not your maid!"

"Of course not. Gee, I'm sorry. You know, Deirdre said you might be upset."

Fury propelled Natalie across the room, but she stopped herself a couple of feet in front of him. Before the rubbery sensation that was attacking her legs could take hold in the rest of her, she struck out. The paralyzing sting of her palm felt oddly pleasant as she glared at him. The lean, hard cheek bore the pale imprint of her hand that he hadn't attempted to stop, the color slowly changing to red while his eyes glittered with cold blue fire.

"I don't want that woman in my house!" Natalie raged.

"Your house?" His voice was searingly soft.

"Yes, my house," she repeated, her wrath too fully aroused to notice Colter's. "I legally sleep with you, which makes it as much my house as yours—if not more, since I take care of it. And I don't want that woman to set foot in it again!"

"If she wants to, Deirdre can come here whenever she likes." Colter's mouth thinned into a forbidding line.

"No! I don't care how many girlfriends you have, but I will not tolerate the humiliation of having them paraded around here! And what about the kids? Do you think they don't—"

He interrupted her with a cutting gesture. "Leave

them out of this. The only things you seem able to tolerate are my money and my home."

"And your touch," Natalie jeered. "Now and then. When I tolerate it."

Colter's eyes narrowed. "What makes you pretend that you don't like all that?" he demanded. "You're a woman. You have physical desires like any other woman."

"Maybe I do, but there's still a major problem here."

"And what is it? Could you be a little more specific?"

"Hell, yes!" she stormed. "Did it ever occur to you that you're madly in love with yourself and no one else? So what makes you think you're so damn irresistible?" She looked him right in the eye with haughty disdain.

Blue diamond eyes raked her body with suggestive thoroughness and Natalie's blood started to race like fire through her veins.

"Shall I show you?" he asked with a growling purr.

The flame in her sputtered and died, her bravado rapidly fading. Her senses were quivering with awareness, traitors to her pride.

Without a word Natalie spun away. A retreat, however cowardly, was more strategic than the unconditional surrender Colter had planned. But he anticipated her move, closing a hand over the soft flesh of her arm and trying to pull her back. She tried even harder to push herself away from his naked chest, a futile attempt that failed when he applied pressure to the small of her back, molding her to his muscular thighs.

His strength was superior. Even when she gained the use of her other hand after he had released her arm, Natalie could not ward him off.

Arched away from him, her face swiftly turned aside to elude his kiss, she felt the scorching touch of his mouth against the slender curve of her throat. Unhurried, Colter explored the pulsing vein of her neck and the hollow of her throat. Then, pushing aside the collar of her blouse, he sought out the sensitive skin of her shoulder.

The sensual assault continued as he retraced his kisses, moving back to her neck and up a little to nibble at her earlobe, sending waves of ecstasy shuddering through her body. That irresistible, primitive desire was growing every second. It was only a matter of time until he claimed her lips and she would be lost.

"Damn you!" Her whispering curse sounded more like a sob. "Let me go!"

His mouth moved along her cheek and she felt it curve into a smile as Colter rubbed his jaw along her smooth skin.

"Not yet." The seductive pitch of his voice was laced with an emotion she couldn't name.

"Stop," Natalie gasped, unwilling to beg for her release, her pride cast aside to be regained, she hoped, when she was free of his touch. "Deirdre can come any time," she promised. The corner of her mouth was being teased by his warm lips. "You can start a harem in the house. I don't care! But let me go!"

"Are you saying I should ignore you? I can't." Colter's voice was husky.

"You have to go to San Antonio," she protested as his mouth slowly began moving over hers. His hand was cupped under her chin, preventing her from moving away.

"Kiss me," he commanded against her mouth.

He was being deliberately provocative, tantalizing her lips with the nearness of his without kissing her. She felt an incredible hunger to know the elemental mastery she had experienced before.

"No," Natalie said, fighting with every stubborn bit of resistance she possessed.

The arm around her back tightened with seductive

force. "Kiss me," Colter coaxed, "or we'll still be here when Missy and Ricky come home."

An inadvertent moan escaped her lips and they parted. Instinct and experience gained from Colter guided the tentative movement of her lips against his. At first he remained passive under her touch, letting Natalie find out for herself the fine art of initiative rather than response as she began an intimate exploration of his lips, growing bolder until she felt the answering warmth of his.

Her actions weren't directed by conscious thought. For Natalie it was almost like drowning, then bursting to the surface and feeling more alive than ever in her life. His bruising ardor was matched by the urgency of her response, causing shock waves of pleasurable sensation.

When Colter gradually eased his mouth from its possessive claim of hers, Natalie was incapable of the slightest movement. Her hands rested on his naked shoulders while her head remained tilted back.

"Tell me again," Colter murmured, totally in control, not reeling from the sensual impact of their embrace as Natalie was, "that you only tolerate my touch."

Tears of hurt anger shimmered in her eyes, stinging and smarting like salt on a wound. "I did what you ordered," said Natalie in a choked, trembling voice. "Now will you let me go?"

An expressive lift of his shoulders was all that happened in the instant before he released her. Yet the distance between them didn't erase the memory of his hard body pressed against hers, or the exciting fire that had consumed her. She couldn't meet his eyes. Natalie walked slowly to the hallway door, pausing in its frame.

Without turning around, Natalie said, "I hate you, Colter. Or is hate another emotion that you don't recognize?"

His only reply to that question was an abrupt laugh.

"Well, I'll be home for dinner tonight, my loving wife. So, no poisonous mushrooms in the chili, please. Unless you want to eat out of the same bowl."

"Shoot," Natalie said sarcastically. "And I was planning to spend the afternoon looking for some really lethal ones." She hurried into the hall, knowing her barbs were ineffectual but needing them all the same.

The next week Natalie threw herself into a frenzy of activity and busywork, cleaning things that didn't need to be cleaned, outdoing herself in the cooking of their meals, taking Missy and Ricky out on little jaunts, working until all hours of the night to avoid the bedroom. She was never entirely sure that Colter was asleep when she did slip between the covers. He never said a word, viewing her devotion to the house and children with what seemed to be detached amusement.

Her weight loss was becoming apparent again and the darkish circles of exhaustion under her eyes were all too plain. Natalie didn't want to think that the telltale signs were obvious to anyone but herself, but she had to acknowledge that they undoubtedly were.

As she glanced into the oval mirror in the dining room, she pinched her cheeks in an old-fashioned effort to bring color to her face before entering the living room to let Colter and Travis know that dinner was ready. As had become her habit lately, Natalie addressed her announcement to Travis, her blue mood lifting a little in the warm glow of his regard.

"Ricky and Missy are at the table, so dinner is ready whenever you are," she said.

"How about giving me five minutes to finish this beer?" Travis asked, holding up his half-empty, still frosty glass.

"I was dreaming of a tall cold one for hours and I hate to guzzle it now."

"It was warm today," Natalie agreed, not looking at Colter, but extremely conscious of his sinewy length stretched out in the chair.

"Warm?" Travis raised a black brow at her understatement. "It was like a blast furnace out at the pens," he said quietly. "A case of cold beer woulda been as refreshing as a blue norther sweeping in from the Plains for the hands out there. I hate to think about tomorrow."

Natalie remembered how gritty Colter had looked an hour ago when he'd come in from the spring roundup. His shirt had been stained with sweat and dirt. The gold-streaked brown of his hair had turned to solid dust even with the shield of his wide-brimmed hat. At the time he had looked hot and tired, not the vitally fresh and masculine man that she could see in her side vision now.

"Why don't you ask Natalie to bring out a case of beer tomorrow afternoon, Travis?" Colter suggested lazily, studying the film of foam coating his empty glass when she glanced at him in surprise.

Travis gave him a long look before draining his glass. "Natalie has plenty to do without running out to the pens."

"Oh, she won't mind." The hard line of his mouth turned upwards at the corners in something that wasn't really a smile. Colter shot a sardonic look at Natalie. "My wife," he said, "enjoys filling every waking hour of the day with chores, whether they need doing or not."

Startled for a split second, she caught the questioning and concerned glance that Travis gave her. A flush of hot color suffused her face. Colter's joke, if it was one, upset her.

Fixing a bright smile on her mouth, she turned to Travis. "Of course, I'll bring out some beer tomorrow.

It won't be any trouble. Now, if you will excuse me, I'll go and dish up the soup."

"We'll be right there," Travis answered.

No other mention was made of the way Natalie was working. During the meal Travis kept the conversation centered on the children and their activities. After they were finished, Travis stayed only for coffee, then left. Natalie had no idea where Colter had disappeared to after the table was cleared. She didn't think she heard the car leave, but she wasn't going to check.

With the same determination that got her through the week, she spent the biggest share of the evening with Ricky and Missy. At eleven o'clock she was still in the kitchen, cleaning the overhead hanging lamp. The night air was still and uncomfortably warm.

Standing on the table top in clean socks—she would scrub and polish it when she was done—Natalie wiped the sweat from her forehead with the back of her hand. The downward movement of her head brought a figure standing in the doorway into focus. She turned with a jerk, nearly upsetting the pan of soapy water at her feet. A little water sloshed over the side, dampening her socks, as she recognized Colter leaning against the door-jamb. She turned quickly back to her work.

"Do you want something?" she asked icily. Grubby as she was, it was hard to maintain her dignity. What was left of it, anyway.

"I thought I would show you the way to get to the cattle pens tomorrow," he answered.

"Tonight?" Natalie managed a laugh. "It's dark outside."

"I meant on the map," Colter responded dryly.

Reaching up to wipe the chain from which the lamp was suspended from the ceiling, Natalie hoped she concealed the guilty flush at her own ignorance.

"I'll be finished here in a minute," she said, striving for the coolness of a moment ago.

"No hurry," Colter drawled.

She had been taking her time, but under his watchful eye, she hurried to finish the task. The exertion of stretching to cover every inch and the heat that radiated from the ceiling brought a sudden wave of lightheadedness. The first one Natalie fought off, but the second one had her reeling with a strange giddiness. In the next instant, a pair of strong hands closed around her waist and lifted her, then set her down on the floor.

"I'm all right," Natalie protested weakly.

Colter let her lean against the table, removing his hands. His touch had disturbed her equilibrium just as much as the heat. "Of course you are," he said mockingly.

"I am. It was just the heat," she insisted.

"Whatever." A thread of impatience was in his voice. "You'll work yourself half to death or collapse from exhaustion if no one stops you. Either way, I'm not the one suffering the consequences. You are. You can stay here and work for another three hours, but I'd like to go to bed. So if you don't mind, I'll show you the map now."

If Natalie had thought to gain his sympathy, he'd let her down in more ways than one. His general indifference really was getting to her. Suddenly she felt hopelessly defeated.

Silently she followed him as he walked from the kitchen to the small study that doubled as the ranch office, a room that she had never entered except to clean, and took rolled tubes of paper from a shelf, selecting one. Her mind had a difficult time concentrating on the pencil tip moving over the large map of the ranch. Nata-lie could only hope that she remembered the way in the morning. It didn't seem too complicated.

"Can you find it?" Colter asked.

"Yes," she answered dully, resolving to return to the study in the morning after Colter had left, to examine the map again.

"Never mind," he sighed. He took a long, close look at her face. "You're too tired to even know your own name. I'll show you this again in the morning."

With that, he turned off the desk lamp, told Natalie a curt goodnight and walked from the room. Dazed by his complete lack of interest, more hurt than she cared to admit that he couldn't even pretend concern and suggest she go to bed too, Natalie stared after him in silence.

He had been right. She was the only one who was suffering. And she had Ricky to think about. What had she hoped to prove? That because Colter was treating her like the household help, she was going to make it worse by slaving from sunup to sundown?

Colter was in bed when she entered the room. He glanced at her uninterestedly and turned on his side. She continued through to the adjoining bathroom, took a shower, and changed into her nightgown. Colter didn't stir when she crawled into bed beside him. A tear slipped from between her lashes for no reason that Natalie could think of and she drifted into a tired, troubled sleep.

The house was nearly immaculate from her earlier efforts so the next day Natalie felt not one twinge of guilt about not doing anything. As he'd said the night before, Colter showed her the route to the cattle pens. It was remarkably easy and she wondered why she hadn't grasped it the night before.

Ricky was home in the morning and they spent most of it outdoors before the sun had reached its zenith. He had always been content playing by himself. This morning Natalie sat idly on a lounge chair and watched.

Lunch wasn't the all-out feast she usually prepared, but just as filling for all its simplicity. She'd learned her lesson. She was not going to prove anything else to Colter Langston. Although Natalie still wasn't certain what it was she had wanted to prove in the first place.

The ice chest was filled with cold beer already chilled in the refrigerator, packed with ice cubes to maintain the frigid temperature inside the cans. It was a struggle loading it in the back seat of the car, but Natalie got it in and started for the cattle pens.

It was almost mid-afternoon and it was hot. To hurry would kick up dust on the dirt roads that laced various sections of the ranch together. Natalie was fine with keeping a leisurely pace.

Again wildflowers dotted the route, pointing up the greenness of the spring grass and the darker green foliage of the live oaks and cedars. She recognized wine cups, bluebonnets, Indian blankets, Mexican hats, and white prickle poppies among the others she couldn't identify. The air was fragrant with their perfume.

Butterflies and moths flitted from blossom to blossom with the bees while birds encouraged their efforts in song. A silver ribbon of water twisted through the meadow, and as Natalie turned onto the road that led to the pens, she heard the stream chuckling over the rocks in its bed.

The sound died away and the bawl of cattle began to grow increasingly louder, reaching its pitch of intensity as Natalie slowed the car to a stop near the dusty haze that hung over the large pens. As she climbed out of the car, the combined heat of man, beast, and sun closed over her almost suffocatingly. The stench of sweat, burning hair, animal excrement, and an unfamiliar medicinal odor was sickening.

There was activity and movement everywhere as Natalie approached the board pens. Dipping, branding, and ear-tagging were carried with steady efficiency by horse and rider or the man on foot. The rope-swinging, leg-slapping, and fast riding so often depicted in Western movies was nowhere in evidence. Despite the acrid smells and unceasing racket, Natalie watched it all with fascination.

Shielding her eyes from the incredible glare of the sun, she studied the human occupants of the pen. A few of the men noticed her standing on the roadside, but she was soon forgotten in the unending demand of their work. All of them were dressed alike: dark blue jeans, the color of their shirts and hats almost indistinguishable now due to the dust that coated everything.

Yet Natalie had no difficulty at all in picking out Colter from the others. Work-stained like them, there was an invisible aura that set him apart. He sat easily in the saddle of a muscular chestnut horse. Natalie knew he was aware of everything going on around him.

Her concentration was centered on Colter. She didn't notice the horse and rider quietly approaching until the buckskin's head blocked her view. Her startled glance was caught by a gentle look from Travis before he swung their attention to the pen.

"What do you think of the exciting, action-packed life of a cowboy?" he asked jokingly. "Heat, stench, noise, and bad-tempered cows. Who do you suppose we can appeal to for better working conditions?"

"Talk to the Man Upstairs." Natalie smiled, tilting her head back to look up at the broad-shouldered rider in the saddle, squinting her eyes when her hand could no longer shield them from the sun's glare.

"You should have a hat if you're going to be out in this sun," Travis said with genuine concern.

Natalie thought of her wide-brimmed straw hat with its bright artificial flowers. It was strictly the garden and poolside kind, a ludicrous sight out here.

"So I've discovered," was her reply. "I'm a true green-horn," she sighed. "I didn't realize there were so many things involved in a roundup."

Travis smiled broadly. "It's more than rounding them up and branding the calves. They all have to be run through chutes and dipped for disease. The sick and crippled have to be separated and doctored. The calves are branded and ear-tagged, the bull calves being castrated to be sold later as feeding steers. None of it is romantic or fun."

Natalie coughed as a cloud of dust swirled around her, kicked up by a cow trying to elude a snaking rope. "I agree," she said in a voice still choked by the dust. "The beer is in the back of the car. Do you want me to get it?"

Travis's gaze shifted out to the pens in a quick assessment. Colter was walking his horse around the small herd in a route that brought him to the front rail where they were.

"What do you think, Colter?" Travis asked. "Break now or finish the rest of this herd?"

Colter's reply was unhesitating and Natalie guessed the decision had been made before he'd ridden over. "We'll finish this group and run the last herd in. They can settle down while the men are resting."

He hadn't even glanced at her. She couldn't stop the rigid tensing of her jaw. "How long will that be?" she asked.

Colter slid a brief look over her face before dismissing her from his attention. "Half an hour or more."

"Am I supposed to stay?" Her voice was taut and weary-sounding as Natalie tried to hide her growing resentment at Colter's impersonal attitude. "I still have to start the roast for dinner, and Missy and Ricky will be coming home soon."

She was pinned by his steely gaze. "You can go or stay, whichever you want," he said after a few moments, "but don't come crying to me about how much you have to do. If you want a shoulder to cry on,"—he barely glanced at the tall, rugged man astride the buckskin—"I'm sure Travis would be more than happy to offer his." A visible flush crept into Travis's tanned cheeks, putting a smile on Colter's ruthless mouth. "As a matter of fact, Travis, why don't you ride to the house with Natalie and bring the pickup back for the ice chest? You'd like that, wouldn't you?"

With a contemptuous light still in his eyes, Colter reined his horse back to the center of the pens. Self-consciously Natalie looked away from Travis. She had guessed that he liked her, but Colter deliberately implied that the foreman's feelings for her were deeper. Which was more humiliating, Colter didn't care.

"That man is too damned observant," Travis muttered savagely beneath his breath. "He notices things that are none of his business."

Natalie studied him through her lashes, although Travis never looked at her as he dismounted and waved to one of the men to take his horse. Angry resentment showed in every controlled move as he vaulted the fence and walked to the car with Natalie trailing in sympathetic embarrassment behind him. In brooding silence, he took the ice chest from the car and carried it easily to a spot of shade under an oak. A jerky movement of his large hand signaled her to drive.

When they were back on the road to the ranch house, Natalie glanced hesitantly at the darkly handsome man in the passenger seat, his arm resting on the opened window, a tightly clenched fist pressed to his lips as he stared unseeingly out of the window.

"Travis, I'm—sorry." Her fingers nervously clutched the wheel. "Colter shouldn't have said that."

"Why? It's true." A muscle in his jaw twitched as he

spoke. "I should've quit the first week you came when I realized the way I felt," he said with calm acceptance.

There was no response she could make to that. She couldn't offer him any encouragement, especially when her feelings toward him were limited to friendship and admiration. Yet the thought of being deprived of his steadying companionship, of facing meals alone with Colter, made her heart constrict.

They were both silent the rest of the way to the ranch. Natalie realized that Travis had not wanted her to speak. For her to say that she was only fond of him would have been just as cruel as giving him false hope. He wasn't the type of guy who'd read what he wanted into her silence. At the same time, she felt a sense of assurance that he would be there if she ever needed him, with no questions asked and no strings attached.

Her mind kept asking if things would have been different if she had met Travis and Colter together at the Fiesta San Antonio. The answer should have been obvious. But there was the uncomfortable discovery that it was not. Another question bothered her. Why would she have chosen Colter over Travis? That answer eluded her as well.

Chapter 7

The start of Ricky's riding lessons had been postponed until after the spring roundup was over. Natalie had decided to wait and refresh her own skills while Ricky learned. When the big day arrived at last, Ricky had awakened when the eastern sky was a lemon dawn. It required nearly all of Natalie's ingenuity and patience to keep him occupied at the house until the hour they were to meet Colter at the barns.

Ricky had persuaded Missy to come and watch, and she was now trailing after Natalie while Ricky blazed the way, hopping from one foot to the other, frustrated with Natalie's slower pace. Colter was just walking out of the corral gate when they arrived. Ricky darted past Colter through the open gate, intent on the horses tied to the rails inside.

"Which one is mine?" he asked excitedly, never taking his round dark eyes from the two horses.

"The bay on the left," Colter answered.

"What's his name?" Ricky breathed. Now that his horse was in plain sight, the need to hurry seemed to have left him.

Colter shrugged. "Joe."

"Just Joe?" Dislike for the name was evident in the boy's tone of voice and his wrinkled nose. "That's not a good name. I'll call him Lightning," Ricky decided.

Natalie studied the two horses in silence. The stocky bay that Colter had identified as Ricky's was the same size as the sorrel standing beside it, maybe even more muscular. She'd anticipated that Ricky's mount would be a pony if not a small horse.

A frown of concern creased her forehead as she glanced at Colter. "Ricky's too small to ride a full-grown horse."

"A small pony can be just as hard to control as a big horse," Colter said firmly. "There isn't a better horse around than Joe. You could set off a stick of dynamite beside him and he wouldn't twitch an ear."

"His name is Lightning," Ricky corrected him. "Can I ride now?"

"Walk over and untie his reins and bring him here," Colter ordered. "Be sure to come up on his side so he can see you."

Ricky was off like a shot. Involuntarily Natalie stepped forward, her mouth opening to add her own warning to Colter's clipped commands. Strong fingers closed over her wrist.

"Let him be." A thread of steel ran through Colter's quiet words. "You can't do everything for him."

Natalie gulped. "He's so small, though." Her gaze skittered away from the blue-green of Colter's eyes and the tawny gold of his hair. She wished for the steadying influence of Travis instead of Colter's unsettling presence.

"If you're going to get emotional over nothing, you can go back to the house."

Pressing her lips together, Natalie resolved not to voice any more of her inner apprehensions. She watched in tight-lipped silence as Ricky was swung into the tiny saddle on the horse's broad back.

All of Colter's instructions during the first lesson were crisply put in a no-nonsense tone. Several times Natalie wanted to explain what Colter said in simpler terms that Ricky could understand, but she didn't, discovering minutes later that Ricky seemed to understand the adult level of Colter's orders. Not until the lesson was over, one that was much too brief as far as Ricky was concerned, did Colter indicate that Natalie should try her horse.

After she'd awkwardly circled the corral the first few times, most of her forgotten skills returned. But under Colter's critically appraising eye, Natalie felt less than adequate. Only once did she feel a glow of satisfaction and it wasn't due to her efforts.

Missy, who had been painfully quiet all the while she sat on the top rail of the corral, watching first Ricky and then Natalie, finally made a comment. "Natalie should keep her heels down, Daddy," she said.

Natalie saw the swift glance he shot at his daughter, but he merely called out to Natalie to confirm Missy's observation. Two thoughts occurred to Natalie simultaneously. The first was that Missy wasn't quite as reluctant to ride as she said, and the second, that Colter was not as indifferent to his daughter as he seemed.

When the lessons were over and the horses were cooled off, unsaddled, and turned out to graze, the four of them walked back to the house. While Ricky was bragging to Missy about his prowess as a rider, Natalie tried to thank Colter for giving the lessons, which she knew were the first of many as she watched the kids run ahead, out of earshot. Somehow, the way she said it managed to convey the wrong impression and she got a cynical look from Colter.

"Are you trying to say that you appreciate my time but you would prefer Travis?"

Her eyes widened. "No," she protested quickly. "I only meant that I appreciated you keeping your word with Ricky and teaching him to ride."

"Did you think I wouldn't?" Again his blue gaze slashed at her.

"No, I did think you would—" Natalie began defensively.

"But you thought I would have someone else teach you. Got it." Colter gave her a humorless smile.

"If you're trying to say that I was looking forward to spending time alone with Travis, then you're mistaken." Her voice cracked as indignant anger took hold.

"I didn't say that at all. You did."

"But you were thinking it," she retorted.

In a series of fluid movements, Colter stopped her in her tracks with a hand on her wrist, turned her to face him, and cupped her face in one hand. There was a mercurial rise of her pulse as she stared into the enigmatic depths of his eyes.

"Do you know what I'm thinking now?" he asked with deceptive softness.

Her legs were suddenly rubbery and her hands reached out instinctively to him for support. A jolting current was transmitted to Natalie, almost rocking her back on her heels.

"The children," she whispered in protest as he made his next move. But those two were far ahead.

His hand moved from her arm to the pliant flesh of her back, obedient to his every command. She felt the warm breath of his silent laughter an instant before his mouth closed over hers. She shuddered once in resistance before yielding to the exquisite sensation of his kiss.

Almost before it had begun, Colter moved away. Natalie swayed slightly toward him. His hand slid from her throat to her shoulder, stopping her. The totally physical reaction she had to his touch forced a sigh of dismay that started from deep in her soul. Would this betrayal of her pride never stop? Basically, she was beginning to hate him. Her lashes fluttered upward, but she saw he wasn't looking at her.

"What is it, Ricky?" Colter asked calmly.

He had run back. With panic-stricken swiftness, Natalie turned her head to the small boy standing in front of them, Colter's hands still holding her prisoner. A thoughtful frown furrowed Ricky's forehead as he stared at Colter.

"Do you like all that kissing stuff?" he asked, screwing his face up disapprovingly.

"It's like spinach," Colter answered in a joking tone. "You begin to like it when you get older."

"Oh." Ricky nodded, the subject no longer of interest to him. "Come on, Nonnie. You said we could have some cookies and milk."

"I'm coming," Natalie murmured, slipping free of Colter's relaxed hold.

Keeping her eyes downcast, she followed Ricky to the house, very aware of Colter's big-cat footsteps behind her.

Her and Ricky's riding lessons continued for a week, held in the cool hours of the morning under Colter's supervision. Ricky's sturdy, good-natured bay was anything but a bolt of lightning, although he obeyed the slightest command—right or wrong—that the reins in Ricky's small hand gave. The commands were more often wrong than right. The uncanny way the horse sensed each time Ricky lost his balance, slowing to a walk or a stop to allow him to regain his seat, endeared it to Natalie's heart.

Her own efforts were much more successful. And she found that under Colter's tutelage, she learned more about riding a horse than just staying in the saddle. There was a glow of accomplishment on her face when she circled the corral at a walk, a trot, and a canter, executed a series of figure eights, and received not one criticism from Colter.

"We'll go out after lunch," he said as Natalie dismounted, "and see how you do in the open country."

She darted him a look of suppressed excitement, wanting to express her joy and knowing he would regard it with mocking amusement. So she simply nodded and walked away to cool her sorrel, keeping the sensation of triumph locked inside.

After the lunch dishes were cleared and Ricky was safely on the school bus for his afternoon session, it was a different story. Natalie paused on her way to the barns to stand beneath an oak tree and gaze at the verdant meadow stretching out below her. Her mind's eye pictured herself cantering the sorrel over the meadow, a breeze blowing her hair. It was an idyllic image that was soon to come true.

She hurried along the path through the trees, breaking into the sunshine a hundred feet from the corral. There she stopped short, the color draining from her face. Her sorrel was hitched to the outside rail of the corral with Colter's blaze-faced chestnut beside it. Colter was tightening the saddle cinch.

But it was the flashy black and white pinto impatiently stamping the ground and tossing its arched neck only a little distance away from Colter that Natalie was staring at, her happiness evaporating like rain in the desert.

Astride the spirited pinto was Deirdre Collins, sophisticated and chic in her split riding skirt worn with a matching vest over a white blouse. A flat-crowned, wide-brimmed hat of the same shade accented the fiery lights of her long hair, caught at the back of her neck. There was smug satisfaction in her emerald green eyes as she studied Natalie's look of stunned dismay.

"There you are, Natalie," Deirdre called out, directing

Colter's unreadable glance in her direction. "Colter and I have been waiting for you."

Natalie bristled at the familiar way Deirdre coupled her name with Colter's. Her chin lifted with pride as she forced her feet to walk her over to the two of them.

"I didn't know you were here or I would have come sooner," Natalie said curtly.

That remark got a melodious laugh from the redhead, which angered Natalie. She cast an accusing glance at Colter. The mocking gleam in his blue-green eyes reminded her of her rash statement after Deirdre's last visit to the ranch, the occasion she had tried to elude his embrace by promising that Deirdre could come anytime. And Natalie flushed in silent outrage.

"Daddy was checking on some cattle not too far from here," Deirdre was saying. "I decided at the last minute to go with him and ride over for a visit. When Colter said he was taking you for your first cross-country trip on horseback, I invited myself along. I hope you don't mind."

"Of course not," Natalie replied stiffly.

"I can't imagine what it's like learning to ride," Deirdre added in a patronizing tone. Her gaze shifted from Natalie to Colter, an intimate expression in their green depths. "Colter and I were practically born in the saddle."

Natalie could feel her confidence already dissolving. Her riding ability was no match for theirs. Her stomach churned sickeningly as she felt herself forgetting everything that Colter had taught her. She fought the urge to flee before she was humiliated by their superior skill.

Colter untied their horses, walking to Natalie and passing her the reins of the sorrel, looking her over with perceptive thoroughness. His height blocked Deirdre's view of Natalie's hands, which shook a little as she took the reins, but he noticed them.

"You forgot your hat," was all he said.

"My hat?" Natalie echoed blankly. "I don't wear a hat."

"Well, there's no need for one in the mornings, but you sure as hell can't ride out in the midday sun without one," Colter stated firmly.

She clutched the reins tightly while an absurd vision of herself in that awful sunhat bedecked with flowers flashed through her mind. Natalie shook her head.

"I don't need one," she answered mutinously, putting a hand on the saddle horn to mount.

But Colter's fingers dug into the sleeve of her blouse. "Go to the house and get your hat. You could keel over in the saddle from too much sun. I'm not going to argue with you."

Fury sparked in her eyes as she met his unrelenting gaze. Then she glanced past him to Deirdre, who was watching their battle of wills with obvious pleasure. Without a word, Natalie wrenched her arm free of his hold and angrily tossed the reins at him. Then she stalked toward the house, resentment making every muscle in her body tense.

How long would they wait for her to return? She had no intention of riding with them, certainly not with that stupid, gaudy hat on top of her head. Natalie slammed the front door behind her and didn't slow her strides until she reached the kitchen. She stood by the table, trying to breathe slowly and deeply to calm herself. It didn't work.

Still and all, she needed a reason to delay going back— as well as a way to work off her angry energy. She couldn't just pitch a hissy fit, tempting as that was.

Yanking a bucket and brush from a closet, Natalie shoved the bucket beneath the sink faucet, poured a generous amount of all-purpose cleaning liquid in the bottom and filled it with hot water. Seconds later she was on her hands and knees on the floor, scrubbing it savagely. She'd done half of it when she heard the front door open and Colter call for her. Her mouth tightened grimly but she didn't answer.

She didn't look up when his footsteps stopped in the doorway of the kitchen. "What the hell are you doing?"

"What does it look like?" she snapped.

"I thought I told you to get a hat."

"I'm busy." She dipped the scrub brush in the soapy water and sloshed it over the floor.

"You are going riding." Colter made sure each word was concisely and emphatically spoken.

"You and Deirdre will find the ride a lot more satisfying by yourselves, I'm sure," Natalie responded sarcastically.

She rose to her feet, setting the bucket of water on the table with a clean rag spread underneath, wondering if domestic martyrdom was ever worth the trouble. She began to scoot the kitchen chairs out of the way, well aware of the steely gaze that followed her every movement, but ignoring it all the same.

"Are we going to go through this again?" Colter demanded. Natalie didn't reply, just kept scooting the chairs. "Are you going to get your hat or am I?"

Natalie shrugged indifferently. "Go and get it if you want, but I'm not going riding."

"Because of Deirdre?"

In a fit of temper, she stamped her foot on the floor, turning to face him at last. "I'm not going to have that woman make fun of me! I don't care what you do, I'm not going to wear that ridiculous hat!"

He tilted his head to the side and smirked. "Ridiculous?" he repeated.

"Yes!" she snapped. "You know very well that the only hat I own is that straw one with the flowers!"

Laughter rumbled from his throat, infuriating her.

"It isn't funny!"

But the low laughter at her expense continued. Before she took the time to consider the consequences, Natalie reached for the bucket on the table and emptied it in his direction, more or less in midair. But he sidestepped the flowing arc of soapy water and only a few scattering drops hit him.

An awful silence filled the room as a giant puddle formed on the floor. Then the glint of reprisal in his narrowed eyes focused on Natalie.

Intimidated in spite of her own anger, she took a hasty step backward as Colter moved forward. She forced herself to stand still, fighting the cowardly inclination to run while her heart pounded in her throat. She succeeded until he towered in front of her. Too late, Natalie tried to pivot away.

Her shoulders were seized in a strong grip and her back was pulled roughly against his chest. The outline of his masculine form was impressed on hers. Quicksilver shivers raced up her spine as Colter buried his mouth in the taut curve of her neck. His hands glided smoothly down her arms, sliding on to her stomach, their erotic caressing igniting suppressed desire in her flesh.

"You made me do it, Colter. You shouldn't have laughed." Charged with emotion, the words vibrated huskily from her tense throat.

Under the powerfully sensual spell of his touch, she didn't have the will to resist when he turned her into his arms. His warm mouth moved with almost bruising intensity over her lips as he easily lifted her off her feet and cradled her in his arms.

"Fight fire with fire," Colter murmured mysteriously, his head moving a tantalizing inch from hers.

Her arms instinctively circled his neck for support. As he burned her mouth with a fiery kiss, his statement wasn't nearly as mysterious as it had seemed a moment ago. Natalie was distantly aware of the smooth strides he was taking. She even felt a fleeting sensation of satisfaction at the thought of Deirdre walking into the house and the scary greenness of her eyes if the redhead saw the way Colter was kissing her.

A blithe, melodious song seemed to fill her hearing like the trill of a bird, and Natalie closed her eyes tighter to really hear the joyful sound. His ardent caresses gave her the buoyant feeling of floating on a cloud. She moaned softly when he took his lips away from hers. A little out of it, she could look at nothing but the provocative curve of his mouth.

"So you wanted to get me wet, did you?" Colter said.

There was a split second of dazed shock at his taunt before she felt him lifting her away from his chest . . . then she was falling. Her mouth opened to call out and water closed around her, bubbling, as she gulped in the chlorinated water of the swimming pool instead.

The lethargy his kiss had induced was immediately gone, her arms flailing the water to get her to the surface. Coughing and spluttering, she reached the tiled edge, pulling herself onto the deck, feeling like a half-drowned house cat.

Pushing straggling, wet locks of hair from her eyes, Natalie turned to glare at Colter. A wide smile split his usually impassive face, the white flash of his teeth bright as he guffawed at her predicament.

Yet Natalie was mesmerized by the smile, the genuine grin. She'd never seen Colter smile like that or laugh and its effect was dazzling.

"I'll convey your apologies to Deirdre," he finally chuckled.

Not until he had disappeared around the side of

the house did Natalie move, shivering in her clinging, wet clothes.

Colter didn't return to the house again that afternoon. But he unexpectedly appeared in the kitchen as she was adding dressing to the spinach salad she'd made for supper. He unceremoniously dumped the boxes in his arms onto the table. Nervously Natalie turned, self-consciously wiping her hands on her apron.

"You have no more excuses for not riding," Colter stated, as if she was about to invent more.

She felt a secret rush of pleasure as she recognized a hatbox from a famous store that sold Western wear. But she forced herself not to hurry as she opened it and removed a gorgeous ivory felt Stetson with a wide brim. The other box contained boot-cut jeans with a matching jacket. She raised her gaze from the new clothes to offer sincere thanks, wondering if his gifts had been motivated by thoughtfulness or practicality.

But Colter spoke before she had a chance. "By the way," he said smoothly, "we're going to have a house guest this weekend. I thought I'd better tell you now so you'll have plenty of time to get the spare room ready."

"One guest?" Ice froze the blood in her veins, almost stopping the beat of her heart. Her temper would never allow her to endure Deirdre's company for an entire weekend.

"Yes, only one." Colter studied the betraying quiver of her chin. "Why?"

"No reason." Natalie shrugged, carefully folding the clothes back into their box. Then she shoved the pants on top of the jacket. "Did you have to invite her here, Colter?" she demanded suddenly in desperate protest.

"Her?" A masculine brow rose high. "I never said the guest was female."

"Oh, stop playing games!" she sighed angrily. "I know

you invited Deirdre to pay me back for trying to splash you. You just want to be sure I remember my place." And what a place it was to be in. Natalie was just as angry at herself for abandoning an uncertain future on her own with Ricky for the reality of life as this unpredictable man's sort-of, sort-of-not spouse.

Spouse had the right sound, she thought bitterly. Legal. Unemotional. She was not and never would be on the intimate terms of a wife. Not with Colter.

"When have I ever done that?" he was asking.

Natalie snapped back to the present moment. He'd shifted his stance a little so that she was cornered by the table and a chair, her escape blocked by his lean body.

"Lots of times. With your coldness, your indifference, your aloof attitude to other people," Natalie answered in a quiet but sad voice. "Even your own flesh and blood. You know who I'm talking about, Colter, and I mean from the get-go. A newborn baby needs more than food and warmth, it has to have affection and attention or that baby can die. Adults aren't all that different. Now, I made a conscious choice to be here, but—" She stopped and searched his eyes. "Colter, don't you truly care about anyone? Isn't someone else's happiness ever important to you?"

"Are you trying to save my soul, Natalie?" There was a wry twist to his mouth.

"I guess I'm trying to find out if you have one—if there's anything else you would sacrifice for the benefit of someone else," she answered softly, an aching throb in her chest.

A surge of restlessness rippled visibly over him. "No." The slicing edge of his one-word answer made Natalie wince. Long strides carried him to the door where he paused to study her with deliberate detachment. "Nor do I have any desire to punish or humiliate you," Colter stated. "Our guest this weekend is Cord Harris. A man."

But Natalie found little comfort in his announcement.

On Friday afternoon, the drone of a small plane sounded above the house. Colter hadn't mentioned their weekend guest again, not even explaining whether he was a friend or business acquaintance. Natalie glanced through the window, seeing the red plane descending toward the ranch before she lost sight of it in the trees. Was this Cord Harris? Colter never said how he was arriving, although she knew there was a dirt airstrip beyond the barns.

In case it was their guest, Natalie set two beer glasses in the freezer section of the refrigerator to frost. Twenty minutes later she heard the front door open and the sound of Colter's voice and that of another man. Smoothing the skirt of her yellow-flowered dress, she walked through the dining room into the living room.

Hesitating, she studied the stranger while waiting for the two men to notice her. Taller than Colter, the man had raven-dark hair and black-brown eyes. High cheekbones emphasized the patrician look of his features. A hint of arrogance was there too, not so blatant as Colter's, owing to the stranger's ready smile.

"Where's Flo?" the man asked in a richly resonant voice. "I expected her to meet us at the door."

At that instant, the man's dark gaze encompassed the living room, where Natalie had already braced herself for the startled, curious look that sprang into his eyes. The very fact that he'd expected to see Colter's aunt indicated he was unaware of Natalie's existence.

"Hello." There was a faint quiver of anger in her voice, her smile taut with the realization that Colter had not mentioned her.

"Didn't I tell you when you called that Flo had retired?"

Colter asked with infuriating calmness. "More or less, anyway. With her church and charity work, she's hardly ever at home."

"No, you didn't tell me." A narrowed look of appraisal was turned on Colter by his guest.

"Then I probably forgot to mention my wife," Colter went on, immune to being judged, as usual. He directed the tall, dark-haired man's attention to her. "This is Natalie."

A rueful smile accompanied the hand Cord Harris extended to her. "I have to apologize for my ignorance."

"Don't, please." Natalie's chin lifted in proud refusal. "It was a very quiet and quickly arranged ceremony."

Colter's level gaze was locked on her face. "What she means is that we met at the Fiesta and slipped across the border to get married."

His terse explanation didn't provide any romantic reasons, true or not, for their hasty wedding. That kept Natalie from having to pretend that their marriage was based on love.

Her anger flashed in her eyes as she swung her gaze to the man at Colter's side. "You see, Mr. Harris, I met all his requirements. I could cook, keep house, and liked children." Before either of them had a chance to respond, she rushed on. "How about a couple of cold ones, you two?"

"Sure," Colter said. "I could go for a beer. Cord?"

With the slight inclination of Cord's head in agreement, Natalie swiftly left the room, her hold on her temper fraying just as fast. In the dining room, she stopped for a few seconds when she overheard the accusing question Cord Harris issued to her husband.

"What kind of marriage is this, Colter?"

"It suits us," was the casual reply. "At least I'm not twisted around a woman's little finger the way you are."

"Huh. That's not how I see my relationship with Stacy. She's everything to me."

"Sorry." Natalie noticed an edge of defensiveness in Colter's voice.

"Are you? Let me tell you something. Some day you're going to get brought to your knees," Cord said sternly. "Love may be the only thing that can humble you. I think you'll find it enlightening."

"I'll let you know," Colter said.

Silently Natalie wished Cord Harris's declaration was prophetic and not wishful thinking. She'd love to see Colter groveling for a woman's affection. She brought them their frosty glasses of cold beer and would have retreated to the kitchen if not for the arrival of Missy and Ricky at that moment, home from school. After a shyly affectionate greeting, Missy dutifully introduced Ricky. As usual, he wasn't the least bit bashful around a stranger.

"Didn't Aunt Stacy and Josh come with you?" Missy asked.

"Not this time." Cord answered with the patient attention of a man who genuinely liked kids. He glanced at Natalie to explain. "Stacy is my wife. She and our little boy usually come with me any time I'm on a horse-buying trip. But our yearly registered quarter horse sale is only a couple of weeks away, so she's busy with that."

"Oh, I see." Natalie supposed that the title of aunt was honorary in this case and Cord's next statement pretty much confirmed it.

"Colter was best man at our wedding—you remember it, don't you, Missy?"

"Kinda," the girl said.

Cord grinned. "Don't let Aunt Stacy hear you say that." He turned to Natalie again. "I know she'll want to meet you, but it'll have to be some other day."

"Soon, I hope. I'd like to meet her too," Natalie said. There was a funny ache in her heart at the loving way he spoke his wife's name and the light that appeared in his eyes whenever he mentioned her.

"How old is your little boy?" Ricky piped up.

"Nearly three," Cord answered.

"He's too young to ride a horse," Ricky told him sadly.

"A bit." A barely suppressed smile edged the corners of Cord's mouth. "Although sometimes he rides with his mother or me."

"I've learned how to ride by myself," Ricky announced importantly. Then he darted a cautious glance at Colter. "Almost," he qualified.

"That's enough visiting for now," Natalie said quietly, knowing Ricky would keep on yakking forever if he had an appreciative audience. "Go change out of your school clothes. And don't forget to change your shoes."

"I'll make sure he does, Natalie," Missy offered tentatively.

Natalie smiled her thanks.

"You know, Missy doesn't seem so shy these days," Cord Harris observed after the two children had left the room.

Colter's glance slid thoughtfully to the taller man. "She's become attached to the boy. She's very fond of him."

Cord fixed his attention on the light reflecting through the amber liquid in his glass. "That's understandable. She had a lot of love to give and no one who seemed to need it."

"You think so? Well . . . we've known each other a long time, Cord." There seemed to be a hidden warning in Colter's statement as well as something left unsaid. The two men exchanged measured looks.

Natalie sensed the sudden tension and imagined she

heard the clang of hard steel, as if two forces of equal strength had just met.

It was almost with relief that she heard the front door open. Travis walked through. There was a veiled look in his brown eyes when he glanced at her, but they still managed to convey a silent greeting before he turned to the other men.

"Karl looked at the plane's engine and carburetor, Mr. Harris," he said. "He couldn't find anything wrong, but he suggested that you call in an aviation mechanic to be on the safe side."

Natalie frowned. "Is something wrong with the plane?"

"It cut out on me twice on the way here, but I didn't have any trouble after the first hour of flight," Cord explained. "The annual inspection on it was just a week ago. I'm sure it's all right." He smiled thoughtfully at Travis. "Thank Karl for checking it out, will you?"

"Sure thing." Travis nodded, and left.

With his departure the two men began discussing the merits of the brood mares Cord Harris had come to see with the thought of purchasing one or more of them. The brief friction that had sparked only minutes before was ignored or deliberately forgotten.

Chapter 8

"Can I have a ride in your airplane, Mr. Harris?" Ricky asked eagerly.

"Ricky!"

Natalie's sharp reproval didn't silence him as he glanced up, a serious frown drawing his brows together as he met her quelling look.

"But I've never been up in a plane," he reasoned.

"Not this time, I can't take you up," Cord Harris said. "Maybe my next visit I'll have more time, but now I have to go home. My little boy is waiting for me." He turned to Natalie and offered his hand. "Thank you for having me here."

"You're welcome to visit any time," she said warmly.

Cord bent to Missy, brushing her cheek with a light kiss. "I'll bring Josh when I come again," he promised with a wink, and she smiled in return.

Then Colter was walking with him to the plane, a red Cessna parked on the edge of the airstrip. Over the weekend, Natalie had noticed that Colter held Cord Harris in high regard. Of course, Cord was a man whom nearly everyone would respect and admire whether they hated him or liked him. The unusual part was that Colter did.

She let out a small sigh as Colter rejoined her and Ricky and Missy. She studied him surreptitiously from the corner of her eye. The man beside her was one she might never understand. She knew him intimately and didn't know him at all.

Natalie wondered if she would ever resolve her ambivalent emotions where he was concerned. On the one hand, she couldn't fathom why he treated her the way he did. On the other, she was deeply drawn to his hidden side and the fiery passion that she seemed to catch glimpses of without ever being sure that it was always there—or that it had anything to do with her.

The scarlet and white plane taxied to the end of the dirt airstrip. The rudders and ailerons were checked. Brakes were set and the engine revved. Then the flaps were partially lowered. Cord saluted them in a final good-bye as he rolled the plane onto the strip, quickly gaining momentum.

As Natalie watched the wheels lifting in as the plane became airborne, she wondered if Cord Harris understood her husband—if he could explain the coldness that so often encased Colter. In Natalie's occasional visits to Flo Donaldsen's cottage, not even she had been able to say why or how he had lost the ability to care.

Lost in the labyrinth of her thoughts, Natalie had been watching the plane without seeing it, deaf to the sputtering sound coming from the engine. Ricky tugged at her arm.

"What's wrong with the plane, Nonnie?"

By then the engine had died completely and the red plane was heading quickly back toward the ground, past the end of the airstrip, without enough altitude to glide safely back. A few scattered trees stood in its path.

The car in which they'd all ridden out there was suddenly in her vision. She glanced in frightened surprise to her side only to discover that Colter was no longer standing next to her. While she had been paralyzed by what was happening, he had been reacting.

"Missy!" Natalie grabbed the young girl by the shoulder, looking down at the thin face, white and terrified as her own. "Run to the barns and get help! As fast as you can!"

Without a word Missy turned and ran with Ricky following. Now Natalie ran, not in the direction of the barns where the children were going, but toward the white rear of the car and the disappearing airplane. The violent crash of metal into earth and trees came next, seeming to go on forever, yet lasting only fleeting seconds.

As she raced by the end of the airstrip through the trees, the sound of a pickup truck came from behind her. Catching her breath against a tree trunk, Natalie glanced over her shoulder, wanting to wait for the help that was arriving and knowing every precious second might count. Resolutely she pushed herself away from the tree and stumbled on.

As she arrived at the crash site, her stomach turned sickeningly at the sight of the twisted wreckage of the red and white plane. Terror filled her heart. A hideous certainty assailed her: no one could possibly come out alive from that mess of tangled steel. Then a movement claimed her attention. It was Colter straining to open the caved-in door. Sobs tore from her throat at his doomed efforts, but he kept on grimly.

The pickup truck squealed to a halt behind her. With rounded, pain-filled eyes, Natalie looked at the men sprinting from the truck, seeing only the broad-shouldered form of Travis McCrea. The shattering of glass sounded from the wreckage and she turned to see Colter start to remove huge shards from the windshield of the plane.

Then her vision was blurred. From her tears, she thought at first. Then her breath caught in her lungs as she realized the cause of the shimmering haze. In confirmation, she heard the crackling of flames. Fear dragged a wrenching scream of agony from her.

"Colter!" This time Natalie screamed a name, her heart filled with terror that he would die along with Cord. "Colter! No!"

Now the fire was visible, hungry flames eating their way from the snarled tail section toward the wings and the ruptured fuel tanks. In that mortal second, Natalie knew she didn't want Colter to die, as she had tempted fate by sometimes thinking. She loved him! She wanted him to live!

With a smothered cry, she started running toward the plane. Gray-white smoke was beginning to change into gray-black smoke, hiding him from her sight. Then her shoulders were caught in a powerful grip she couldn't escape. She struggled uselessly against it, sobbing Colter's name with every breath she drew.

"You'll get yourself killed!" Travis shouted angrily.

"I don't care!" Natalie cried. "I've got to reach him! Colter—" Tears gushed from her eyes as Travis ignored her plea.

Then she heard his whispered, "My God!"

Twisting around, Natalie saw a man emerging from the smoke. With a sharp stab of relief, she recognized Colter's lanky frame and the bulk of Cord Harris's tall, heavy body in his arms. At that moment, the flames reached the fuel tanks. The force of the explosion knocked Natalie off her feet, catapulting her to the ground with Travis's protective weight shielding her from the bits of debris.

Flames and black smoke billowed into the air. Suffocating, searing heat tore at her lungs before she was pulled to her feet by Travis and pushed away from the inferno. The green leaves of the surrounding trees were transformed into curled ashes floating aimlessly through the air, suspended by the torrid air from the fire.

The impetus of Travis's hand got her several feet away. But Natalie had no thought of saving herself. Turning back, she wanted only to reach Colter. The ranch hands were of the same mind—she saw them racing to his prone body, spreadeagled over Cord Harris in an instinctive effort to protect the injured man from the exploding flames.

Two of the men pulled Colter to his feet. Semi-conscious and dazed, he was half-carried a safe distance from the blazing wreck. The other men, Travis among them, were making a human stretcher of their arms and carrying the inert body of Cord Harris to safety.

The screaming wail of sirens in the distance cut through the commotion as Natalie rushed to Colter's side. Crimson blood stained his chest, arms, and hands. His hair had been singed by the flames.

"Colter, are you all right? Are you hurt?" Tiny sobs shook her voice.

"Don't worry about me." Despite the growling force of his words, there was a glazed look to his eyes as he pushed her away. She was in the way of his view of the two men bending over Cord Harris. "We've got to get him to the hospital."

"The ambulance and fire trucks are here now." Travis appeared beside them, putting a restraining arm across Colter's chest. "I'm afraid it's too late."

The words wiped the glazed look from Colter's face. With a lightning movement, he pushed Travis's arm away, swinging his hand up in a vicious backhand slap that staggered Travis.

"No!" Colter shouted. Cold fury twisted his filthy face.

"Damn it! He's not dead! He was alive when I pulled him from that plane!"

"Colter, don't," Natalie sobbed, trying to stop him as he made his way toward the limp form on the ground.

The only hands he respected were those of the paramedics scrambling out of the ambulance. The look in his eyes terrified Natalie as he stared at the blood-streaked face of the man on the ground. It was as if he was willing Cord back from the dead.

"Get his pressure . . . internal bleeding . . . could be severe . . ." Natalie heard one of the paramedics mutter.

"I feel a pulse," another one whispered as though he was afraid he would frighten it away. "Weak, but it's there."

With practiced skill, they slipped the injured man onto a stretcher and stabilized his head and neck in an aluminum frame, putting a silver blanket over him to keep him warm. Cord had to be in shock and gravely injured. They carried him to the ambulance as Colter followed, linked by some invisible wire to the unconscious but still alive Cord Harris. As the ambulance doors were swung shut and latched, Natalie turned to Travis.

"Get Flo to watch the children," she ordered.

Without giving him time to say yes, she raced for the white car, sliding behind the wheel and putting it in reverse almost before the motor turned over. The ambulance siren screamed, and she followed the sound, its wavering shriek so like the ebb and flow of life.

At the hospital, the admitting nurse directed Natalie to the trauma center waiting area. There she found Colter sitting on a couch in a small alcove off the corridor. He was leaning forward, elbows on his knees, his hands clasped in front of him, staring at the closed doors marked *Surgery* that led to the operating area. His gaze flicked to her as he scrubbed at his face with a damp towel he'd been given, pressing against a nick from the windshield glass to stanch the trickle of blood. Except for the hand she placed on his thigh as she sat down beside him, she made no gesture, said no words of reassurance. At the moment, all of them seemed without meaning.

The minutes dragged by with immeasurable slowness and they waited in silence. Colter was like a statue carved from stone, tense and rigid, unmoving except for his eyes that followed every person who left or entered those fateful doors.

With no conception of how much time had passed, Natalie saw his gaze narrow as a short, older man came through, not wearing surgical scrubs. A white coat flapped around his legs as he walked purposefully toward them, frowning.

"I thought I told you to get those taken care of," he said to Colter.

"They're only scratches," Colter growled.

"No. More like gashes. And filled with dirt and glass too."

Colter waved the other man's concern away with a stiff hand that had curled into a claw. "I'm not going away from here, doc."

"There's nothing you can do," the other man said after a little while, not without compassion. "He'll be in there for hours while they try to put all the pieces back together."

His attempt at hospital humor fell flat. "Cord is going to live," Colter said with sudden vehemence.

"Are you asking me or telling me?" the doctor said. "Because if you're asking me, the only one who can answer that question is God Almighty. All that can be humanly done is being done. A hospital social worker has notified his family."

"His wife—"

"She's flying in, although I don't know how she has

the guts after what happened to her husband." The doctor reached down, taking a firm grip on Colter's arm. "Come on. Let's get those injuries cleaned up."

There was an instant of stiff resistance. Then Colter got to his feet, an impatient spring to his steps as he followed the doctor down the corridor. Natalie went along. She wanted to close her eyes to the sight of the slashes on his hands and arms from the broken windshield of the plane. The depth of her love for Colter made her feel the pain he seemed to be impervious to.

Then his bloodstained and torn shirt was put back on, covering most of his bandages except the ones on his hands. Their silent watch was resumed outside the doors leading to the surgery area. A nurse's aide brought them coffee which Natalie sipped sporadically and Colter ignored.

More time inched by. Light, hurried footsteps sounded in the hall, accompanied by long, masculine strides. Colter was on his feet as Travis appeared with an attractive brunette at his side. She walked straight to Colter, her hands reaching out for his while she mutely smiled a tremulous greeting.

"Are you all right?" Travis asked Natalie quietly.

"Yes," she whispered.

"Dr. Matthews called and suggested I meet Cord's wife at the airport," he explained.

Natalie's gaze turned to the other woman and she was barely aware of the comforting hand Travis placed on the back of her waist. She marveled at the control in Stacy Harris's voice when she spoke.

"Travis told me the way you risked your life to save Cord." The brunette's words were spoken quietly, without the trembling that made it so hard for Natalie to talk. "There aren't enough words to thank you, Colter."

"Stacy, when Cord opens his eyes and says something,

anything, that'll be enough for me. More than enough."
A muscle twitched in Colter's jaw.

Stacy Harris glanced over her shoulder, following
Colter's gaze to the doors that led to the surgery area.
"He's still in there, isn't he?" A shudder went through
her and she hugged her arms around herself as if to
ward off cold.

"They said it would be some time yet before he's out,"
Natalie offered in a weak voice.

It was more than two hours before a tall, heavyset man
emerged from the doors, weary and grim, a mask hanging down the front of his green scrubs. He told them
that Cord had survived the surgery, implying that he
considered it a miracle. His injuries were extensive and
serious, ranging from a severe concussion and broken
bones to internal injuries.

"When can I see him?" Stacy asked.

"They'll be taking him from the recovery room later
to intensive care. It'll be some time," the surgeon said.
"He's fighting every inch of the way, Mrs. Harris, and
that's about all I can tell you."

"Thank you." A solitary tear slipped from Stacy's
lashes, the first one Natalie had seen.

A quaking sigh of relief came from Natalie. Travis's
gaze flew down to her in concern and understanding.
When the doctor left, he took the edgy silence with him.
Colter walked to the window looking out to the west and
stared at the sunset sky, shot with crimson arrows.

Without glancing at her, he asked, "Is Flo watching
the kids?"

"Yes."

"He's going to make it," Colter stated.

"Yes," Natalie agreed.

"I'm sending Travis back to the ranch." His gaze

flicked from the window to her face. "I know you want to go with him, but you're staying here with Stacy."

Natalie's head jerked as if he had physically struck her. "I planned to stay anyway," she said through the tight lump of pain in her throat. It felt like her heart. "You're in no condition to drive home with those injuries."

He looked down at his bandaged hands as if he'd completely forgotten about them. Offering no acknowledgment, Colter turned away and walked back to the small alcove where Stacy waited.

Natalie reminded herself that he'd always had the power to hurt her—and now, with the newfound love she felt, he had even more.

At midnight, Stacy was allowed to see Cord. She returned to the waiting area pale and shaken, but showing a lot of self-control. His condition hadn't worsened but it hadn't improved either.

The doctor who'd disinfected and bandaged Colter's arms came bustling down the hospital corridor at two in the morning. At the sight of him, Colter stiffened. There was a taut line to his mouth before he spoke.

"What happened, Matthews?" Colter demanded.

"Are you still here, Langston?" the doctor asked.

"What happened?" he repeated.

"Your friend isn't the only patient in this hospital. You're going to be next if you don't go home and rest up." The doctor turned to Natalie. "Take your husband home. The next few days are going to be rough going. He might as well get some sleep while he has a chance. I've already made arrangements for Mrs. Harris to sleep here at the hospital. The nurses will see that she's as well cared for as her husband."

"I don't need any sleep," Colter said in an expressionless tone.

"Please go home. I can have you thrown out, you

know." The doctor's mock threat didn't make much of an impression on Colter. He looked at Natalie, who only shrugged. The doctor sighed and his expression softened. "I'll notify you personally if there's the slightest change either way, Colter, but go home."

"Please," Stacy said softly. "You and Natalie have done so much already. If the doctor doesn't call you, I will."

Natalie would have added her own plea to theirs except that she knew Colter wouldn't listen to hers. For once, though, Colter obeyed someone else's orders.

And he let her do the driving. Within a few minutes, the two of them were in the car and bound for the ranch. Not one word was spoken between them until Natalie stopped the car in front of the house.

"Would you like me to help you wash?"

"I can manage."

When they entered, Flo appeared in the living room wearing a long robe to cover her nightgown. Colter didn't even glance at his aunt, but strode purposefully down the hall to their bedroom. It was left to Natalie to bring Flo Donaldsen up to date.

"Travis told me it was a miracle Cord was still alive," Flo said with a weary shake of her head when Natalie had told her all she knew.

A wave of nausea swept over Natalie as she remembered the terror that had gripped her. "I still don't know how Colter got him out of that plane before it exploded."

The gray-haired woman looked intently at Natalie. "I once accused Colter of not even having emotions. I was so wrong. So very wrong."

Natalie's eyes glowed with sudden brilliance. Colter's reactions had been totally emotional. After risking his own life to save his friend, he had refused to believe that Cord was dead, and he had been proved right. At the hospital, she'd had glimpses of a very different side of him. Colter had depths she'd had no idea of. His cold, hard shell was real enough—though it had been pierced today. She took a deep breath, feeling a tumultuous leap of her heart.

"You must be tired," Flo Donaldsen announced. "The children went to bed hours ago and it's time you did the same."

"Yes, I am tired," Natalie said, but she actually felt incredibly awake.

"I'll take care of breakfast in the morning for the children," Flo offered. "You two sleep in."

"Please wake us if there are any phone calls from the hospital," Natalie said as she started down the hall after Colter.

"I will," Flo smiled. "No matter what the news is."

The bedroom light was on. She found his bloody, torn shirt in the bathroom and the evidence that Colter had washed.

But he wasn't there. Natalie tiptoed into Missy's room and then Ricky's room, thinking he might have felt the need to check in on them. He wasn't in either room. Surely he wouldn't have gone back to the hospital, she thought wildly.

Hurrying through the rest of the house, she saw from the living room window that the car was still parked in the driveway. A light was on in his study. When Natalie returned to the living room, she felt a breeze of night air blow on her face. The French doors to the back patio stood open.

Stepping into the darkness, Natalie saw Colter indistinctly. He was sitting in one of the chairs, his legs stretched out in front of him and his head tilted back to stare blankly at the crescent moon. She started to speak but happened to glance at the can of beer in his bandaged hand, the aluminum catching the faint glow of the moonlight. As she watched, his fingers slowly tightened around the can, unconsciously crushing it without his even noticing the liquid that spilled down his hand.

"You're supposed to drink the beer," she said softly, walking over to remove the can from his hand, "not spill it all over the place."

Colter sighed but didn't reply, although she sensed his gaze had moved to her face.

"It's going on four o'clock." Natalie smiled at him gently, loving him so very much that it was almost a physical ache. "Come on to bed."

In a slow, reluctant motion, he rose to his feet, but made no move to enter the house. She wanted desperately to tell him that she understood the silent anguish he was going through. Fear held her words in check, fear that he would reject her sympathy. She stood uncertainly at his side, wondering if she should repeat her question or simply leave him.

"Colter." She said his name with an aching throb in her voice. "You need to rest."

"Do I?" His voice, husky and warm, vibrated around her, physically touching her with its evocative tone.

"Yes, you do," she whispered.

With a fluid turn, Colter faced her, his features in shadow, the moon trailing silvery light over his hair.

"How long has it been since I've touched you, wildcat?" Behind the sensuality of his words was the harshness of mockery that she knew so well. Her knees threatened to buckle.

"Please, Colter." She pushed aside the surging need his question had aroused. "I want you to rest."

A soft chuckle came from him. "But that's not what I want." Hard decisiveness laced his words.

Her breath was drawn in sharply as his hands closed over her hips and she was pulled against his very male body. Before she could control the sudden explosion of her senses, his mouth was covering hers with searing hunger. Her lips parted on contact, allowing him to take all the sustenance he desired. His appetite was ravenous as he demanded the full satisfaction of the melting softness of her body.

Then Colter broke free and an inaudible sigh broke from Natalie's lips. She wanted to feel again the consuming fire of his kiss—but steel fingers closed over her wrist. Ignoring her cry of pain, he pulled her through the open patio doors, the glass rattling in the frame as he slammed them shut. The momentum of her shaking legs carried her to his side. Using it, Colter swept her into his arms, the gauze of his bandages scraping the bare skin of her arms. For an instant it broke the seductive spell of his touch.

"Colter, please," Natalie protested faintly. "You're hurt!"

There was no reply until they reached the bedroom, where he let her feet swing to the floor. His arm still circled her waist, molding her against his length while his hand brushed the hair from her cheek.

"Then don't fight me tonight, Natalie," he murmured.

Her heart beat wildly as the bedroom light illuminated his expression an instant before he switched it off. The forbidding set of his jaw was there and the unrelenting line of his mouth, but there was no indifference in his eyes. They blazed with desire. For her.

Chapter 9

Sunlight danced over her face, warming her skin with its golden kiss. Natalie snuggled deeper into the embrace of the strong arms that held her.

"I was beginning to think you were going to sleep until noon," a low voice whispered into her hair.

Keeping her eyes tightly closed, Natalie smiled dreamily and slowly moved the top of her head against Colter's chin. The scent of his maleness was like a heady wine. She was afraid to speak, afraid to let all the sensations of love come spilling out.

"You're a funny little critter, Natalie," Colter murmured, shifting her into a more comfortable position and bringing her nearer to his face on the pillow.

"Why do you say that?"

The smile remained when her lips moved to ask the throaty question. Her lashes fluttered and her eyes opened to drink their fill of his handsome face.

With his usual arrogance, he ignored her question. "I'm hungry. Get up and fix me some breakfast." The teasing order was softly given, closer to being a request than a command.

Reluctantly Natalie untangled herself from his arms,

instantly missing the warmth of his bare flesh against hers. In the darkness of last night, it had been easy to conceal her love from him. The brilliant sunlight would undoubtedly reveal all the feelings she wasn't ready to acknowledge.

She couldn't fight the desire to keep it to herself a little while longer. Colter was much too observant for her to hide it from him indefinitely. Besides, she wanted him to know. But she wanted to tell him at a moment that wasn't heavy with the aftereffects of passion.

Her gold robe was lying on the foot of the bed and Natalie reached for it as she slipped from beneath the covers. Quickly shrugging into it, she zipped it up to the top, then glanced at Colter. He had pushed himself into a half-sitting position with the pillows at his back. The white of his bandages stood out starkly against the tanned skin of his chest. The half-closed look he gave her was suffused with a lazy thoughtfulness. She had to smile.

"Bacon and eggs?" Natalie questioned, and he nodded. She started toward the door. "It shouldn't take long. Would you like me to bring it on a tray?"

"I'm not an invalid," he said dryly, "but if I don't show when it's ready, I guess you could bring it in here."

The hands of the kitchen clock indicated that it was nearly mid-morning. Missy was in school and from the window over the sink, Natalie could see Flo Donaldsen sitting in one of the patio chairs. She guessed accurately from his shouts that Ricky was playing somewhere nearby.

As she began her preparations by putting bread in the toaster and starting up the coffeemaker, finishing with placing strips of bacon in the square skillet, the door in the kitchen that led outside opened. With a happy smile, Natalie turned to greet Flo, but it was Travis who walked in. He stopped at the sight of her, the expression on his rugged face freezing a little.

"Good morning, Travis." Some of the joy that love had brought her crept into her voice, adding an airy lilt.

His mouth moved into a smile that didn't reach his eyes as her greeting seemed to unfreeze him. "Morning, Natalie. I was just bringing in the mail." He tossed envelopes and magazines on the table.

"Is there anything important I should take to Colter?"

"Not that I noticed," Travis answered slowly. "Is that his breakfast you're cooking?"

"Yes, he's still in bed," Natalie said.

There was a husky undertone in her voice, put there by the vivid memories of their passionate lovemaking before the sun came up.

"Oh. Well, you look especially radiant this morning." His flat observation dimmed the sparkle in her eyes. The hand holding the fork above the bacon-filled skillet paused as Travis asked, "Is there a reason for that?"

"Yes," she answered, suddenly conscious of his feelings toward her.

His hands were resting on his hips in a vaguely challenging stance. "The look of a woman in love, right?"

She bent her head for an instant, wishing she didn't have to hurt him, although she'd never once thought that she might be in love with him. Then she slowly turned to him, giving him a faint look of apology but not regret.

"You must have known how I felt," Natalie said gently. Travis had been there at the crash site when she had discovered that she really did love Colter.

Dark lashes shut out the look in his brown eyes, a momentary flash of pain that was gone when Travis opened his eyes. "I guess I couldn't believe that it happened."

"It did happen." Natalie smiled a little. "And I wouldn't change the way I feel for all the money in the world."

His long legs moved him toward her at a deliberate pace, his earnest gaze searching her face. "I want you to be happy, Natalie," he said tightly. "May I—kiss the happy bride-to-be?"

She hesitated for only a second before she turned her face up to his. With both hands, Travis framed her face as if memorizing every feature. Tears shimmered in his amber eyes at his pain. He lowered his head to her lips.

"For all the times I'll never hold you, Natalie," he said in a raw, aching whisper.

Then he was kissing her, barely controlled passion making the mouth that claimed hers tremble. But his moment of possession was short, and he soon drew away from her, breathing in deeply. The twisting pain of lost love showed in his face in the instant before he spun away toward the door. Natalie wanted to call out to him, to say something that would ease his hurt. She was the cause of his anguish, so there were no comforting words she could offer.

Robbed of a little of her joy, even sobered by the reminder of love's harsh side, Natalie turned back to the breakfast she was preparing for Colter. Her finger pressed the button on the toaster and she took the juice out of the fridge. Minutes later, she was sliding the eggs onto a warmed plate and adding the bacon. Adding juice, coffee, and toast to the tray took just a little while longer.

Humming lightly to herself, Natalie picked up the tray and started for the door. It burst open before she reached it and Ricky tumbled in.

"Morning, Nonnie," he cried gaily.

"Hey, Ricky. Good morning, Flo," she said brightly to the older woman, who had followed Ricky at a more sedate pace.

"Are you just eating breakfast?" Ricky exclaimed in a scolding tone. "I'm going to help Flo make my lunch."

"I'll take this to Colter and come back to help you." Natalie winked at Flo.

"Colter isn't here." Flo frowned in surprise at Natalie's words. "Ricky and I just talked to him in the driveway. He's on his way to the hospital."

"But he asked me to get breakfast." She stared in blank confusion at the older woman.

"All I know," Flo said with a touch of sympathy, "is that he said he'd phoned the hospital. He didn't sound happy with the information they gave him. I imagine he forgot all about eating."

"He could have told me he was leaving," Natalie said in a protesting murmur.

"Colter isn't in the habit of informing anyone about his plans," Flo reminded her.

That was true, Natalie admitted silently. She had rarely known where he was during the day. Yet surely after last night—she shook that memory away. His thoughtlessness this morning was a result of his concern for Cord Harris. She couldn't fault him for that.

Colter didn't come back for supper, although Natalie postponed serving it for nearly an hour in the hope he would come. Nor was Travis there, sending word to the house in the afternoon that chores would be taking him to the far boundary of the ranch. Flo had naturally returned to her cottage, which left only Missy, Ricky, and Natalie sitting around the large dining room table.

It was after midnight when Natalie heard the crunch of tires in the gravel drive. Uncurling her legs from the sofa, she closed the book in her hand, completely aware that she had been reading the same page for over an hour without taking in a word, and tossed it on the adjacent cushion. She opened the front door before Colter's hand could touch the knob.

"H-hello." Natalie smiled in accompaniment to her breathless greeting.

"I thought you'd be in bed." His gaze flicked over her tiredly as he walked by.

"I waited up for you," she explained unnecessarily. "I wasn't sure if you'd eaten and I wanted to know how Cord was doing."

"He's still listed as critical, but his condition is improving, so the doctors say," he sighed with bitter scorn. "I'm not hungry. Deirdre and I ate at the hospital cafeteria."

"Deirdre?" Natalie asked hesitantly. "You mean Stacy."

"No, they sent up a tray for her so she could stay with Cord."

Unconsciously she followed as he walked down the hallway to their bedroom, briskly removing his jacket as he went. She tried to ignore the sinking in her heart.

"What was Deirdre doing there?" She had to know, despite her pride. Jealousy goaded her.

"She heard about the accident. So she came to the hospital to see how he was and if there was anything she could do to help," Colter answered sharply.

"Does she—know Cord and Stacy?"

"No," he said sarcastically. "Deirdre always offers her sympathy to complete strangers. Of course she knows them!" he snapped.

As he tugged at the sleeves of his shirt, Natalie saw him wince involuntarily when the material caught in the adhesive of his bandages.

"Let me help you," she said quickly, stepping forward to ease the shirt over the gauze.

"Save your mothering for the kids." Colter pulled away

from her touch, giving her a look of savage irritation. "I don't need it."

Hurt pride lifted her chin to a defiant angle as Natalie turned away, leaving him to struggle on his own. With jerky movements, she began her own preparations for bed, trying to convince herself that Colter was tired and worried. Slipping the nightgown over her head, she heard the bed accepting his weight.

"Flo said she would stay with the children tomorrow," Natalie said stiffly.

"What for?" Cord asked without interest.

Natalie glanced over her shoulder, her gaze stopped by the impersonal hardness of his. "So I could stay with Stacy," she said, not liking the remoteness in his eyes.

"There's no need to do that."

"Why not?" Natalie challenged him, the clinging nightgown whirling about her legs when she turned around. "You wanted me to last night."

"That was because you were available."

"And I suppose that Deirdre will be at the hospital tomorrow," she murmured cattily.

His gaze narrowed. "Yes, she'll be there and so will I. You're a stranger to Stacy. Deirdre and I have known her since she married Cord. Besides, it's more convenient."

"What do you mean?" Natalie demanded, jealousy tearing at her heart.

"Because Deirdre has an apartment in town. She can be at the hospital in minutes if Stacy needs her."

There was a betraying quiver of her chin as she met his mocking eyes. "Maybe you should stay there then," she suggested icily as she walked to the bed. "It would be more convenient than driving back and forth."

"I'll consider it," Colter said levelly and rolled onto his side.

The trembling of her chin started other quivers

through her body. Her emotions, muddled and confused, touched off conflicting urges. She wanted to scream at Colter to go to Deirdre now, to throw things at him and arouse him out of his indifference, if only to get a reaction. She wanted to bury her head in the pillow and cry with frustration and futility. Most of all, she wanted to touch him, to apologize, to make him understand that she didn't want to fight him—she wanted to love him.

In the end, Natalie did none of those, but switched off the light and slid beneath the covers to lie in rigid silence listening to his even breathing. Why had she thought anything had changed, she asked herself, simply because Colter had desired her the night before?

Natalie was awakened the next morning by the sound of closet doors opening and closing. Through her lashes, she watched Colter slip on a blue chambray shirt and tuck it into the waistband of his jeans. As if he sensed her eyes on him, his piercing gaze swung to her. Its discerning quality made faking sleep impossible. Natalie forced her eyes to open all the way, stretching her body in a drowsy way.

"Don't bother to get breakfast for me," Colter drawled, reaching for the jacket on the chair.

"Will you be home for dinner tonight?" she asked as though having him there was no big deal to her.

"If I'm not here, eat without me," was his clipped reply.

But the very fact that he'd answered in that way forewarned Natalie that he wouldn't be home. The entire day and night she was tortured by fears that her spiteful words had driven him to Deirdre, although she silently realized that no one could make Colter do anything he hadn't already decided to do.

Refusing to humiliate herself by waiting up for him

again, she went to bed shortly after Missy and Ricky did, tossing and turning until she fell into a troubled sleep. She didn't hear him return. The only evidence that he had consisted of the clothes he'd worn lying on the chair, and the rumpled pillow beside her own.

For two days, Natalie didn't see Colter, only signs that he'd come back to the ranch. On the afternoon of the third day, she, Ricky, and Missy were at the corrals where Ricky was resuming the riding lessons that had been interrupted. This time they were under Travis's supervision, since Ricky had appealed to him the night before.

Ricky was cantering the stocky bay around the enclosure. The horse's front hoof struck an outsized chunk of earth and he lurched forward before regaining his rhythmic stride. The minor mishap was all it took for Ricky to lose his balance and tumble to the ground. Travis reached him almost before the first wail broke from Ricky's lips. Natalie and Missy were only a step behind.

"Ricky, honey, are you hurt?" Natalie reached anxiously for the crying boy as Travis helped him get up. His little arms wrapped tightly around her as Ricky buried his face in her neck and continued to sob uncontrollably.

"Put him back on the horse." The snapped command came from behind them.

Natalie's arms tightened protectively around Ricky as she turned to glare at Colter, striding toward them, his face a mask of tight-lipped coldness.

"He took a tumble," she protested, but Colter's hands were pulling Ricky away in spite of his efforts to cling to Natalie and hers to keep him there.

Ignoring the little boy's loud wails, Colter carried him to the patiently standing bay and sat him in the saddle, picking up the loose reins and handing them to Ricky.

"Nonnie!" Ricky clutched the saddle horn and ignored the reins Colter was placing in his hands.

Natalie tried to rescue him, but Colter's arm swept her away. "What are you doing? He could be hurt—"

"Are you, Ricky?" Colter turned his steel-blue gaze to the crying boy, and received a tiny nod. "Where? What hurts?" When Ricky failed to answer, Colter frowned. "Thought so. You're afraid, is all."

Ricky's cries became gasping sobs as he stared wide-eyed at Colter's impassive face.

"Of course he's frightened," Natalie said defensively. "That's a long way for a little boy to fall."

"He's going to fall off again if he doesn't take those reins," Colter stated grimly, looping them around the horse's neck within Ricky's reach.

Before Natalie could guess what Colter planned, he slapped the horse on the rump, sending it trotting away. Her heart jumped into her throat. There was a terrified look on Ricky's face as he started to slide from the saddle again. Immediately the docile bay slowed to a shuffling walk and Ricky pulled himself upright in the saddle.

"Now pick up those reins," Colter commanded. Without any directing hands on the reins, the bay stopped. Ricky's hands were frozen on the saddle horn. "Pick them up or I'll get the horse going again."

"Colter, for God's sake!" Travis exclaimed angrily.

Colter ignored the protest as he took a step toward the horse. Ricky immediately took the reins in his hand, still shaking and wide-eyed, but the sobbing had stopped.

"Walk the horse around the corral." The harsh edge was gone from Colter's voice but the firmness remained. After a hesitant glance at Natalie, Ricky obeyed. At a walk and a trot, Colter made him circle the corral several times. "Now, canter Joe around the corral once," he ordered.

Natalie's mouth opened in instant outrage, only to

close in disbelief when she heard Ricky speak. "His name is Lightning." And it was Lightning he nudged into a canter.

"I did a good job, didn't I?" Ricky smiled from ear to ear as he stopped the horse in front of Colter.

"Yes, you did," he agreed, lifting Ricky out of the saddle onto the ground. Natalie started to step forward, but Colter was already instructing Ricky to cool the bay. Then he turned to Missy. "Do you see how it's done?"

The young girl dropped her gaze at his question, her thin face pale and drawn. Without a glance at either Travis or Natalie, Colter walked to his daughter and swung her slender length into his arms. There was mute appeal in the troubled look Missy gave her father.

But Colter stepped through the corral gate and to Natalie's sorrel horse tied to an outside post. He set Missy in the saddle, untied the reins, and climbed up behind her. His arms protectively circled her as he walked the horse away from the corral in the direction of the open meadow beyond the stand of trees.

It was two hours later that Missy came rushing into the house, her face flushed and excited, her eyes sparkling with pride. Her words tumbled out in her hurry to tell Natalie and Ricky that she had conquered her fear of riding.

"Daddy said I shouldn't be ashamed that I was afraid. He said being afraid of horses was like being afraid of the dark and I had to learn there was nothing that would intentionally harm me. He rode with me for a long way just talking and making me relax and remember how much fun I used to have riding. Then he got off and I rode by myself for a while. And Daddy said I was almost as good as I used to be, and with practice, I would get better."

Natalie's smile was mixed with astonishment at the happiness in the young girl's face. She couldn't ever remember Missy being so confident or so talkative. And she wasn't finished yet.

"We talked about a lot of other things on the way back," Missy continued. "Daddy said I wasn't a little girl anymore, that I was becoming a young lady and maybe it was time I stopped wearing my hair in braids. Do you think I should get it cut, Natalie?"

"I can make an appointment with the hairdresser, sure. I think you'd look very pretty with short hair," Natalie said.

"Oh, do you think so? I told Daddy I was skinny and plain, but he said I was probably one of those girls that would bloom in my late teens and just knock everyone off their feet. Can you imagine that?" Missy breathed. "Should I change into a dress for dinner? Daddy said I would look good in blue because it matches my eyes."

"Why not?" Natalie was amused by Missy's eagerness.

"Come with me, Ricky," Missy said to the boy, who hadn't been able to get a word in edgewise. "You can help me brush my hair."

Ricky didn't seem to mind being enlisted for that. As Natalie watched the two of them dash from the dining room, she decided it was amazing what a man's attention could do for a girl. She had always sensed that Colter could be overwhelmingly charming if he chose to be. In the face of Missy's transformation, it was difficult to hold a grudge against him for the way he'd treated Ricky. Particularly because Colter had been right.

Chapter 10

Colter didn't come to the house until it was exactly mealtime, seeming so calm that his demeanor belied Missy's account of their afternoon ride. He pulled out the chair at the head of the dining room table and sat down.

"Aren't we going to wait for Travis?" Natalie asked.

"He won't be eating here." The answer was clipped out with no explanation.

Natalie could only guess that Travis had made other plans so as not to have to hang out with her and Colter, knowing how she felt. She ladled the soup into bowls.

"How is Cord?"

"He responded lucidly to the doctors today. They don't have any more reservations about his recovery." Again that impersonal tone marked his words.

Apart from Natalie's expression of relief at that news, Colter's statement brought an end to the conversation. Without Travis there for after-dinner coffee and with the children excused from the table, Natalie found the continued silence scraping at her nerves.

"Are you going to the hospital tomorrow?" she asked, feeling so awkward that she took a sip of the coffee when it was still too hot to drink.

"No, I'll be needed at the ranch now." One arm was draped over the back of his chair as Colter stared with brooding thoughtfulness at his china cup.

Natalie glanced at him quizzically. There had seemed to be a hidden meaning in his reply. His impassive gaze caught her look and the line of his mouth hardened.

"You might as well know," he said in a measured tone, "I've fired Travis." He glanced at his wristwatch. "He oughta be packed and gone by now."

"You fired him?" she repeated incredulously. "But why? What did he do?"

"That's none of your business."

"Surely he'll stop to say good-bye to Missy and Ricky," Natalie persisted, unable to think of a reason for Travis's abrupt dismissal.

"Don't you want to say good-bye to him?" Colter said mockingly.

"Oh—oh, of course," she stammered. "Travis has been very kind to me." The sound of disgust that Colter made irked her to no end. "And he's been a gentleman," she added sharply, "regardless of what you think!"

"He's a man," Colter jeered softly. "I can't believe that there weren't a few stolen kisses."

Uncontrollably Natalie flushed, remembering the innocent kiss she and Travis had exchanged the morning after the crash. Colter would never regard it as innocent.

"Where is Travis going?" she asked instead, striving for composure. "Did he say what he was going to do?"

"Isn't it strange?" Colter chuckled without humor. "You're more upset by his leaving than he is. When I told him he was through, he seemed relieved. I had the feeling you two had made contingency plans or something."

"What do you mean?" Her voice was unsteady.

"I hope you aren't thinking of running away with him. Wouldn't, if I were you. Unless you want a miserable life."

Hurt anger trembled violently through her. "More miserable than it is right now?" Natalie taunted. "I think that's impossible!"

The muscles along his jaw leaped. "Aren't you forgetting something? We made an agreement. And you're going to keep it!"

"And how are you going to make me do that? Lock me in every night? Post a guard at the door whenever you're gone? I'm not your slave, Colter Langston! I'm not chained to you!"

Her hands were on the tabletop next to her cup, clenched into fists. With a lightning move, his fingers closed over one of her wrists in an unshakable grip as he leaned toward her.

"You will do as I say and like it!"

Her reaction to his angry arrogance was instantaneous. Her free hand gripped the coffee cup and threw the hot liquid into his face. Frightened by his cry of pain, Natalie raced to the front door, hearing the crash of china and chairs as Colter began his pursuit.

Through the door and into the moonless night she ran. Fear for her own safety was replaced by prayer that she had not injured Colter. Yet she couldn't go back and endure any more of his insults and indifference. Both wounded her more than the falseness of his not-exactly-subtle accusations.

Madly racing for the concealment of the oak trees, Natalie reached them as the front door slammed behind Colter. The black trees hid her from his sight, but the darkness also worked against her. She stumbled over tree roots, was slapped in the face by low-hanging branches, and only the light from the barns behind the grove of trees kept her going in the same direction. As she burst into the open, she heard Colter crashing through the trees.

She had no destination in mind. Her only aim was to

escape, for the moment at least, Colter's payback for her throwing coffee in his face.

The light from the barns flickered over a large blocky shape—it was a pickup truck. Then a tall figure separated itself from the truck, rushing out to meet her. For a screaming second, she thought it was Colter.

"Natalie?" Travis's low voice was mixed with surprise and concern.

With a gasping sob, she threw herself into his arms, clinging to the broad chest with what little energy she had left. Holding her close, Travis brushed the tangled hair from her face.

"What's wrong? What has he done to you?" he demanded.

"Nothing. Everything," she whispered wildly. "He told me—"

"Take your hands off my wife, McCrea!" Colter's harsh voice sliced off the rest of Natalie's explanation.

"I don't work for you anymore, Colter," was Travis's low reply. "I don't take orders."

As Colter came closer, Travis set Natalie to the side and stepped in front of her, shielding her with his body. "To get to her, you're going to have to go through me," Travis said, in that same soft undertone that sent shivers of fear racing down Natalie's spine.

"Don't threaten me, McCrea," Colter warned. "I've whupped bigger and stronger men than you."

"You're going to have to do it again. I've stood by and watched long enough when you bossed Natalie around just like you boss everyone. I'm not going to keep quiet about it—"

"Travis, please!" Natalie clutched at his elbow to restrain him, feeling the muscles flexed and ready in his arm.

"Don't want to be quiet, huh? You managed it when you held her in your arms and kissed her!"

The tall, dark-haired man took a threatening step forward. Natalie eluded the arm that tried to keep her behind him and raced in front of Travis, spreading her fingers on his broad chest to block him.

"Stop it! Both of you!" she cried in desperate anger. A hasty glance at the furious faces of both men told her that her plea was useless.

"Colter, if Natalie wouldn't end up hating me," Travis went on, "I'd kill you for that remark."

Colter laughed harshly. "Are you trying to deny it? Natalie's already admitted that you kissed her!"

"Yes, he did! Once!" Natalie yelled, trying to stop a fight that neither man could win. "But not the way you think!" Beneath her hand, she felt a sudden stillness come over Travis.

"Why should it matter to you, Colter, that another guy wants your wife?" There was an odd watchfulness in his brown eyes as Travis studied the man challenging him. "It never bothered you when men made a play for the first Mrs. Langston. Not even when they succeeded. Why does it concern you that I want Natalie? Or is it that you're afraid that she wants me?"

"She's staying here," was the snarling reply. As Colter took another step closer, the light illuminated his face, revealing the incredible intensity in his gaze. "All the plans you've made to run away together don't mean squat. There's no place you can go that I won't find you!"

"What's one woman more or less?" Travis taunted.

"Get out of the way, Natalie," Colter ordered in an ominously calm voice.

"No." She refused weakly at first, then gathered her strength. "No!" Travis made no attempt to stop her as she raced to Colter, digging her fingers into the iron bands of his arms. "I won't let you fight!"

With a fierce shrug, Colter broke free of her grip. The

harsh glitter of his eyes swept her face as he took her by the shoulders, mocking her puny attempt to stop him.

"It won't do you any good to try to protect him," Colter told her coldly.

"You crazy, blind fool!" Travis laughed bitterly. "It's not me she's protecting. It's you!"

A snort of disgust came from Colter as he flicked his gaze from Natalie's pleading eyes to challenge Travis. "You don't expect me to believe that, do you?"

"You've finally joined the rest of us mortals, haven't you, Colter?" A heavy sigh broke from the other man's lips as the tension of battle left his muscles. "You've left your mountain lair and now you know what it's like to love someone until it feels like your guts are being torn out."

Natalie gasped at Travis's declaration, unable to believe there was any truth in it. The hands gripping her shoulders increased their viselike hold. Her doubting gaze moved over Colter's face. Unthinkable pain distorted his hard features as he stared beyond her at Travis.

"Is it true?" she whispered. Her hands touched his waist, her body swaying closer despite the punishing grip of his fingers. "Oh, Colter, please—is it true? Do you love me?"

With aching hunger in their depths, his eyes swept her upturned face before he crushed her against his chest, holding her so tightly that she could barely breathe. His chin and cheek rubbed the top and sides of her hair, a rough, feline caress from a mountain lion.

"Yes," Colter groaned. "Yes, I love you, Natalie."

Racking sobs of happiness shook her body and tears of joy streamed from her eyes. She hadn't believed it was possible. Drowning in the overflowing release of emotion, she was too choked up to speak as she surrendered then and there in his arms.

But in the blink of an eye, he set her away from him, striding from her into the shadowy oak trees without a backward glance. Stunned by his unexpected action, Natalie could only stare after him for a paralyzed moment.

"I never thought anyone could reach him." She pivoted sharply toward Travis's quiet voice, having forgotten he was there. "Without you he'll die, Natalie," he murmured.

There was pain in the brown eyes that looked at her. "And you," she asked softly, compassion forcing her back to the present moment, "what will you do?"

He smiled wryly. "I'll live. I only adored you from afar anyway. I won't have those memories of holding you in my arms in the middle of the night."

"You don't have to leave," she whispered.

"Yes, I do. You know that." Travis breathed in deeply, seeming to shrug off the pain. "I've saved up some. I think I'll get a place of my own."

"I wish you all the happiness in the world."

He turned toward the pickup. "Colter left so he wouldn't stand in the way of what you wanted. He's never placed anyone's desires above his own before. Don't take that for granted, Natalie."

She began to edge backward. "Good night, Travis," was all she could manage to say before she turned and made a mad dash to the house.

The impetus of her love made it feel more like floating. Flinging open the door, she paused on the threshold, halted by the stark pain in Colter's eyes as he stood in the hallway.

"I knew you wouldn't leave without Ricky," he muttered, turning his head away. "May God give me the strength to let you go again—"

The sound of the pickup's engine grinding to life and the crunch of its big tires on the gravel drive interrupted him.

"Travis is leaving," Natalie said softly. "I'm not going

with him and I'm not going to meet him. I never
planned to."

"What do you take me for? A complete idiot?" Colter
exploded. A savage fury broke around her as his blazing
look hit her. "I came down that morning to have the
breakfast I thought you were lovingly preparing. I heard
you tell Travis that you loved him and all the money in
the world didn't matter to you! I saw the look in your
eyes, all soft and warm, before he kissed you."

"Oh, Colter, no!" She ran to him, her hands touching
the muscles of his chest, tense with rage. "I was telling
Travis that I loved *you*! Whatever I said about money was
to let him know that I didn't care if you were rich or
poor. Then he asked if he could kiss the bride-to-be . . ."
She trailed off, when Colter turned away from her, obviously not believing a word.

"Yeah," was all he said.

"I swear it's the truth," Natalie vowed. "How could I go
into another man's bed after what we shared that night?
I love only you."

He stared at her, searching her face, wanting to believe.

"Don't you see," she beseeched him. "That's why it
hurt so much tonight when you kept accusing me of
having an affair with Travis. I love you, not him!"

"You said life was miserable with me," he snapped.

Colter flinched when her fingers touched the muscle
leaping so wildly in his jaw. "Isn't life miserable when you
think the one you love doesn't love you?" Natalie argued
softly.

"It's hell!"

As he spoke the words, he was sweeping her into his
arms, burning his brand onto her mouth. She savored the
urgent caresses of his hands, needing the physical sensation of his love as much as she needed hers. For long moments they stayed like that, until Colter reluctantly pulled

his mouth from hers, gently cupping her face with his hands, breathing raggedly as he rubbed her forehead with his in a surrendering gesture.

"After the way I acted, I have no right to your love," he muttered. "Even now, I feel like you should hate me."

Natalie pressed herself more tightly against him. "I told myself a thousand times that I did. There were a couple of moments when I wished you were dead. But Colter—when I saw the plane catch fire and imagined you could be killed, I realized I didn't want to live without you. Suddenly I didn't care why you had married me or why you took me to your bed."

A convulsive shudder rocked his body.

"I never thought I was capable of feeling much. The sight of Cord trapped in that wreckage shattered that once and for all." Colter sighed, lifting his head to gaze into her face. "And when you walked into the hospital and sat down beside me, not saying a word, just touching me to let me know you were there if I needed you, I felt like the lowest critter that ever walked the earth. I understood why Cord cried his wife's name when I pulled him from the wreck. I had this terrible need to have you with me. And there you were."

"Deirdre?" she asked softly.

He looked deep into her glowing topaz eyes. "I never saw her except when she was at the ranch the times you knew about and at the hospital. She's nothing but trouble and she's nothing to me. The only woman I want is my reluctant wife."

Gently Natalie kissed his lips. "I love you."

There was a humble light in his eyes, the proud arrogance gone, the aloof remoteness something belonging to the past.

"There's a lot you're going to have to teach me." Colter smiled ruefully. "I don't know anything about being a husband or a father. I'd like to get to know my daughter. It's my fault she's so shy and insecure. Now I really do understand the agony of believing that the one you adore doesn't care for you."

"It's simple, honey," Natalie whispered. "All we have to do is draw Missy into the circle of our love."

"And Ricky . . . and all the other children we're going to have," Colter added with a smile. Then he kissed her again.

And again.

SWEET
PROMISE

Chapter 1

The music was a slow, sentimental ballad, spinning its love theme for the few couples on the floor. The subdued lighting added to the magic of the moment, creating another romantic spell.

A happy sigh escaped Erica's lips as she felt Forest's chin rest lightly on her head. Her fingers curled tighter around his neck while she gently rubbed the side of her face along his jaw in a feline gesture, smiling when she felt him press a kiss into her dark hair.

Tilting her head back, she gazed up at him, admiring the commanding strength conveyed by his square jaw and the cleft in his chin, the carved line of his mouth, and the velvet look in his brown eyes as they possessively examined her face.

To speak in a normal voice might break the spell, so Erica whispered softly instead. "Would it sound very corny or silly if I said that I could do this all night?"

"With me or with anyone?" Forest murmured. A thick eyebrow, the same light brown as his hair, arched to tease her.

"That's another thing I like about you. You never take me for granted." Her soft voice trembled with the depth of her emotion and Erica buried her head in his shoulder, knowing that her violet eyes were much too expressive of her thoughts.

"What else do you like about me?" His lips were moving against the silken strands of her hair, igniting warm fires elsewhere.

"Conceited?" she teased him, but there was a catch in her husky voice.

"Where you're concerned, I need all the reassurance I can get." The arm around her waist tightened, holding her closer to his muscular body as if he expected her to slip away. "Tell me." His growling order was a mock threat, but one Erica was only too happy to obey.

Hesitant to reveal how deeply she cared for this man, who was, truth be told, a little notorious for his careless and carefree association with women, she kept her tone light.

"For starters, don't make all those affirmative noises when Daddy is around. You're independent and financially secure."

He tried not to smirk. "Go on."

"Too bad you're much too handsome for any girl's peace of mind," she sighed. "Elusive, that's the word for you. Always managing to dodge getting led to the altar."

"Yeah, with a ring through my nose," he laughed. "No thanks."

"But you are good at making me believe I'm the only woman in your life." Erica raised her head from his shoulder and encountered the smoldering gleam in his eyes. With her lashes, she shielded the answering gleam in her own. "Gee whiz, a girl just forgets everything her parents taught her when she's with you," she said coquettishly.

He understood that she was teasing. "Not all girls." His hand cupped her chin, lifting it so he could gaze thoughtfully into her face. "Certainly not you. That first night I took you out, I was ready to confirm all the rumors about you being an ice maiden."

"Don't believe everything you read online," she said dryly.

"Do I look that stupid?" He laughed. "Seriously, Erica, you were a challenge in the beginning and that's no lie." White teeth flashed as he grinned. "I don't believe anyone has said no to me as many times as you have."

She forced herself to breathe evenly. "Do you mean all those times you invited me to your apartment, it wasn't to see your art collection?" Her eyes widened with fake surprise.

"Only the one in my bedroom." The laughter left his face as he studied her. "Every time I touch you or kiss you, I sense that you're holding back. Look, you are Vance Wakefield's daughter—"

"The great and powerful Vance Wakefield," she said sarcastically.

"Well, uh, yeah, he is. And a lot of guys must have taken you out just because of that. Besides the fact that you're beautiful," he added hastily.

"Thanks."

"Hey, you know me well enough by now to realize that I don't care who your father is."

"Thanks for that too," she said softly. Their steps had almost ceased as they simply swayed in tempo to the music.

"Not that I haven't taken into account that he is your father and very important in your life, of course," Forest added. "That's the way it should be, even though I know he doesn't totally approve of me."

"Your personality isn't the issue. It's your reputation," she said bluntly.

Forest groaned under his breath. "Maybe he still sees you as his little girl."

"No, not really," she said with a humorless smile. "Daddy isn't an ogre. He sees me as an adult, more or less. And he realizes that my relationships with other people are on an adult level."

There was no need to add that if Vance Wakefield felt his daughter was being used, he would go after the offender with all the weight his money and power could bring to bear. Yet that wasn't a comforting thought to Erica. Almost all her life, she'd tried very hard to become close to her father. He was a strong, indomitable, sometimes ruthless man who despised weakness of any kind. She seriously doubted if he'd mourned long for his wife, her mother, after her untimely death.

In her early years, Erica had fought for his love, always terrified that her handsome father would marry again and she would have to compete with a new wife and possibly another kid or two for the attention she wanted so desperately. No other woman had entered his household, but he became essentially married to his business, a more demanding rival than a little girl could ever compete against, let alone prevail over. Still she struggled for every ounce of attention that she could steal, using every weapon from open rebellion and stormy scenes to humiliatingly obvious neediness.

It had taken her nearly twenty years to come to terms with the fact that he loved her in his own way—and that the relationship was never going to be warm and fuzzy and safe. As strong as their bond was, she was still female. Weak, at least in his mindset. As a result, Erica got good at concealing any mistake she made for fear of seeming vulnerable. She hated to risk lowering his opinion of her when it wasn't high to begin with.

"If you're not afraid of your dad, why do you keep saying no to me?" A frown of puzzlement drew Forest's brows together. "You aren't an ice maiden—uh, I just said that. Sometimes when I get you close you're almost too hot to hold. Don't you want me as much as I want you? Or don't you trust me?"

"Oh, no, I don't trust myself," she corrected him quickly. She could feel the glowing heat of a certain memory rising in her cheeks and murmured a silent prayer of thanks for the dimness in the room that concealed it.

"And you've been afraid to do something in the heat of the moment you would regret in the cold light of day," he finished for her, a gentle and satisfied smile easing the strong line of his mouth.

"Right. Yeah. That's what I've been afraid of," Erica said jokingly. But the fear she hid was real enough.

The last note of the song was tapering into silence. For a second, Forest retained his hold, keeping her pressed against his long length, and Erica wondered if he'd caught the genuine truth in her reply. She modified it a little to herself. She *had* been afraid. But she wasn't any longer.

Two months wasn't a very long time to know a man. Still, Erica was positive that what she felt for Forest was more than friendship, more than sexual attraction, but something deeper, something like love.

A musician in the small combo announced a short break and all the couples had left the dance floor by the time Forest guided Erica back to their table. His arm kept its possessive hold on her waist and he let her go only when they were seated, their chairs pushed close together.

"I'm beginning to understand more things about you," Forest said softly, resting his arm on the back of her chair to caress her bare shoulders. "But I've been making even stranger discoveries about myself."

"Really? Like what?" Erica tucked a strand of shoulder-length dark hair behind her ear so it wouldn't interfere with her view of him.

"Like—" His gaze wandered over her face, lingering on her lips. "Like has nothing to do with it. I'll give it to you straight. I've fallen in love with you."

Her gasp was a mixture of disbelief and elation. She hadn't ever dared to hope that he might care as much as she believed she did. The wonder of it made her eyes shine with a mist of tears.

"I love you too," Erica breathed. "I never believed—I never thought it was possible that you might love me."

"Only a man in love would take no for an answer as many times as I have." He smiled and something in his smile confirmed the truth of his words.

She wanted to wind her arms around his neck and feel the warmth of his lips against hers, but just then laughter sounded from one of the tables near theirs and Erica was reminded that they were not alone.

"If you doubted my feelings," Forest murmured, his hand intimately caressing the curve of her neck, "can you imagine how I wondered about yours? I felt you were bound to distrust me because of my, uh, reputation."

"Oh, that," she said lightly.

He gave her a rather sheepish smile before he went on. "I've heard some of the rumors about me. Some were based on fact."

"I never cared what anyone said about you."

She wanted to explain that one of the things that had attracted her to him was his somewhat diehard bachelor attitude, but to do that would mean explaining her reasons and she didn't have the courage to do that yet.

"Okay. Let's drink a toast. To each other?" His fingers closed around the stem of his martini glass and Erica reached for her much smaller glass. Compared to the strong-smelling vodka of his, her sherry seemed tame.

Their eyes met over the glasses as they raised them, sending a silent message of hope and trust. The expensive crystal rang true when their glasses clinked.

"Hey, I think there's something in my martini," Forest declared after his first sip, putting the glass nearer the light to study it.

"Besides the olive?" Her tremulous smile was to cover the fluttering of her heart as she studied his thoughtful face.

"Would you look at this?" His voice was amused and vaguely triumphant as he directed his gaze to the miniature plastic spear in his hand. He'd poked it through the pimento-stuffed olive, all the way through, and picked up a ring, delicately fashioned even if it was dripping with vodka. The muted candlelight touched the stone and reflected myriad colors.

"This must be yours." At his announcement, Erica swung her stunned look to him.

"No." She had to deny it.

He wiped it dry with his handkerchief and handed the ring to her. "I hope you're going to accept it," he said. "It might be poetic justice to have the first girl I've ever proposed to turn me down. But after all this time of saying no, now that I'm asking you to marry me, please say yes, honey."

Somehow she eluded his move to slide the ring on her finger, taking it instead and clutching it between the fingers of both hands. The diamond solitaire winked back at her until her head throbbed with pain. Erica fought to stem the hysteria rising inside her.

"Don't you like it?" His voice was low and controlled, but with a definite edge to it.

The face she turned to him was unnaturally pale and strained. "Oh, Forest, I love it," she gulped, tearing her gaze from the mocking sparkle of the ring to meet his eyes, unable to stop the single tear that slipped from her lashes. Solitary as the diamond, the tear blazed a hot trail down her cheek, but she quickly wiped it away.

"Please—can we go?"

"Of course."

Erica knew Forest would misinterpret her reasons for wanting to go, figuring that she would want a less public place to cry. She told herself that they would be tears of happiness. The salty tang on her lips right now was bitter, produced by the misery of the moment.

With the ease of a man who knew his way around, Forest took care of the check, collected the light shawl that matched the layered chiffon dress she wore, and had the parking valet bring the car around to the front of the club.

Moments later he'd turned the car onto a quiet San Antonio street and was switching off the engine. Not one word had he said to her, and he didn't now as he drew her into his arms. Her lips hungrily sought his descending mouth, welcoming and returning the warmth of his touch while his hands arched her toward him. Her uninhibited response unnerved both of them and it was a little while before they managed to talk again.

Forest's mouth was moving over her eyes and cheeks. "C'mon, Erica, marry me." His breath caressed her skin as he spoke. "Or do I have to sweep you off your feet and carry you away to make you say yes?"

"I want to marry you," Erica whispered, a poignant catch in her voice. "More than anything else, I want you to believe that."

Despite her reassurance, his searching kiss stopped, halted by the unspoken qualification in her reply. His tense stiffness made her heart ache for him. The ring was still in her hand, a hard lump in her sensitive palm.

"But I can't accept your ring." She added the words Forest seemed to be bracing himself to hear.

"Why?" The demand was combined with the tightening of his grip just before she let go of the breath she'd been holding. "You do love me?" He released her.

"Yes, I love you. Honestly, I do," Erica vowed, caressing his cheek. "But I just can't accept your ring. At least not now."

There was a slightly bemused look on his face. "You know, I got that you were more old-fashioned than most, but I never guessed that you would want me to speak to your father first."

"No, that's not what I meant!" Her cry was almost panicked.

"I don't understand." Forest sighed, wearily rubbing the back of his neck. "Do you want to marry me or not?"

"Yes, I want to—oh, please, Forest, I can't take your ring. It wouldn't be fair." She silently begged for his understanding, to have the touch of his hands become loving once more.

"What gives? Are you engaged to someone else?" An incredulous anger narrowed his gaze.

"No!" She pressed her fingertips against the sudden pounding pain between her eyes. "I can't explain and I have to ask you not to back me into a corner. I swear it's true that I love you, but I—I need time."

He stared at her for a long moment, his expression unreadable before his slow smile broke the tension. "It's a big step. I've had plenty of time to think it over, but you haven't. Not one hint from me, was there? Guess I pulled off that part pretty well."

Let him think so. Time to make a decision was not what Erica meant, but she was very willing to take advantage of the suggestion. The shadowy light streaming through the car windows made the many facets of the large diamond sparkle.

"It is a big step," she agreed, taking a deep breath. "Not something that's done on the spur of the moment." The only smile she could summon was rueful. "Marry in haste, repent at leisure. Isn't that the saying? I don't want it to be that way with us, Forest."

"Neither do I. I want you to be as sure as I am," he stated.

Although she didn't look up, she could feel the warm regard of his eyes. The determination in his voice almost made her want to put the ring on her finger and damn the consequences, but she steeled herself against doing anything that dumb. Slowly she stretched out her hand, palm upward, the engagement ring in the center.

"Would you keep this for me?" she asked. As she met his controlled gaze, the pain at giving back his ring softened and she sought to reassure him. "I think I'll be wanting it soon, so don't give it to some other girl, okay?"

"There isn't one. Not even a ghost of a one. I cleared a lot of old phone numbers out of my cell phone's memory weeks ago, if you really want to know." His brown hair gleamed golden in the pale light as he reached out to retrieve his ring.

When it was safely in his pocket, his velvet brown gaze moved over her face, its oval perfection framed by the rich brown hair combed away from it. His searching glance came to a full stop on the curves of her mouth.

"Don't make me wait too long, Erica." It wasn't a request, not with that autocratic edge to his voice. It wasn't a threat, either, since undeniable passion throbbed beneath the surface.

"I won't." The starlight touched the air with a faint shimmer as she waited in anticipation of the moment when Forest would hold her close.

His hand trailed lightly over the hollow of her cheek

back to the nape of her neck, sliding under her hair as a thumb gently rubbed the pulsing vein in her neck.

"No woman has ever dangled me on a string before," he told her, his expression paradoxically tender and hard. "I don't like it." Erica started to initiate the movement that would bring her body against his muscular chest, but he checked her with a shake of his head. Then he released her and turned to the front. "I'm taking you home. Keep in mind that I'm not the world's most patient guy. The sooner you make the decision, the better."

Erica had no opportunity to argue as he started the car and drove it back onto the street. Part of her wanted the evening to last forever, not so she could keep on exasperating Forest by not answering, but to postpone what she was going to be forced to do if she wanted to marry him. And Erica was sure that she did want to.

The closer they came to her home on the outskirts of the city, the more her thoughts became preoccupied with her dilemma. When Forest walked her to the door, the kiss she gave him appeared natural enough on the surface, but underneath her nerves were becoming raw from the strain of her decision.

When she stepped inside the house, she discovered her legs were trembling. Their weakness was not caused by Forest's lusty kiss. Her widened eyes, like fully opened violets, darted to the closed door of the study, almost the only room in the large, rambling house that her father used. Erica sighed unhappily. It was all too easy to envision his freezing scorn and contempt, his inevitable response if she went to him with her problem.

It had never been his contempt that she had feared. There had been times in the past when she'd deliberately provoked his wrath to get his attention, unfortunately. Only once had her actions backfired on her, the very last time she had done it. Only afterward had she realized how foolish her childish behavior had been.

But that time, it had succeeded in forcing her to grow up. And Erica had finally realized that her father was incapable of loving her as much as she loved him. In many ways their temperaments were alike. They could be equally bullheaded and stubborn, and equally quick to anger. Yet Vance Wakefield just wasn't able to give of himself and he had never been able to understand her need as a little girl to be constantly assured of his affection.

Her coming of age had opened her eyes to this one flaw of her father's. In the past two years—almost two years—Erica had stopped demanding more than he was capable of giving, emotionally anyway. Their relationship had reached a level of casual companionship that she had never thought they could attain. To go to him now would destroy it.

Her teeth sank into her lower lip to bite back the sob of despair. Casting a last furtive glance at the study, she hurried down the hallway to her bedroom. When the oak door was closed behind her, she leaned weakly against it, then pushed herself away to cross the Persian carpet of a richly patterned blue and gold. Her fingers closed tightly around the carved oak bedpost while her darkly clouded eyes stared at the brilliant sea of blue of the bedspread.

Her first impulse was to throw herself on the bed and wallow in regret that she had ever been crazy enough to get into such a situation. Instead Erica shook her head to clear it, banishing the idea of a pity party for one as a waste of energy. She tipped her head back and breathed in deeply to ease her jumping nerves. Low laughter surged through the tight muscles of her throat, its echo taunting her as she moved through the room and sat on the edge of the bed.

You've spent nearly two years dreading this day, she chided herself. *Hiding from it. Stupidly thinking that it would all work itself out on its own.*

She buried her face in her hands, refusing to cry as she forced her mind to search for a solution—any solution that would not involve going to her father. Lifting her face, she sighed dispiritedly. If only she had someone to talk to. Someone close who would understand what had prompted her to do what she had done. It had happened long ago, but it wasn't over. She refused to take the chance of confiding in Forest and risk the loss of his love.

She had no close girlfriends, at least none she would trust with damaging information like this. When she was growing up, her father had insisted that she attend private schools, snobbishly believing they offered a better and broader education. At the time, Erica had thought that he'd sent her far from home because he didn't care about her. Only now could she see that he just hadn't known what to do with a young child under his roof after her mother's death from cancer.

She knew her only from a few photos, pre-digital era photos that were fading fast, even though they were kept tucked in albums. Her father kept talking about having them copied but he never got around to it, and Erica felt that the pretty woman in them somehow wasn't real.

As for friends, the few she'd made in her young life now lived in other parts of the country and after more than four years of separation, she'd stopped checking their Facebook pages and leaving messages. Not even on Christmas.

Lawrence Darby, her father's longtime assistant, had always been a sympathetic sounding board in the past, but Erica was totally aware that he automatically informed Vance Wakefield of problems big and small, something she wanted to avoid. Not that Lawrence would deliberately betray her. He would only be turning to the man he knew had the connections and influence to resolve just about anything.

When it came to relatives, Erica did have aunts and uncles and cousins, but none who were close or particularly concerned about her personal problems or even whether she had any. She drew in a breath when she thought of something at last.

"Uncle Jules," she muttered. Of course. He was her go-to guy for this one.

Jules Blackwell wasn't actually related to her, but he'd grown up with Vance Wakefield and was one of her father's rare friends. When Erica was born, Jules Blackwell had appointed himself as her godparent and taken an active interest in her life. She'd never doubted his affection—in fact, she sort of took it for granted.

Jules's position and profession were independent of her father's, which gave Jules a better perspective. To him, her father was a lifelong friend and not the powerful Vance Wakefield, former corporate raider and influential consultant to Fortune 500 companies.

Of course, her father was home a lot and no longer traveled much on business or kept a suite of offices. He relied on a laptop and Lawrence, and boasted that he made even more money that way. But it hadn't brought them closer.

She'd decided on her own to call Jules her uncle. And he was aware of the struggle she had made to claim a little paternal affection. He could be trusted not to share her confidences with her father.

Fortunately for her, Jules Blackwell was a well-respected attorney for a lot of good reasons. For the first time in nearly two years, the shame and guilt she'd hidden away in her heart eased a little. Erica wanted to cry with relief, but she still refused to let herself. The time for weeping was when success was in her grasp. She got up, ready to make her first move.

Going to the polished oak chest of drawers, she rummaged through the expensive lingerie until her fingers closed around a knotted handkerchief buried in one corner. Hot color flushed her face at the feel of the heavy but small metal object poking into the material. Handling it as if it were radioactive, she buried it again, this time at the bottom of her purse.

Sleep eluded her so that most of her rest came in fitful dozes. Still Erica lingered in bed as long as she could the next morning to avoid meeting her father. When she arrived in the sunny yellow breakfast room, only Lawrence was still seated.

"Sleep late?" He smiled, his eyes crinkling behind wire-rimmed glasses. He was only two years older than Forest, but his receding hairline and thinness added about ten years. "You're usually down at least an hour earlier."

"Yup," Erica fibbed, helping herself to toast and marmalade before pouring a cup of coffee to go with it.

"Vance has already eaten, obviously, but he asked me to pass a message on to you."

"What's that?" Subconsciously she was holding her breath as she took a chair opposite Lawrence.

"One, to remind you about the dinner tonight at the Mendelsens and, two, he suggested that you invite Forest Granger to bring you."

Her surprised glance took in the rather smug look on his face. Her father's suggestions were virtually royal commands, and he'd never so much as hinted that one of her dates could be included in an invitation extended to them as father and daughter.

"Did you have any part in that, Lawrence?" A knowing smile played around the corners of her mouth.

"No one makes decisions for your dad." But there was a twinkle in the pale blue eyes that indicated he had undoubtedly introduced Forest's name into the conversation. "I think Vance is beginning to get a clue that there might be something serious developing between you two."

Not very subtle. The remark was obviously meant to encourage her to fill him in. But Erica knew her reply would be passed on to her father. It was his indirect way of remaining involved in her life without taking the time to ask her anything himself.

"Well, it's kind of soon to be sure, but it could be serious." It was a lot more serious than anyone knew, for about a thousand reasons, but Erica didn't want to admit to any of it. "I'll call Forest when I get to the boutique and find out if he's free tonight."

"How is business?" Lawrence inquired.

"I believe Daddy is going to be very surprised when he receives my monthly report," she declared, concentrating next on sipping her coffee.

More than a year ago, Erica had persuaded her father that she needed an outside interest. Call it a reason for getting up in the morning. He seemed to think it was beneath the great and glorious name of Wakefield for her to be employed by someone. Erica had doubted that he actually believed in her, but to keep the peace, he'd financed a boutique for her to run. On her own, she'd done a potential profit-and-loss statement that impressed him and come up with a business plan, as well as a report on the staggering number of people who visited San Antonio's world-renowned Riverwalk each year.

Along with some of his other traits, Erica turned out to have inherited his business acumen. At the end of her first year, the exclusive dress boutique had broken even.

Now, partly due to her excellent and slightly eccentric taste in fashion and her knack for management, it was beginning to show a profit. Being responsible for its success or failure had also helped Erica really understand the demands her father's multiple interests made on him.

The instant Lawrence left the breakfast nook, all conscious thought of the boutique vanished. The haste that made Erica leave her toast and coffee half-finished was due to her desire to arrive at the shop and call Jules Blackwell in privacy, where there was absolutely no risk that her father or his assistant would overhear her.

The boutique, which she'd named after herself, would already be open when she got there. As she locked the door of her sports car before making the short walk down to the river promenade, she said a silent prayer of thanks that she had a manager as trustworthy and conscientious as Donna Kemper, a pretty blonde in her early thirties, divorced with two little girls. With Donna in charge of the rotation of part-time staff and a couple of full-time assistants, Erica had discovered that the shop could survive—and even thrive—without her constant supervision.

There was only one customer on the floor when she walked in. Smiling a hello to the woman, Erica murmured a friendly greeting to Donna.

"The shipment arrived from Logan's," Donna informed her. "Bree is unpacking it in the back and there's another girl coming in to help her with the steaming."

Wrinkles were the bane of every clothing retailer, but the staffers seemed to enjoy getting them out with the expensive machine made for the purpose.

Erica nodded in acknowledgment. "I have some calls to make, then I'll be out to help all of you with the display."

A smile of understanding spread across the woman's face. "We've waited this long to receive it. Another few hours before the goods are racked won't make much difference."

Then the customer required Donna's attention and Erica walked to the back of the store to the small alcove in the storage area. After she dialed Jules's office number, she sifted through the mail Donna had placed on the desk, trying to force her hammering heart to slow down.

It was several minutes before his secretary was able to connect her with Jules. He was plainly delighted and surprised that she had called. The easygoing fondness in his voice made her wish she'd turned to him sooner.

"I was calling to see if you'd be free around lunchtime, Uncle Jules," Erica explained in answer to his question.

"Are you taking me out to lunch, young lady?" His teasing laugh lifted her spirits. "Because if you are, I'm accepting."

"Actually, yes. This is on me." She smiled at the receiver of the old beige phone, visualizing the round, usually smiling face on the opposite end.

"Good. Where would you like me to meet you?"

Erica hesitated. "I . . . I was hoping I could see you for a few minutes at your office."

Her statement was followed by a small silence before he spoke again, the laughter giving way to a solemn tone of voice. "Are you and Vance having problems again?"

"No, not exactly," she hedged.

He must have sensed her unwillingness to discuss it over the phone. "All right. I'll expect you here at eleven-thirty. How's that?"

"Thank you," she sighed.

"Don't worry. Uncle Jules will fix it, whatever it is."

When Erica hung up, a tentative smile was gleaming in her eyes. With her burden lightened, she called Forest, who very willingly accepted the invitation her father had extended.

Chapter 2

Promptly at eleven-thirty, Erica entered the spacious reception area of the Blackwell & Todd law firm. The receptionist glanced up, taking in the details of what she was wearing, a simple white dress with vivid blue flowers against a background of white, something they were featuring at the boutique.

"Good morning, Miss Wakefield," she greeted Erica. "Mr. Blackwell said to send you right in the second you arrived."

Erica nodded her thanks, her fingers tightening nervously on the strap of her white purse. Between unpacking the shipment of new fashions that had arrived at the shop and waiting on customers, there had been little time to mentally prepare for her meeting with Jules. She would have welcomed a few minutes' delay.

The door to his office was open and a moderately heavyset man was sitting behind the desk, his dark hair liberally peppered with gray. He bent over a heap of paperwork, preoccupied. At her light rap, his head raised, the stern expression of concentration replaced by a jovial smile that seemed to better fit his overall roundness.

She smiled back. "Hello, Uncle Jules." She stepped

into the room as he pushed himself out of the large leather chair.

"Close the door." His hand wagged in the air in accompaniment of his order. By the time Erica had complied, he was standing in front of her, only an inch or two taller than she was. "I don't want the associates getting on my case because they saw me kissing a beautiful young lady," he declared with a broad wink. After he had placed an affectionate and very respectable kiss on her proffered cheek, he pulled out a chair for her near his desk. "It's been two months—no, three months—since I last saw you. That's much too long, Erica."

The mild reproof changed her smile to one of apology. "I'm sorry, Uncle Jules. It doesn't seem that long, but what with one thing and another, time slipped away."

"Oh, it's okay. From all I've heard, your dress shop is doing well," he said, scooching his chair closer to Erica's when he sat down. "I also heard you and Forest Granger are an item," he added with a twinkle. "If he's lasted this long, you must be more than just fond of him."

Erica had forgotten how easy it was to confide in Jules. "I am," she admitted, glancing down at his desk. Unlike a lawyer, she didn't have the knack of reading things upside down, so whatever secrets were there were safe. "As a matter of fact, I'm in love with him." She tossed her head back, sending her long brunette hair tumbling around her shoulders. "Last night, Forest asked me to marry him."

"Mmm." A thoughtfully serious look crept into his otherwise smiling expression. "I understand Forest is the love-em-and-leave-em type. Until now. Until you, I mean," he corrected himself.

"He swears he's deleted the numbers of every girl he used to know from his cellphone."

Jules guffawed. "In my generation, you burned the

love letters. I gotta tell you, Erica, even in my tomcat days—and I did have them, no matter what I look like now—I knew better than to put anything in writing. Not even on a candy heart. *Be Mine*—forget it, you could get sued just for two little words, never mind the three little words. I always tell my clients that but they never listen, which is how I make so much money—"

She smiled. "Jules, you were saying?"

"Oh, right. Where was I?" He snapped his fingers. "Granger. His reputation is not exactly sterling, in your father's never-humble opinion. Is that what you wanted to see me about? Do you want me to use my world-class charm to convince Vance that you found the right guy?"

"No, I—I don't think Daddy is bothered by that." Now that it was time to tell Jules why she was here, Erica found herself faltering. "Daddy isn't going to be a problem."

"But something else is," he prodded gently.

The deep breath she'd taken was exhaled slowly so that her yes came out as a sigh. "Do you remember—it was about two years ago, in January—when I insisted that Daddy go on vacation with me?"

"To Acapulco? Yes, I remember," Jules smiled. "As I recall, you came to me then to enlist me for the persuasion effort. Considering the improvement in the relationship between you two after you came back, I think spending time alone with each other was the best thing that could have happened. It's a shame you didn't vacation together before."

"The whole thing was a fiasco, a terrible disaster," Erica declared in a trembling voice.

She stared at the rows of law books behind his desk, no longer trying to stop the flow of vivid memories. Her voice was flat and unemotional as she related the events that had taken place. It was a judiciously censored version, to be sure, but she gave him the basic facts.

* * *

The idea for the vacation had developed from an obsessive need to be the sole object of her father's attention. Only by separating him from his business could she succeed. Once too often in her growing years Vance Wakefield had hired some glorified nanny from an agency and sent Erica off in her company to an exclusive resort. Never took a vacation himself, or so she remembered. He was a classic workaholic and self-made multimillionaire.

That didn't matter to her. Enlisting the aid of his inner circle, Erica had forced a reluctant agreement from her father to take a break. Her first clue that her plans were not going the way she intended was when her father made reservations for the three of them, explaining that Lawrence hadn't had any vacation in the four years he'd worked for him.

Not until they'd gotten off the jet and were registered and shown to the most expensive suite of a luxurious Acapulco hotel did Erica fully realize that, to Vance Wakefield, a vacation meant conducting business long distance and online. Her first reaction had been anger, then a complete denial that she wanted his company at all as she commandeered Lawrence with her father's permission.

Lawrence tagged faithfully after her that first afternoon when Erica fled the hotel for the sun-kissed beaches of Acapulco. Anger boosted up a notch while self-pity stayed just below the surface as she realized that Lawrence was to be her companion and bodyguard, a male babysitter not fundamentally different from the nannies her father had foisted her off on in the past. As the toes of her sandals dug into the golden beach, she knew her father was probably congratulating himself over his twofold use of Lawrence: an assistant when he needed one and a trustworthy companion who could show Erica the sights. And at the same time he was providing Lawrence with a so-called vacation in a posh place. Vance Wakefield was quite capable of thinking along exactly those lines.

"Poor Lawrence," she murmured aloud, staring at the vast expanse of blue water, broken only by curling whitecaps, the occasional boat and the heads of swimmers.

"Huh? Why poor me?" he asked quietly, stopping beside her, his jacket thrown over one shoulder with his tie sticking out of its pocket. His white shirt, open at the throat, made his pale skin seem almost ghostly.

"You've worked for Daddy for so long, Lawrence. This just isn't fair. You're constantly at his beck and call, and you have to put up with me." Erica felt almost as sorry for him as she did for herself.

Lawrence shrugged. "I don't mind." His light blue eyes gazed back at her through his wire-rimmed glasses.

"Well, you should mind!" She wanted to stamp her feet, but the childish satisfaction she would get out of doing it would be negated by the soft sand. "Why should you have to be responsible for Vance Wakefield's daughter? And I am his daughter, whether he likes it or not!" She wanted to howl at the sun as her outrage gave way to despair. "Oh, Lawrie, why can't he be like other parents? Is it so much to ask to have him spend two weeks with me? Out of twenty-one years of pretty much pretending I didn't exist?"

"Point taken. Anyway, no, he isn't like other parents, Erica, because he's Vance Wakefield," Lawrence said calmly, very accustomed to Erica's swift changes from anger to tears. "You have to see him the way he is and not the way you want him to be."

"In other words, enjoy the sun and fun of Acapulco

but don't make waves," Erica said scathingly. "Forget that I have any rights to his time."

"In his own way, he cares very much about you."

The comment sounded flat and rehearsed, and only made her madder. "I'm not giving up." Her voice was charged with determination and her chin was tilted at a defiant angle. "My dear old dad just isn't going to ignore me for two solid weeks."

"Don't do anything foolish," Lawrence cautioned.

Erica didn't answer but there was a mischievous glint in her eyes as she hooked her arm around his elbow. "Let's walk down by the water," she commanded.

"We can't go far," he said, leading her toward the gentle waves rolling onto the beach. "Your father will be expecting us back."

"So what?" Erica replied. "I've waited for him long enough. Let him wait for me for a change."

Her rebellious mood brought a worried frown to his thin face, but Erica ignored it. She focused her attention on the beach, enjoying the warmth of the sun on her shoulders, glad she'd changed out of her practical traveling clothes to a sundress with polka dots. The salty breeze from the Pacific fanned her cheeks, lifting long strands of her hair and cooling her neck.

Her gaze skipped over the scanty attire of the swimmers and sunbathers, noting instead the thatched, open shelters on the beach to provide places for shaded afternoon siestas. Behind those were gently swaying palm trees and rows of high-rise hotels that curved around the bay. Beyond them were the mountains, gray, craggy sentinels guarding the golden sand and sapphire-blue sea.

"It reminds me of Hawaii," she commented idly. She laughed a little. "Remember the person Daddy hired the last time, Lawrie?"

"Vaguely. What was her name?"

"Prudence Mulier. She used to get so outraged if anyone tried to flirt with me, but you could tell she was dying for them to look at her."

"Was that the one with the good figure and the platinum blond hair that was black at the roots?" He chuckled.

"That's Prudence!" Erica grinned as Lawrence pulled her out of reach of an adventurous wave, its foamy edge lapping at the golden sand in front of them. She turned to him eagerly. "Let's wade in."

"Not me." He shook his head. Reaching up to smooth back the hair the breeze had ruffled, revealing his receding hairline. "Go ahead if you want to."

Before the words were out of his mouth, Erica had slipped off her sandals and was walking toward the water. The smooth sand beneath her toes was deliciously warm from the sun, as were the wavelets that curled around her ankles. Wading was really fun and she pitied Lawrence who was too staid and self-conscious to give it a whirl.

Twenty feet or more in front of her, a swimmer broke the water, rising majestically to stand hip-deep before he began to wade ashore. His lean, muscular torso gleamed golden bronze in the sun and a medallion winked at Erica from the sexy sprinkling of jet black hair on his chest. Almost in spite of herself, her gaze moved up to his face. Wow. Handsome and then some. He gave the impression of darkness in the brilliant light—his hair, his eyebrows, his eyes, were all black, glistening and shining from the water, but no other shade than black.

She was struck by the masculine quality of his patrician good looks: straight nose, strong jaw and chin, high cheekbones. It was as if a natural nobility had been stamped on his features. As Erica waded closer, their paths intersecting, she was conscious of his height. She was five feet six inches, and south of the border, few men towered over her, but this one did.

His glance flicked dismissively over her as he strode by without splashing a drop on her. Erica was accustomed to being checked out by men. His lack of interest stung. She looked around for Lawrence, who was strolling out of reach of the tiniest waves, but parallel to her, carrying her sandals. Her joy in wading in the warm ocean was gone, somehow disrupted by the dark stranger. She went back to Lawrence's side, using his arm as a support while she slipped on her sandals.

Yet the pull of the bronze shoulders tapering down to a narrow waist and hips magnetically drew her gaze. There was something utterly compelling about the man. He was handsome, but not in the wholesome, boyish way of the American men Erica knew. His looks were foreign. Ultimately male. The proud way he carried himself gave the impression of underlying steel.

Erica wasn't aware that Lawrence had noticed the direction of her gaze until he spoke. "He's quite something, isn't he? Lord of all he surveys."

"Yes," she agreed absently, wondering how her father's assistant would define himself. Lawrence was . . . neuter, she decided. Which probably made him the perfect type of personality to work for someone as traditionally macho as Vance Wakefield.

Macho was a good word for the stranger too. But he was a lot younger than her father, although obviously older than her.

Just why are you so damn interested in him anyway? She ignored the little voice in her head that asked the question and went back to watching him. The stranger approached one of the thatched shelters nearest them. At the same instant a golden arm reached for a fresh, folded white towel and she saw the woman reclining there.

Even at this distance, Erica could tell that the woman was no longer youthful. Her first instinct was that the woman was his relative until she saw the blond hair beneath the sunhat. There was a flash of white as the man smiled at some comment the woman made. Erica glanced at Lawrence, curious to get his take on the pair.

"Who do you suppose she is?" she asked.

"I don't know what the current term is, but I would say he's the woman's lover—you know, for a fee," Lawrence replied.

"Are you serious?"

"C'mon, you're not that naïve. It's a fairly common occupation in resorts like this," he laughed at her open-mouthed expression. "A lot of wealthy women come here. I bet a lot of them would be happy to have an escort who looked like that."

Silently Erica agreed, knowing there were definitely some older women who'd adore that arrogant, lordly air. Kind of like the club chicks who loved any Eurotrash male, so long as they claimed to be impoverished dukes or counts.

And, of course, she'd heard of male escorts. She just had never seen one in action, that was all. But Lawrence hadn't meant to be snotty.

Her back stiffened when she remembered the dismissive look the stranger had given her. She was so anxious to be out of his sight that she raised no objections when Lawrence directed her back to their hotel.

The following morning Lawrence rented a car. The plans made the evening before were that all three of them—Lawrence, Erica, and her father—would take a trip to the colorful open-air market. At breakfast, Vance Wakefield bailed, insisting that he had to stay at the hotel to participate in an online videoconference.

"Is it that important?" she asked wistfully.

"Sure is. Business is business. You know how it is."

"I wish I didn't."

He proffered a wad of cash. "Here you go. Buy yourself something."

Her resentment smoldered, defying Lawrence's obvious attempts to lighten the mood. Erica barely glanced at the extensive display of handcrafted items, not appreciating the wonderful things created by artisans that she would have loved if she'd been in a better mood.

She bought a lot of stuff anyway, getting a certain satisfaction in spending every cent of the money her father had given her. Nearly everything she purchased was likely to annoy him. Too garish. Too noisy. Too badly made. She didn't bother to bargain.

It was nearly two o'clock in the afternoon when Lawrence drove up to the hotel entrance and patiently unloaded everything.

"Do you suppose you can get one of the bellboys to lug all this up to our rooms?" Lawrence asked with a teasing smile as he wiped the sweat from his forehead. "I'll go and park the car."

Erica nodded reluctantly, feeling suddenly hot, sticky, and irritable, and wishing she hadn't gone on a spree, with its resulting mound of shopping bags and boxes. Glancing toward the hotel entrance, she searched for the ever present uniformed bellhops, but there were none in sight. As she moved toward the car to get Lawrence and send him into the lobby, it pulled away from the curb. An exasperated sigh came from her. It would be stupid to leave all this stuff unattended while she went to look for assistance.

An impatient, what-now shake of her head brought a tall man into view, his long strides bringing him closer to Erica. She scowled as she recognized the stranger from yesterday. The white tropical-weight suit he was wearing enhanced his dark attractiveness but he still had that intriguing wild look.

Her hand raised to summon him. When her violet eyes locked with the blackness of his, it was Erica who came away with the feeling of being bruised.

"You wish something, *señorita?*" The condescension of his inquiry annoyed her, so much so that she missed the flawless English and the seductive pitch of his voice. Her chin raised a fraction of an inch higher.

"Yes. I would like you to carry these packages into the hotel for me." Her words were spoken not as a request, but as a command. Erica noticed that his expression changed radically.

"I do not work for the hotel," he informed her in an icy voice.

The rapier thrust of his gaze sent adrenalin pumping through her system, heightening her senses as she extracted some money from her purse. The Great Persuader, her father called it. She needed help, so whatever it took . . . Erica extended a handful of bills toward him. When he failed to accept it, she frowned.

He of all people ought to be accustomed to accepting money from women. Yet she didn't dare say something so obnoxious out loud.

Yet she conveyed an unmistakable certainty that he was there to wait on her. Why didn't he just take the bills, she wondered. His gaze traveled with insolent slowness over her body until it stopped once again on her face. A mirthless smile curved the hard line of his mouth at the red flags that had run up her cheeks.

Stupid, stupid, stupid. She could think of other names to call herself but stupid covered it.

Another Mexican guy, much shorter and wearing the hotel's uniform, appeared at her side. "Would you like me to take your packages, *señorita?*" he asked in heavily accented English.

Her hands still held the folded bills. Erica looked directly at the taller man. "Thanks, but no. He can do it," she said to dismiss the hotel employee, but she wasn't prepared for the torrent of protest.

"Oh no, *señorita!*" the bellhop declared in a horrified voice. A stream of rapid Spanish followed the outburst while he darted wary looks at the taller man now regarding Erica with smug amusement.

When the incomprehensible flood stopped, the stranger replied in Spanish, speaking almost as fast. Erica looked at them blankly. She had no doubt they were using a lot of local slang and she really didn't have a chance of understanding any of it at that speed. The only words she could make out were "*turista*" and "*Americana.*"

No compliments. Not in the tone of voice both men were using.

Aristocratic fingers took the money from Erica's still outstretched hand and gave it to the uniformed Mexican. Her mouth opened to protest, but the tall stranger forestalled her.

"It is his job, *señorita.*" The chiseled face inclined graciously toward her. His polite smile didn't fool her, not when his black lashes didn't hide the bold mockery in his gaze. "Or would you have me take money from the mouths of his hungry family?"

His gaze flicked distastefully over the odd assortment of purchases, silently reminding her that a lot of people couldn't remotely afford the ridiculous spree she'd been on. Erica felt ashamed.

In a sense, she had been spoiled since her father had never deprived her of anything money could buy, but she had never flaunted the family wealth. And she wasn't about to explain to this stranger, no matter how good his

English was, the reason for her meaningless extravagance this time, which she knew very well was over the top. She didn't bother to reply to his taunting question as she pivoted and marched toward the hotel doors with the laden-down bellhop following in her wake.

On the fifth day in Acapulco, Erica rose early in the morning. Restless and thwarted in her attempts to spend time with her father, she wandered onto the beach, peacefully silent and empty at that hour of the morning. The temperature was mild and warm, although the wind blowing off the ocean was unusually strong. She hoped that an early morning swim might do good things for her and put her in a better mood before she met her father and Lawrence at the breakfast table.

Slipping off the decorative lace beach jacket, she laid it beside her towel and sandals. She took her time wading into the foaming surf, watching the soaring gulls and feeling better by the minute. Not until she was almost hip-deep did she realize she'd forgotten to put on her bathing cap.

With a sigh, she turned back to the shore. Walking into the waves, she hadn't noticed their force as they broke around her. Her thoughts had been scattered, not registering the choppiness of the normally calm sea.

Her foot slipped on something slimy—for a second she hoped it wasn't a dead jellyfish—at the same time a strong wave struck the back of her knees. Already off balance, she was swept from her feet by an even stronger undertow and her cry of surprise was cut off as she was suddenly submerged in salt water. Erica struggled for the surface, trying to get her feet beneath her again. A toe touched bottom. She gulped for air and another wave covered her, its retreating flow dragging her into deeper water.

An iron grip closed over one of her arms, then another hand was taking the opposite shoulder and drawing her to the surface. Instinctively she reached out to cling to her rescuer, coughing out the water she had involuntarily swallowed. Her hands closed around the muscular bicep of his strong arm and her legs treaded water.

"There's another wave, *señorita*," he gasped, "brace yourself against me."

Obeying instantly, Erica slid her arms around his waist and pressed her head to his chest. Through the watery spikes of her lashes, she saw the gold medallion in the curling black hair on his chest.

At that moment, the wave broke around and over them. Its force pushed her hard against him, her motion stopped by the taut muscles in his thighs and legs. The severe constriction of her lungs, robbing her of breath, wasn't from being pounded with what felt like an ocean's worth of foaming surf but from being molded by it against his water-sleek body.

When the wave receded, Erica reluctantly tilted back her head to look, frightened and bewildered, into his face. He raised a hand to brush the drenched hair from her eyes.

"Th-thank you." Her sincere words were met by an impassive look.

"Come." His arm was firmly around her waist and he was half dragging, half carrying her to shore. "You can catch your breath in the shallow water."

Her mind, her senses, her body were in a chaotic state. Her mind was insisting that she reject the gratitude that surged through her for her rescuer, the stranger who'd antagonized her. All the while her senses were reacting to his male virility and her body was still tingling from the burning warmth of his.

They didn't stop in the shallows, but continued all the way to the shore. His arm was no longer supporting her as Erica walked out of the water, but his hand on her lower back guided her steps. When they reached her small pile of belongings, the pressure on her back was taken away, stealing some of the strength in her legs as it went. She sank gratefully to her knees, using the thick towel to rub her shivering skin, wondering how she could be so cold when she felt so warm inside.

"It isn't wise to swim alone, *señorita*, especially when the beach is so deserted," he said curtly.

The stern reprimand jerked her head up. He towered above her, his hands resting on the band of his black swimming trunks. Her gaze swung away from the unnerving, masterful stance and searched the empty beach.

"You were," she pointed out.

A black eyebrow flicked upward, the small movement reinforcing Erica's impression that he was not accustomed to being questioned.

"I am familiar with the beach and tides, *señorita*. You are not."

"No," Erica agreed dryly. "I am a tourist. An American tourist."

The eyebrow descended to its usual place and she sensed a softening in his attitude. "Who spends many dollars in my country." Amusement flashed in his eyes. "It is good that I saved you to spend more, no?"

"I . . ." Patches of red appeared on her face at his mention of her embarrassing spree, and Erica bent her head to let her wet hair cover the betraying flush as she reached for her lace jacket. "I'm grateful you were here." But her thanks didn't match the sincerity of her earlier words. "I honestly didn't believe anyone else was around."

"Then it is lucky I saw you as you came down to the beach and heard your cry."

Erica slipped on her jacket and scrambled to her feet, clutching her towel and sandals in front of her as if they were a shield, although her bikini was a lot more modest than some she had seen.

Again she was jolted by the sight of so much bronze skin. His. As if, she scolded herself, you never saw a bare-chested man in swim trunks before. Come on. But this man had an unmistakable, almost animal magnetism that compelled her to look at him even as she silently reminded herself that he was nothing but a gigolo, escorting wealthy older women for the monetary favors they would bestow.

"You are not going to swim more?" The lilting inflection of his low voice turned the sentence into a question.

Swallowing nervously under the intense regard of his eyes, Erica shook her head firmly. "No, I only take a short dip before breakfast." Her hand self-consciously touched her dripping hair. "My father will be expecting me."

He nodded. "Of course."

"Thank you again," she added over her shoulder as she turned to leave.

"*De nada.*" But there was a vague smile of acceptance on his lips.

Erica wondered a little breathlessly as she hurried away how devastating a genuine smile of his would be. Then she pushed the conjecture from her mind and fervently hoped she never saw him again.

But she did the following day, although she was sure he didn't see her. He'd been with that blonde from the beach. Under the stranger's spell, the older woman had seemed suddenly youthful and a lot more animated.

Erica had been disgusted.

Chapter 3

Erica hesitated on the edge of the hotel grounds. She wasn't in the mood for sunbathing or swimming, and she felt if she had to spend one more minute looking at the endless rows of bright beach umbrellas stretching to a vanishing point far away, she would scream.

She was one of ten thousand tourists in this huge hotel—okay, she was exaggerating but she probably was the only one who didn't really want to be here.

Exactly what she did want was an open question.

They had been in Acapulco a full week. Apart from the marketplace, the hotel, the cliff divers, and the beach, Erica had seen nothing. They could have easily been in Miami Beach instead of Mexico for all she had seen of the country.

Her father had even claimed Lawrence to help him crunch numbers for an upcoming presentation, telling Erica to enjoy the sunshine. She tucked her book deeper under her arm. It was a well-written, fascinating history of Mexico, crammed with odd facts. Her father had given it to her, no doubt in the interests of improving her mind. She'd entrusted her laptop to the hotel safe so as not to leave it in her suite and not asked for it back once. To hell with social networking. Her friends and friends of her friends and forty billion photos of them all partying just didn't do it for her lately.

Her brain certainly wasn't getting much of a workout otherwise. In fact, she would swear it had dissolved in the fragrant smoke of shrimp being broiled in a palm-thatched hut on the beach and served up with cold beer. She walked away from it until there was only the scent of coconut oil on the sun worshippers, but still found the beach too hot.

She intended to find a secluded nook in the hotel gardens and read. Now even that thought didn't appeal to her.

Sighing dejectedly, Erica strolled down one of the leafier walks. Her heartbeat quickened as she recognized the stranger walking toward her. As yet, Mr. Tall-Dark-And-Handsome hadn't seen her. Unsure of exactly why she wanted to avoid meeting him again, attracted and evasive at the same time, Erica tried to dodge behind a high shrub and slip through the foliage to another walk she knew was only a few feet away.

In her haste, she forgot the book tucked under her arm and it tumbled to the ground, landing with a resounding thud. For a split second, she froze behind the concealing leaves, staring at the book now lying in the center of the walk. That second's hesitation deprived her of the chance to get away unseen as the purposeful footsteps slowed as he neared the book.

Silently cursing her clumsiness, Erica stepped into the walkway as he bent over to retrieve her book. "It's mine. I dropped it," she said stiffly.

"*Señorita.*" He nodded in recognition. There was speculation in the glance that darted from her to the shrub.

"I was taking a shortcut to the other path." The defensive thrust of her chin dared him to ask why.

But the glitter of amusement in his dark eyes told her he had guessed. His gaze traveled down to the book in his hand before he held it out to her.

"It is a pity to read about Mexico when you are here and can see it firsthand," he commented.

His observation was an exact echo of her own sentiments. Her fingers tightened on the book.

"The way things are going, I'll have to be satisfied with this." Dissatisfaction and self-pity made her voice tense. "My father is much too busy for sightseeing." She darted him a sideways look that didn't quite reach his face, although she was all too aware of the muscled chest under his white polo shirt and the deep blue jeans that did nice things for his athletic thighs. "Thank you for giving me back my book, *señor*." She started to turn away.

"*Señorita.*" The authoritative ring of his voice halted her, only to become mellow when he spoke again. "I would be pleased to show you around this afternoon if you are free."

"No, thank you." Her denial was vigorous, causing her sable-brown hair to dance around her shoulders. Erica didn't care to experience the potent sexual attraction that threatened to captivate her whenever she saw him.

"Why not?" Again she got the impression of arrogance, of a man who wasn't accustomed to having his invitations refused.

Her amethyst eyes darkened a little. "I wouldn't like to make your . . . your lady friend jealous and deprive you of what must be very hard-earned money."

"My lady friend?" His lips thinned as her arrow found its target.

"Yes." Her expression was smug. "The blonde. I've seen you with her several times, on the beach and other places."

"Ah, you mean Helen." He nodded, a trace of laughter in his eyes.

"I really wouldn't know what her name is." Erica shrugged. "All I noticed is that the tan she's working to get only makes her look older."

"I would think someone as young and beautiful as you are could be sympathetic to a woman who finds her beauty fading with each rising of the sun."

The gentle, almost poetic reproof made Erica feel ashamed. She did feel sorry for the woman, and at the same time, a dash of heartless pity for someone attempting to recapture her lost youth in this man's arms.

"Maybe," was the only admission she made.

"Helen is visiting friends this afternoon, so don't think you are stealing me away from her by accepting this invitation," he mocked.

"It never occurred to me to try to steal you away." Her eyes widened with genuine innocence.

"Then if you don't mind doing a little trespassing and you truly would like to see the city, there is no reason for you to refuse my offer."

His logical statement figuratively removed the ground from beneath her feet. "I—I suppose not," she faltered.

"Then do you accept?"

"Um, I suppose so," she said uncertainly. So long as they stayed in public places with a lot of people, she would be all right. And she would choose the taxi from the stand in front of the hotel and pay for it too.

"If we are going to spend the afternoon together, I cannot keep calling you *señorita*." A smile curved his mouth. "What is your name?"

"Erica—" Then she stopped. Even in Acapulco, she had discovered that the name Wakefield was known. This man already assumed she was a rich tourist and she would rather he didn't know how rich. "My name is Erica."

"Erica." His pronunciation lightly rolled the "r," giving her name a caressing sound. "My name is Rafael."

Like Erica, he added no more than that. Unlike him, she didn't test the sound of it on her lips. The unusual name was too much like its owner, smooth and commanding, like satin covering steel.

"Do you wish to tell your father where you are going?" Rafael asked.

"As long as I'm back by five and he can reach me on my cell, he won't care where I am," Erica sighed. Then she realized that that was definitely a little too much information.

She couldn't blame her father for everything, not since she'd turned twenty-one. Put it this way: Vance Wakefield was too involved with some pending presentation to a corporate board and too confident of her ability to take care of herself. His trust was a compliment if Erica had chosen to look at it that way.

Rafael didn't seem surprised by her remark as he stepped to the side, gesturing for her to precede him in the direction from which he had just come.

"My car is parked over here," he told her.

"Oh. I thought we'd take a taxi." She wasn't about to get into a strange man's car no matter how nice it was.

And his car was gorgeous. It was a very expensive European sports car in a gleaming silver-gray, the luxurious interior upholstery a blend of black and silver.

"Is this your car or . . . Helen's?" she asked, stalling for time. She didn't want to insult him, but she didn't really know him, and she wasn't going to get in his car, be driven off and never seen alive again.

Just then a prosperous-looking man in a bespoke suit came out into the parking lot and waved to Rafael, then shouted a greeting to him—and to Erica, when he recognized her.

It was the hotel manager, who she'd been introduced to in the restaurant. Her father had known him for years. His wife bustled out next, scampering in her high heels to bestow an old-friends kiss on Rafael while her husband watched, chattering in rapid-fire Spanish.

Erica smiled and nodded to hold up her end of the conversation, picking up enough of it to understand that Rafael was not only well-known around here but highly thought of. Also that he was under strict instructions to be very, very nice to "Ehrrreeka" or he would be chopped up and fed to the nearest chihuahua. The hotel manager's wife waved her sparkly manicure at both of them, blew a final kiss, and got into her husband's car and drove off with him.

As ad hoc recommendations went, it would do. For all Erica knew, the hotel had gigolos on staff. If he was one, which she was beginning to doubt, it was probably just a job. She told herself not to be judgmental.

He opened her door for her, and she got in, enjoying the sleek elegance of the vehicle. Rafael glanced at her casually before turning the key in the ignition. The powerful motor sprang to life.

"Do you think I can afford a car like this?" he asked.

"No, I guess not," she said with a shake of her head.

The beginning of their drive took them along the familiar bay as Rafael identified the small rocky island as La Roqueta, suggesting that Erica take the glass-bottom boat to see the submerged shrine of our Lady of Guadalupe near the island. When she wondered aloud about some of the bigger yachts sailing in the harbor, he took her to the docks where many were moored.

He pointed out a mammoth vessel and said, "That is— where I am staying."

Erica glanced at him in surprise. "I thought you stayed at the hotel."

"No, it is only a popular place." Rafael shrugged.

She looked back at the yacht, its name indecipherable at this distance. "Helen must be very rich."

"I believe she is." He shifted gears and drove the car away from the water.

From the yacht club they went to the San Diego Fort overlooking the bay. Rafael took her through the museum in the reconstructed star-shaped fort, the original buildings destroyed by an earthquake. Erica was surprised to discover that Rafael knew so much about the history of the area. On her own she wouldn't have found the sights as enjoyable or as interesting.

The next stop was the Plaza de Toros; Erica needed no one to translate the sign. This was the place of the bull-fights. She glanced sharply at Rafael.

"I really don't care to go here," she said firmly.

"You don't like bullfights?" The question was asked as if he knew that her answer would be negative.

Erica didn't disappoint him. "No, I don't."

"They are only held on Sundays and holidays, and today is neither." His expression held some amusement. "I thought you might like to see the inside of a bullring, however, when it is empty. Wait here while I get permission to take you in," he instructed her.

A few minutes later he returned and guided Erica into the Plaza de Toros, admitted by an elderly Mexican who nodded deferentially to both of them. Erica listened with half an ear while Rafael explained the ritual of the blood sport, the parts played by the mounted picadors, the banderillos who enabled the matador to observe the fighting characteristics of the bull, and the matador himself, bound by custom to execute difficult passes to prove his skill to the crowd.

Mostly Erica was caught up in the eerie atmosphere of the empty stadium, the blood-red color of the wooden barrier that separated the crowd from the ring, the sawdust-and-sand area. She had only to close her eyes to hear the cries of the crowd and visualize the black bull charging the magenta cape of a gold-bedecked matador in the traditional suit of lights.

"You find the thought of the contest revolting?" Rafael's quiet voice asked.

"I'm afraid I would be rooting for the bull," Erica said. He was standing beside her, a faint smile on his face. "Have you ever fought one?"

"I would guess that all Mexicans have, if not in reality, then in their minds." He turned his dark gaze on her.

"But you actually did, didn't you?" Instinct told her that she'd guessed correctly. "Why? To prove that man is superior to beast? Or did you want to find out how you would react at—what do they call that—the moment of truth?"

"Some consider it a test of manhood," Rafael said sardonically. An enigmatic light in his eyes held her captive. "But I have found there are much more difficult moments of truth to be faced in a man's life than the one that offers a fighting bull. Moments in which a man's future and his happiness hang in the balance."

A spell had been cast upon her. Rafael's words seemed to hold a portent that Erica couldn't understand. Lost in thought, she noticed a glimmer of white when he smiled and took her arm.

"Have you seen enough? Should we go back to the car and continue your guided tour?"

"Yes, yes, of course," Erica replied, trying to snap out of her odd mood.

The silver car drove up the road into the mountains guarding the city, hugging the switchback curves as it climbed higher and higher. Erica was inwardly analyzing that moment in the Plaza de Toros while absently responding to Rafael's questions. Not until they were nearly at the top did she realize that her answers had dealt mainly with her childhood and her relationship with her father. Some defense mechanism in her mind had prevented her from giving specifics, but thinking back she was aware that her replies had given him a very accurate picture of her life. She was not usually so open with strangers and she resented his ability to get through the gates.

"And you are twenty-one years old, you said." His gaze left the road long enough to see her affirmative nod.

"How old are you?" Erica asked quickly.

"Almost twelve years older than you are." Rafael switched down to a lower gear as he braked and eased the car into a wide turnout. "This is what I wanted to show you."

As the car rolled slowly to a stop, Erica stared at the panoramic view before her, barely conscious of the brakes being set and the engine switched off. When Rafael opened her car door, she stepped eagerly onto the gravel.

The vividly blue water of the bay below them was ringed by the golden beach. The multistory hotels looked more like miniature blocks while the boats on the water were no more than white dots. West of the city were the mountains they'd driven through, and beyond the mountains was another range of mountains. The sky was as blue as the sea, its brilliant color only disrupted by thin tails of high, filmy clouds.

"At night the view is just as beautiful," he told her.

"I can believe it," Erica breathed, walking forward to expand her nearly limitless view.

"Careful!" His voice rang out at the same instant his fingers closed over her arm, drawing her away from the edge.

The suddenness with which he drew her back made her lose her balance so that she fell heavily against him and his other hand gripped her waist to steady her. Her palms felt the burning warmth of the hard chest beneath his shirt.

"The edge is sometimes unstable," he explained.

Erica's heart was racing, the closeness of his muscular body erasing all other thought. She tilted her head back to gaze into the face so tantalizingly near her own. His dark eyes were focused on her parted lips, the sensual line of his mouth only inches away.

Erica was consumed by an overwhelming desire for Rafael to kiss her and for a split second she was sure he would. Then his gaze flicked to the ardent glow in her eyes and he . . . set her away from him.

She stared at him for a long moment. "Why didn't you kiss me?" she asked, fighting the pangs of rejection.

An expression of amazed amusement lifted one corner of his mouth. "Women from the US are always this forthright, are they?"

"I wouldn't know," she said, "there's only one me. I can't speak for all of them."

"Boldly seeking answers."

The hint of criticism brought a faint tinge of pink to her cheeks, but Erica wasn't deterred. "If you don't ask, you don't learn," she answered calmly.

"Since you wish me to be honest, Erica, why did you want to kiss me?" Aloof, he nonetheless studied her heightened color. "Did you want to find out if all the stories about Latin lovers were true? A little experimenting for a hot holiday, perhaps?"

Erica averted her head, nervously brushing her hair away from her face. "If you really want to know, I wasn't thinking about your nationality at the time."

It was his overpowering maleness that seemed to make her gravitate toward him. She glanced at him from beneath her lashes and saw the doubt on his face.

"It's the truth," she asserted, "although I wouldn't be surprised if you were a professional. Your experience puts you in the class of a Don Juan."

"Do you believe the mark of a great lover is the number of women he possesses?" he asked, watching her reaction intently.

"Don't you?" Erica snapped.

"I think the test of a lover is keeping one woman happy for her entire life." Rafael's seductively quiet voice vibrated with firm conviction.

"That—" Shivers raced down her spine at his words. She paused to subdue the sudden catch in her voice before answering boldly. "That still doesn't answer why you didn't kiss me. You said before that I was beautiful."

He was silent for a little while, thinking over what he would say, was her guess. At last he spoke. "A real man does not seek only outer beauty. That can be found easily enough. It is inner beauty that is rare."

"What about me?" The question was reluctantly asked as she proudly lifted her chin.

"I think," answered Rafael slowly, "that inside you are a bit selfish." He ignored her gasp of anger. "You claim to have deep affection for your father, but you try to separate him from his work, which gives him great pride and pleasure. If you truly love someone, you want their happiness above yours."

"That's a terrible thing to say!" There was a betraying quiver of her chin. Her hand raised to slap away the superior expression from his face, but his own lightning quick movement stopped her, her wrist held in a tight grip.

She fumed.

"I was about to add," Rafael continued calmly, a wicked look of laughter in his eyes, "that you are very sensitive and would not knowingly hurt anyone."

"Oh yeah? Let me go and I will!" Erica tried to twist her wrist free without success. "I don't want you to touch me!"

"A moment ago you wanted me to kiss you." His other hand slipped beneath her hair to cup the back of her head. "Or are you trying to prove that you aren't hurt by pretending that you don't care?"

"It's called pride," she said, breathing heavily with anger and frustration. "You should know all about that. You seem to have way too much of it."

"I did not kiss you because I don't like being used. And I could not be certain whether you regarded me as a man or as a Mexican," he stated.

Erica blinked in disbelief. "How could any woman *not* be aware of you as a man?" It was a thought she hadn't realized she had spoken until she saw the satisfaction in his eyes.

Oh my.

The sensual expertise of the mouth that covered hers banished her hold on reality. She should protest, struggle free, her mind told her, but with a shuddering sigh she clung to him, letting herself be kissed as she had never been kissed before. Some latent instinct arched her body closer to his, a gesture of surrender.

Immediately his hold on her tightened, giving her more pleasure as his kiss became urgent and possessive, as if he was staking an ownership that Erica couldn't deny and didn't want to deny.

Then Rafael was untangling the hands she'd wound around his neck and placing them in her lap. Erica still trembled from her total, elemental awareness of him. Her round eyes gazed at him, her skin still tingling with the electric shock of the best kiss, bar none, of her life.

"It is late," he said firmly, a strong hand on her shoulder to guide her to the car. "I will take you back to your hotel."

At that moment his hold over her was so complete that Erica would have done anything he asked. Too aware of the dizzying heights his kiss had taken her to, she found it temporarily impossible to regard him as a paid escort or a fortune hunter, but his distant air when he helped her into the car forced her to do so.

The pangs of humiliation set in as Erica realized the embarrassing situation she'd gotten herself into. She turned her head to the car window to hide the burning surge of heat in her face.

They were halfway down the mountain before Rafael broke the silence. "You should not kiss a man in that way, Erica."

Pride surfaced with a rush of spirit. "Isn't that the way your women usually kiss you?" Keeping her head turned, she made sure she didn't flinch under the obsidian glitter of his swift and thoughtful regard.

"You are new to fiery passion, I see." His tone was ironic.

"I am not."

He shook his head. "Men and women can be consumed by the flames. You should not flirt so dangerously."

"Kissing you doesn't mean I want to go to bed with you," Erica retorted.

"Ah, but when you kiss a man that way, it is he who wants his possession to be complete."

An awkward silence hung in the air between them as his low-voiced statement robbed Erica of any halfway clever reply. Her own response to him was much too vivid in her mind, and Rafael was not a man to be challenged or bluffed by girlish lies to the contrary.

When he stopped the car in front of the hotel entrance, Erica wanted to dash through the grand double doors, but she told herself to remain in the passenger seat as he walked around the car to open her door. The sun was warm, yet Erica shivered when he politely took her arm and guided her to the doors. His dark vitality was much too overpowering and his sensual virility made her feel vulnerable and young.

Rafael inclined his head toward the doorman who

held the gold-enscrolled doors. The naturalness of the inherently superior movement put her off and she stopped a few yards inside the entrance.

"There's no need for you to accompany me any further," she said.

His arrogant demeanor didn't change as he turned to her, his head back, his eyes narrowing into black diamond chips. "I hope you found most of the afternoon enjoyable, *señorita*."

She felt a flash of pique at his reversion to the impersonal term of address. Out of the corner of her eye, Erica saw her father and Lawrence entering the lobby, and really felt the sharp, questioning look she received when Vance Wakefield saw her with Rafael.

"It was very informative. Thank you." Her nod was dismissive.

His gaze centered for a brief moment on her mouth, mocking the coldness that came from the lips that had trembled beneath his.

"*Adiós*." Then Rafael was striding away from her. Erica hesitated for a second, drawing an audible breath to calm the wild beating of her heart. With a determinedly bright smile, she turned toward her father and Lawrence.

It was unlikely that Lawrence had forgotten that first afternoon when they had seen Rafael with the aging blonde. The polar-blue color of her father's eyes as they met hers told Erica that Lawrence had passed on the information. Refusing to be daunted by his displeasure, she lightly brushed a kiss across her father's cheek.

"If you two will give me a few minutes to change, I'll join you downstairs for drinks before dinner," she said, keeping her tone airy so they wouldn't guess anything was wrong.

"What were you doing with that man?" her father

demanded, with his usual knack for getting straight to the point.

"Who? Rafael? Oh, he took me on a tour of the city this afternoon."

"Do you mean you hired him?"

"Yes," she fibbed, adding a shrug to make it sound more plausible. "You and Lawrence were busy this afternoon and I didn't feel like sitting around the hotel."

Vance Wakefield wasn't an easy man to fool. As he inclined his leonine head toward her, his expression was doubting and laced with parental concern.

"You do know what kind of man he is. He's an adventurer, a fortune hunter, living like a parasite off rich women." The undertone of his low voice was warning her in no uncertain terms.

"How thrilling." She couldn't resist teasing him.

"Erica—"

"I know what he is, Daddy," she said calmly.

Lawrence glanced at her apologetically and she smiled in return. To his way of thinking he had only been doing what he thought was best. It would never have occurred to Lawrence to say nothing of their having seen Rafael on the beach.

"That type of man is completely mercenary and without morals," her father continued. "I will not have my daughter getting mixed up with the likes of him. Do you hear me, Erica?"

"Yes, Daddy."

"I've put up with a lot of your shenanigans in the past but this is one thing I won't tolerate. Now go and change and we'll meet you in the lounge."

Chapter 4

Vance Wakefield never gave warnings lightly and he never saw the need to repeat them. If he ever found out that Erica was attracted to Rafael, however much she fought against said attraction, she would have to suffer the consequences.

When she had rejoined her father and Lawrence for cocktails, his earlier disapproval must have been assuaged by her explanation. As if to reward her supposed good sense, he agreed to attend the performance of a locally renowned singer appearing in a very upscale club the following evening—a concession that surprised Erica, since she'd tried many times to persuade him to go with zero success.

The next day, Erica credited her new, improved attitude to her father's business to his giving in. She hadn't been swayed in the least by Rafael pointing out that she was a little selfish—anyway, who wasn't a little selfish? That wasn't necessarily all that bad.

The evening of the performance, Erica took her time about choosing what she would wear. Her father had capitulated; she owed it to him to make the evening special. She fingered the cream silk of her long gown and smiled. The material molded her curves and the color highlighted the rich darkness of her hair and her violet eyes.

Picking up a matching evening bag studded with cultured pearls, Erica moved softly toward the connecting door of the suite, rapped once and walked in. Her father was restlessly pacing the room and Lawrence was at the round table, surrounded by papers, a laptop open in front of him. He was running numbers.

"Aren't you even dressed yet, Daddy?" she scolded him lightly.

He stopped pacing, pushed back the cuff of his long-sleeved shirt and looked at his gold watch. "Shoot. I didn't realize it was that late." He shook his head ruefully.

"Well, it is," Erica said good-naturedly. "Do you want me to lay out your black tie stuff while you shower?"

"I'm afraid I'm not going to be able to make it tonight, honey," he said as he walked over to take her hands in his.

The obvious insincerity of the gesture hit her hard. For a moment Erica could only stare at him in frozen silence.

"What do you mean?" she demanded hoarsely.

"That Houston deal looks like it's going to blow up in my face. We're going into midnight negotiations to salvage it." His sigh accented the lines of strain around his mouth, but his explanation evoked no sympathy from Erica. "I hope we can anyway."

"What does that have to do with tonight?" She jerked her hands free. "Houston is more than a thousand miles away."

"Didn't you get an A-plus in geography once?" He chucked her under the chin. "Guess those fancy-pants schools were worth it."

"What do you mean?"

He harrumphed. "We're going to start the negotiations by phone. Lawrence can't get much of a wireless signal, so teleconferencing, which would be quickest, isn't going to happen. For security reasons, we don't want to use the hotel's Internet service."

"Woo hoo," she said sarcastically. "How James Bond. What's at stake? The future of the free world?"

He looked at her levelly. "Several hundred million dollars. So we—I—have to beg off the concert tonight. You can still go, of course."

"Thank you very much." She practically spat the words out.

"Sorry," he said briskly. Then, as if she wasn't even there, he looked over Lawrence's shoulder to see what he was doing.

She could practically feel steam coming out of her ears. "I don't know why you bothered to come to Acapulco at all! You haven't even been outside the hotel since we came. All you think about is business, business, business. What about me? I'm your daughter! Don't I deserve some of your time?"

He straightened. "For God's sake, will you listen to reason? I didn't just dream up this crisis to avoid taking you somewhere." His own quick temper was beginning to show.

"Didn't you?" Erica jeered.

"If this damn singer is so important to you," he growled, "I guess I can spare Lawrence again."

His assistant sat there, mutely fiddling with a pencil.

"Oh no." She backed away, her hand raising rigidly in protest. "You don't have to provide me with an escort. Not this time. That's always been your solution but it won't work anymore. I'm quite capable of entertaining myself. There isn't any need for you to pay someone to do that. From now on that's going to be my choice!"

"Damn it, Erica! You'll be sorry for this," her father declared, his body tense with anger.

"I'm not the one who'll be sorry, Daddy. You'll be," she hissed.

Erica stormed out of the room, hearing the phone ring just as she slammed the door. Her steps didn't slow up until they had carried her to the garden area and through it to the beach. She paused briefly on the edge of the sand and kicked off her heels so she wouldn't sink in, swinging them from one hand.

She walked aimlessly up the beach. A copper moon floated in the heavens like a giant metallic balloon for some party she wasn't invited to. Its light tinted the whispering ocean waves, their iridescent sheen adding to the magic of the warm night. Now and then the night breeze rattled the spiky fronds of the palm trees.

She felt as unsteady as if she were drunk but she was stone cold sober. It was her imagination that seemed to be spinning. Gradually her steps slowed even more to a meandering pace. But frustration and loneliness still burned inside with vengeful fire. Her heart cried bitterly for what she had never had and never would have: unconditional love. Erica stared at the gentle waves rolling onto shore, bringing little shells and tiny treasures for anyone to find the next morning until the tide took it all away again.

A long shadow fell on the sand beside her.

"I hope you aren't thinking of taking a swim at this hour of the night."

Her pulse raced as Erica slowly turned to face Rafael, bracing herself against the force of his compelling attraction. The tip of her tongue moistened her lips as a fantastic thought entered her mind. She shook the dark mane of her hair and willed her body to relax.

"Actually, I was only admiring the beauty of the evening," she lied, giving him her most alluring smile.

"Tropical nights are indeed beautiful," Rafael observed,

not taking his gaze from her moonlit face. "Warm and languid and tantalizing."

Her heart thumped violently against her ribs. She was just about sure that the wild thoughts running through her mind were visible on her face. What she was contemplating was risky, even if she succeeded. She turned away from him, momentarily frightened by what she was going to do.

"Is something wrong?" Rafael moved nearer as she perhaps subconsciously guessed he would.

A strange excitement consumed her as her senses reacted to his vital maleness and her mind whirled with thoughts of revenge. His hand lightly touched her shoulder and she leaned against it a little. The warmth of his skin burned away the last chill of apprehension. She gazed into his eyes as if she was trying to hypnotize him.

"What is it?" he asked.

"Rafael . . ." She breathed his name as if they were lying naked in bed together, their bodies touching, her voice vibrating huskily. "Will you marry me?"

"What?" His dark, intense gaze seemed to withdraw, although he was still looking directly at her.

"Have I shocked you?" she whispered.

"No. But your question is surprising. I feel as if you have welcomed me into a hidden fantasy."

Not quite. But she was charmed by his thoughtful response. And giddy at being looked at the way he was looking at her right now.

"Have you had too much champagne, Erica?" he asked lightly.

"No. Not one drop. I'm not drunk."

"But you are giddy. Are you feverish?"

She moved her head to avoid his hand. "No."

His searching gaze was infinitely tender. "I shouldn't have said what I did. Forgive me."

"But you did." His finger touched her chin to raise it.

"Do you truly wish to marry me even though you know—what type of man I am?" Rafael demanded, his thick dark lashes further veiling the unreadable expression in his eyes.

She nodded, not trusting herself to speak.

"Perhaps it is destiny," he mused. "It is said that the ones we are meant to truly love are foreordained. Whether that is true or not, I could not say."

Erica was not sure what he meant—that he thought they were meant to be together, she supposed. Well and good.

"That doesn't matter to me, not at all," she assured him fervently. Her hand raised in a natural movement to let her fingertips caress his lean cheek. "I only want to marry you, now, tonight."

A muscle in his jaw tightened beneath her intimate touch. "What about your family . . . and mine? Didn't you think I had a family?"

"Oh—oh, of course." Her breathing was becoming uneven under his shadowed but intense regard. Erica searched his face in desperation, trying to discern the reason for his question. A frightening thought struck her. "Rafael, you aren't planning to marry Helen, are you?"

"Since she is already married, it is unlikely," he answered smoothly. A dark brow arched at her stunned look. "Does knowing that upset you? Have you had a change of heart?"

"No. I mean—no, it doesn't matter," she added hastily, her cheeks taking on a rosy hue. "I just want to marry you."

"Tonight? With no one from our families present? That is a very selfish request."

"Is it so wrong to be selfish? I could make you happy if you let me."

There. She had come as close as she dared to suggesting a—a fling. Disguised as a marriage, of course. Would he take the bait?

He hesitated.

"Is it so wrong to want this night for ourselves alone? To not want to share this moment with anyone?"

There was a peculiar ring of truth in her voice that even Erica didn't understand. Yet it existed. A marveling light sparkled in her eyes when Rafael's hands tightened around her waist.

Willingly, eagerly, she slid into the hard circle of his arms, burying her head in the hollow of his throat and inhaling the intoxicating scent of his maleness. The firm pressure of his thighs sent scorching fires racing through her blood, leaving her body weak and yielding. His low, seductive voice spoke almost inaudibly in Spanish, his warm breath stirring her hair.

"Oh, Rafael," she moaned. "Please, I don't want to be alone any more."

Again his hand captured her chin, forcing her to look into the unfathomable blackness of his gaze. "Then you must marry me, Erica." Her name rolled caressingly from his mouth. "It is I who ask you."

"Yes," she whispered, wondering at the strange catch in her voice.

She ignored a premonition that the game she was playing could not be won. She was blindsided by his dark virility, swept along by forces she couldn't control. But this was what she'd wanted, what she'd planned. The risks had been swiftly calculated as soon as the idea had come to her. The first obstacle, getting Rafael to agree, was passed. Everything else would follow that somehow. Or so she hoped.

With a heart that was light and untroubled, she waited in the foyer of an old but handsomely furnished building that Rafael had brought her to while he saw to the details of their hurry-up wedding. Her blithe unconcern lasted through much of the ceremony, which was conducted entirely in Spanish, another reason she felt so detached from the proceedings. Rafael's gentle promptings ensured that she made the proper responses to the solemn-faced official.

Then he removed the gold ring from his little finger and slipped it onto her ring finger. Its heaviness, still retaining the warmth of his hand, reminded her of the seriousness of the vows she hadn't even understood. She tore her gaze away from the silver, double-headed eagle engraved on it to look helplessly into his dark eyes. She moistened her dry lips and swallowed the lump of fear in her throat.

The official's voice had stopped its flow of rhythmic Spanish. Feeling paralyzed, Erica could only watch as Rafael bent toward her. Her heartbeat fluctuated wildly when his mouth touched hers, breathing warm life into the icy places in her heart. As he drew away, she clung to his arm, nodding in numbed shock at the smiling official and the woman witness at his side.

Distantly she heard Rafael accepting their congratulations while the realization set in that she was married to him. For a moment she was terrified by the swiftness with which it had happened, before she consoled herself with the thought that a quickie divorce was no big deal, and, failing that, annulments were arranged all the time.

But her legs were wobbly when Rafael led her to the car and she knew her face was pale. The interior light went on automatically when he opened the door, and his observant gaze immediately noticed her pallor. He looked at her again when he slid behind the wheel.

"Are you not well?" His eyes lingered on her trembling lips. She pressed them together. They still held a trace of the sweet taste of his.

Erica ran a hand over her cheek to her hair to distract him. "I feel a little dizzy," she admitted, cutting off the hysterical laugh that accompanied her words. "I just realized I haven't eaten since breakfast."

"Then we must remedy that with a wedding dinner, no?" The devastating effect of his smile made her empty stomach tighten violently.

"Yes," Erica said. Having something to eat—a little something, she could just nibble on a roll—would combat the weakness flowing through her body.

Evidently eating only a "little something" wasn't allowed in a fine Mexican restaurant. She watched as a waiter prepared their steaks on a cooking trolley beside their table. The restaurant served authentic cuisine and most of the well-dressed customers were nationals instead of the usual tourists from the hotels. Beautifully scrolled wrought iron separated the dining area from the lounge, allowing a strolling guitarist playing quiet folksongs to serenade both sections.

The soothing, intimate mood of the place allowed Erica to relax and enjoy her meal without any twinge of anxiety. When the dishes were cleared, she picked up her wineglass to finish the last of the sangria.

The signet ring on her finger clinked against the crystal, reminding her sharply of her new status. Over the rim of her glass, she looked at Rafael leaning back against his chair, a thin cheroot between his fingers, calm and composed. Nonetheless, there was something very watchful about him. Erica replaced her glass and smiled as naturally as she could.

"Would you excuse me?" she asked lightly as she reached for her evening bag. "This blushing bride needs to fix her makeup."

As she rose to her feet, Rafael was there holding her chair, his gaze moving over her face as if he saw only perfection in it, but he didn't object. Her pulse beat rapidly in her throat. Erica had to force herself to walk slowly in the direction of the powder room.

By a stroke of luck, there was a pay phone by it. Using her extremely limited, phrasebook Spanish, she succeeded in having a local operator connect her with the hotel. In a nervous, breathless voice, she asked for Vance Wakefield's room.

A feeling of triumph that was utterly irrational filled her when she imagined her father's reaction to hearing that she'd married his worst nightmare, a fortune hunter. His multimillion-dollar business deal would suddenly seem a whole hell of a lot less important. In the blink of an eye, he would see to it that the marriage was annulled. But first, there would be a gigantic, angry scene. He was sure to roar at her for doing such a stupid thing, but her father wouldn't be able to ignore her.

"*Señor* Wakefield is not here," the operator's voice informed her.

Icy panic gripped her throat. "What do you mean, he isn't there? Please have him paged," she asked. "This is his daughter and it's imperative that I reach him."

"One moment, *por favor.*"

On hold. Her fingers curled over the black receiver as the seconds dragged by. He had to be in the hotel, she told herself.

Another voice came on, a man's. "*Señorita* Wakefield?"

"Yes. Where is my father?" she demanded, hysteria edging her voice.

"*Señor* Wakefield has returned to the US—"

"That's impossible!" Erica broke in. "There's no flight at this hour!"

"I believe he has chartered a jet, *señorita,*" the man replied patiently. "He has made reservations for you to return tomorrow and he left a message at the desk for you. Would you like me to read it?"

"No," she answered numbly, as if to protest what she was hearing. "No, that won't be necessary."

"I believe it was an emergency, *señorita*."

"Yes." A bitter laugh stopped in her throat. "A business deal. Thank you. Thank you very much."

Her mouth twisted with the irony of it as she hung up. His business had won and she had lost. Erica stared at the ring on her finger. She was married and her father wasn't around to rescue her. What was she going to do? What could she do?

Her first instinct was to flee. To get as far away from Rafael as she could, as soon as she could. She would send him a message explaining that it was all a mistake—hers. She didn't have much money in her personal account, but to a man like him, it would be a small fortune. But how would she go about getting a divorce? She pressed her fingertips to her temples, fighting the panic that threatened to surface. She desperately needed time to think. But Rafael was waiting in the dining room for her to rejoin him.

With the same impulsiveness that had gotten her into this situation, Erica decided to leave a message for Rafael that she was returning to her hotel. The manager could summon a cab for her. In the sanctity of her room, she would come up with a solution. As she turned to carry out her decision, Rafael appeared before her.

She couldn't help noticing the hard line of his mouth, momentarily softened by a smile of concern. Cowardice reigned supreme inside her. There was something indomitable about his personality. Her father might be a match for Rafael but she wasn't.

"Did you think I wasn't coming back?" she asked with forced friendliness as she glided toward him.

"Should I have thought that?" He studied her intently.

"Well—" Erica's smile was hard to maintain when she

answered as truthfully as she dared, "I admit to bride's nerves. That's all."

His regard of her eased, and she saw a wicked glimmer of arrogant amusement in his dark eyes. The firm touch of his fingers on her elbow seemed to reinforce his right of possession, if that was the phrase, as he led her into the restaurant.

"That is understandable," he said. "Do you wish to leave or would you like a drink in the lounge?"

"Oh, um, the lounge," Erica said, stalling for time to cope with this new complication.

The guitarist was still performing, his nimble fingers caressing the neck of the instrument. The throbbing notes matched the wild song in her heart. Erica clutched the margarita that Rafael had ordered for her, taking quick sips of the tart drink and hoping the tequila in it would have a calming effect. Her attention was centered on the guitarist to avoid looking at the wide shoulders of the man she'd just married.

"Do you enjoy the music?" Rafael asked.

"Yes, he's very good." Her gaze skittered away from her husband—*that is the right word, Erica,* she told herself. *Husband.*

"Would you like another drink?"

Erica glanced in surprise at her empty glass and quickly agreed. Time elapsed with unnerving slowness. She slurped a second margarita and a third, which didn't get her any closer to a solution. She didn't dare have another drink because her head was swimming. There was no alternative except to agree when Rafael suggested they leave.

The freshness of the night air seemed to heighten the potency of the tequila. She was now a little *too* relaxed and her mind refused to function properly. She sat silently as Rafael started the car and drove away from the restaurant. The bright lights of the hotel row beckoned, but he wasn't heading that way.

"Aren't we going to the hotel?" Erica asked. A lightning thought occurred to her and she seized upon it immediately. "My things are there. I'll need them."

Once at the hotel she would be safe. It was suddenly essential that Rafael take her there. In her room she would be able to assert her father's authority. Rafael wouldn't be able to argue with that.

"Not yet," Rafael replied, glancing swiftly at the oncoming traffic as he turned down a street. "I thought I would take you to the yacht. Have you ever been aboard one?"

"Not one that size," she admitted, her heart sinking as she realized that, short of ordering him to take her to the hotel, she had no alternative but to agree. "Isn't Helen there?" she asked hopefully.

"One of the engines is being overhauled, so she is staying with friends," he explained, looking amused at her hesitant question.

"I see," Erica murmured. If Helen had been there, she would have had an excellent reason to beg off. As it was, she had to resign herself to going there.

Minutes later they were at the yacht basin and Rafael was switching off the ignition. Erica waited nervously as he walked around the silver car to open her door. Again his hand was firmly holding her arm, guiding her along the dock past the silent boats toward the majestic monolith at the far end.

The heel of her satin shoe caught on the ridge of the yacht's gangplank and she stumbled. Instantly Rafael's arm was around her as he swung her off her feet and carried her the few remaining steps to the polished deck. It happened so swiftly that Erica didn't have time to protest, the unexpected contact with his steel-strong frame depriving her of speech. The power of his attrac-

tion was never more formidable than at that moment.
When he set her on her feet, she leaned weakly against
him, her head against his arm.

"Welcome aboard, *Señora*—" Rafael said caressingly,
his dark head inclining toward her, but his sentence
went unfinished as brisk footsteps approached them and
he straightened.

"Buenas noches, señor."

Erica blinked rather bewilderedly in the direction of
the voice that had granted her a reprieve. A man in a
gleaming white uniform stood in front of them, obviously one of the yacht's crew. In spite of his deferential
attitude, Erica sensed curiosity when the man's gaze
shifted from Rafael to her.

"Buenos noches, Pedro," Rafael replied. The rest of his
swift Spanish Erica couldn't follow, but she thought she
guessed accurately that he was explaining who she was
and his purpose in bringing her aboard.

Rafael introduced the man as a crew member, Pedro—
and the rest of the name escaped Erica in the fluent roll
of his Spanish. Unbidden, the thought came to her that
she was going to have to learn Spanish since she was married to a Mexican. There was a moment of horror as she
realized how permanent she was making the marriage
sound. When the man nodded respectfully toward her,
she was incapable of speech and her head inclined stiffly
in answer.

Sobering instantly, Erica succumbed readily to the
pressure of Rafael's hand at her back, eager to complete
the tour of the yacht and be taken ashore to her hotel.
The change in her manner brought his quizzically
watchful gaze to bear on her. She attempted to conceal
her haste as he led her into the main salon.

"What is the name of the ship?" she asked, the barest
tremor of nerves in her voice.

"She is called *Mañana*—tomorrow." His enigmatic dark gaze held hers. "A suggestion of sweet promise, no?"

There was something suggestive in his statement. Her skin stretched with white tautness over her knuckles as her viselike grip on the pearl evening bag increased. It seemed to her that tomorrow would never come and not with any promise of sweetness.

Turning away from him, she made a show of studying the salon, admiring it, in spite of her emotional state, the bold, clean lines and the elegant Spanish décor. She would never have associated the vivid colors with Rafael's blond mistress. They just didn't go together at all.

She felt like lingering in the tastefully appointed room, but Erica denied herself that pleasure. She wandered into the dining room, keeping her comments to a minimum as Rafael showed her the lounge, the well-equipped galley, and pointed out the direction of the crew's quarters. Her interest was aroused by the book-lined study, but she forced herself to glance around with polite indifference.

"Last of all, the staterooms," Rafael announced.

Erica paused in the carpeted passageway, her gaze sliding away from his aristocratic features. He certainly *looked* like he belonged on a yacht, even if he didn't own this one. Or any one.

"I don't want to see . . . hers." The admission came out tautly, a strange feeling burning in her chest.

"As you wish." There was a trace of humor in his voice.

Rafael opened the doors of two guestrooms for her to see, pointedly ignored a third and fourth door and led her to the last one in the passageway.

"These are my quarters," he told her as he opened the door.

Female curiosity got her inside, but the startling décor invited her to step farther into the spacious room. The sophisticated use of rich browns and blacks was arrest-

ing, their darkness relieved by a shade of muted gold.
There was nothing dreary about it. The atmosphere was
luxurious, sensuous, and masculine.

Erica experienced a feeling that was difficult to define—
a need to escape, perhaps, before a mystical spell was
woven. Rafael was standing behind her, his wide shoulder
blocking her view of the door. Undercurrents of emotion
vibrated between them. She took in the unwavering gaze
that pinned her in place, the tapering length of his well-
built body, the expensive material of the pants stretched
over muscular thighs, the raven blackness of his hair and
eyes, the aura of masterfulness—all of him. The air was so
charged that Erica hardly dared to breathe.

With slow, deliberate movements, Rafael's hand reached
out to touch her cheek, his thumb caressing the bone, his
touch releasing a torrent of tiny, erotic sensations. Her
lashes fluttered down to conceal her response. She had to
steel herself not to react, not to melt in his arms as she had
done before and as Helen had undoubtedly done many
times before in this very room. Unexpected pain made her
press her lips tightly together.

"No one has been in this room except myself and the
crew, Erica."

Her eyes opened wide in surprise at his uncanny perception of her thoughts. The look on his bronzed face was
impossible for her to define, but it made her heart pound
like a trip hammer. His thumb moved down to the corner
of her mouth and traced the outline of its feminine softness. When his hand moved to the side of her neck, her
lips trembled in unwilling protest of its departure.

The descent of his dark head was unhurried, her lips
parting in anticipation of the moment when Rafael
would claim them. His kiss was a lick of flame, igniting
her already kindled desire. Possession was immediate
with no tender, probing search for a response by Rafael.

A swirling mist of lascivious weakness swayed Erica against him. Her shoulders were seized as she was pulled to the rock wall of his chest. The mastery of his embrace was a seduction of the senses. The total exploration by his mouth of her face and neck and shoulder was beyond her power to halt had she wanted it to stop. He alternately gave and took, demanded, received, and returned her passion.

In a moment, she would be lost beyond recall, absorbed by a personality more forceful than any she'd ever known. It was fear of this that enabled her to whirl away from him when every other warning had been swept aside.

Her freedom from his touch lasted only an instant as her hair was brushed aside and his mouth gently kissed the sensitive cord of her neck. Erica gulped for life-giving air, her trembling fingers closing over the lean hands spreading across her curves, drawing her back against his rising male hardness. One hand allowed itself to be pushed away. Her temporary resistance was ended when Erica felt the zipper sliding quietly open down her back. She ached to feel his touch against the nakedness of her flesh. The intoxicating desire to submit was overpowering.

She turned back to him, her hands clutching the bodice of the cream silk gown that threatened to slip away. Her face reddened as she saw his gaze lingering on the tantalizing shadow between her breasts. Her luminous eyes silently beseeched him.

"Do not be ashamed." His seductively soft voice caressed her. "You are my wife, Erica." Again the smoldering light in his eyes swept over her breasts, the intimacy of the look causing her to draw a deep breath that only made the light burn brighter when it returned to her face. "Every inch of you is beautiful to me. Don't be frightened, *querida*."

She wasn't. Her arms willingly wound themselves around his neck as he carried her to the bed, setting her on her feet beside it. She was his wife, he had said. A delicious sensation of bliss washed over her.

His jacket was off, his shirt unbuttoned, being tugged free of his pants. The sight of the golden chest, the bare skin being revealed as he removed the shirt, made her hesitate despite her extraordinary desire for him. Her fingers tightened convulsively on her loosened gown.

"I—I have to go back to the hotel. Now," she said huskily.

Rafael looked at her for a long moment, his arms gently circling her. "If that is what you wish, *querida*, I will take you there," he murmured. "Speak now or let us speak no more."

But the fruit of temptation was there before her and the age-old desire to bite into its sweetness was supreme. Her hands slipped around his waist as she tilted her head to receive his kiss.

Later . . .

Rafael cradled her in his arms, murmuring reassuring words in Spanish that she didn't understand. Tenderly, patiently, he eased her lingering fear before he initiated her, sweeping her into the dizzying rapture of sensual and emotional love. When the last sigh of ecstasy shuddered through her, he held her against his bare chest, pressing her head to the uneven beat of his heart.

"Esta mañana, querida," he whispered softly.

Chapter 5

Erica stirred restlessly beneath the leaden band that held her down. The pressure eased slightly and she shifted into a more comfortable position on her side. In a state of near wakefulness, she became aware of an unfamiliar warmth and touch. Instantly all her senses were alert, her skin tingling where the hand possessively cupped the rounded firmness of her breast. She realized that Rafael was lying beside her.

Gently she rolled away from his unresisting hand, hugging the edge of the bed so as not to wake him up. Her mind raced in panic as she stared at the shadow-darkened form in the bed. What had she done? Confusion and shame assailed her. Was she really so desperately needy that she'd married a virtual stranger? She thought back to the unknown Mexican official who had mumbled legal words she hadn't even understood.

She could forgive herself for wanting no-strings-attached sex. But to allow herself to be seduced by a man she knew was a fortune hunter was just plain risky. To marry him was insane. Her father, Vance Wakefield, most likely would never forgive her, even after the high-priced lawyers he would undoubtedly hire got through taking Rafael apart in court.

Erica backed away from the bed. Frantically she grabbed at her gown lying on the floor and the rest of her garments scattered nearby. Keeping an eye on the sleeping man in the bed, she dressed with fear-driven swiftness. Her muscles were stiff and resisting. Guilt consumed her.

Carrying her shoes and evening bag in her hand, she tiptoed into the hallway, quietly closing the door of the stateroom behind her and listening for any sign or sound that Rafael might hear her leave. The yacht was quiet except for the waves licking the hull. Pausing in the doorway to the deck, Erica glanced furtively around, afraid of running into a member of the crew.

Nothing. She was alone.

She hurried as quickly as she dared to the gangplank and didn't stop running until she was ashore.

The sky was pitch black. By the time she was able to wave down a cab and arrive at her hotel, the first glimmers of dawn were lighting the sky in the east. The night life of Acapulco ran from dusk until dawn, and most of the hotel staffers barely noticed her return.

Once in her room, Erica walked directly to the shower, stuffing her gown into the wastebasket. She turned the showerhead on full force, willing the stinging spray to banish the sensual memories that burned so vividly. It was futile. His caresses were scorched into her mind.

As she reentered her room, the door to the connecting suite opened. For a split second, she froze in terror, half expecting to see Rafael standing in the doorway. Instead it was Lawrence, a maroon velour robe tied around his waist, his fingers raking his thinning hair.

"I thought I heard someone stirring in here." A yawn punctuated his remark. "What are you doing up at this hour?"

Erica was between Lawrence and the bed. Chances were he hadn't seen that it hadn't been slept in and he obviously believed she had come in much earlier. She was too ashamed and humiliated by her own conduct to tell him what had happened.

"I'm getting ready to leave," she said tautly.

"Vance had a maid pack most of your things." A sleepy smile crooked his thin mouth. "He left me behind to make sure that you caught your flight—which, by the way, doesn't leave for hours."

Something told Erica that if she didn't leave the hotel within the hour, Rafael would be here to get her and the whole pathetic story would be out.

"We're leaving now," she declared.

Lawrence frowned. "There aren't any scheduled flights at this hour of the morning."

"Then we'll charter a jet like Daddy did!" A strange mixture of torment and temper showed in her eyes. "*Right* now!"

He gave a shake of his head as if he'd given up trying to understand her mercurial moods. "Okay, okay. I'll meet you downstairs in twenty minutes."

Only after Lawrence had left the room did Erica notice she was still wearing Rafael's ring on her finger. She hurriedly stuffed it in the bottom of one of her suitcases and got dressed. Less than an hour later, their chartered jet was leaving the runway with not a sign of Rafael anywhere.

They didn't return to San Antonio, flying into Houston instead where Vance Wakefield had gone. He was too involved in negotiations to notice Erica's agitated behavior. The rare moments he spent in her company were too short for her to confide in him. But it wasn't about finding the time. When it came right down to it, she didn't have the courage to confess.

* * *

"So I never told Daddy." Erica sighed as she finished recounting her story to Jules Blackwell. "I've never told anyone until today."

"And you say the marriage was consummated?"

"Yes." She didn't try to hide the scarlet shame in her face.

"Sorry. I hate to embarrass you. Anyway, nowadays that doesn't matter one way or another, not the way it once did. But that fact probably will come up in the annulment proceedings, so I needed to know," her uncle said.

"I have to tell someone," she sniffled.

"Now, now," he said, patting her hand affectionately. "Don't beat up on yourself. I have a feeling you've done enough of that already."

Erica smiled at him ruefully. "Thank you for not telling me what an idiot I am to get into a mess like this."

He nodded. "We have to think about an easy way to get you out of it, that's all." He heaved his rotund body out of the chair beside her and walked around to his desk. "You haven't seen the guy since you left Acapulco, right?"

"No, I haven't."

But she remembered the irrational fear and indecisiveness when she had waited. And waited. She'd bought and used five drugstore pregnancy tests over several weeks just to be absolutely sure she was in the clear, even though they'd used condoms.

Worrying about when Rafael would walk back into her life had been even more consuming. She'd been completely blindsided by her uncontrollably passionate response to him. Funny, because, her subsequent totally controlled behavior around other men really had earned her the nickname of Ice Maiden. Forest liked to tease her about that.

"Do you know where he lives?" Jules was asking.

Erica shook her head. "No, I don't."

"What's his full name?"

She looked into his gently inquiring gaze, a bubble of hysterical laughter escaping her throat before she could stop it. "I don't know that either. Or what he was saying sometimes—San Antonio has always been my home, but I grew up in boarding schools. I never learned basic Spanish other than 'good morning' and 'thank you.' I took private lessons so I could chat with some of the customers in my boutique. But then"—she shrugged—"in Acapulco, I couldn't follow the pronunciation. Isn't it funny, Uncle Jules? I'm married and I don't even know what my name is."

"What about the marriage certificate?" he asked, giving her a chance to dwell on another example of her world-class stupidity.

"Rafael must have it. I vaguely recall signing my name but I suppose he put it in his pocket."

"It's a legal document, so it will be on file. I can get a copy of it," he assured her as he removed the ring from the handkerchief Erica had given him. The silver eagle with two heads stamped on the face of the ring stared back at him. "This signet ring could be a family crest, but it's unlikely."

Erica watched the attorney anxiously. "Do you think I'll have to pay off Rafael to get a quickie divorce?"

"It depends on how wealthy he thinks you are and whether he's discovered that you're Vance Wakefield's daughter," Jules answered. The look he gave her was sincerely apologetic. "Some husband you picked."

"Don't call him that! And don't joke about it!" Her tempestuous pride made her snap.

Jules seemed glad to see evidence of her fighting spirit.

"One way or another, he did it for the money. I doubt he'll settle for a token kiss-off."

"I don't have a lot of money, Uncle Jules, outside of the allowance Daddy gives me. You know how the trust fund is tied up." Her teeth nibbled at her lower lip. "Daddy will ask a lot of questions if I hit him up for serious bucks. And he'll find out why I want it. Shoot," she said vehemently. "We get along so well now." The last sentence was a despairing sigh.

"I know."

A mirthless smile lasted about a second on her face. "If I'd had an affair with Rafael, my dad could have forgiven that. But to marry him? And keep it a secret all this time?"

Jules gave her a worried look.

Erica rushed on, the words tumbling out. "I just can't let Daddy find out no matter how much Rafael demands. I'll have to find a way of scraping it together on my own."

"You're worrying about a bridge we may not have to cross, honey," Jules scolded. "There's time enough for that later when I've located your one-night husband." He held out his hand to her. "Are you going to take me out to lunch or not?"

His gruff tone was meant to coax her out of her obsessing and it worked pretty well. "Of course."

After lunch they paused outside the restaurant. Jules's happy, well-fed grin converted to an expression of professional reassurance. "Thanks, kid. I'll begin making discreet inquiries when I get back to the office," he promised. "I'll let you know as soon as I find out anything."

"It would be best if you contacted me at the boutique or on my cell. I don't want Daddy getting suspicious." Erica hesitated for a second. "When you do find Rafael, I . . . I don't want to see him."

His wink said he would take care of that. "Give Vance my regards."

"I will, Uncle Jules, and thank you."

He waved aside her gratitude as they parted. Following the meandering San Antonio River to her shop, Erica discovered she wasn't as relieved as she had thought she would be. Her burden had been somewhat lightened, though, and she was confident that Jules Blackwell would be able to find Rafael and arrange for an annulment or fast divorce. Yet she was restless, curiously on edge, as if there was something she hadn't taken into account.

The ominous gray cloud was still hovering on the horizon when she dressed for dinner that night. The vibrantly yellow cocktail dress was chosen especially to chase it away. Erica tried to take some satisfaction in the calm way her father included Forest in the conversation en route to the Mendelsens' home. Vance Wakefield could be really cutting if he didn't like or approve of a particular person. But her inner preoccupation made her cheerfulness forced, although no one appeared to notice it but herself.

John Mendelsen greeted the trio at the door of his Spanish-style house. He was a distinguished-looking man, a contemporary of Vance Wakefield's and a sometime business associate, friend, and golfing partner. His blond hair had long ago lightened to silver and his tan contrasted sharply with it and the ice-blue of his eyes.

"Where's that beautiful wife of yours?" Vance demanded in a laughing voice.

"Luisa is on the patio with the rest of our guests. You're the last to arrive, as usual, Vance, but there's still plenty of time for a couple of drinks before dinner," John assured him. "I'm sure Luisa will stop flitting among our guests long enough to see that your thirst is quenched."

"Luisa is much too aristocratic to flit," Vance joked.

Erica smiled in silent agreement. John Mendelsen's wife was petite but somehow imposing, a descendant of an old and respected Mexican-American family, innately proud and regal.

"Who did Luisa invite this time?" Vance asked as John began leading them through the cool hallways.

"We have our usual group—George and Mary Saunders, the Cliftons, the Mateos and their daughter, and Reina Cruz." Their host shrugged. "If Luisa seems to be preening a bit, it's because she succeeded in persuading Torres to come this evening. He's the head of an old Mexican family and an authority on Latin American history. He's in San Antonio to oversee the installation of a new exhibit at the Mexican Cultural Institute."

"I should have brushed up on my Spanish," Vance mused.

"No worries. He speaks perfect English."

Erica and Forest were walking a few steps behind her father and John Mendelsen. With the two older men engrossed in conversation, Forest leaned in a little toward Erica.

"Have I told you that you look sensational?" He practically growled the compliment.

She darted him a sparkling, flirtatious smile. "No, tell me."

His hand tightened around her waist. "If we were alone, I'd do more than tell you."

Erica glanced up at his face, noting the light in his warm brown eyes. Only for a second, her imagination played tricks on her and she saw smoldering black eyes. Her stomach constricted painfully before she could blink away the tantalizing image and she was once more seeing Forest's square face.

"Have you mentioned us to your father?" Forest asked.

"I haven't said yes to you yet," she whispered with

forced lightness. In her heart, she knew she couldn't give him an answer until the Rafael situation was resolved once and for all.

"But you will say yes. If I wasn't sure of that, I—" They had entered the patio and Forest was unable to complete his sentence.

Erica understood the urgency in his voice. In her own way she felt the same.

The first of the guests to notice their arrival and step forward to greet them was Reina Cruz, a pretty widow in her late thirties. Her smile encompassed all of them, but Erica thought that it lingered a little longer on her father. In the past, if any woman singled him out for attention, Erica was sure to dislike her on the spot. But her recently learned, hard-won attitude toward her father no longer dictated that reaction. She liked and admired Reina, and even wished her good luck if the woman really did have her eye on her father.

"I have heard a lot about you, Forest." Reina smiled after Erica had introduced him. "I am glad to meet you. Erica is very lucky."

"I hope to make her luckier some time soon." Forest flicked a possessive glance over the dark-haired girl at his side.

"So you've arrived, Vance."

"You know I wouldn't miss one of your dinner parties, Luisa," her father declared in his typically diplomatic and offhand way.

"Erica, you are gorgeous." John Mendelsen looked on approvingly as his wife brushed the younger woman's cheek with a kiss that was affectionate without being effusive. Just as graciously she turned to Forest. "And I'm so glad you were able to come, Forest."

He nodded. "It was really nice of you to invite me."

Luisa's dark eyes sparkled at Erica. "It seemed the best way to make sure that Erica could join us."

She felt her father's eyes rest on her thoughtfully, but Erica made no reply to the leading comment except to smile calmly. Luisa Mendelsen linked her arm with Vance's.

"Come, all of you. I want you to meet my guest of honor," she said.

Luisa was active in civic organizations and projects that had to do with the Spanish-American history of Texas and San Antonio in particular. Her dinner parties usually included a Latin American dignitary—cultural, political, or artistic—so Erica wasn't surprised that one was here this evening. She glanced idly ahead of her father and their hostess to see the elderly historian from Mexico.

Among the familiar faces of the other guests was . . . oh no. Bronzed face. Pitch black hair and eyes. Tall. Him.

Erica's knees almost buckled beneath her. Her vision blurred and for a second she thought she was going to faint. Briefly she leaned against Forest before her sight cleared and blood flowed again.

Controlled by a sense of numb inevitability, Erica let Forest escort her to Rafael, bracing herself for the moment when he would see her. As if from a great distance, she heard Luisa call to him and the dark, arrogant face she knew so well turned to answer. His aloof gaze swept the group of guests. Erica couldn't be certain, but it seemed as if his gaze narrowed on her for a lightning second before it stopped on Luisa. A polite smile lifted the firm line of his mouth, firmer than Erica remembered.

"I would like you all to meet Don Rafael Alejandro de la Torres," Luisa said.

Erica dug her fingernails into the palms of her hands. She glanced anxiously at her father as he was presented to Rafael. There was no recognition in his face. Any second she expected Rafael to blurt out that he was Vance's son-in-law, then gradually she realized that he wasn't going to.

"This is Vance's daughter, Miss Erica Wakefield."

Luisa's introduction directed Rafael's gaze to her. His lean, chiseled face had a courteous expression, but the intense scrutiny he gave her stripped from it what little color remained in Erica's face.

"Miss, is it? How charmingly old-fashioned. You are not married, Miss Wakefield?" Rafael asked dryly as he offered his hand in greeting.

Her hand trembled as she forced it to touch his, remembering the way those strong fingers had caressed her body with erotic intimacy. That same heat seemed to scorch every inch of her.

"Ah—no. I'm not." Her quivering chin lifted proudly.

Then her hand was released and Rafael was turning toward Forest as Luisa made the introduction again, adding in explanation that he was Erica's friend. There was no reaction by Rafael to that statement. A server arrived with a tray of drinks. Instantly the other guests, friends of long standing, moved forward to greet them and Erica was able to slip away from the circle that included Rafael.

Yet the eagerness with which she threw herself into the conversation with the new group didn't make Erica any less conscious of Rafael's presence. Never once did she look in his direction, but she saw the way the other women gravitated toward him. At times, she could hear his low voice and icy chills of apprehension danced along her spine.

Had he come here to find her? Was the exhibit at the Mexican Cultural Institute just an excuse? Or was he an impostor? In Acapulco he had pretty much admitted that he was a fortune hunter. Erica herself had seen him with a woman who was definitely a lot older than he was.

But he'd remained silent about their hasty, clandestine marriage. Did that mean he intended to use it to manipulate her somehow? There was no question any more that he knew who her father was.

Erica knew she had to find out where he was staying so she could let her uncle know. Yet she shrank from asking him directly and asking the others at the party would only arouse curiosity. And Forest . . . what would he think? Her head pounded with the multitude of her questions. She hadn't wanted to see or speak to Rafael again, but the choice had been taken out of her hands.

If Rafael planned to use their secret against her for whatever reason, then to run to avoid seeing him would show cowardice and increase his hold over her. Maybe the best thing to do would be to seek him out, apart from the others, and let him realize that she wasn't afraid of him. But it was inconceivable that such an occasion would arise. His personality was too compelling for him to be alone in a group of people unless he chose to be. A dark look of despair shadowed her eyes.

Dinner was announced. Erica discovered her father was seated opposite Rafael, who was on the hostess's right, while she was down the table and across from him, a position that promised that any time his gaze moved it would include her. Even Forest was separated from her so that she could no longer use him as a shield.

The carefully prepared meal seemed tasteless. Erica spent most of her time pushing the food around her plate and making sure her eyes didn't stray to Rafael. Tension was beginning to etch tight lines around her smile when the dessert dishes were cleared and Luisa suggested they move to the living room.

Forest started toward her, only to be waylaid by

George Saunders. Rafael was talking to her father a few steps away and Erica glanced desperately around for a haven. With a smile of relief, she saw Julie Mateo, only a year younger than herself, entering the living room.

"What have you been doing lately, Julie?" Erica asked brightly to get the girl over to her side. Not that she'd changed. Same auburn hair, same makeup.

"Very little, actually. Helping out at the hospital part-time." Julie was quiet and unassuming. It was only in the past few months that Erica had gotten to know her at all. "I like your dress. Is it from your shop?"

"As a matter of fact, it is," Erica admitted with a self-consciously proud smile.

Julie grinned. "That's a fabulous way to advertise your boutique."

"Do you own a boutique, Erica?" There was a knowing gleam in Rafael's eyes as he watched the startled turn of her head.

"It's a joint venture between my father and myself." In spite of her effort to reply calmly, her voice sounded overly cool.

Vance Wakefield smiled at her indulgently. "I get bragging rights. My daughter has great business sense. She picked out the location on the Riverwalk and except for a little advice from me, she's run the place all by herself."

Rafael's raven-black head tilted patronizingly toward her. "Ah. I think I know it. Is it called Erica's?"

"Yes, it is," she said defensively. "Not very original, I admit."

"What a coincidence." One corner of his mouth curved in a mocking smile. "I stopped there today around noon to buy a gift for my sister. I'm quite sure I would have remembered if I'd seen you there, Erica."

"I believe I was out to lunch at the time." She froze inside as the irony of the situation struck her. Right when she and Jules Blackwell had been discussing her elopement with Rafael, he'd been in her boutique. "I hope Donna was able to find something just right for your sister."

"She did." The instant the reply had been made, Rafael turned to her father, seeming bored both with Erica and the subject of the conversation.

"What do you think of San Antonio, Don Rafael?" her father asked. "Have you been here before?"

"Not for some time," he replied, answering the last question first. "San Antonio is like a grand old lady. Proud of her rich heritage and culture, and looking to the future as well. Even with all the new buildings and development, the city has never lost the grace and old-world charm it is so famous for. Truly, it deserves to be one of the four unique cities in the United States."

Erica stared at him in silence, stunned by the way he'd put her feelings for the city into well-turned words. He could be giving a speech. She'd forgotten how very charming Rafael could be. How she hated him at that moment. It took all her willpower to prevent her from telling the entire gathering what a despicable person he was. Bottom line: he'd married her for her money and he was here to collect some of it.

Her rage seethed inside her as she watched the way he dominated the room. The center of interest was always where Rafael was. Erica stood on the fringes of various different conversations, not trusting herself to say a word. The subjects the other guests discussed never seemed to stray far from Rafael.

When the small group she was standing with began to gravitate toward him, Erica pretended an interest in an alarming-looking Aztec statue. Forest was on the far side of the room leading some discussion with Matt Clifton and Ed Mateo. Both were nodding in agreement with what he was saying. She tried to be glad that Forest was mingling with ease, but she wanted to be away from this house and Rafael, to feel the comfort of Forest's arms around her. From past experience, she knew the party would drag on for another hour or more.

"The statue is an excellent example of early Aztec art." Erica's back stiffened as she became aware that Rafael was standing nonchalantly by her side. His black gaze ridiculed her obvious annoyance—he had to know that appearing just like that would upset her. "I'm afraid this will have to do," he murmured mysteriously.

A confused look entered her eyes as she regarded him. "I don't know what you mean."

"I believe you wished to speak to me privately. This is as private as we can get, unless you wish to cause comment by leaving the room in my company."

"What are you doing here?" Erica hissed, staring at the statue and wishing she could throw it at him.

"Didn't our hosts explain? I am here with an exhibit from Mexico," he answered in an amused voice.

"Don't play games!" she snapped, whirling around to face him. "You know very well what I'm talking about!"

Her anger seemed to amuse him more. "Do you really wish to discuss it here, *mi esposa*?" Erica caught her breath sharply as his eyes seemed to physically touch her upper body, traveling with unnerving slowness. "You are my wife, Erica de la Torres, by word and by deed."

Coloring furiously at his unnecessary reminder, she glared her resentment. "No, we won't discuss it here," she said grudgingly.

His nod of acknowledgment indicated that he'd known very well it could be no other way. "I am staying at the Palacio del Rio," he said and gave her his room number. "May I expect you there at noon tomorrow?"

"Yes," she snapped.

"I shall look forward to the pleasure of your company."
The sensual line of his mouth curved ever so slightly.

The only satisfaction Erica could get out of all this was
the fact that Jules Blackwell and not her would meet
Rafael tomorrow. At least she would be spared another
disturbing encounter with him.

As Erica predicted earlier, all the guests lingered for
the better part of an hour. Rafael was standing with Luisa
and John Mendelsen as the others got through the good-
byes. Forest was standing behind her, his arm loosely circling her waist, so she rested lightly against him. There
was a sense of protection in his casual embrace as they
waited for her father to finish speaking to his host.

"I didn't really expect to enjoy myself tonight," Forest
murmured near her ear. "Your father's friends aren't
nearly as stuffy as I expected them to be."

Erica bent her head back and to the side to gaze into
his young, handsome face. "I would have much rather
been somewhere else," she said decisively.

"Damn, but you're beautiful!" Fire leaped into his
brown eyes as his lips possessively touched hers, unmindful of watching eyes.

Erica held his ardent gaze a second longer, his tender
caress touching her deeply, before she turned to see if her
father was ready to leave. Her softly luminous eyes were
pinned by the ominous blackness of Rafael's, his handsome features etched with proud disapproval. Erica's
heart raced under his gaze, until he turned away and she
was free.

Still, she had to wonder how long it would be before
she was truly free.

Later, in her own home, Vance Wakefield discreetly
made himself scarce so Erica and Forest could say their
good-nights in private. Erica went eagerly into his arms,

responding with forced ardor to his kisses. Yet she found she couldn't block out the events that had taken place.

Worse, she realized she was trying to compare her reaction to Forest with the way Rafael had made her feel. Even in Acapulco, she would have sworn that she disliked Rafael—and was sexually attracted to him at the same time. But the comparison was pointless. Sensations aroused the first time that a man awakened a woman to her hidden desires would never be as stunning or overwhelming again.

Chapter 6

Erica pressed a hand to her churning stomach, then pulled open the door to the hotel's Riverwalk entrance. She had phoned Jules the instant she'd arrived at the boutique that morning. The receptionist had informed her that he was out of the city and not expected back until Tuesday or Wednesday of the following week. The cell phone number she had for him went straight to voicemail after the first ring several times, so he wasn't answering it.

During the rest of the morning, Erica had deliberated over calling Rafael to cancel her appointment with him. As reluctant as she was to see him again, she was also aware that she desperately needed to know what his demands were so that she would have time to figure out her side of it. The sooner she found out how difficult it was going to be, the sooner she could find a way of dealing with it. Besides, she wasn't sure she could put Rafael off until Jules came back. It was conceivable that he might try to contact her at the boutique or at home.

There was no sign of Rafael in the restaurant on the river level or in the lobby's cocktail lounge. Her watch showed exactly twelve noon. With her heart beating unevenly, Erica walked to the house phone and dialed his suite. Her hand nervously clutched the white receiver.

"Yes?" His rich voice flowed smoothly in her ear.

She faltered momentarily. "Th-this is Erica. Um, should I meet you in the lounge?"

He gave a low laugh. "You indicated that you wanted a private discussion, then you pick a public place to have it. Don't you want to talk to me where no one can overhear us?"

"Yes—"

"Then come to my suite," Rafael commanded and told her the number. He hung up.

Erica held the phone to her ear for a long moment, her throat choked by the refusal she hadn't had a chance to say. As if she wasn't already angry with him . . . well, now she was furious.

She walked self-consciously toward the elevators, glancing furtively around in case someone she knew saw her. It was one thing to pretend that she had accidentally bumped into Rafael in the crowded lobby and it was another to be seen going into or coming out of his room.

For once luck was on her side as the doors yawned open to admit her to an empty elevator. There was no one around on Rafael's floor either and Erica walked swiftly to his room, praying that he wouldn't make her wait too long in the hallway before opening the door.

When it opened, she quickly darted in, not drawing a breath until she heard the door close behind her. Then she swung to face Rafael. Being upset didn't keep her from noticing how good he looked in the suit he was wearing. His hand made a polite gesture toward a small sofa. Erica walked toward it, trying to calm her chaotic thoughts and emotions.

"Would you like anything to drink?"

"Water, please."

She accepted it, more to have something to occupy her hands to ease their nervous trembling. The last thing she wanted was to drink anything that would cloud her thinking. Stay alert, she told herself.

Rafael sat down in a bulky armchair next to the sofa. His manner reminded Erica of a lord about to listen dutifully to the problems of one of his lowly subjects. Her lips tightened.

"You wished to discuss our marriage," Rafael prompted with infuriating calm.

"No, our divorce."

"Why did you wait for over a year and a half, Erica?" His voice sounded disinterested, but his dark eyes glowed.

Erica glanced down at her glass of water. "I didn't know how to reach you or where you lived."

"And you made no effort to find out."

"No." She refused to be intimidated, even though the whole thing had been her idea and her fault. "Once I left, that was that. I guess you think I owe you an explanation, but—well, I can't explain."

"Ah." He paused. "But now you know who I really am."

"It's immaterial," she answered coldly. "I want a divorce."

He nodded. "Last night I heard talk that you and this Forest Granger are in love."

Hard to say what annoyed her more, his words or his tone of voice. Erica didn't comment.

"Perhaps he is the reason for your sudden decision."

Her chin raised to a defiant angle. "We are in love with each other. Let's get back to the subject of the divorce."

Rafael studied her for a long moment. "Do you know that there has never been a divorce in my family?"

She shot him a look, thinking that there had to have been more than one wife who'd wanted out if the rest of the Torres men were this arrogant. "It's not that big of a deal. Especially considering that we hardly knew each other."

"Still, it will take time."

Ice ran through her blood, sending shivers through her. Erica stared at him, trying to will him to understand her side of it.

"I don't think you understand," she said firmly. "I don't love you. I'm in love with Forest."

He gave her a wry look. "Have you told him about me?"

"Hell, no." Her protest was shocked and indignant.

"I assume you don't want him to know."

"Rafael, that's my business. Not yours." Her anger was nearly beyond control as she rose on shaking legs, her hands doubled into fists at her side. She glared at him, fighting to check her temper. "I don't have to explain anything to you. Got that?"

"Yes, I do." He pushed himself out of the armchair to tower over her. "You seem to think that you have the right to do whatever you want, whenever you want. With no consequences."

With a flash of guilt, she silently acknowledged that he had a point. The mad impulse that had made her marry him seemed to have happened long ago, and she still didn't understand how she could have been so foolish. "That was then and this is now."

"It seems to me you are forgetting something, *querida*," he said. "Our night together—"

"One night," she retorted. "One single night. That's all it was." But the memory of the sensual bliss she'd found in his arms and his expert lovemaking made her blush. She hoped he didn't notice.

"Nothing more than that?"

She held up a hand to get him to stop. "If you're going to talk about it, I'm going to leave, right now."

"Very well. Then I won't."

Erica took a deep breath. "If it's money that you want, that's open to discussion."

He gave her an aristocratic nod. "How civilized. But I don't need money."

"Oh. I see. Um, it would involve lawyers, so maybe it's best if you and I don't get into that."

He gave her a long look. "Is there anything else we need to discuss? I assume that you did not become pregnant as a result of your indiscretion."

He ought to know. His bachelor lair on the yacht had been stocked with condoms and he'd used them. She wouldn't have had sex with him if not, but nothing provided 100 percent protection. The chilly note in his voice repelled her. "No. I didn't get pregnant," she said with equal coldness. "But thanks for asking."

"I didn't ask, I merely assumed that you had not. I wonder now if you would have bothered to tell me if that had happened."

She whirled around. "You don't have a very high opinion of me, do you?" Her eyes searched his and saw his silent answer there. "Think what you want. But if you really need to know, yes, if I'd been pregnant, I—I would have told you. Eventually."

"Nice to know."

She was suddenly consumed with curiosity. "Do you have children?"

"No. But I want to."

Without wanting to, she imagined what a child of his would look like—a dark-eyed boy who was a miniature of the man before her—then shook her head to make the thought go away.

He shrugged. "Clearly, you do not. Or at least not with me, though you are my wife."

"Rafael, I'm not. I'm just not. It never should have happened. I was young and inexperienced and I—I don't even remember what I was thinking that night!" she burst out.

He looked steadily at her. "Try," he said. "I would like to know why you did what you did."

Did he mean her going through with the incomprehensible ceremony . . . or the night of passion they'd shared?

"It doesn't matter," she said at last. "I'm not going to stay married to a man I don't love."

"That is something you should have considered before you married me," he snapped harshly.

"I did!" The fear that made her breath catch was masked by a sudden show of bravado. "Oh God—I never intended the marriage to last more than an hour. The only reason I married you was to get back at my father for always putting his business ahead of me. I knew he would pay off that official, pronto, to put an end to it, whatever it took. Document revoked, papers shredded, end of story."

"But your plan backfired, no?" Rafael smiled.

Erica didn't want to look at him. "Yeah, it did. I couldn't reach him. He'd flown back to the States on a chartered jet," she said bitterly.

"Why didn't you tell me that night?" he asked quietly.

"I was freaked out and confused," she said over her shoulder. "And—and afraid, yes, that you'd be angry. I was no match for you. I thought if I could go back to the hotel I'd be safe. But you didn't take me back to the hotel."

Rafael studied her thoughtfully. "Did you sleep with me because you were afraid of me?"

Erica swallowed nervously. The memory of his fiery caresses and how deeply she had ultimately responded to them was too much for her even now. A feeling of shame reddened her cheeks as she recalled the way she'd welcomed his intimate touch.

"Not at first," she answered with dangerous honesty. "But afterward, y-yes. I was. That's why I ran out first chance I got, while you were sleeping." It took all of her pride to look into his face without faltering. "How can you possibly want to stay married to me when you know why I did something so stupid? And when you know I love someone else?"

"What I want and what I must accept are two very different things, Erica," Rafael said.

He was way too good at dodging direct questions and the tactic was making her extremely nervous. "Well, I won't accept it!" Her cry rang angrily through the room. "I'll have my attorney file for divorce immediately."

"Suit yourself. He will have me served at the hotel with the papers, of course, which will be full of the usual lurid nonsense." He scowled. "And filed in the public records. Available to anyone. Vance Wakefield will not be happy to see your name in blogs and newspapers." Rafael gave a wave of his hand as he began to invent some headlines. "*Mexican Madness! San Antonio Beauty Marries For One Night!* He will be appalled."

She narrowed her eyes. "Are you trying to intimidate me?"

"No," he said blandly. "Just pointing out the consequences, because again, you are proceeding without thinking."

She started toward him, the light of battle in her eyes, but he stood his ground.

"It would be interesting to discover what your boyfriend's reaction would be, but I can promise you that he will never hear it from me."

"You wouldn't dare," Erica whispered.

"I am not doing anything but explaining what happens when someone files for divorce. Ask anyone who's been through it or look it up yourself. Your family's name is well-known and the filing, as I said, is public. It will include the grounds for the request of the dissolution of the marriage, and relevant dates, and where it took place. Does it surprise you that reporters sniff out such news? It shouldn't."

"I don't read gossip columns," she said tightly.

"Millions of other people do."

She had no idea what he was getting at. "So what?"

"You don't want a mud-slinging divorce. You want a quiet one so your father will never find out what you did."

Erica gasped, at a complete loss for words. Unfortunately, he was right.

"I have a suggestion, however."

She didn't want to hear it and he waited a little while to speak. His voice was low, almost husky when he did. "Give me a chance, Erica. One more chance, in honor of that one night. It was real," he insisted. "To have you in my arms for that brief time meant so much to me."

She heaved an involuntary, almost inaudible sigh.

"And now that I have seen you again"—he hesitated—"the memory means even more."

His steady regard unnerved her. The indefinable look in his eyes reminded her so strongly of that one night that she gasped again, more softly.

"No—no, that wouldn't be a good idea."

"Are you so sure of that?" His voice was soothing, almost hypnotic, without the cold edge it'd had before. "If it is only a memory, than it will fade away. If what happened between us is meant to last . . ."

She didn't want him to finish the sentence.

"I will be in San Antonio for several weeks," he continued, "for as long as the exhibition is on display. We can begin again, as lovers. Allow me to court you."

"But I have a—a lover," she stammered. Somehow that utterly romantic term sounded odd when she used it to describe Forest.

He smiled ruefully. "Now you have two."

"One is more than enough for me," she said, feeling overwhelmed.

"May the best man win," he murmured.

Erica looked at him, hoping her conflicting emotions didn't show in her eyes. "I think he has, Rafael. I'm not going to tell him to go jump off a cliff just because you showed up."

She hugged her arms around herself just so he couldn't do it himself. If he got physical with her . . . she knew all too well how smoothly sensual his moves were . . . she would give in. Again.

"No one has to know of our marriage. Or of that night." His dark eyes pleaded with her, but not from weakness. Only from the strength of his desire. It warmed her through and through, as hot and golden as the sun the day she'd first seen him.

"I can hear your mind racing," Rafael said, a trace of resignation in his voice. But not defeat. "I don't ask you to agree with me today. Take the time you need to think over what I've said. I will give you one week. See what happens if you meet me halfway."

Her body seemed curiously drawn to him, even though a mental alarm was warning her away.

She didn't say yes. And she didn't say no. Erica picked up her bag and left without saying anything more.

His words echoed in her mind all the way back to the boutique. Erica had escaped from him once, but it hadn't really been an escape, just a postponement. Giving Rafael a second chance would mean explaining to her father why she suddenly had two handsome men in her life. A barrage of painful questions was sure to follow and he'd get the whole story out of her sooner rather than later.

No, never.

She wouldn't explain anything to Vance Wakefield

ever again. She didn't even want to think about his possible reaction.

As she pushed open the shop door, Erica knew she would never be able to get through the afternoon pretending nothing was wrong. The throbbing pain in her temples was nearly blinding her. Her statement to Donna that she wasn't feeling well was barely out of her mouth before her store manager was agreeing with her.

"Go on home, Erica. I didn't think you were feeling well this morning. Now there's hardly any color at all in your face. I'll take care of everything, don't you worry."

For the rest of the afternoon and all of Sunday, Erica shut herself in her room, using the pretense of illness to break her date with Forest. Each passing hour made her realize that she was farther than ever from a decision.

She alternately sobbed into her pillow and pounded it with frustration. When she wasn't doing either, she was up and out of the bed, pacing the floor.

Did her father's love, such as it was, and respect, on his limited terms, matter more to her than her own future? A divorce would focus public attention on what had happened, and not in a positive way. She came up with a headline or two on her own. *Erica and Rafael: A Fling or the Real Thing?* Or how about . . . *She Left Her Heart In Acapulco.*

Forest would be the butt of endless jokes, and he hadn't done anything to deserve that kind of humiliation.

Yet Erica couldn't conceive of actually being Rafael's wife. She had radically misjudged and underestimated him: he was the scion of a distinguished family and highly educated. And handsome as ever, that hadn't changed. And sexy—oh, was he ever sexy. In a way that seemed to make her dangerously unstable and prone to doing things that were just plain crazy.

But she wanted a love that didn't make her do that,

real love she could count on forever. Not just for one night. A husband who would cherish and adore her, put her first, give her all the affection that her father hadn't been able to demonstrate.

It occurred to her that everything she wanted might be more than one man could give.

Well, whether or not Rafael loved her the way she wanted to be loved, she just didn't love him. Never mind what it felt like to melt in the sensual bliss of his embrace. She was very, very sure she loved someone else: Forest.

Erica lay back on the bed and crumpled the much-abused pillow, which by now was leaking a few tiny feathers, under her head. She stared at the blank ceiling. In her overheated and overtaxed imagination, the faces of both men floated over her.

Forest. Good-looking in his athletic way but somehow callow, compared to Rafael. whose dark, soulful eyes burned right through her doubts. She knew which man she wanted more. But she wasn't going to give him a second chance. She just couldn't.

Monday morning arrived and she was still no closer to a decision. But she couldn't keep on hiding out in her room. Besides, Rafael had said she could take the time she needed to make up her mind. Maybe her uncle Jules would have a brilliant solution when he came back from wherever he was. With that slightly encouraging thought, Erica pulled herself together, got dressed, and went off to work at the boutique.

Forest had a meeting on Monday morning so it wasn't until Tuesday noon that she saw him. Her doubts and questions had come back by then, more numerous than before. She felt a little sorry for him. He didn't know the first thing about the reasons why.

He took her to lunch at one of the sidewalk cafes on the Riverwalk. They sat in the shade of a giant market umbrella. He was feeling romantic, evidently, but Erica avoided the tenderly possessive look in his eyes.

She toyed with the guacamole and freshly made tortilla chips she'd ordered. "Forest, I have a question for you."

"Ask away."

"Do you consider yourself ambitious?"

"Hell yeah," he said indignantly. "Is that a bad thing?" His gaze was speculative when it touched her face. "There was something behind that question. What's up, Erica?"

"Nothing." She wished she hadn't shot off her mouth. Rafael was right about her being impulsive. But Forest didn't accept her dismissal of the subject.

"Honey, are you afraid I'm marrying you because of your dad?"

She looked at him warily. "What do you mean?"

"Hey, just knowing him is an education in itself," he began.

In so many ways, she thought. Not all good. "Right," was all she said.

"He's connected at the highest levels," Forest went on. "So that right there can further my career."

"Got it."

He patted her hand. "Don't worry. He's just gravy. You're the main course."

Erica winced. "Uh, thanks."

"Look, kidding aside, I'm successful because I work hard, Erica," he said, "and that was true before you and I ever hooked up."

"I know," Erica assured him quickly, gazing into his square-jawed face. "And I know how much it means to you that you've gotten as far as you have because of your own ability."

"Then why the question?" An amused frown creased his forehead.

"I was . . . only wondering how important your work was to you," she hedged.

"Really important. Every guy has to stay ahead of the competition and these days, I have plenty."

She swallowed hard, thinking of Rafael.

"But I do get how much you resented the demands that your father's empire made on him. You aren't asking me to cut back my hours or anything, I hope."

"If I did, would you?" Erica tried to make it sound like a joke, as his answer didn't matter.

"No," Forest stated unequivocally. "I love you a lot, but you'll have to marry me the way I am."

"Okay," she whispered, suddenly sorry she'd put him on the spot. "Anyway, I do love you the way you are."

The dimple in his chin deepened as he smiled. "Then you'd better hurry up and say yes so I can put that ring on your finger."

A noncommittal reply came to her mind but it never got past her lips. A stricken look stole over her face as she saw Rafael approaching their table in the company of another man.

"Hello. Nice to see the two of you again," he said when Forest glanced away from Erica's face.

"Don Rafael," Forest acknowledged, rising from his chair.

Rafael's eyes were mockingly amused when he saw Erica hide her shaking hands beneath the table.

"I'd like you to meet *Señor* Esteban Rivera, a noted archaeologist from my country," he said, introducing the man who was with him. He introduced Erica and Forest to him in Spanish.

"*Buenas días, señorita, señor.*" The man nodded graciously to them both.

"It's a pleasure, *Señor* Rivera," Forest said, smiling.

Accustomed now to talking with Mexican-American

customers in her shop, Erica automatically replied in Spanish, adding that she hoped he was enjoying the beauty of San Antonio. She thought nothing of it until she encountered the piercing intentness of Rafael's gaze.

In deliberately rapid Spanish, he demanded, "How long have you been fluent in my language?"

Erica glanced hesitantly at Forest, whose grasp of Spanish was very limited. He seemed extremely curious about what had been said and a little suspicious of the tone.

"Only recently." She answered Rafael in English, her tone stiff and defiant. "It's useful in the shop. Our customers come from all over."

Rafael took in that information. "Of course."

"Would you care to join us for coffee?" Forest offered.

"I'm sorry. *Señor* Rivera and I are expected elsewhere. Perhaps another time," he replied, declining the invitation with a patronizing nod.

"Why do you figure he stopped?" Forest said thoughtfully after the two men had disappeared.

Erica shifted uncomfortably. "I imagine he was just being polite."

"Maybe." But Forest didn't seem convinced and neither was Erica.

Jules Blackwell called her at the boutique the following morning, before she'd had a chance to see if he was back from his trip.

"Okay, I found out a few things, Erica. Some of them may surprise you," he said, continuing before she had a chance to tell him about Rafael's presence in San Antonio. "Your husband didn't marry you for your money, believe it or not. Honey, you married into a very old Mexican family that has extensive holdings in Central and South America, and a hefty family fortune to boot."

"I know—not every detail, maybe, but the gist of it. Uncle Jules, he's here. In San Antonio," she said.

There was a moment of startled silence. "Have you talked to him?"

Erica sighed heavily and proceeded to tell Jules what had happened while he was gone. When she concluded, it was his turn to sigh.

"This puts a different spin on things, that's for sure." Erica could visualize his frown of concentration. "I guess I could go to see him at his hotel. At this point, it certainly can't hurt."

"Would you, Uncle Jules?" Emotion choked her throat.

"We can't give up without a fight," he said jokingly. "Let's see how it goes. I'll call you right after I meet with him."

Then he hung up.

"You're awfully quiet tonight, Erica," Forest commented, touching a fingertip to her mouth. "What's on your mind?"

"Sorry. I was just thinking." Erica breathed in deeply and glanced around the intimate lounge.

"About me, I hope." He smiled and his arm tightened affectionately around her shoulder.

"Actually, about the shop," she laughed. In truth, she'd been mentally reviewing her conversation with Jules Blackwell. He had called back the following afternoon after having met Rafael—not a very productive meeting, according to Jules. More like a standoff, in fact. Rafael, who wasn't stupid, hadn't said much and there was a limit to how much Jules would say to him.

When she'd asked his advice on how to proceed, Jules had hesitated and then insisted that this was a decision only she could make. He refused to advise her one way or another.

"Having problems at the boutique?" Forest asked.

Erica shrugged. "Nothing important."

"Then let's talk about us instead of the shop."

"N-not yet." She swallowed nervously, knowing there was no way she could tell him she hadn't made up her mind about that.

He sighed impatiently and moved away from her, darting her a glance that couldn't be mistaken for anything but angry, even in the dim light of the room.

"I'm sorry, Forest," Erica apologized. "I don't have an answer for you and it isn't fair to lead you on. I'm trying to be honest with you." Or as honest as she could be under the circumstances.

"Thanks." The single word had an edge. He stared at his drink for an uncomfortable moment. "You didn't deserve that. It's my turn to apologize, honey."

"I understand," she said, nodding.

"Well, well, well. Will you look at who just walked in?" he murmured cynically. "I wonder if it's another coincidence."

Erica glanced toward the entrance and immediately averted her head when she recognized the man entering the lounge. Her heart thudded against her ribs. She clutched her glass, wishing she could make herself small so Rafael wouldn't see her.

"Is he coming over here?" she asked tautly.

"He's with some other people," Forest replied, watching Rafael openly. "They're taking a table on the other side. I don't think he's even seen us. I guess I was wrong."

A nervous laugh of relief bubbled from her. "What made you think Don Rafael was following us in the first place?"

"I don't know." He shrugged, glancing at Erica, then back at the table where Rafael was seated. "I had a hazy impression at the dinner party the other night that he was interested in you. He always seemed to know where you were and who was with you."

Her cheeks flushed hotly. "Really? I didn't notice that he paid any special attention to me," she protested with false lightness.

"It was just an impression. I could have been mistaken." He smiled a crooked smile. "Tell me, did you notice him?"

"Oh, Forest!" Erica tilted her head to one side in simulated amusement. "Who wouldn't? I mean—he does stand out. A woman would have to be blind not to notice him and even then she would probably pick up on his vibrations."

"You know, I've never been jealous before," he chuckled. "Dance with me, Erica. I really feel like holding you all of a sudden."

Being in his arms wasn't easy. She felt that she ought to savor every moment together and yet . . . Rafael's distant presence was a distraction. The song ended much too soon, forcing her to open her eyes and move away from Forest's broad chest.

Her gaze focused immediately on Rafael sitting at a table on the edge of the dance floor. Sardonic amusement lit up his black eyes when he glanced at Forest. It was impossible for her not to acknowledge his presence without being blatantly rude. She ought to say something, anything—but Forest was already filling the void.

"We meet again, Don Rafael," he said politely.

Rafael rose and extended a hand to Forest in greeting, leaving him no choice except to cross the few feet to accept it. The two couples with him were quickly introduced before Rafael insisted that Forest and Erica allow him to buy them drinks.

Erica silently raged at the way Rafael was maneuvering. She'd wanted this evening with Forest to be special.

She wished she'd had the courage to persuade Forest to leave when Rafael had arrived at the club, but she hadn't wanted to spark any curious questions. Now she was seated between Rafael and Forest, feeling stiff and uncomfortable, knowing that Rafael had arranged it that way deliberately.

Her skin went hot as Forest rested his arm along the back of her chair as if staking a territorial claim to her. Her violet eyes darkened with resentment that she couldn't respond the way she wanted to. Rafael's presence was a reminder, at least to her, that she wasn't free. As if he knew what she was thinking, Rafael smiled.

The conversation started, trivial and impersonal, until Forest suddenly asked a question. "Rafael, are you married? Just curious. You never did say."

Erica wanted to slide out of her chair like a six-year-old and crawl under the table. All she could do was sit up super-straight, not sure which man she should glare at. Rafael gave Forest a humorless smile but he looked at her.

"The woman I want has not yet consented to my proposal," he stated ambiguously. He turned his gaze to Forest. "But I have no doubt she will soon make her decision."

Forest glanced quickly at Erica, a suspicious jealousy darkening his brown eyes. Her hands were rigidly clasped in her lap as she tried to ignore the crackling electricity in the air.

"Maybe, Don Rafael," she murmured in an even voice, "she needs more time." Deliberately she looked at Forest. "Marriage is a lifetime commitment. Or it should be."

"I agree, Erica," his seductive voice said. "To leap into it hastily could have disastrous results. And unpleasant consequences for all parties concerned."

One of the other members of his group spoke up and the subject was changed, for which she was grateful. Erica knew she'd sidetracked Forest's suspicions by looking at him when she'd made her comment to Rafael, but she hated tricking him that way. She was angry at Rafael for putting her in a position where she was forced to do it. She wondered what he would do next, but what he said to Forest left her in no doubt.

"May I have this dance with Erica?" he asked. His ridiculously macho courtesy—as if either man had a right to say yes or no for her!—was infuriating.

But Forest did say yes, without thinking twice. She wondered which of them deserved the cold-drink-in-the-face treatment more and decided it was, ha ha, a tossup.

So as not to make a scene, she found herself not fighting Rafael when he led her onto the dance floor.

There, he took her in his arms and Erica wondered how she could've ever forgotten how powerful his physical attraction was. Her senses vibrated with the provocative pressure of his lean fingers on the small of her back and the implicit emotional connection in the hand that clasped hers. She distrusted whatever it was that he stirred in her.

"Why can't you leave me alone?" she whispered, staring at the whiteness of his shirt and wondering if he still wore the gold medallion.

"I thought women liked to have their husbands pay attention to them," Rafael said.

"You may not be my husband for long," was her tart reply.

He laughed softly, his warm breath stirring the hair near her face. "That is up to you. It is not as if I or anyone else can tell you what to do."

"Exactly."

He gave her a considering look. "But what if you decide you do want to be my wife?"

"That's a really big *if*, Rafael."

"True. But so long as it is a possibility, I will wait to find out. I am old enough to know what I want." His mouth curved into a smile. "Which also means I only blame myself for your reluctance. If you'd known what you wanted all those months ago, our marriage would not be a secret today."

She closed her eyes, wishing for a fraction of a second that she had the power to make him vanish. And Forest, while she was at it. She was ready to start again from square one, a little older and a whole lot wiser.

Rafael's warm gaze showed his feelings for her when he returned her to Forest at the end of the song. There was no denying the strength and loving sensuality she saw, but Erica was still struggling to forget the look in Rafael's eyes when Forest took her home.

She tried to find the same quality in Forest's embrace and failed.

Chapter 7

Erica snapped open her evening bag to make sure she had transferred the house key from her other handbag. The gold key winked reassuringly back at her. She glanced at her bracelet watch as she stepped into the hallway from her room. Forest would be arriving at any minute.

"Another date with that Granger guy?" her father's not-very-interested voice asked.

"Yes, the symphony orchestra is giving a concert tonight," she said, smiling.

"I don't think he's going to pay much attention," Vance Wakefield commented, his gaze running over the pale, utterly feminine chiffon of her gown.

"That's the idea, Daddy," Erica replied, widening her violet eyes mischievously.

He laughed and walked into his study. Her mouth tightened, knowing that as he shut the door, her father also shut out his thoughts of her. Not to be mean, but simply because there was no reason for him to worry about her.

The doorbell chimed and Erica pushed her self-pity aside. She intended to enjoy herself tonight. Tilting her head at a happy angle, she opened the front door.

"You!" she breathed in astonishment.

Rafael just stood there and studied her. Black sweater, black jacket—the picture of cool.

"Yes, it's me." He favored her with a smile that was hard to read. "Aren't you going to invite me in?"

Her fingers tightened on the edge of the door, but she didn't step aside to admit him. In fact, she was effectively paralyzed by surprise.

"What are you doing here?" Her demand came out in an anxious whisper.

"You are going out this evening?"

It was a rhetorical question that required no response but she gave it anyway. "Yes, I'm going to a concert," she murmured self-consciously, glancing behind him in anticipation of Forest's arrival. "You—you haven't answered my question. What are you doing here?"

His black eyes seemed to mock her persistence. "Your week has passed," Rafael stated.

"I still have tonight," Erica whispered desperately, nervousness tightening her throat. Her eyes searched his, looking for some indication that he wasn't going to hold her to that ridiculous stipulation. "Is that why you're here? For my answer?"

"I am here to see your father," he replied in a more easy-going tone. "There is something I wish to discuss with him."

"So you came to tell him a-about us." Panic made her stutter a little.

"Should I?" he parried, the blackness of his gaze piercing her hope.

A car door slammed and Erica saw Forest walking swiftly over the flagstone path to the door. Rafael glanced at the approaching man, then brought his gaze to her face. He seemed amused by her dilemma.

"You wouldn't tell my dad, would you?" she asked in a

whisper. He stared at her and smiled. "Please, Rafael, don't!"

She hated the ironic gleam in his eyes. But all he said was, "I will await your decision, Erica."

With Forest only a few steps away, she was forced to open the door and admit both of them. Rafael's statement should have reassured her, but it didn't. Forest greeted him casually enough, but there was suspicion in his eyes all the same.

"I'll let Daddy know you're here, *Señor* Torres," Erica mumbled, turning awkwardly away from him.

Her father showed no surprise when she announced from his study door that Rafael was here to see him. Deliberately, she didn't look at Rafael's face as he walked past her into the study and shut the door behind him.

"What does he want?" Forest asked, taking her arm a little possessively.

Erica gave a nervous glance at the closed study door. "To talk business with Daddy, I guess." She hoped Forest believed that. She certainly didn't.

There was only one subject that Rafael and Vance Wakefield could possibly have to discuss and that was her. Rafael hadn't exactly said that he wouldn't tell all, but the implication had been there that he would keep silent. Yet she didn't trust him.

The evening was ruined from the get-go. Halfway through the performance, Erica knew that she had to return home. At this very moment, Rafael might be relating the entire sordid tale to her father. The complete lack of color in her face and the tightly drawn lines of strain around her mouth convinced Forest more than her words that she wasn't feeling well. His solicitous concern made her feel guilty, but not so guilty that she didn't take advantage of it.

With the lingering gentleness of Forest's goodnight

kiss still on her lips, Erica rapped lightly on the study door and entered. Angry sparks flashed in her eyes when she saw Rafael sitting in a chair opposite her father, lordly grace in every line of his body. She'd seen his car parked in the driveway, of course, and knew he hadn't left, but she feigned surprise at seeing Rafael still there.

"Is the concert over already?" Her father frowned as he glanced at the heavy gold watch on his wrist.

"No. Forest got a phone call at intermission that required his immediate attention," Erica lied. "I decided to come home rather than sit through the concert alone."

"A business call at this hour?" Vance questioned.

"You know how that goes, Daddy." She shrugged, trying to read the pensive look in her father's eyes to figure out what he and Rafael had been discussing. "I've gotten used to it."

"What a pity," Rafael drawled, "to become accustomed to such a thing."

His sardonic expression was extremely annoying and Erica knew he had guessed why she'd returned. He wasn't at all surprised by her sudden arrival. She had a feeling that he'd anticipated it.

"I've learned to live with it, *señor*," she said softly, putting a faint sarcastic emphasis on the last word.

He only raised one jet-black eyebrow. Then Rafael turned away from her. "It is getting late, *Señor* Wakefield, and I have taken up too much of your time."

"Not at all, not at all." Her father rose to his feet when Rafael did, waving aside the formally worded apology. "I—"—he cast an oblique glance at Erica—"enjoyed our discussion."

"I'll see Don Rafael to the door, Daddy," she offered quickly as her father started around his desk.

The absent-minded thoughtfulness in his blue eyes scared her a little. The discussion that had taken place before her arrival had to have been about her or her father wouldn't be looking at her so strangely.

"Yes, you do that, Erica," he agreed and quickly wished Rafael a good night.

Erica didn't trust herself to look at Rafael until the study door closed in back of them. Then she whirled around, the delicate chiffon of her gown billowing around her.

"What did you tell him?" she hissed angrily.

"What do you think I told him?" Rafael countered, his sensual gaze caressing her face.

Erica ignored his undeniable attractiveness. "You told him about us, didn't you?" She hated his air of detachment. Her anger didn't ruffle him in the least.

"I said I would await your decision," he reminded her coolly.

"I *know* what you said," she whispered. "But I didn't believe you then and I don't now!"

"Do not push me, Erica." The warning was reinforced in the clenched line of his lean jaw.

"I want to know what you told him," she repeated. "Did you say anything that would make me look bad?"

His gaze narrowed on her upturned face. "You are not a little girl, Erica. So don't talk like one."

She sputtered with indignation, ready to slap him. Hard.

Rafael kept on talking. "Your father has his own rigid code that he lives by and expects others to live by. I doubt that anyone could influence him, least of all a stranger."

"Never mind that," Erica snapped. "Do you honestly expect me to believe that you said nothing about us?"

He took her by the shoulders, gently enough, but she sensed the remarkable strength he was controlling. Still, the icy look in his eyes took her breath away.

"Are you questioning my integrity, Erica? While your lips are still warm from another man's kisses."

How had he known that? She guessed men weren't as

stupid as they pretended to be most of the time. "So what," she gasped, unable to free herself from his hold.

He pulled her against his chest and it felt . . . good. The muscular hardness of his body drained what little strength she possessed.

"Just pointing out the difference between what you say and what you do," he countered smoothly.

"I don't need you to teach me that," she said, "or anything else."

"No? Then what do you need, Erica? Or should I say, what do you want?"

"You don't have a right to ask me questions like that!" She still couldn't get free but she had to admit, if only to herself, that she didn't entirely want to.

"Let me guess. You crave the gentle touch of a lover. But which one?"

"Shut up, Rafael," she said with heat.

He didn't. "That man—did you wish for him and not me?"

The bold question brought tears to her eyes, crystal drops that shimmered, threatening to fall. She dashed them away.

Rafael released her. "You will have to decide. And I will have to take my chances."

"You don't have a chance," she said, shaking. "Not a single one—oh!"

His mouth claimed hers with sensual speed as his hands lightly caressed her upper arms. His stroking fingers might as well have been iron bands that kept her in place. She was incapable of resistance. He kissed her passionately, thoroughly, making her forget who she was and where they were for several long, delirious moments. When he let her go for the second time, her emotions were as bruised as her swollen lips.

He stepped back and once again became the image of masculine reserve.

"I will pick you up tomorrow afternoon at two," he told her. "I will expect your answer then."

"Go to hell!" Erica whispered, pressing the back of her hand to her throbbing mouth.

A cynical smile curved his lips. "With you, maybe I am condemned to that."

"Then why make demands on me?" she protested.

"Because you are my wife," Rafael said simply and turned away.

"Oh, I see," she said. "That makes perfect sense. I'm just supposed to obey, right? Well, I'm not going to. Listen, Rafael, north of the border, you don't have a legal right to be that macho."

He suppressed a snort of amusement, which puzzled her, and left without another word. Erica hovered for uncertain moments in the hallway, her senses recovering from the erotic experience of his touch. Then the door to her father's study opened and she spun around to gaze blankly at her father.

"He's gone. What did he want, anyway?" she asked, striving for an air of uninterested curiosity.

Her dad still had that thoughtful look on his face. "He came to see me about some property I own. At least, he said that was why he had come. But he asked for my permission to see you, Erica."

"He did?" she breathed. Antagonism surfaced for a brief moment. How could Rafael be so certain that she would ultimately agree to be his wife for real and forever? "What was your answer?"

"I told him—well—" He hesitated, wryly shaking his head. "My first instinct was to laugh until I realized he was actually serious. Then I told him that you were seeing Forest Granger, but I did say that he could see you if you wanted to see him. The whole thing seemed a little silly to me, but he seemed serious. Or maybe the word is gallant."

"Gallant? How fabulously old-fashioned."

"Is that bad?" her father asked. "I mean, in the age of hookups and guys who just aren't that into you or whatever the phrase is, wouldn't women want men who mean what they say?"

"I can't speak for every female on the planet, Daddy."

"No. Of course not. I was just thinking aloud."

She took a deep breath. "Anyway, he asked me out for tomorrow."

"Oh." Her father studied her for a long moment. Erica hoped she didn't look too disheveled from Rafael's kiss. "Did you accept?"

"Yes," she said, smoothing her hair. She couldn't very well tell her father that the invitation had been something like an ultimatum.

"How serious are you about Granger?" It was the first time in her memory that he had ever asked such a pointed question. Usually her father would have someone else do it for him and relay the answer.

"I'm not sure, Daddy," Erica hedged.

"You know what? I sometimes forget I'm your father," he said absently. The comment didn't surprise her, although it wasn't meant to be unkind. "I'm always too busy, aren't I?"

"No, not really. Anyway, I understand how it is. I'm a big girl now." She smiled wistfully, wishing they were close enough, emotionally speaking, that she could go into his arms and be hugged.

"Forest is independent and ambitious. He isn't intimidated by me either," Vance mused. "His career, his business, are truly important to him—that's unavoidable for a young man."

"Well, that's true for just about everybody these days,"

she pointed out. "Men and women both." There were times when her father's view of the world seemed so hopelessly out of date that it was no use correcting him.

"Family ought to come first sometimes," he argued. "The all-American business model doesn't allow for that. I can't help thinking about what we miss out on. People from other countries do things differently."

A deeper understanding came to her. "Are you referring to Don Rafael?"

"Not specifically, no," her father replied casually. "Although I'd guess that family is a priority with him."

Really. Erica thought bitterly that family and tradition were probably so important to Rafael that he intended to try and keep her as his wife whether she loved him or not. Even though he'd said that life with her would be hell for him.

"Maybe you should think about how much a family means to you before you make any commitment to Forest," her father suggested, running a hand through his thick mane.

Slow anger burned within her. "Did Ra—did Don Rafael make that suggestion?"

"Of course not!" His reply was plainly astonished. "Whatever made you think that?"

She shifted self-consciously under his piercing gaze. "You don't normally talk this way."

"No?" Once again the withdrawn look set in as his mind began to wander. "No, I suppose not. Good night, Erica."

He was already walking into his study and the door was swinging shut when she added her good night. She doubted that he'd heard her. That moment of concern about her future disappeared as rapidly and unexpectedly as it had come.

* * *

The hot October sun blazed down with the heat of a thousand hells. Erica gritted her teeth as she accepted the hand Rafael extended to her as she stepped out of the air-conditioned coolness of his car. She had barely said five words to him since he had picked her up at the house promptly at two o'clock. The amused look on his face indicated that her freeze-out tactics hadn't worked. She'd displayed no interest in their destination and he deliberately hadn't enlightened her.

Defiantly tossing back her long hair, Erica glanced around the downtown section of San Antonio. The Tower of the Americas loomed benevolently above them, firmly planted in the Hemisfair Plaza. Maybe he was going to take her to the top and throw her off, she thought crossly, thus removing the obstacle of their marriage.

But it wasn't to the tower or the plaza that Rafael led her. Instead he guided her to one of the many sets of stairs leading from the street level of San Antonio down some twenty feet to the picturesque stone paths along the river banks. He strolled with her by the quaint shops, open-air cafés and nightclubs in the commercial area of the Riverwalk, indifferent to Erica's annoyance.

The cool serenity of the river, the lush tropical foliage of the gardens, and the old trees that shielded the walk from the direct rays of the burning sun soon had an effect on Erica. She had never been able to remain unmoved by the serenity and beauty of this unique place.

Rafael paused to light a thin cheroot, and she wrinkled her nose. He took it out of his mouth. "I won't if you don't like it."

Reluctant to concede anything to him, she shook her head. "It's all right. So long as we're by the river." The cigar must have been an expensive one, because its aromatic smell was actually pleasant.

He put it back in his mouth, puffing gently as his aristocratic fingers hooked themselves in the pockets of his finely tailored trousers as he resumed his leisurely pace.

"It is rare that a man's dreams come true," he said idly, as if voicing his thoughts aloud. For a second Erica thought he was speaking personally and her relaxed expression hardened. "To think it was once proposed to cover this river with concrete and turn it into a sewer."

"Richard Hugman was a visionary architect," she agreed.

"The conservationists who supported him knew what they were doing."

Erica smiled, wondering if the architect had ever dreamed that so many people from all over the world would come to enjoy the graceful beauty of the arched footbridges over the river and the luxuriant greenery everywhere. Everywhere was natural beauty, enhanced but never overpowered by man's touch.

Her glance at Rafael was appraising. "I hadn't realized you were familiar with San Antonio and its history."

"You have forgotten, Erica," he smiled at her absently, "that I am a historian. And I think you have forgotten that most of the Southwest was once ruled by Spain, then by Mexico."

"Does it bother you to be here in the city that boasts the Shrine of Texas Liberty? Otherwise known as the Alamo." A gleam of battle came into her eyes.

He looked at her like someone who couldn't be bothered with such a childish challenge. "I think you are referring to the thirteen-day siege of the Alamo by the dictator General Santa Anna. Am I wrong?"

"No. And don't forget the 187 men who died there to be free," Erica tossed back.

"Are you claiming an exclusive right on that?" he asked lazily. "Have you heard the bugle call 'Deguello,' the song of no quarter? It was not only Americans who defended the Alamo to the death, but Mexicans as well. One of your more famous Texas patriots was Jose Antonio Navarro, who signed the Texas Declaration of Independence. Yet you prefer to look on me as Santa Anna, I think."

The smoke from the cheroot blew her way and she waved it away angrily. "If the boot fits, Rafael, it fits. You don't have to fight me," she said. "Just let me be free."

"That is not something I would do willingly." His voice was tinged with resignation. "I also fight for what I believe in."

Her hand lifted the heavy weight of her hair and massaged the tense muscles at the back of her neck. She had known all along that he wasn't likely to acquiesce and do things her way. Not just like that. Whatever. She had to try. But if he wanted a fight, he would get one.

He extinguished his cheroot and tossed the butt into a trashcan. "Don't expect me to concur with your low opinion of me, Erica," he was saying, a note of impatience in his voice. "You seem to think I am worse than General Santa Anna himself."

"Not necessarily. And don't go off on tangents."

Too late. He was taking a deep breath, warming to the subject. "It is true that he was ruthlessly cruel to the people of Texas before the rebellion, but there was only one of him."

She wasn't going to give him the satisfaction of saying that he was right about that.

"Look at the missions founded by the Spaniards throughout your country, Erica. So many have endured—"

"Get to the point," she said sweetly but thinly.

"Character is individual, not national."

She blew out a sigh. "I am so sorry we ever got into this. I feel like I'm out on a date with a walking, talking historical marker."

He gave her a wry smile. "Very funny. I like your sense of humor, even when it is directed at me."

"Plenty more where that came from," she said almost cheerfully.

"Is there anything you like about me, Erica?" he asked after a little while as they continued to stroll.

"List your best qualities. I'll pick."

He clasped his hands behind his back. The action made the musculature of his chest stand out underneath his shirt. Well, that was one, she thought desperately.

"I'm a kind person, or so I have been told."

She threw him a look that said she doubted that.

"And intelligent, I suppose."

"If you're so smart," she burst out, "why can't you see that I don't want to be married to you? Better yet, accept it, so we can both move on."

"Ah, Erica. Emotions are very different. 'The heart has its reasons, which reason does not know.'"

"William Shakespeare. Don't tell me," she said.

He nodded, seeming pleased with her. "You too are intelligent, Erica."

She shook her head. "My dad says I don't seem to know that." Thinking of her father made her irritable, overwhelmingly so. "I need a drink."

"Lemonade—?"

"No. A real drink. It isn't too early for margaritas."

An hour later, a half pitcher of frosty lime slush mixed with potent tequila got her and Rafael deep into a conversation that bordered on the surreal.

"You will enjoy being my wife in more than name," he said seductively. "I won't ask for your love in return, but only your loyalty to the vows we took. That will be the only demand I make of you."

Erica laughed without humor. "Is that really a choice?

Sorry, I don't see myself in that wedding picture." Her voice even lacked emotion.

"Is that an answer?"

Immediately her temper blazed. "Don't assume anything, Rafael. I might be your wife out of pure spite. Has that ever occurred to you?"

"I would agree to those terms," he said.

"Are you a glutton for punishment or what?" she asked in disbelief.

"No. But I think I could win you over."

The margaritas were getting to her. She answered too quickly. "Ah . . . maybe so."

A hotly sexual aura seemed to shimmer around the powerful body under his immaculately pressed shirt. His eyes glowed. "Give me a chance."

"Wh-what I need," she began, "is a chance to prove that I don't need you. And even though tequila and logic don't mix, I think that makes sense." She finished the dangerously refreshing slush in her glass. "Besides, I sort of like making my dad angry. Worth it just for that." She covered a small burp with her hand. "Maybe."

"What is worth it?" he asked carefully.

Dimly, Erica reminded herself that he, pound for pound, could out-drink, out-argue, and out-wrestle her into bed again. Where she would have no defense whatsoever against his incredible physical magnetism.

"Marrying you," she said a little thickly. "Again. For real. Let's just do whatever it is you've been trying to talk me into all day—that's what's worth it. Just so long as you aren't looking for true love from me."

He seemed uneasy during her impassioned speech. When she drew a breath to continue, he raised a hand to silence her.

"I am aware of your feelings on that subject, so there is no need to keep repeating these things. But I think you should inform your father of the precise nature of our relationship."

"Why? You talked to him about it already." She eyed him, feeling woozy.

"We didn't get into the details."

"Hope not. And you shouldn't. Vance Wakefield hates messy situations."

Rafael straightened and gave her a sad look. "Then maybe he will agree that there is no need to maintain the pretense of starry-eyed romance when he does know."

"There's no telling what he'll think." She put her purse on the table and took out a compact and lipstick, touching up a face that looked a little blurry in the tiny mirror. "Or do. Can we get out of here?"

"Have we come to an agreement?"

His clipped question brought her abruptly back to reality somehow. She felt herself pale as she put away the makeup. "I think so. You and I are . . . what we are. We can make up the rules as we go along."

"You really do not want to—"

"I didn't say that," she snapped. Then, more slowly, she said, "It's Forest, I guess. How do I tell him that I actually am married when he wants to marry me?"

"Just do it."

She shook her head almost imperceptibly. "I wish it was that easy."

"Hmm." He sat back, folding his arms over his chest. A waiter came over from the bar and removed their empty glasses and the margarita pitcher. "So, do you prefer to elope with me and stay away until the furor subsides, rather than face the awkward moment when you reject Forest for me?"

Erica looked into his eyes, wondering at his easy perception of her innermost thoughts. Some of her thoughts, anyway. Her mind was so muddled by having heavy-duty drinks on a warm afternoon, she scarcely knew what she'd said. *Herewith*, she thought miserably, *I absolve my bad self of all responsibility until I am sober.*

As much as she disliked Rafael, she had to admit that the pull of his dark attraction was stronger than ever. That strikingly handsome face and superb body were too much to resist.

"I'm not a very good liar." She paused. It occurred to her that she was getting better at it by the minute, what with all this practice, and that made her feel ashamed. "I doubt that Forest will believe me if I tell him I'm in love with you and not him."

"When we are remarried, he will have no choice but to accept it," Rafael stated. "He has asked you to marry him, hasn't he?"

"How did you know?" Erica frowned, aware she had never mentioned that, margaritas or no margaritas.

"Your attorney Jules Blackwell told me, but I would have guessed it anyway. Had Forest wanted to just fool around, as he probably calls it, and not get married, you wouldn't have been so quick to demand a divorce from me." He studied the check that the waiter brought, added a generous tip, took a credit card out of his wallet and put it into the folder.

"Forest thinks I love him. I told him so." Oh dear. That was the margaritas talking. Her avowal of feelings for good old Forest didn't sound very convincing or compelling, if he only thought she loved him.

Rafael seemed to have picked up on that. "People fall out of love." He shrugged dismissively. "Sometimes feelings are just physical."

Trust you to come up with an answer like that, Erica thought dejectedly as she turned away from his unnervingly penetrating regard. At the same moment she counted herself lucky for recognizing that she only found

Rafael sexually attractive and had not foolishly believed herself to be in love with him. A heavy sigh vibrated her body. Now she wished she had been blind to the difference, because she was about to tempt fate and turn her life upside down over him, still fighting a losing battle with her indifferent father.

She was stuck in an emotional rut. And hopelessly confused. Erica looked at Rafael from under her lashes. Wow, he was beautiful in a totally male way. She wanted that. She could manage that. It was love which was dangerous. Was it ever all right to just want *that* and not all the rest?

Not if you're engaged to someone your father likes, she told herself. Get real, she added, even though she didn't know how the phrase actually applied to her or where to begin. She was so rattled by having Rafael back in her life that her brain was going to take a while to recover.

"Can we get out of here?"

He put his hands on the table in a gesture of finality and pushed himself up. "Yes, of course."

"Unless you want to gloat a little longer over talking me into something I'm not sure I want to do."

He scowled as they walked out, ignoring the ill-concealed smirk of the hostess who overheard the exchange as she leaned over a seating diagram on the counter. "I didn't talk you into anything, Erica."

"Okay, then I talked myself into it." The sun outside dazzled her eyes painfully and her head began to ache. Precisely what she had said evaporated from her memory.

"I think you enjoy provoking me." A muscle twitched in his jaw and it was clear that his temper wasn't fully under control despite the evenness of his voice. "Come, I will take you back to your home."

The brooding silence during the return trip had Erica shifting uncomfortably in her seat. She tried unsuccessfully

to block him out of her thoughts, to ignore him as completely as he was ignoring her, but his dark good looks and
animal attractiveness made that impossible. Even in broad
daylight, he was as sleek and elegant as a jungle cat, and
like a jungle cat there was a strain of wildness that civilization could never entirely erase.

Until a court dissolved the marriage, this man *was* her
husband. And, in a couple of hours in his company, she
had just committed herself to new variations on the
theme of said marriage to him, even saying that they
could make up the rules as they went along.

What had she been thinking? More like what had she
been drinking, she thought, regretting the margaritas.

A sense of unease took over at the thought of explor-
ing too many possibilities with Rafael. True love was un-
charted territory and she didn't want to go there, no
matter how good-looking he was.

When the car stopped, it took Erica a full second to
realize that they were in the driveway of her home. She
blushed as she accepted his hand to help her out of
the car. It bothered her a lot to realize how susceptible
she was to his touch. Instead of starting toward the
house, he tightened his hand on hers to keep her beside
the car. Erica glanced at him curiously.

"Forest is coming—no, don't turn around. He's driving
in now."

"Just my luck," she groaned.

"More like fate, I think." He looked down at her possessively. "All you have to do is kiss me, Erica. He can inter-
pret it however he likes."

She breathed in sharply, wanting to resist but knowing
that she doubted she could convince Forest in words
that it was Rafael she preferred. She looked pleadingly
at Rafael, wishing he was not such a Prince Charming.
Where was an ogre when you really needed one?

"Decide quickly, Erica," he murmured.

Slowly she moved nearer to him, drawn more by the seductive sound of his voice than a desire to demonstrate her change of heart to Forest. Her hands rested on Rafael's chest and picked up the steady beat of his heart as she tilted her head to receive his kiss. The gentle insistence of his kiss disarmed her and a pleasant warmth relaxed her tense muscles. A hunger that she had long denied parted her lips so that she was pliant to his touch.

The slam of the car door was unexpected. She sprang guiltily away from Rafael, forgetting completely that the scene had been staged for Forest's benefit. She turned red at her shameful lapse, hating that strange power that Rafael had over her physically.

"I couldn't believe it when Lawrence told me you were out with him!" Forest muttered hoarsely. His face was pale with rage.

The fierce pain in her heart throttled any words of denial she wanted to say as she gazed hopelessly at him. How could she have been so mean?

"Erica is free to see whoever she wants to see. There is no understanding between you two, is there?" Rafael asked blandly.

"I was stupid enough to think so, yeah," Forest growled, flicking a furious look at Erica. "Guess you just gave me your real answer, Erica. Hell, I never realized you were so cold-blooded. That must have been how you got tagged as an ice maiden."

When that last contemptuous sneer had been delivered, Forest pivoted and stalked back to his car. Her hand raised in a feeble attempt to call him back and explain.

"Forest . . ." Her voice shook as she took a step toward his retreating form.

But Rafael reached out and stopped her. "Let him go,

Erica," he said firmly. "Don't prolong his agony. Just let him go."

Unshed tears glimmered in her eyes, but the fiery light that blazed in the violet-blue depths showed her resentment.

"You told me to be merciful," she jeered, "when there isn't any mercy in your heart!"

"You're wrong," Rafael said. "Although I spoke of it for Forest, I meant it for you. I don't want you to imagine a love you will never have with him. Make a clean break and do it quickly. I will never mention him again if that is what you prefer—"

"How can you talk like that?" Erica cried, letting go of his hand.

"Like what?"

"As if you and I are going to be together. Forever."

"We are married, *mi esposa*. It is not as if we had never known each other in the biblical sense." A lazy, sensual smile emphasized his meaning. "And I know that Forest has never held you in his arms in the middle of the night, or he would know that there is no ice in your veins— eh, *querida*?"

Her cheeks were scorched by the memory of her lack of self-control. She refused to meet his gaze and raced away from him to the house, wondering how many times in the future she would flee from him when she was left with no weapons to attack him with.

Chapter 8

There were lots of eyebrows raised over Erica's sudden break with Forest and plenty of talk when she was seen repeatedly in Rafael's company over the next two weeks.

Their evenings together were always spent attending a concert, theater production, or a similar event where there wasn't much need for small talk between them. The distraction of having something to occupy her attention was welcome, although she was never able to completely ignore Rafael. He was much too masculine, and charming when he chose to be, for any woman to ignore. But Erica still kept her distance.

All of her friends and acquaintances thought she was incredibly lucky to have a man as hot as Rafael paying so much attention to her. When her replies were less than enthusiastic, they laughed them off as a sign that she wasn't sure she could hold him. Considering the number of her female friends who wandered over during intermissions or when they met in town on the pretext of saying hello to her, she almost marveled at Rafael's seeming indifference to them.

The tinkling of the bell on the shop door announced the arrival of another customer. Donna was in the back room, freshening up after her lunch break. Managing a welcome smile, Erica stopped straightening the rack of new dresses to turn and greet the person who'd just walked in. Only it wasn't a customer. It was Rafael.

His dark glance slid past her startled expression to the back of the boutique, and the wide smile he gave her indicated that Donna must have stepped into view. Erica was always surprised at how that smile of his could take her breath away, even when it had nothing to do with her.

There was only a slight hint of the confusion he also caused in her when she greeted him. "Rafael—um, hi. I didn't expect to see you today."

"It is often the unexpected that brings the most pleasure."

Don't flatter yourself, she wanted to reply, but the caressing tone of his voice was too soothing to say something like that.

"I found myself with the afternoon free and only one person I wanted to spend it with."

His black eyes were regarding her with such intensity that Erica almost melted, until she remembered that Donna was listening. "I hope you mean me," she answered in a half-hearted tease.

His brows drew together in a quizzical frown. "Do you not understand that I have eyes only for you?" he asked, so softly that Erica doubted Donna had heard him.

"I think you will have to convince me of that," she whispered.

"Erica." The impatient way he said her name quickly changed, replaced by a low, cajoling tone. "First I will take you to lunch. You haven't eaten, have you?" At the negative shake of her head, Rafael continued, "Then I have something I want to show you."

The last statement astounded her. Their previous dates had been among crowds of people who served as emotional insulation, so to speak. Erica balked visibly at the prospect of being alone with him.

"Can we do this some other time?" she blurted out. "My lunch break today isn't very long and I promised—"

"We're never busy on Tuesday," Donna spoke up. "I'm sure I can manage by myself for a few hours, Erica."

Erica drew in her breath to keep her temper under control. Rafael didn't make it any easier by looking at her with open amusement.

"If that's settled," he said at last, "we can go."

She shot him an exasperated look. "I have to get my bag. Give me a minute."

A few minutes later they were walking out of the boutique. Donna smiled a good-bye with the enthusiasm of someone who'd done a good deed.

Erica had become accustomed to Rafael's habit of putting a hand at the small of her back when they walked, but today she took exception to it.

"There isn't anyone watching us," she told him, "so there's no need for you to touch me."

"What is it that's made you angry? I do not believe it is that." He raised his dark eyebrows.

"Maybe I'm just now getting in touch with my anger, while we're talking about touch," Erica retorted, looking defiantly in his direction. "And let's not forget good old resentment."

"That too?" His inquiry was annoyingly courteous.

"Hell yes. I feel more and more like I got manipulated into this agreement."

They had reached a staircase leading from the Riverwalk to street level. Erica was on the first step when Rafael made her turn around to face him. The one-step advantage brought her eyes level with the ebony blackness of his.

"I wonder what it is you resent so much. The agreement, such as it is? Or that you consented to it?" Something in his expression kept her close when what she wanted to do was pull away.

She was steamed and found it difficult to speak clearly. "Don't split hairs, Rafael. All of it is wrong." She was much too conscious of how very near those masculine lips were.

"If you say so." He shrugged, laughing silently at her refusal to differentiate. "Why do you hold yourself so rigidly, Erica?"

"I don't see any need to keep up a big show of devotion in private, do you?"

He looked annoyed. "How else will you learn to be natural with me?"

"I could never react naturally to you," she declared.

An exasperated sigh came from him when he moved to the side. She could run away right now if she wanted to, but . . . she didn't want to. They were back to square one.

"Let us go and eat before my appetite is ruined by your stubbornness," he was saying.

What little appetite Erica had was gone. Rafael didn't eat much either, as electric currents of tension charged the air between them.

"I'd like to go back to the boutique now," Erica said the minute they were outside the small restaurant.

"This side trip will take only a few moments of your precious time," he said.

Erica discovered that his edgy response had the power to hurt. There was a sickish feeling in the pit of her stomach that she didn't quite understand.

"Where are we going?" she asked hesitantly as he opened the car door for her.

He didn't bother to reply until he was seated behind the wheel and had maneuvered the car into traffic. Even then his response was indifferent, as if he regretted insisting on this trip.

"A friend of mine bought a house here in San Antonio. It needs a great deal of repair." He shot her a brief glance. "Since neither my friend nor his wife is able to be here right now, he asked if I knew of anyone—any woman who had good taste—who would look at the house from a woman's point of view and recommend improvements."

"That's why you're taking me to see it," Erica murmured.

"What did you think?" Rafael asked softly. "That perhaps I was luring you out so I could seduce you all over again?"

"I don't know what you had in mind," she said primly. "But since you are my husband, I don't think it would actually count as a seduction."

"Give me a chance," he said.

"You keep saying that."

It seemed to her that he wasn't exactly teasing. "No. There's Forest and—and a few other things that have to be resolved."

"That's a vague answer."

"It'll have to do, Rafael." She was a little afraid he might try to prove his point and seduce her for all he was worth, and she wasn't entirely sure she would say no.

They had arrived, and she was thankful. The large Mediterranean-style house was bustling with activity. Three gardeners were clearing brush, and shaping the abundant foliage around the front of the house. Towering oaks arched gracefully over the cream yellow façade, clearing the terra cotta tile roof. Other workmen were repairing the loosened mortar of the courtyard walls and replacing broken roof tiles.

Rafael led her through an ornate wrought-iron gate into a courtyard with overgrown walkways and a gazebo choked with vines. From there they went into the house, where painters covered the walls with a fresh coat of oyster white in some rooms and stripped the old varnish from the woodwork in others.

In spite of the chaos of renovation, Erica was drawn to the proud character of the old house. The enormous living room with its high ceiling and mammoth fireplace captured her imagination. It was easy to imagine it furnished with a touch of grandeur: she thought heavy carved sofas and tables of Spanish design would be just right.

They moved on. The breakfast area was surrounded by glass, the individual panes stacked from floor to ceiling.

"So. Any thoughts on the décor?" Rafael asked her opinion for the first time since the tour had begun.

"I wouldn't change a thing." She did picture the glassed-in breakfast area filled with greenhouse plants to enhance the outdoor effect. "Not if you mean knocking out walls and altering the basic layout," she hastened to add.

"Then you like it?"

"Yes." She looked at him, making no attempt to hide her radiant smile. "Your friend is very lucky. This house is fabulous."

"Hmm." He acknowledged her statement with a nod. "Well, then. I have to confess that I told a small lie." Rafael turned his enigmatic gaze to the garden beyond the stacked windows. "My friend does not own this house. It belongs to me—to us."

Erica stiffened indignantly. "Nice trick. Why did you do that? Lie, I mean."

He lifted his head high so that he was looking down at her. "I am sure that if I had told you that it was ours, you never would have come with me."

She shifted uncomfortably away from his intent gaze, unwilling to admit there might be some truth to his observation.

"You live in Mexico. Why did you buy this?" she asked, her tone cold.

He muttered something under his breath, then moved her around to face him. "How can you ask that?" he said impatiently. "Yes, Mexico is my home just as Texas is yours. I thought it might please you to have a home in San Antonio so that we . . ." He didn't finish the sentence.

"What? Just tell me, okay?"

"If you decide in my favor, you will want a home here. Near your friends and family."

Erica took a deep breath, his thoughtfulness touching her even though she would be wise to reject it. He was jumping the gun, to say the least. His willingness to throw money around to make his point was more than a little alarming—he seemed to have that in common with her dear old dad.

But she wasn't going to be bribed to make up her mind and she wasn't ready to believe that he was solely concerned with *her* happiness. If she deluded herself to that extent, she'd be lost. Rafael's basic motivation was getting his own way, and she realized that he was expert at it.

But for a moment she had actually believed that he'd been making a grand gesture to please her.

"Rafael, the idea of sharing any home with you is really out there. I'm not going to fall at your feet or even say thank you."

His fingers tightened on her shoulders for only a second before he let her go. Erica's heart was beating much too fast when he did. But she'd meant every word she said.

That episode, although the house was never mentioned again, made a definite change in their relationship. They still went out several evenings a week. She'd decided that she couldn't say no to everything, not when she hadn't made up her mind once and for all.

Any onlooker would have deemed Rafael to be a gentleman at all times, but only Erica knew that the heat between them had definitely cooled. So what. It was easier to think when his eyes weren't so warm and his touch so seductive.

But whenever she returned from one of their dates, she was haunted by the specter of those first weeks. Maybe it was just plain pique or even her vanity that made her smiles and looks convey an undertone of intimacy, as if she wanted a similar response from Rafael. But her attempts to flirt with him were checkmated by chilly courtesy.

She was beginning to think that there was nothing between them except a bitter tomorrow with no promise of any sweetness.

The evening before, one of Erica's friends, Mary Ann Silver, had spent a little too much time talking to Rafael about the exhibit he was supervising at the Mexican Cultural Institute.

Although his hand had been resting possessively on the back of her waist, Rafael hadn't addressed a single remark to Erica. When Erica's patience had been stretched to the breaking point, Mary Ann had glanced at her with a superior smile.

"Have you seen the exhibit, Erica?"

Rafael's smile was aimed in her general direction as he replied before Erica had a chance. "No, I'm taking her on a personally conducted tour tomorrow afternoon."

Erica didn't confirm or deny it, knowing the thought hadn't occurred to him until that very second. But he'd somehow managed to convey that he was eager for Erica to learn about his other passion in life.

Besides romancing her.

A gentle breeze stirred Erica's hair as she and Rafael

walked by the Aztec-style sculptures of fearsome creatures that marked the entrance and exit of the Mexican Plaza on the Hemisfair grounds. Exhaling softly, Erica managed to conceal her dispirited sigh. The exhibit could have been interesting, but Rafael's impersonal tour had taken away the fascination. Wistfully, she remembered the tour of Acapulco he'd given her. Now that had been informative and entertaining.

"Where are we going now?" Erica asked as she repressed another sigh.

"Where would you like to go?" Rafael said blandly.

"Oh, it doesn't matter." Annoyed, she increased her pace so that she was a little ahead of him.

If she'd hoped he would catch up with her or reach out to slow her down, Erica was disappointed. Resolutely, she refused to slow her steps, needing to show him that his indifference didn't impress her.

In the small square ahead there was a bustle of activity. Pretending a curiosity that she didn't really feel, she headed toward it. The defiant way she tossed her hair indicated that Rafael could follow if he chose.

Then a smile shattered the strained lines around her mouth. She turned to Rafael almost eagerly as she exclaimed, "Look! They're going to have an armadillo race!"

As she reached the fringes of the group, he did catch up. But she was distracted by the excitement and happy laughter that surrounded her. In the center of a cleared circle was the starting point of the race. The owner-handlers of the armadillos were just entering the circle, carrying the funny little animals with their tiny ears and thin faces and long, bony-plated tails.

"I missed the annual spring race," Erica commented as she glanced back at Rafael. "It's quite an event. One year they had over twenty-five thousand people."

The handlers were kneeling down on the pavement,

each holding the tail of his armadillo with one hand and cupping the hard breastplate with the other.

"Which one do you think will win?" She was too delighted by the impromptu event to notice Rafael's reaction. "I pick the one on the right side. He's rarin' to go!"

"I'll pick the quiet one next to yours," Rafael said in an indulgent tone. "He is wise not to waste his energies so soon."

"He's probably too spooked to move," Erica warned with an impish glance at him. "Mine will beat him easily."

A half smile of doubt was on his lips when the order was given to release the critters. Erica's armadillo scampered immediately away, only to stop within a few feet, while Rafael's raced directly into the crowd and won.

Erica was ready to laughingly admit defeat and she found herself jostled against him by the crowd. The sudden contact with his hard and warm length made her gasp with shock. His hands tightened in support, drawing her inches closer. The sensual gleam in his eyes made it difficult for her to breathe.

"I haven't heard you laugh like that for a long time, Erica." Gently, he set her apart from him and began to guide her toward the car. "What happens to the armadillo now?" He seemed to want to change the subject to something less personal.

Erica fought off the magnetic pull that made her want so to be back in his arms. "They make terrible pets, so they're turned loose where they happened to be caught."

Rafael only nodded. Now that the inspired silliness of the little race was over, his aloof air was back.

A strange, cold restlessness had plagued Erica for the past three days, but she couldn't put a finger on exactly what was troubling her. She'd sent Donna home and locked up the boutique over an hour ago. There had been no need for her to go home since she had the evening free.

A purpling dusk had begun to settle over the city, adding to her melancholy mood. Her wandering footsteps were drawing near one of the sidewalk cafés. It was still too early for the night life along the river to begin and the tables were empty. Normally she avoided drinking except at social functions and she especially avoided drinking alone. Yet she found herself sitting down at one of the tables and ordering a glass of wine. Without taking a sip, she was idly fingering the stem of the glass when a familiar voice startled her out of her reverie.

"My, my. If it isn't the one and only Erica Wakefield. Without her Romeo."

Her stomach tightened sickeningly as she turned around. "Forest!" His name came out in an achingly tormented sound.

"I wondered if you would even recognize me." His regular features were etched in sardonic lines.

Erica hadn't seen him since that Sunday afternoon when he'd rejected her, believing that she preferred Rafael to him. Tears welled up when she saw the harshness in his brown eyes, and no warmth at all.

"I thought Don Rafael was occupying all of your time now," Forest said.

She cringed a little at that jab. "Don't, Forest. Please don't." She bent her head, letting her hair swing down to cover the tear that slipped from her lashes.

He cursed. In the next instant, she heard swift footsteps carrying him down the flagstone steps to the Riverwalk. Erica sprang up and raced down the steps after him.

The pain hurt too badly for her to let him go this way, and, selfishly, she needed the reassurance that he cared, that somebody cared. Her carefree days with Forest before Rafael had unexpectedly reappeared in her life seemed so uncomplicated compared to the twisted path of life she was walking on now.

"Forest!" she called out breathlessly.

He hesitated, then turned around. His forehead was creased with anger. "Erica, there really isn't anything more to say. And I damn sure don't need your pity!"

"I miss you," she whispered, standing in suspended motion before him.

For a second, a hungry light flashed in his gaze before his jaw was clenched in a rejecting line. "You can't have both of us. You made your choice."

"But it wasn't the one I wanted to make." Her honest protest came out before she could stop it.

He stared at her in silence, then ran his hand through his thick brown hair. "You aren't making any sense," he growled, and started to turn away again.

Her fingers closed over his arm to stop him. "I know I'm not making any sense," she murmured. "I only wish I could explain it to you."

The touch of her hand seemed to break his self-control. He took her by the shoulders and pulled her into his arms. Roughly his mouth caressed her hair as he crushed her even closer to him.

"I must be insane," he said softly. "When I saw you sitting there, I should've walked away."

"I'm so glad you didn't," Erica sighed. The suffocating embrace was easing the cold ache in her heart.

"Why, Erica, why?" He cradled her face in his large hands and tilted it back so he could really look at her.

Closing her eyes tightly against his beseeching voice, she shook her head slightly, unable to reply for a fraction of a second. Her courage failed when it came to the moment of explaining her decision.

"If I told you," she finally said in a forlorn whisper, "you would only hate me more than you do already."

"I *should* hate you. I actually believed that you loved me as much as I loved you. I thought you were seriously considering marrying me. This last month when everyone has so kindly made sure I knew every place you went with that—that—"

The touch of her fingers silenced the sarcastic flow from his mouth. Forest breathed in deeply to regain control.

"I'd almost convinced myself that I didn't care about you any more," he continued with a rueful sigh, "until today. And then all the hurt came back."

"I thought it had settled down myself." Erica couldn't keep the sadness out of her smile.

The sound of the tourist boat came from the hidden bend of the river and Forest eased his hold. Reluctantly Erica moved away, wishing they were alone so he could hold her so tightly she would forget Rafael. Forest held out his hand to her.

"Shall we walk?" he asked quietly.

"I—I don't think we'd better." Erica shook her head.

He looked away grimly. "A minute ago I was holding you in my arms. Now you're saying that you won't even walk with me? Are you trying to drive me out of my mind?"

"I don't know what I'm doing," she admitted wryly. Her thoughts were just too jumbled to keep straight. She had made an odd sort of commitment to Rafael. Seeing Forest again hadn't changed that—or the circumstances that had prompted her commitment.

"Then explain what's going on," Forest said crisply. "Are you—what's the right word—stuck on Rafael? Is that it? Were you testing me to make sure that our love was the real deal? That would be ironic, wouldn't it?" He laughed bitterly. "I never even gave you a chance to explain on that day. Why didn't you come to me and tell me what a fool I was?"

"Because you weren't a fool," Erica protested.

"What does that mean? You can't be in love with both of us."

"Please, just don't ask questions I can't answer."

"They're simple questions," Forest snapped. "Are you in love with me?"

"Yes, but—" That strange, restless confusion returned, leaving her uncertain and apprehensive.

"Are you in love with Rafael?"

"No!" Her response was more emphatic than she intended and Erica experienced a pang of guilt she didn't quite understand. It was silly, because she couldn't possibly care for Rafael.

"Then what's going on?" he demanded. "If you're not in love with the guy, why are you letting everyone, including me, think that you are?"

"I can't tell you." Her voice was choked with frustration.

"Is your father behind this?"

"Whatever made you think that?" she asked in an astonished tone.

"Because this isn't like you at all, Erica. Is he making you see Rafael because they have a business deal in the works?" His voice had become threateningly soft.

Erica's response was immediate and indignant. "Of course not! How could you accuse my father of such a thing? Daddy is insensitive at times, but never to that extent!"

Forest shook his head, frustrated at his inability to get through the wall she'd erected. "I get the feeling you're afraid of something. You imply that all this is happening against your will. The only one who's ever been able to make you do something that you didn't want to do is your father, but you tell me he has nothing to do with it."

"He doesn't." She took a hasty step backward, regretting the impulse that had prompted her to speak to Forest when he would have willingly left her. She should have made a clean break and not let herself get tangled up in any kind of a relationship with Forest again.

"Erica, let me help you. I love you," he said earnestly. "I don't really know what's going on, but whatever it is we can face it together."

"You don't know what you're saying." She retreated again. "I think I'd better go."

"Don't you think I'd protect you from whatever it is that's got you so scared?" Forest demanded.

"I h-have to work it out by myself," Erica said, knowing how dangerously easy it would be to confide in Forest right now. "I can't involve you."

"I love you," he said quietly. "I am involved."

"Stop—saying that," she breathed. Her hand was raised, as if to ward off the temptation.

"We'll go somewhere else and start over again," he suggested as he saw the slight weakening of her stand. "If—"

"No!"

The second after the strident cry of denial was sounded Erica was running away from him. Her chest heaved with sobs, but fortunately Forest didn't pursue her. As much as she tried to shut them out, his last words kept echoing in her mind.

Maybe she'd misjudged the depth of his love after all. Maybe he wouldn't desert her if she did go through with a divorce from Rafael. Her father would be spectacularly angry, but if Forest was there to support her, she might be able to deal with Vance Wakefield.

Then anger and resentment began to build against Rafael. He'd undoubtedly guessed that Forest was the weak link in his plans. He'd probably congratulated himself for getting Forest out of the way so early. Alone, Erica had been vulnerable to his games and malleable to his proposal. She brushed the tears from her eyes, another impulsive plan taking shape, a plan that could bring her the happiness she had believed was impossible.

In the past her impulsiveness had gotten her into serious trouble—including this crazy marriage to Rafael. This time she would think it over very carefully, and weigh the risks and advantages before leaping in.

Chapter 9

Erica prowled restlessly around her bedroom, casting impatient glances out the window at the snail-slow progress of the rising sun. The oval clock on her dressing table indicated half-past six when, with an angry movement, she grabbed her bag and bolted from the room.

She had been up half the night making her decision. Even now there were frightened butterflies in her stomach. Rafael had been right when he told her that she had spent a lot of her life trying to run from things she didn't like. He'd used that trait to his own advantage just as he'd done everything else. Somehow, he had her half-convinced that staying married to him and seeing what happened next would be the right thing to do.

His reasoning was about to backfire. Even thinking about agreeing to give him a chance again had been another way of running. She hadn't wanted to face her father's anger or deal with his inevitable condemnation. She hadn't wanted to take another chance: that she would lose Forest's love. When it came right down to it, she had only been taking the path that seemed easiest.

Elation swelled inside her as she imagined Rafael's reaction when she finally told him no. She really doubted he would even offer token opposition to a divorce. After all, if his family was so important to him, he wouldn't want to shock them with the details of their on-the-spot marriage.

It upset her to imagine how long it would have taken her to make up her mind if she hadn't seen Forest. Either way, the whole thing might blow up in her face. Her father could, at least figuratively, disown her. Forest might not want anything to do with her once he understood the lie she'd been living, but she would be free.

The traffic was heavy with people on their way to work. It was seven o'clock before Erica had parked her car and hurried into the hotel where Rafael was staying. The light of victory was in her eyes as she started for the elevator doors. Then she changed her mind. She would call Rafael's suite first and let him wonder why she'd come to see him at this hour of the morning. She wanted him to be thinking it over before she got into the explanation. It was going to be a long one.

She picked up the house phone and smiled ironically as she remembered how childishly frightened she had been the first time. Today was going to be a whole lot different.

On the other end the unanswered ring sounded again and again, and it didn't go through to guest voicemail. Erica nibbled impatiently on her lower lip. She hadn't thought of the possibility that Rafael might not be in his room. With a sigh of exasperation, she hung up and dialed the front desk.

"Would you please page Rafael de la Torres?" she asked. "I didn't get any response when I called his room."

"One moment, please," the courteous voice on the other end replied.

Seconds later she heard his name on the public-address system. Interminable minutes later, the operator came back on the line.

"I'm sorry, he doesn't answer the page."

"Would you try his room again then?"

Quickly she gave the number of Rafael's suite. There was a slight pause before the voice responded. "I'm sorry, that suite is not occupied."

Erica frowned. "But I know he's staying here."

There was another request for her to wait and more seconds ticked slowly by. "*Señor* de la Torres checked out a week ago, miss," the operator told her.

"Checked out? That's impossible."

"He left a forwarding address here in the city," Erica was informed.

"May I have it, please?" She rummaged hurriedly through her bag for a pen and scrap of paper.

With the address in her hand, it wasn't until Erica was back in her car that she realized the address the hotel had given her was the one for the house Rafael had bought. He had obviously been living there for the past week and she wondered why on earth he hadn't mentioned it. Of course, she hadn't shown much interest in what he did, so she figured he just hadn't bothered to tell her.

When she parked her car in front of the house, she was surprised at the transformation in it in such a short time. The riotous foliage was still thick around the front of the house, but it was definitely under control. The stone fountain had been scrubbed clean of the dirty moss and snarled vines so that the water sparkled clearly in its basin.

The scrolled iron gate had a new coat of black enamel and the courtyard walls were solid once more. The shady walkways were no longer losing the battle with the shrubs and the view of the freshly painted gazebo wasn't obscured by the previous overgrowth. With an excited quickness to her step, Erica hurried toward the door, eager to see what had been accomplished with the interior of the stately house.

Only when she rang the doorbell did she remember that her reason for coming had nothing to do with the renovation of the house. In fact, it shouldn't concern her at all, since she would never be living here. As footsteps approached the door from the other side, she tilted her head to its haughtiest angle.

This about-to-happen moment was one she was going to enjoy tremendously. Rafael had been far too sure of himself. She was going to get a lot of satisfaction out of putting him in his place.

A cool smile teased her lips as the door swung open and she was surveyed by a pair of dark eyes.

Not his. A servant's. The man wasn't in uniform, though.

"I would like to talk to Don Rafael. Is he in?" she asked, keeping her tone pleasant.

"Yes, he is in, but" the man hesitated—"I don't believe he is available."

"I'm Erica Wakefield. Would you just say that I'd like to see him?"

Her clipped request got no more than an expressive lift of the man's shoulders. He seemed to doubt that her name would impress his boss, but he nodded. "*Sí.* I will tell him."

There was another instant of hesitation when the man thought over letting her wait outside or inviting her into the foyer. He evidently decided that she might be somebody important and politely asked her to come inside.

While Erica waited in the foyer, she listened to the click of the man's heels on the polished tile floors as he carried her message to Rafael. Her view of the other rooms of the house was limited, but she could see it was now sparsely furnished.

The Mediterranean décor was what she would have chosen to match the house's character. She longed for a peek at the glassed-in breakfast nook, but had to squelch her curiosity when she heard the same footsteps coming back.

She stepped forward as the man reappeared. His dark head inclined graciously toward her, then he smiled apologetically.

"I am sorry, *señorita.* Don Rafael is unable to see you. He asks that you return in an hour."

She drew in her breath to control her temper, saving that for Rafael. "I will not return in an hour," she said firmly. "Please tell Don Rafael that I want to see him now."

The man sighed as if his life would be infinitely easier if she went away, but for some reason he decided not to refuse her. Again he left her standing in the foyer and disappeared down the cool hallway. His eyes were lit with amusement when he returned a few minutes later. Furiously Erica wondered what Rafael had said.

"Don Rafael will see you now. This way, please," the man said with only a suggestion of a smile.

The servant walked rapidly the way he had come and Erica had to hasten her steps to keep up. They passed the living room and the library, and Erica couldn't help blinking in surprise when the man started up the staircase to the second floor.

When Rafael had shown her the house, the staircase was under repair and she hadn't been able to go through the rooms above. He had said at the time that there were only bedrooms on the second floor. She realized it was still early, but she hadn't expected that he wouldn't be up. The anger she'd let build up began to recede—it would be unfair, somehow, to yell at someone in pajamas.

As the servant opened one of the doors at the top of the stairs, she nervously clutched the strap of her bag, as if she could swing it like a weapon. She almost wished she'd waited an hour per the polite request, especially when she saw the ornate wooden bed, still unmade. Thank goodness it was empty.

Her heart was thumping unevenly as she went into the room. The French doors to the balcony were ajar and the aroma of freshly brewed coffee hung in the air. The man was leading her right to those doors.

Rafael glanced up as she hovered just inside. "Bring Miss Wakefield a chair and some coffee, Carlos," he instructed calmly.

A large wicker chair was pushed up to the round table where Rafael was seated. Erica was uncomfortably aware of the black robe that Rafael wore. Tied at the waist. Revealing the bareness of his legs. As she walked toward the chair, she caught the scent of soap and shaving gel. Her gaze bounced off the glistening wetness of his black hair as she realized Rafael had just stepped out of the shower.

A plate of *pan dulce,* sweet breakfast bread, sat in the center of the table and a bowl of fresh chunked pineapple was in front of Rafael. Erica shifted uneasily in the cushions of the winged wicker chair. Carlos reappeared with a steaming cup of coffee and set it in front of her.

"Would you like something to eat, Erica?" Rafael asked.

It was difficult to look right at him, even though the robe covered up all the best parts. She spoke to Carlos instead. "No, thank you." Out of the corner of her eye, she saw the nod of dismissal that Rafael gave Carlos.

At the soft click of the closing bedroom door, she felt the penetrating darkness of Rafael's gaze directed at her. He was just too good at getting her off balance. Her chin lifted in challenge—she was determined that wouldn't happen this time.

"Then forgive me, Erica. I haven't had my breakfast and

I am ravenous." There was little apology in his low voice. "Whatever brought you here must be quite serious—it is very early. I hope you don't mind if we postpone it until after my meal."

She exhaled an impatient breath, aware that she was being rude and not caring very much. He didn't seem at all concerned, despite his polite words, about what was on her mind, she thought crossly. He was probably totally sure of himself, as usual.

"I don't mind," she said all the same, thinking silently that he was entitled to his last meal.

But she was the one who was nervous and not Rafael. Making an effort to keep her composure, Erica concentrated on her coffee, trying to ignore the strong white teeth biting into the juicy pineapple. She couldn't deny the naturalness of their intimacy, sitting where she was across the breakfast table with Rafael. The gold medallion he always wore winked at her from the vee of his robe.

Finally the pineapple was gone and Rafael seemed disinclined to have more sweet bread. She watched him refill her cup, then his, from the coffee jug on the table. Leaning back in his chair, he took a sip and savored it before he swallowed.

"Would you care to begin?" he murmured.

Erica glared at him, hating the fact that he was so relaxed while she was perched on the edge of her chair. She folded her hands in her lap.

"I'm not going to accept your second proposal," she replied in a voice that was coldly emphatic.

A dark brow registered amusement instead of surprise. "So you have decided."

"Yes," she declared. "I'm filing for divorce as soon as I can. We might as well get it over with."

"I see," Rafael replied calmly.

He rose from the wicker chair and walked over to the

balcony railing. Through the wrought iron, elaborate
as Spanish lace, the courtyard was visible. The golden
light of the morning sun was just beginning to dispel the
shadows. Erica stared at him in amazement, searching
for any sign of anger, any gesture that would indicate his
reaction.

He glanced over his shoulder. "The courtyard is beautiful again, isn't it?"

Erica pushed herself out of her chair. He was deliberately ignoring her announcement, as if it had come from
a peevish child.

"I know you heard what I said. I guess you're too arrogant to believe it," she fumed.

His gaze moved indolently over her, then returned to
the profusion of green below. "Of course, I believe you.
I don't think you would say what you don't mean." He
shrugged, his manner indicating that the matter wasn't
important to him. "The gardener suggested planting
climbing roses against the wall. What do you think?"

Erica's mouth opened in amazement. She scowled at
him as she crossed the few steps to the iron railing.

"I didn't come here to discuss gardening, Rafael," she
said hotly.

"No?" He just looked at her. "What else, then? Are you
unsure about your decision to file?"

"Not at all," she avowed, lifting her chin defiantly.

He gave an abbreviated wave. "Then what is there
to discuss? You must have another reason to be here
besides that."

A short, confused laugh came from her throat. She
had expected anger, a noisy scene, but really not indifference, a much more difficult thing to combat.

"More than anything else, I came to tell you I was calling your bluff. Your plan isn't going to work. I'm not
going to be manipulated into becoming your wife. Even

though I am," she declared, bewilderedly wondering why she was explaining at all.

"Yes, yes. More or less what you just said, Erica. But you didn't have to come here to announce all that. Why not just let that lawyer do the honors?"

Her hands raised in confusion. "I wanted you to know!"

"Why?" Rafael countered.

"I . . ." His question baffled her and she struggled to answer it. "I suppose I thought it was fair."

He lifted a quizzical brow. "But according to you, I am manipulative. Why should you be fair?"

"I don't know," Erica said angrily. "This isn't making any sense."

"I agree." He smiled. "But I doubt if you have guessed why." He turned slightly. "I would like to know what prompted your decision."

This was firmer ground and Erica looked at him with renewed determination. "I saw Forest last night."

"Ah yes. My arch rival," he said mockingly. "So you discovered that you couldn't live without him."

"No, I discovered that I couldn't live with you!" she retorted. "I don't care how much maneuvering you do. I don't care if Daddy throws me out of the house. And if Forest decides he doesn't want the emotional risk, that doesn't matter either. I'm just not going to be your wife any longer!" Her eyes narrowed. "Let's keep it simple and not get into a battle over nothing. You don't want a messy, expensive divorce."

"No," was all he said for a moment. Then, "I believe, Erica, that you have finally grown up."

She looked at him blankly. His resigned acceptance was simply too startling. In a daze, she turned toward the courtyard, her fingers closing over the railing as she tried to fathom the reason for his attitude. That very male smell of good soap and shaving gel came to her again.

"By the way, did you ever tell your father and Forest of our marriage?" Rafael was standing beside her, his eyes as black as the robe that covered most of him.

She sighed. "Not yet." She glanced his way. "And why do you want to know? Do you still think you have a snowball's chance in hell of talking me out of it?"

His handsome face was pensive. "I am done asking you to give me a chance, Erica."

"Really?"

"It is a pity, though. Our children would have been beautiful and intelligent, but perhaps too impulsive, no?" He smiled.

His comment brought an unaccountable flush to her cheeks. "They would be impossible brats!"

"*Si*, everyone has faults," he agreed with a mocking grin. "But it would be arrogant to try to talk you out of your decision. The only way I could persuade you to change your mind was if you loved me. And, of course, you don't."

"No," Erica breathed. A tremor raced down her spine, vibrating her nerve ends as she realized how very close Rafael was to her.

"Have you ever wondered what might have happened if you hadn't left my yacht in such a hurry after our one night?" he asked quietly.

"Your yacht?" She turned in surprise.

"You cannot still believe it belonged to Helen." Rafael chuckled. "I am sorry. You misunderstood so much and I didn't correct you."

"Taking me down a peg?"

The phrase puzzled him but only for a second. "Ah yes. I suppose so. You seemed determined to see the worst in everybody at the time. Helen happens to be my uncle's wife, and she was actually staying at your hotel. She had decided not to go with him to South America on family business. He joined her in Acapulco a few days after you left. And it was a very happy reunion."

"But she was an—"

"An American, yes," he supplied the word for her. "It isn't uncommon for the Torres men to marry outside their country. My maternal grandmother was French."

"I don't know much about you," Erica mused.

"Very little, in fact." Rafael's gaze moved over her thoughtful face. "I know a great deal more about you, though I have to say I lack understanding. For instance, I know you married me to spite your father." The breeze had tossed a lock of hair across her forehead and Rafael reached out and tucked it behind her ear. He let his fingers trail down her neck. "Why did you not have me take you back to the hotel when I said I would?"

She lowered her eyes, shifting nervously under his gentle stroking, suddenly and vividly reminded of much more sensual caresses. The marriage was a mistake, a big one, but it had been a heavenly wedding night in every way.

"Please, I—I don't want to discuss that."

His fingers stopped on her exposed collarbone. "I did not mean to hurt you, Erica." The sincere tenderness in his voice brought an aching throb to her chest. "It only seemed to me . . . that it was meant to be. You asked me to marry you. I said yes. I do not regret one second of that night."

"Yes. I mean, no, I have, but—" She was tongue-tied again as she found herself unable to speak of it at all.

Gently he lifted her chin. "In the morning, I intended to tell you that you were a very satisfying and passionate lover. I never guessed that you would run from me after we had shared so much."

"Rafael, please!" Her own weakness kept her by him even then.

"I do love the way you say my name." A smile curved his mouth, the hard, tempting mouth that she couldn't stop looking at. "Now, what is it you want of me this time?"

"I don't know," she whispered, her lashes closing, trying to make sense of her chaotic thoughts.

"Do you remember that time in Acapulco when we had just met, and you asked me why I didn't kiss you? Where is that boldness now?" he chided.

Desperately Erica summoned it up. "Stop it—just stop it. Why aren't you angry? I'm going to divorce you!"

"I know." His voice remained gentle and subtly seductive. "You are only trying to follow your heart."

She wanted to smack him . . . or kiss him with all her strength.

"I can't be angry at you because of that." He fell silent for a few moments. "Perhaps if I believed you were leaving me for another man, I would be."

Erica gasped, her eyes opening in time to see the flash of his smile.

"It is your freedom you want," he said. "Not Forest."

"What makes you think that?" she demanded in protest.

"Have you not learned that it isn't the same when he touches you? The same as it is with us?" Rafael countered. "His caress is adequate, I am sure. But not the same. It cannot be."

"I don't know what you mean or how you can even think that," she said heatedly. "I mean, it is different, or was, but that's because I was so inexperienced before. I do love Forest."

"So you keep saying."

The words were no sooner spoken than Erica felt the touch of his mouth against hers. Lightly he explored her lips, warming them with the kindled flame of his kiss.

Desperately she tried to be analytical in her comparison of his embrace and Forest's, but the passionately sensual reaction Rafael evoked in her put paid to that. His arms slid down her back and gently arched her toward him while her hands encountered the nakedness of his chest.

In a heartbeat, she knew that her response to Forest had been more or less automatic, with none of this wild joy. Touching Rafael's superb body was an irresistible pleasure. Her hands slipped inside his robe to wrap around his waist. Now she pulled them free and pressed her palms against his chest.

But she didn't have to struggle as Rafael gently let her step back, his hands steadying her for a moment before he released her completely. The intensity of his gaze was too disturbing and her pulse was already behaving much too erratically.

"I—I think I'd better leave." Erica whispered after she'd taken a panicky but deep breath.

"It's a pity you could not love me." He studied the high color in her face. "We began something beautiful."

"It would have been perfect for you, wouldn't it? A bride, a baby, and you're all set." Her words were unkind, but she had to be blunt with him.

His lips thinned. "No other woman will do. That is the truth. You may have your freedom but I will still be bound by my own chains."

"Oh, please." She felt obliged to mock his dramatic statement with those two little words, but she didn't feel better for doing it. "You mean you aren't going to contest the divorce?"

"On one condition—an easy one."

"Let's hear it," she said uneasily.

"That you tell your father and Forest the truth." The gentleness that had softened his manner in the previous moments was replaced by a calmness that upset her for some reason. "Not such a terrible price to pay," he went on, "since it is what you would have had to do if I'd fought the dissolution of our marriage."

Perplexed, she shook her head. "I don't understand. Why are you giving in?"

"I could not force you to honor our vows, although you acted as if that was my intention sometimes," he said wearily.

"I don't believe you," Erica murmured, watching him and wondering what ploy he would think of next. "I think you thought you could succeed in seducing me again, though, just to get me to do what you wanted. Whatever. Your methods are effective. I broke off with Forest."

He only shrugged. "Was I seducing you? I would call it persuasion."

"Don't act innocent, Rafael. It really doesn't suit you."

He gave her a wolfish grin but didn't reply.

"Why did you go through the rigmarole of taking me out for a month if you didn't intend to marry me? I mean, marry me again, in public."

"I hoped you might begin to care for me," he said evenly. "But I would rather sleep alone for the rest of my life than have a woman who resents my presence in the bed."

He meant what he said, apparently—she could tell that much by the look in his eyes. Although the chances of him sleeping alone for very long were next to nil, she understood that he was serious when he said that he wouldn't marry again. She felt a sharp flash of guilt for having treated their vows so casually.

With the right man, that wouldn't have happened, she told herself. When she married again, she wanted it to be forever, to a man who loved her, who needed her.

"Rafael, you have to marry again," she whispered.

"Is that pity in your voice? Spare me," he said dryly. "I

was aware of the risks when I married you. And like you, I will pay the price."

"I wish there was something I could do." Pain tore at her heart.

"There is." He sighed bitterly. "You can be my wife."

Erica pivoted away, regretting the damage she'd done to both their lives. There was a muffled curse from Rafael, then silence. She glanced hesitantly behind her, only to discover that she was the sole occupant of the balcony. The sound of impatient movements came from the bedroom and she walked slowly through the open French doors. Rafael was viciously yanking a shirt from a hanger as she entered.

"What are you doing?" The question seemed to irk him even more.

"I am getting dressed." He took a pair of pants from the closet.

She stood motionless until she saw him unknotting the sash of his robe. Then she quickly turned around, his laughter mocking her movement.

"You are still shy, Erica," Rafael said.

He could call her whatever he liked. "I'd better leave," she murmured nervously and started for the door.

"Wait," he commanded, catching her by the arm before she reached the door. "Give me a moment and I will go with you."

From the corner of her eye, she could see that he had his pants on, but his bronze chest was still bare. "I'm going home," she said curtly.

"I'm going with you."

"Why?" The single word was an accusation.

His eyes narrowed into black diamonds, hard and cutting. "Because I want to be there when you tell your father about us."

"Don't you think I'll keep my word?" She felt hurt by his lack of trust.

His fingers tightened for a fraction of a second before he let go of her arm. "I have no doubt that you'll tell him," he answered tautly. "I realize that you don't think much of me, but I will help you deal with him. I am sure he will be furious."

She was taken aback. "Are you going to do it because you're my husband?"

"Yes. Exactly. Do you think I would make you face him alone?" He turned away from her in disgust.

"Rafael?" She said his name hesitantly.

"What?" he snapped. He thrust his strong arms through the sleeves of his shirt, showing blatant disregard for the expensive material.

"Thank you," she whispered.

He glanced over his shoulder, his grim expression softening. "You are welcome." An unreadable emotion burned in his eyes.

Chapter 10

After Rafael was dressed, he asked Erica's indulgence for a few minutes so that he could make the calls to postpone his appointments for the morning. Then he followed in his own car as she drove back to her home.

Parking her car in front of the garage, Erica waited nervously on the flagstone walk for Rafael to join her. As she watched the lean, dark figure approaching her, so calm and controlled, she was suddenly grateful for that underlying steel she'd always sensed beneath his courtesy.

Before, when it had surfaced, she had fought it as an unruly, frightened horse would fight a commanding hand on the reins.

No one, not even Forest, had ever guessed at her hidden desire to be protected. Independence had been thrust on her and Erica's headstrong willfulness had seized it as a shield to hide her weakness. Yet Rafael knew instinctively that she cringed from her father's disapproval even when she deliberately incurred it. New emotions welled up as she viewed Rafael in this fresh light. He was no longer threatening her happiness but promising to guard it in some indefinable way.

Her hand reached out for his physical support,

strength flowing from his firm grasp of her cold, shaking fingers. She tried to conceal her need for him with a false smile of bravado.

"Shall we go in?" she said brightly.

Rafael touched her mouth, where tremors of fear were betraying the lack of genuineness in her smile. "Do not be frightened, *querida.*"

She wanted to tell him how safe she felt with him at her side, but the admission wouldn't come out. If she admitted to her feelings of security, she would have to confess to something else.

The masculine line of his mouth straightened more as Rafael released her hand, letting his arm curve around the back of her waist. He guided her along the walk to the front of the house.

A car pulled into the driveway as they neared the entrance. With a start of surprise, Erica recognized the driver almost instantly. Forest parked the car and walked toward them.

"What are you doing here, Forest?" she asked, glancing hesitantly at Rafael's unrevealing expression.

"I thought for a minute I was going to be treated to another extended PDA," Forest answered grimly, flashing a look of open dislike at Rafael. "That's Personal Display of Affection to you, dude. Someone texted me to get here pronto. What's going on, Erica?"

"Uh, I . . ." She nodded uncertainly at Rafael.

"I left the message," Rafael stated, ignoring Forest's obvious challenge to explain quietly to Erica, "I believe it would be best if you only had to tell your story once."

She pressed her lips tightly together, moved by his gentle understanding.

She had never expected to find security in his embrace but now she wanted to seek it in his arms. Before, the chemistry between them had owed everything to the potent combination of male and female. Only this minute did she realize that his presence offered something more than sexual attraction.

"Thank you," she whispered.

Rafael stared at the brightness of her violet eyes for a long moment, his dark gaze intense, then he abruptly looked elsewhere.

"Let's go in." His curt words were directed to Forest.

"By all means," Forest jeered.

Suddenly, in Erica's eyes, Forest turned into a stranger, someone she barely knew at all, and Erica found herself edging closer to Rafael. It was difficult to remember that she had despised him and his mind games only a few hours ago.

Lawrence was in the hallway outside her father's study as the trio entered the house. There was undisguised speculation in the look he darted at the three of them, but his voice was professionally calm when he spoke.

"Mr. Wakefield is expecting you if you'd like to go right in," he said, motioning in the direction of the closed study door.

Rafael had evidently contacted her father at the same time as Forest, Erica decided, feeling a sense of relief that they weren't barging in totally unexpectedly. The reassuring pressure of the hand on her back was removed as Rafael stepped forward to open the door. It wasn't replaced as he allowed Erica and Forest to go ahead of him into the room.

Vance Wakefield seemed to be in an amiable mood as he rose from his desk to greet the two men and his daughter.

The smile on his face didn't cover the sharpness in his blue eyes when he turned to her. "I see I've been chosen to referee this lover's triangle. Can't say I'm exactly looking forward to it."

Erica perched on the edge of a chair. Her gaze skittered across the room to where Rafael had settled himself into a large leather armchair and then to Forest, who was sitting near her in a watchful silence.

"You're not the ref, Daddy," she responded quietly, twisting her fingers together in her lap.

"Guess not. I don't have the striped shirt and black pants," he said.

The joke fell flat.

Erica breathed in deeply, searching her mind for a place to begin. "I don't know of any way to start without sounding melodramatic." She smiled weakly at her father's ice-blue regard. Her gaze darted immediately to Rafael, and she felt reassured by the warmth she saw in his eyes. "You see, Daddy, Rafael and I are married."

"*What?*" The expected explosion came from Forest instead of her father. "Do you mean that you had me come over here just to learn that you'd married *him?* You cold-blooded little—" He started to push himself out of his chair before he could say the last word.

He never got a chance to say it. "Sit down, *Señor* Granger," came Rafael's clipped order. "You will hear my wife out before you judge her."

Forest glared at him, then sat back in his chair. Erica turned away from the disgust in his expression, her heart leaping at Rafael's quick defense of her.

"This is kind of sudden, isn't it, Erica?" Her father spoke quietly with a hint of underlying disapprobation. "Not that I have any objections to Don Rafael."

"Actually . . ." She stared at her clenched fingers. "I met him almost two years ago when we were in Acapulco. I didn't know who he was at the time—that is, I thought I knew." A red flush of embarrassment stained her cheeks as she raised her head. "I believed he was a fortune hunter. I married him the night you flew to Houston, Daddy."

An uncompromising coldness entered her father's expression. "Are you saying that you've been married to him for nearly two years?" he demanded.

She nodded, squarely meeting his eyes, seeing the anger building there. "I did it to spite you. I know it sounds childish and stupid, and it was. Back then I only wanted to make you sorry for ignoring me when it was supposed to be our vacation. When I found out you'd left, I was too frightened to tell you what I'd done."

Vance Wakefield made no comment. He simply looked at her with icy incredulity as if saying that he wasn't surprised she'd behaved so foolishly. She was a willful female without an ounce of sense.

"I suppose he's been blackmailing you all this time," Forest muttered, glancing at Vance Wakefield. "We have only his word that he is who he says he is."

There was an edge of finely honed steel in Rafael's voice as he responded to Forest's implication. "I assume you can use a computer. Investigate me. I have nothing to hide. And *Señor* Wakefield has already made discreet inquiries of the Mexican consul to verify my identity."

"That's true, I did," her father replied without any apology.

"And he's why you didn't accept my proposal, isn't he?" Forest said grimly.

"I couldn't very well agree to marry you when I was already married to Rafael." Erica almost wanted to laugh.

"At least you were sensible about that," her father said dryly. "I suppose I should be grateful that you didn't get yourself into a bigger mess. Or pregnant."

"Your criticism of Erica is unwarranted," Rafael said calmly as she flinched at her father's cutting remark. "Everyone is capable of mistakes."

Vance Wakefield bristled. "My daughter has a penchant for trouble, and she usually expects me to get her out of it. I don't think I would be wrong if I said she's made this confession today in order for me to arrange an annulment so that she'll be free to marry Forest."

"Technically, an annulment isn't possible. But I understand that the letter of the law is not so strictly interpreted nowadays."

A stunned silence followed Rafael's softly spoken words and Erica flushed under Forest's accusing glare. "It is true that Erica ran away after we were married, but not until the morning after the wedding."

Forest cursed beneath his breath, while her father's eyes narrowed into ice chips of polar blue. Erica couldn't bear their joint disapproval and bounded to her feet, turning her back to them and hugging her arms around her churning stomach.

"If you intended to divorce him, how come you've been seeing him constantly this past month?" Forest demanded. Erica glanced over her shoulder at Rafael, strangely unwilling to explain how he'd made her see him. He returned her look steadily and answered the question for her, speaking to Forest.

"Because my wife believed that I would not grant her a divorce."

"We're not living in medieval times, man," Forest said rudely. "If she wanted to divorce you, she could have."

Rafael nodded. "Of course. But I thought I would try to win her. I went about it in very much the wrong way."

Forest snorted. "I don't believe I'm hearing this, do you, Vance?"

"Go on," the older man said to Rafael.

"I told her if she didn't break off with you and begin seeing me, I would tell her father about our secret marriage, knowing how much she wanted him to think well of her. Erica came to me this morning and informed me she was going to tell her father the whole truth and face the consequences."

"I would like to know why you married my daughter and kept silent about it." Her father's sharp gaze swung from her to Rafael.

But Rafael seemed immune to his disapproval as he studied Erica's face before replying. "I married your daughter because I loved her and for no other reason."

"That's not true," Erica gasped.

"But you never asked why I married you," Rafael reminded her cynically. "You have never considered what my reasons might have been."

"So let's hear 'em," her father said. "Generally speaking, I have been wondering why anyone still does get married in this day and age. Aren't hookups, as your generation calls them, a whole hell of a lot easier?"

Rafael seemed to be taking the question quite seriously, unlike Vance, Erica noted silently. Score one for him.

"Why marry, generally speaking? Oh, for one thing, I want children," Rafael said.

"You sure?" Vance asked cynically, casting a self-pitying glance at his only daughter.

"Yes. But there were and are plenty of women who would have married me and given me children. Erica, I guessed that you didn't love me the night I married you, or at least not as fully as I loved you. But in my arrogance—"—he smiled in self-mockery—"I believed you would come to return my love in time. I never expected to find you gone in the morning."

Erica stared at him in wordless amazement, the knowledge that he loved her jolting through her like an electric current.

"As you once pointed out, *querida*," Rafael continued, "I have a lot of pride. When I found you in San Antonio, you demanded a divorce and claimed to be in love with another man. I could hardly fall to my knees and declare I adored you under those circumstances."

"If you knew she loved me," Forest inserted, "why didn't you do the right thing and set her free?"

Rafael's aloof gaze swung to Forest. "Because I knew you could never make her happy. Oh, perhaps for a little while." His hand moved in a short, dismissive gesture. "But you are too much like her father. A few months after the wedding, you would begin taking her for granted, pushing her aside to further your career. You might have one or two children to occupy her time, but the love for a child should not take the place of the love that a man and woman can share. I had hoped that Erica might begin to care for me in this past month, but she has not. So I have agreed to her request for a divorce and will not contest it."

He rose easily to his feet and turned to her father. "Do not be harsh with Erica. The sensitivity that you see as a weakness, I see as strength. She accepts your affection and returns it tenfold. Not all parents can say that of their grown children. And she is grown." His glance encompassed Erica and Forest. "There is no more to say than that. My presence is no longer required. *Buenas dias.*"

Silently, almost in a daze, Erica watched him walk past her to the door, with no more than a gracious nod in her direction. When the door closed behind him, she knew that she would never see him again. There was no elation, no sense of relief, no feeling of victory that she had finally achieved her freedom. In word if not yet in deed. There was only a frightening emptiness, a void, as if some precious part of her had walked out the door as well.

"I'll call Jules," her father said gruffly. "He can get started on the divorce papers."

"No!" The denial was spontaneous and firm. "No, there will be no divorce," Erica declared.

"Don't be idiotic," Forest said angrily. "The dude's giving up. Get the divorce so we can be married."

"I don't want to marry you." She looked into the strong, square-jawed face, seeing beyond the all-American handsomeness of it for the first time. "I don't love you, Forest. I'm sorry, but you're just a shadow of my father. You two are so similar in some ways I'm surprised I didn't see it before. I love my father, but I don't want to be married to a man like him."

"You certainly don't think you're in love with Rafael, do you?" Forest laughed with disbelief.

Erica said nothing for a second before she replied slowly and with increasing sureness. "Actually, yes. I think I am."

"Don't make another mistake, Erica," her father cautioned, but there was nothing dictatorial in his voice.

But Erica was already racing out of the house and around to the side where Rafael had parked his car. The door was open and he was about to get in when he saw her. She stopped, then hesitantly walked toward him, searching his impassive face for some sign that she wasn't too late.

"Rafael." The name came from her mouth in a croaking whisper. She wondered if a matador felt like this when he faced the black bull in the ring.

"Yes? What do you want?" Impatience edged his low voice.

Erica moistened her lips nervously. "I don't want a divorce, Rafael."

If anything, his expression hardened. "I do not need your pity. Leave me alone."

"I don't pity you, Rafael," she insisted. "I pity myself for finding out, maybe too late, that I really love you. I know there's nothing I can say to make you believe me, but it's true all the same. I do love you."

"You are only grateful," he corrected her, "because I

shouldered some of the blame for our mutual stupidity and blunted your father's anger. Don't hide words of thanks in words of love."

"I don't know when I began to love you," Erica went on stubbornly. "I only know I realized it a few moments ago when you walked out of the study and part of me went with you." She refused to give up. "It was like a fog lifted and I understood why you have so much power over me every time you touch me. Don't you see, Rafael? I could never let myself love you before because I thought you'd married me for my money. I pretended that I let you make love to me just because I thought you were so incredibly sexy. Then I scared myself into thinking only that mattered. But no other man made me feel the way you do, not even Forest."

He nodded, giving her a chance to take a breath.

She continued in a rush of words. "When you came here and I discovered you weren't a fortune hunter, you backed me into a corner and demanded that the marriage become a reality. But I believed you wanted that just so your family wouldn't think you were—" She broke off.

"The word you want is *loco*," he said wryly.

"Well, both of us were. For just one night. It seemed to me that a single mistake shouldn't have consequences like that."

"Like what?" he asked evenly.

"You know. To have and to hold. Forsaking all others."

"Those are bad things," he said in a flat voice.

Was he being sarcastic? Not sure of his meaning, she held back a bitter laugh. Tears scalded her eyes and trickled down her cheeks as she turned away from him. "That was all just a ruse in there with my father, wasn't it? You only said you loved me to save my pride. You never expected me to take you seriously, but I don't care!" she said wildly. "You wanted a wife and children. Well, I happen to *be* your wife and—"

"Stop it!" Rafael took her by the shoulders and turned her around. The iron control was gone and an inverted anger was in its place. Despite that, the tears didn't stop as she gazed at him with the full futility of her love in her eyes. "You are giving into an impulse. You do not know what you are saying," he snapped.

"Really? Maybe you're just too arrogant to believe me!" she cried.

In the next instant, the arms that had so rigidly held her away brought her against the hardness of his chest, locking her in an embrace that was exquisite punishment. His hungry mouth covered hers until she throbbed with a feverish ache for him. Even when he later untwined her arms from around his neck, she was blissfully aware of his reluctance.

"I do love you, Erica, *mi esposa*," Rafael declared huskily. The burning fire in his gaze convinced her beyond all doubt.

"Why did you wait so long to come for me?" she whispered, touching the face that she now had a right to caress.

"So long?" He laughed softly. "Ah, my love, when I found you were not aboard the yacht, then later discovered you had checked out of the hotel, I flew to San Antonio immediately. No one could or would tell me where you were. I waited here for nearly two weeks before I received word that my father had suffered a stroke. I had to return to Mexico. Circumstances kept me there all this time."

"And your father?" Erica asked anxiously.

Pain flickered in his eyes. "He died last spring."

"Oh, Rafael, I'm so sorry." Her lips trembled in sympathy. "I wish I'd been there with you."

"You did not love me then." Rafael kissed her lightly

so she would know he meant to inflict no pain with those words.

"Now I do," Erica sighed, resting her head contentedly against his shoulder as his arms tightened around her. "With my whole heart."

"You must tell me that tomorrow and every tomorrow after that." The husky command was muffled by the soft skin of her throat.

"I promise I will," she whispered as she felt her body relax into the heat of his fiery caress.

"Every morning that I woke without you in my arms made the night that we shared so bittersweet," Rafael said in a raw, low voice. "Several times I have thought you were about to discover you loved me. Then I gave up hope. When you were with me, you seemed to become more unhappy and I knew I had to set you free."

"I'm not sure I deserve you. You were right when you said I was selfish." She gazed sadly into his face.

"I hope you cannot bear to let me out of your sight," he vowed. "It has been so difficult to be so near to you and not touch you or show you how much I cared. If you had learned Spanish before, you would have known how much I loved you on our wedding night aboard the yacht."

"Where is the yacht?" asked Erica, now cherishing the memories of that strange but wonderful night.

"In Acapulco, waiting for you to return," he answered.

"*Mañana*," she murmured the name of the yacht. "Let's go there."

"We will spend our honeymoon on it after we fly to my home tomorrow so my family can meet you," he declared.

"Do they know about me?"

"Yes." Rafael smiled tenderly. "Not that you are my wife, but I have spoken of you and of my intentions to make you my wife. My pride would not let them think you had done anything wrong, or permit them to pity me because I'd lost you. We will have another small wedding in the village near my home. You do not mind?"

"No. I'd like to say our vows again. But Rafael—" A shy pink blush filled her cheeks as the desire to feel his touch swept over her. "Must we wait?"

He drew in his breath. "You *are* my wife." From his pocket, he removed the signet ring and slipped it on her finger. "Your friend Jules Blackwell returned it to me. I told him I loved you and would not leave until you were wearing this again."

That was all the reassurance she needed. Erica melted in his warm arms.

More by Bestselling Author
Hannah Howell